THE

SOUND

OF

FOREVER

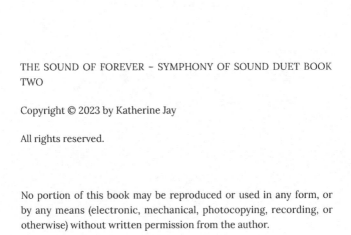

THE SOUND OF FOREVER – SYMPHONY OF SOUND DUET BOOK TWO

Copyright © 2023 by Katherine Jay

This is a work of fiction. Names, characters, places, brands, media, and incidents are either the product of the author's imagination or are used fictitiously. Any resemblance to actual persons, living or dead, events, or locales is entirely coincidental.

Cover design by © Books and Moods

Editing by Happily Editing Anns

CONTENTS

AUTHOR'S NOTE

This book contains subject matter that some people may find triggering. A list of the main potential triggers can be found on Katherine's website:

http://www.katherinejayauthor.com

Please note, triggers are not listed here to avoid spoilers for the book.

PLAYLIST

Symphony of Sound Duet

The Sound Of Silence - Disturbed
Perfectly Broken - Banners
Pieces (Hushed) - Andrew Belle
Creep - Radiohead
Blinding Lights - The Weeknd
I Wish It Would Rain Down - Phil Collins
Until I Found You - Stephen Sanchez
I Write Sins Not Tragedies - Panic! At The Disco
Chandelier - Sia
Silence - Sarah McLachlan, Delerium
Battle Scars - Guy Sebastian, Lupe Fiasco
Too Much Love Will Kill You - Queen
Lover - Taylor Swift
Bring Me To Life - Evanescence
White Noise - Coasts
Incomplete - Backstreet Boys
Forever Now - Cold Chisel
Everybody Hurts - R.E.M.
What's Left Of You - Chord Overstreet
Take It Slowly - Garrett Kato
Oceans - Seafret
Breathe Again - Harrison Storm
Bitter Sweet Symphony - The Verve
Firework - Katy Perry
Carry You - Ruelle, Fleurie
Hold On - Chord Overstreet
Forever and Ever and Always - Ryan Mack

This one goes out to the readers who love getting their heart ripped out, trampled on, broken into a million pieces… and then put back together by the end.

For those who want stories with a love worth fighting for…. This one's for you.

PROLOGUE
Jesse

Twelve Years Ago – Age Sixteen

I stand in some kind of awe-like trance as the girl I've only ever watched from a distance walks toward me. At first glance she appears confident, but a hint of hesitation sneaks through in her smile.

Yeah, I wasn't expecting this either.

Her friend stops a few feet in front of us and waves. "Thanks for meeting me here," she says a little nervously, her eyes bouncing between us. "I...ahh..." She stumbles over her words, her expression uncertain until Tate puts out his cigarette and steps forward.

"I'm Captain America," he says, pointing proudly at his chest. "And this is...Robin Hood," he adds, waving his hand in my direction. "The Men in Tights version."

"The fuck?" Asshole. I almost tell them my real name until the beautiful girl in front of me giggles, her eyes locked on mine.

Alright, Tate, you can have that one.

"Can we get nicknames too?" she asks, waggling her eyebrows, hesitation long gone.

I shake my head before answering but Tate cuts me off. "I think that can be arranged," he says with a smirk. "What do you say, Robin?"

I cringe at the idea, but the name Buttercup instantly pops into my mind. It's what I've been calling her since I first saw her. But I can't say that. It's corny.

Buttercup eyes me curiously until her lips pull into a mischievous grin. "You thought of something, didn't you?" she says with excitement in her gaze. "Is it Maid Marian?"

I bite back a laugh. While I never would have suggested that name, I like that her first thought was for us to be connected.

"Buttercup," I mumble, but it's so quick, she doesn't hear me.

"What?" she asks, her head tilted to the side.

"He calls you Buttercup," Tate confirms loudly and I swear he's asking for trouble.

I shoot a glare his way, before turning back to the girls with a tight grin. "He's kidding, how about—"

"I like Buttercup," she says almost shyly. "It's from that movie, right?"

"It's from The Princess Bride, yes." Though it's not the reason I call her that.

"Buttercup it is." She nods as her smile grows. "And my friend here is..."

"Lily," Tate calls out, sticking with the flower theme.

"Lily sounds good," Buttercup says as her gaze flashes to Lily's. "But now that we have that figured out, what the hell are we doing here?" Her smile fades as she crosses her arms over her chest. Her thick, blonde hair blows across her face but she ignores it, intent on maintaining her composure. Her sass.

I like it. A lot.

I knew I'd like her from the little glimpses I'd already seen of her around town. The moments she never noticed. God, if she knew I'd been thinking about her for years, she'd undoubtedly turn and run.

No one speaks, so Buttercup asks again, her tone somewhat sterner. "What's. Going. On?" she practically growls.

A hint of uncertainty flashes across Tate's face, but it's gone before I've had the chance to process it. "I'd like some alone time with your friend," he tells her before smiling at Lily.

"Yeah, that's not going to happen. You can have privacy, but I'm not leaving J...Lily alone. With anyone."

Smart girl. I like her even more now.

Buttercup walks over to the rocks, just out of earshot, and sits down, signaling for me to join her. "We'll be right here," she calls out with a pointed look. "Stay where I can see you."

I bite my cheek so I don't laugh, and happily follow her, only glancing back at Tate for a brief moment. He can handle himself.

"What do you think they're talking about over there?" Buttercup asks after we've been chatting for a few minutes. "Lily hasn't mentioned 'Captain America' at all." She rolls her eyes. "We usually tell each other everything. It's J... Lily and me against the world. I'm a little confused."

"Join the club. Although even Lily looked confused when you first got here. Maybe they met online?" I throw the idea out there before really thinking about how unlikely it is. I'm not even sure Tate's on social media. If he is, he's never mentioned it.

Buttercup scrunches her nose, seemingly thinking it through, until an idea hits her. "Lily's a gamer; maybe they met that way? Is the Cap a gamer?"

"Definitely not." I laugh. Even if we had some kind of console or streaming service, I doubt he'd play.

"Damn, I thought that might explain why he has a nickname." She laughs. "Though it doesn't explain why you do. Unless you're a gamer? Care to fill me in?" She bites back a smile as she looks my way, drawing my eyes to her shiny pink lips. I can't figure out if she's wearing gloss, or if she wet them with her tongue. Either way, it makes me want to kiss her.

"So..." she drawls, bringing my attention back to the conversation.

I'd almost forgotten she'd asked me a question.

With a small shrug, I give her the answer Tate gave me. "It's because I want to steal from the rich to help the poor." Although his exact words were, "do you think you're going to steal from the rich to pleasure the poor?" And in that scenario, it would be Buttercup I was stealing, and I'm the poor. He's an asshole.

Buttercup laughs and there's something about her that makes me think she'd laugh at the truth too.

"What a hero," she says, fake gushing. "Although, because Cap mentioned it, all I can picture is the Men in Tights version of you. We're in a forest; perhaps you'd like to dance?"

"Fucking Tate," I grumble, but fail to hide my suppressed grin.

Buttercup laughs again. "I think it's cute."

"Cute?" Goddammit. "I am not cute."

"You are a little bit cute." She scrunches her nose as she shrugs, making me want to show her just how "not cute" I am. But I don't want to scare her away. I'm sure that will happen on its own.

Buttercup's sassy grin returns, and she rolls her eyes again. "Okay, you're not cute. Let's move on. Tell me, what do you do when you're not at school?"

As we talk, Buttercup draws pictures in the dirt, and for some reason, I commit them all to memory. It's nothing spectacular—a sun, some trees, even a dog, or maybe it's a horse; she's not exactly an artist—but there's one that really holds my attention, and while it could be described as a scribble, it feels like more than that. It almost looks like script or cursive writing, but it's impossible to make out what it says. That is, until I realize she's singing along as she writes. She's writing the title of the song.

I run a broken fingernail across my wrist, mindlessly copying her design onto my skin, only looking away when I notice a faint red outline appear.

"I still can't believe I've never seen you before," Buttercup muses without looking up, cutting into my thoughts.

"I've seen you," I say without thinking, then freeze, dropping my hand as her eyes flash to mine.

"You have?"

"Ah, yeah. I have," I say, nervously running a hand through my hair. Dammit. How do I get out of this without looking like a stalker? "I think you were getting ice cream, near the library in Mossman Hills." At least she was the last time I saw her, but there have been many moments.

"Ooh busted. That was definitely me. I often catch the bus there when I don't want to go home. It gives me time to walk around unnoticed. Although, turns out I'm not completely unnoticed." She bites her lip as she smirks my way, and I huff out a laugh. I'm the one that's been busted. "Maybe next time I can visit with a purpose?" she proposes, crinkling her nose again, and I have to stop myself from blurting out yes. I'd do anything to see her again...to talk to her more. There's always been something about her reeling me in.

"If you do, I can show you where the locals get desserts," I say with a shrug, trying to appear casual.

Buttercup stands up beside me. "Yes!" she says excitedly. "That would be heaven. I love sweet things when I'm stressed, and let's just say my family has been driving me to sugar lately."

She huffs out a shy laugh and apologizes under her breath before launching into an explanation. "I don't usually spill, but—"

"Trust me, I get it. Sometimes we just need to vent."

"Again. Yes!" Her voice rises before she covers her mouth with her hand and winces. "Oh God, that was a little too enthusiastic."

She grabs my arm as she giggles to herself, and I involuntarily flinch from the pain. Since she's laughing, I expect her not to notice. But I'm wrong.

"What happened?" she asks, her hand hovering over my sleeve as though she's itching to check for damage.

My heart races as I consider lying, but something has me wanting to tell her everything.

"I got in a fight," I say, lifting my tee to show her the bruises.

"Jesus!" She reaches out to touch but stops herself. "Do you get in many fights?"

I *pause, wondering if she's judging me or genuinely concerned.* "I don't seek them out if that's what you're asking."

"I'm not," she rushes out. "This just looks more like—" *Buttercup pauses, cutting herself off, but I can finish for her. Abuse. It looks like I was beat up. And she's not wrong.*

Our eyes lock and whatever she sees in mine has her expression turning to anger. "Who?" *she snaps, like she's protecting me, making me swallow back a laugh.*

I shake my head without answering and her eyes flash to Tate, the glare she gives him highlighting her thoughts.

"It's not him," *I say, but it's obvious she doesn't believe me, so for some stupid reason, I decide to be honest.* "He's been there too," *I say, referring to Tate. Although, he found a way to avoid it.*

Buttercup frowns. "And you said he's your foster brother?"

"I did."

Her eyes widen as a gasp escapes her, easily forming the correct conclusion. My foster dad. Not that "Dad" is the right word for him.

"Have you told anyone?"

"There's no point. They always put it back on the kids. It's happened to me before, and if they move me somewhere else, it could happen again."

At this point, I'm just accepting it in the hope that he messes up in another way, so Tate and I get moved.

But I can't see that happening anytime soon. I think the little luck I had has run dry.

"God, I feel like such a bitch for ever thinking I had a bad home life," Buttercup says as her eyes flash with guilt. "Sorry, I shouldn't have said that."

"Don't. Don't do that. I didn't tell you that to make you feel bad. In fact, I don't even know why I told you." *Except that I get this feeling we're the same. That deep down, we're both just trying to make it through this life as we wait for the next one. I've seen it in her eyes. The longing. The sadness.*

Buttercup smiles as she takes a step closer, her hand brushing against mine. "Maybe you trust me," she says with a slight lift of her shoulders. "Or maybe you feel the same connection I do?" The slightest pink tinge flushes across her cheeks, and I've never seen anything more beautiful.

"Or maybe it's both," I rasp, hesitantly connecting our fingers without drawing attention to it.

Yes, we've been talking since she arrived on the mountain, and it feels like we know each other, but this is still only the first time we've had a conversation. Though, there's no denying the connection. I've felt it since the first time I saw her.

"Robin..." she whispers, trailing off, making me once again regret playing the fake name game. *I want to hear her call me Jesse. I want to hear my name whispered from her lips as I make her mine.*

"Buttercup—"

"I think you should kiss me," she rushes out and I freeze. Fuck, I want that. But—

"Don't think about the reasons you shouldn't... and just do it," she adds, cutting me off.

Well, okay then.

Leaning forward, I brush my lips slowly against hers, testing it out a couple of times, before deciding not to waste what will likely be my one shot. When she figures out that my life is so much worse than I admitted, she's going to run for the hills. Or down them in this case.

Pulling her close, I sink my free hand into her hair and angle her face toward me, staring into her striking green eyes as I ignore the images that try to push themselves into my mind.

I've just leaned in to kiss her again when we hear raised voices from behind us and spring apart.

"Fuck, are they arguing?" Buttercup asks, her eyes flashing toward Tate and Lily. I haven't been able to focus on anything other than Buttercup since she walked into the clearing, so I have no idea what's happening between them.

But when I look over and see Tate pocket something, I internally cringe. Motherfucker. I know exactly what he's doing.

"It definitely looks heated. But—"

"We're leaving!" Lily yells as she marches toward us, aggressively grabbing Buttercup's wrist to pull her away.

An unwelcome image flashes through my mind as I picture the bruise bracelet she'll have come tomorrow, *but I hold back my rage when Buttercup rips her arm away.*

"What the hell, Jade? What's going on?" she asks with a rage of her own.

"We have to go," Lily...Jade says, grabbing Buttercup again. "Now!" She takes off in a run, dragging Buttercup behind her, and it's enough to make me see red.

"Stop!" I yell at the same time Tate does, before we both run after them.

I slow to let him catch up, grabbing his arm when he reaches my side. "Why the hell didn't you tell me this was a drug deal?" I grate, gritting my teeth.

And why the hell didn't I figure that out sooner?

1
Willow

P resent Day

My eyes glaze over as everyone around me speaks at once. If I could shut off my hearing I would. Although, their chatter will forever be better than the silence.

Surprisingly, Pippa's the first to notice I've zoned out. She squeezes my shoulder and whispers "sorry" in my ear before yelling at everyone to shut up.

Of course, it doesn't work.

Mom starts speaking again as soon as everyone else goes quiet, her arms folded over her chest. "I can't believe you'd do that without telling anyone where you were going," she scolds. *Again.* "Do you even understand what you put us through? We almost lost you once before, Willow. That was enough for a lifetime."

Okay, now I feel a little bad, but I didn't think I'd be up there that long. And I definitely didn't think I'd end up back in the hospital.

When Alex told me he could help me figure out what happened, I almost laughed in his face, assuming it was another ploy to get me to say yes to a date. But then I remembered he'd alluded to knowing more information before, and the curiosity almost got me.

If Jesse hadn't come into my life, I probably would have said yes. I would have taken the easy road and listened to what Alex had to say. Hung on his every word. *Trusted him.*

Instead, I decided it was time I figured out the truth. On my own. And I knew the best place to start. I just didn't know I'd roll my ankle and get stuck there.

"Willow's been through a lot, Mom. How about we give her the night to rest. The nurses will look after her. She's tired, hurt and... Let's just give her some space."

Broken. She was going to say broken. And she'd be right.

My heart broke on that mountain. And right now, I'm using all my strength to bury that feeling deep within me. Because it freaking hurts. I'd gladly take a million rolled ankles or walk a mile on broken glass if I could take this pain away.

Jesse was there. Jesse was somehow involved in Jade's death. Jesse lied.

And God, that kills me.

All that time he knew what had happened to me, and he never said a word.

Even when I asked.

"Pippa's right. I think it's time you *all* left," I say as Mom argues. "I need to be alone." *And I need a chance to process all of my thoughts.*

I watch as my family all walk away, one by one, honoring my request, but as my Mom reaches the door, she looks back at me with a frown set in her features, shaking her head in disappointment.

I know that if I ever have kids, I'll probably look back on this moment and regret it—that I told my mom to leave. But for now, I can't handle her being here. Yes, I know she's just worried about me, but she has an awful way of showing it.

When I'm finally alone, it's not as satisfying as I would have hoped. In fact, being alone with my thoughts is probably not my smartest idea. I reach for my phone to distract myself, just as movement near the door catches my eye, but when I look up, no one's there. *God, I'm even imagining things now.*

Taking a deep breath, I contemplate who to contact when Sara sneaks back into the room, saving me from myself. "You didn't mean me, right?" she says with a hopeful grin, making me smile.

"Why were you creeping around near the door?" I laugh to myself. "I originally meant *everyone*, but I'm

glad you're back. I'm just about done with thinking."
Turns out, thinking makes it worse.

"I wasn't... Doesn't matter." She pulls up a seat next to my hospital bed and frowns. "Want to talk about it?"

God, I hate this. My ankle's fine. This all feels unnecessary. Though, I'm sure it's not the real reason I'm here. I heard mention of my mental health.

When I look Sara's way, she's staring back at me in nervous anticipation, and I hate that I'm still not ready to talk. "Not yet. Maybe soon." I shrug. *Or maybe not.*

"I understand," Sara says as she pats my arm before sitting up straighter in her chair. "Want to know what happened to Grant on the farm today? It involves mud." She bites back a smile and bounces her eyebrows, changing the subject without further question.

And I adore her for it. "Absolutely." I smile.

With a beaming grin of her own, Sara regales me with the tale of her husband's "literal fall from grace"—as she calls it. And rightly so. He apparently fell off their horse, Grace, straight into the mud. It's exactly what I needed to hear, and even though I'm ninety percent sure she made the entire thing up for my benefit, because Grant's an amazing rider, it still makes me laugh. Something I didn't think would be possible today.

"So, next on my list is candy," she says when she's finished her story, sitting back proudly.

"Your list?" I ask hesitantly, looking at her hands.

Sara reaches down to something and giggles. "I wrote down a list of things I could do to cheer you up."

Okay. "How did you know I'd need that much cheering up?" Yes, I rolled my ankle and got stuck at the top of a mountain. But she didn't know that before arriving here.

Sara sighs. "Because of the look on Jesse's face when he raced out the door to find you, and the look on yours when you came back."

Oh. Are we that obvious?

"I promise I'm not fishing for answers," she adds before I can speak. "I know you'll talk when you're ready. I just want you to know, I'm trying." She squeezes my arm before leaning over and pulling several bags of candy out of nowhere. I didn't even see her bring anything in.

"Thank you. I know you are. And I appreciate it. It's a great start. But I am curious, what's next?"

Sara grins and I can't help but smile in return. "Next is a rom-com, specifically one from the nineties."

"That's good. I like it."

"Then I have music and wine. Though you're probably not supposed to have wine right now." She grimaces. "Anyway, last, I have…" She hesitates before cringing. "Jesse."

"Jesse?" I bolt upright as my eyes flash to the door, as though I'll see him standing there, waiting. But he's not. Sara scrunches her nose but doesn't answer right away.

"Well?"

"He's still out there." She tenses. "And from the broken look on his face, I'm going to guess something happened between the two of you, only I wasn't sure if speaking to him would help or hinder the situation. Which is why he's last on my list. Sort of an *if-all-else-fails*, backup plan."

Her reasoning is good, I'll give her that, but I'm stuck on the words "he's still out there." I was under the impression he left. Probably because I was *told* he left. I don't know how I feel knowing that he hasn't.

Sara frowns exaggeratedly. "It was a bad idea, wasn't it?"

"No, not a *bad* idea. I'm just not sure it's a good one."

"Do you want to know what he's doing?"

Do I? That doesn't seem like progress. Although it would be nice to know that he's hurting as much as I am. "Sure." I shrug.

"He's moping around and begging to see you."

"Good."

"Good?" Sara stares at me in shock until I smile.

"Trust me, he deserves it."

"I'll always trust you. You know that. Want me to get Grant to kick his ass?"

I'd love to say yes, but something tells me he's been through enough already. And if anyone's going to kick his ass, it's going to be me.

Sara puts on *My Best Friend's Wedding*—I needed something that didn't end in a mushy happily ever after—then heads off to pick up her son, Benji, leaving me with her laptop.

I've just reached the part where they sing "I Say A Little Prayer," when Ashley, of all people, wanders in without apology.

"You need to put that boy out of his misery and either tell him to leave, or invite him in to talk. It's humiliating for him."

That almost came across as genuine concern until she kept talking.

"Thank you for the unsolicited advice," I say, holding back an eye roll. "I'll be sure to take it under consideration."

"Ugh, I can't believe your attitude's back. I was actually starting to like the pleasant Willow you'd become. Pity Pippa returned and ruined it all."

Bitch! I wish it was Pippa. Speaking of Pippa though...

"You know you're the one in the wrong, when it comes to your relationship with her. Right? *Your* attitude toward Pippa isn't warranted. At all."

Okay, maybe that's not the complete truth considering Pippa had been sleeping with Jonah. But that's a different story.

Ashley smirks, not even flinching at my comments. "How does it feel knowing you did the same thing I did?" She folds her arms over her chest as she raises her perfectly shaped eyebrows. "I'm not stupid; it's obvious that guy has feelings for you."

My jaw drops. Surely Mom filled her in on the truth around Pippa's fake relationship.

"You all know Pippa's with Ryan. She was never with Jesse."

"We know that *now*. Question is...did you know that when you went after him?"

I swallow a lump in my throat. *Jesus*. Am I just as bad as she is? True, I never did anything until I found out it was fake, but I *felt* things.

"That's what I thought," Ashley says without letting me answer.

And it hits me.

"It's guilt," I say with a little too much enthusiasm.

"What?"

"Your vendetta against Pippa *isn't* because of Pippa at all. You do it to make yourself feel better. Because every time she snaps back, it takes away some of your guilt. You get to tell yourself she's a horrible person. That she deserved it."

Ashley stares at me in shock and I know I'm right. I can't believe I didn't see it before. It also explains Jesse's attitude toward me when he first arrived in town. It may have morphed into his need to push me away, but it started as guilt. I'm sure of it. He knew who I was the second he saw me. And God, I want to hate him for that.

"You know what? Maybe I will put Jesse out of his misery," I say, pulling myself out of bed, motivated by my need to get away from Ashley.

Crutches in hand, I turn toward the door. "Where is he?"

2

Jesse

T welve Years Ago – Age Sixteen

Tate doesn't answer me about the drugs, but I don't need him to. His grim expression says it all. And it makes me want to deck him. The only thing holding me back is knowing that he's doing all this to avoid a beating in the first place. Something I now refuse to do. I'd rather take the pain.

"She looks younger than us," I say, making sure he knows how disappointed I am.

"It's her or me, Jesse. I'm just saving my own ass. And in a way, I'm saving yours too. I'm not forcing her into drugs. She contacted me."

He may be right, but fuck, it feels wrong. She can't be older than fifteen, and she's already into drugs. Or getting into them. Jesus. "Come on, we have to stop them," I say, picking up my pace again. "Lily looks angry, and the last thing we need is trouble at home if she spills."

23

3
Jesse

"**G**et up. You need to get down there and make sure Willow keeps her mouth shut."

My thoughts are a tangled mess of the past and the present, with Tate's last words playing on repeat in my mind. When he appeared on the mountain, I assumed things were going to change between us, that he was there to help. But then he threw that line at me, laced with anger, and now I'm back to wondering if he's a threat.

Making me even more desperate to see Willow.

"Snap out of it," Pippa says as she shoves me over on the bench just outside the hospital doors and sits down. "She's not going to let you in."

Tell me something I don't know. "It doesn't matter. I'm staying."

I can't walk away after everything that happened on that mountain. Apart from needing to know she's okay, I need her to know that I'm sorry. *And I need to know what she remembers.*

"What if we don't want you to stay?" Pippa says, and I freeze.

We? Ouch. My eyes flash to hers as she watches me, her face shadowed in disappointment.

"You don't even know what happened."

"It doesn't matter." She throws my words back at me. "She's my sister."

"So that's that. You're just going to judge me, without knowing any of the information?" I don't know why I'm arguing when she'd only judge me *more* if she did know the truth.

Seth steps forward and hesitantly reaches for my shoulder. "We have to get back anyway, Jesse. We've got meetings, and—"

"I don't give a fuck about any of that right now. I left her before; I won't do it again."

Seth sighs as his eyes flash to Pippa's for a beat. "Yes, you left her. But you left because you don't belong here. This isn't your world anymore. You're not a small-town guy. You live in San Francisco. In an apartment. With a doorman. You're on *billboards*. This isn't your life. You left her here with unanswered questions, and none of that's changed. Jesse…"

He continues on, but I don't bother listening to the rest of his grand speech, because he's wrong. Yes, I left her yesterday to go back to my life, or was it the day before? God, I don't know. But that's not the time I'm referring to. And I can't do it to her again.

"Would you have left Amber?" I ask, because it worked for me earlier today. *Fuck, has it really only been hours since I first found out she was missing?*

Seth scowls, reading through my intentions, but then shocks me with his response. "I did *fucking* leave her!" He raises his voice. "I knew it would be the end of us...and I left."

"What?" My jaw actually drops.

"All you need to know is that we were married over a decade ago and I left. We got divorced. We were done. And yet we still made our way back to each other. You don't need to work it all out today, Jesse. You have a lifetime."

When he's finished, Seth shrugs as though he didn't just rewrite my belief of his history while I stare at him blankly. I have so many questions, but since none of them are going to help me in this situation, I store them away for later.

"You don't understand. I *need* to see her."

I feel like a broken record but they're just not getting it.

"You're right. We don't understand," Pippa jumps in, standing up with her arms in the air. "So, tell us. What the hell happened up there? And why was Tate involved?"

"What about Tate?"

Goddammit.

Of course, Willow's dad chooses that moment to walk outside, making us all fall silent for a beat.

"How do you know Tate?" Pippa eventually asks, and even I know it's a stupid question. He was their goddamn school principal.

He raises a single eyebrow before his gaze flashes to mine, his usual calm demeanor gone. "I just came out here for some air. But Jesse, Willow doesn't want any visitors. It's probably best if you go."

Yeah, that's not happening.

I open my mouth to argue but Pippa cuts me off.

"Go home, Jesse!" she cries out before sympathy fills her eyes. "Please just go."

Seth's gaze bores a hole in the side of my face as I lock eyes with Pippa's, warring with her in silence. Bit by bit her gaze softens until I think I've got her. "Pippa—"

"No, Jesse!" Willow's surprisingly powerful voice booms from the doorway, instantly drawing my attention.

My heart sparks at the sight of her, and the world around me fades away. At least, until I register the anger in her eyes. Eyes that, even filled with loathing, have me locked in a chokehold.

"Willow?"

"No, Jesse," she repeats, only softer this time, her beautiful soul pleading with me to listen.

And this time I do.

Because everything I've done has been for *her*, and I'm not about to stop that now.

"I meant what I said up there, Willow," I tell her, without saying the private words out loud, hoping she'll understand. And from the small nod she gives me, I know that she does.

I fucking love her.

"I need you to leave," she says anyway. "And I don't just mean the hospital. I need you to go back to San Francisco. Back to your life. And leave me alone."

Jesus. That's like a bullet to the heart. "Willow—"

"Please," she begs. "I'm not ready and I want you to respect that."

She turns and hobbles inside without even a backward glance, and then all eyes are on me. I stay strong under the scrutiny, but inside it feels like my heart's been smashed into a million pieces. The last thing I want to do is walk away. I want to storm inside and demand that she forgive me. I want to fall to my knees and beg her to talk to me because she doesn't know all the facts.

But I can't do that because I can't tell her all the facts, or any of them. And it's tearing me apart.

"Let's go," I say, turning to Seth as I ignore all the unspoken questions aimed my way.

I know when to accept defeat, but as I said the last time I walked away... I'll be back.

***

I make Seth drive back into Hepburn Falls before we head to the airport, even though it's out of our way. I need to see Tate before I go. I have to know he's not going to cause any trouble for Willow.

When we arrive, I keep an eye out for his motorcycle, and find it exactly where I assumed it would be...parked across from the bar. Relief fills me knowing I'm not going to have to search for long, but the instant I see him, my blood boils. Tate's hovering outside, in a heated discussion with Alex, and even though it's dark, I can tell neither of them look happy.

"Pull in here. I'll just be a minute," I say as I unbuckle my seat belt, jumping out of the car as soon as Seth comes to a stop.

Alex is the first to notice me, and his angry expression quickly morphs into one of cocky intrigue. "Hockey man, to what do we owe the pleasure?" he says with a smirk as I picture my fist connecting with his jaw.

Tate spins around to face me, his eyes widening briefly before he schools his features. "You should be long gone, Jesse. Don't you have a grand life in another state?"

My brow furrows at the sudden change in his attitude, but I stand tall. "Don't you? Why are you still here?" I ask, now looking at both of them.

Tate laughs. "I'm from here, remember? Or did that information slip your mind?"

How could it slip my mind—the guilt of that still eats away at me—but right now, it's concerning.

"When are you going back to Seattle?" I say, ignoring his question.

Alex steps forward but Tate throws his hand out, stopping him from getting too close. "We'll leave when we're ready," Alex says at the same time Tate grunts, "tomorrow," putting my mind at ease. A little.

"Good." I nod. "Then we'll all be gone and this can be over."

"What can be over?" Alex asks, his brows raised in question. "Do tell me what's had the two of you so worked up this week. Tate was all for me talking to Willow, but now he's changed his tune. Anyone want to fill me in?"

Fuck. I can't for the life of me work Alex out, but I don't like it. And from the look on Tate's face, neither does he. "I don't know about Tate," I say, lying. "But Pippa didn't think you were the right guy for Willow, and I'm just helping her out."

"Whatever you say. This entire week has been a fucking waste." He throws his hands in the air and walks inside the bar, but not before giving Tate some kind of knowing look.

"Tate," I begin when Alex is out of sight. "We—"

"We're leaving," he says, cutting me off, glancing toward the bar before his eyes settle back on mine. "Be satisfied with that. It's the best you're going to get. You'll just have to trust me."

All I can do is nod. I've trusted him for twelve goddamn years. Longer if you count the years before Jade's accident. But for the first time, I'm not so sure. And I definitely don't trust Alex. But they're leaving, so at least I've got that.

When I get back in the car, I'm a little on edge but I try to hide it, until Seth busts out one of his usual nervous jokes and I snap.

"How's that blood pressure going?"

"Are you fucking kidding me right now? I've just left Willow. I'm not in the mood."

"I know. But I can't ask you what I really want to ask."

My eyes flash to his, but all he does is shrug. I want to know what he's referring to, but I also don't, because I know I'm not going to be able to answer his question.

"I'm going to sleep," I snap instead. "Wake me when we get close."

I don't sleep. At all. I'm awake for each excruciating second but keep my eyes closed to avoid conversation. When enough time passes that I feel like we must be close, I open my eyes and fake a yawn, pretending to wake up. But Seth calls me out.

"God, you're an asshole. I could hear your mind ticking that entire time. We've got twenty minutes to go."

I shoot him a thanks and pull out my phone, seeing a text from the same unknown number as earlier today.

Unknown: Decided to leave tonight. We're on our way home.

My chest hollows as I huff out in relief, hopeful that's the end of it, and after bringing up my recent calls, I hover over Willow's number. I want to call her, but I can't. She won't answer. So, instead, I text. If there's a chance I can put her mind at ease about one thing, I'm going to do it.

Jesse: In case it's on your mind, you don't have to worry about Tate or Alex. They left.

While I may not fully trust either of them, for now, they're out of the picture and that's gotta mean something. I hope. And when Willow sends me a *thank you* text a little while later, I feel like I can relax.

I stare at my phone after that, only looking up as we're pulling into the rental returns at the airport. We've just found our parking bay when Seth's assistant texts to say the band needed their private jet back and we'll have to wait until the next morning to get a flight, forcing us to spend the night in a motel close by. While it's a shame the jet's no longer an option, God, am I grateful for the band in the first place. I don't know what I would have done without them, and Dylan.

By the time we get home Monday afternoon, I'm mentally and physically drained, and yet, when night falls, I can't sleep. Again. I hate being here knowing that Willow's hurting and she won't let me see her.

But there's nothing I can do to change that. I just have to wait it out, and wait it out, I will.

I'm staring at the ceiling when my alarm goes off Tuesday morning. Before my visit to Hepburn Falls, I had a great relationship with sleep. I considered it part of my hockey performance routine. Now I'm fucked. And there's only a month before preseason begins and I'm back to high-intensity training. My body needs rest. And I need Willow.

My day drags as I mope around my apartment, not really sure what to do with myself. It may have only been a week but now my life feels all wrong without her.

I need a distraction.

My door buzzes ten minutes after I've ordered takeout, and I stare at the intercom with suspicion. There's no way that's them. So...

It buzzes again and I snap into action, rushing over to answer. "Yup."

"Jesse, it's me."

"Pippa?" *She's back?*

"Yeah, do you mind if I come in and get my keys?"

Keys...right. "Yeah, I'll open up."

I stand by the door, waiting for her to arrive, because I have nothing else to do, but when she steps into view, I regret it. Watching her give herself a pep talk about *not* ripping my head off isn't my idea of fun.

"Shit!" Pippa startles when she sees me.

"Yep." I say, giving her nothing.

She cringes, realizing she's been caught, and then owns it. "Trust me, *that* was needed."

"I get it."

"Do you? Because if you know *why* I want to yell at you, why aren't you doing anything to fix it?"

I stare at her blankly to stop myself from giving her a piece of my mind. "You were there," I say with my voice void of emotion. "You told me to leave. Willow doesn't want me to fix it."

"That's bullshit and you know it."

Yeah, it is. But Willow only wants me to fix it by telling her everything. And I can't. Not yet. Not until I'm sure she can handle it.

"I guess you and Willow agree on one thing... Neither of you are willing to open up about what happened on that mountain."

Relief hits me but I try not to outwardly react. If Willow's not talking, we're all safe. *For now.*

"It's not my place to tell you if Willow doesn't want to. And I'll talk to *her* when she's ready. Here's your key."

I grab the key off the stand near the door and hold it out for her. "It's parked on level five, spot number two forty-seven, near the elevator. The code to get out of the gate is six, six, five, four.

Pippa rushes to pull her phone out of her purse and quickly punches in the details, as though I'm such an asshole that I wouldn't repeat them if she forgot.

"Thank you," she says with a forced grin. "No matter how I feel about you right now, I promise to be a professional at work, and I promise I'm not about to throw you to the media wolves."

"Thanks." *I think.* Though I'm not sure I love the "no matter how I feel," line.

"I'll clear up our relationship with the media too," she adds. "I'll give them the 'just friends' line. Ryan's even said I can tell them we're together."

"Wow."

"Yep. I think he likes me." *Obviously.* I hold back an eye roll.

"He more than likes you. And he's a good guy. You deserve that. He'll be a much better boyfriend than I would have been." I shrug.

Pippa's lips pull into a small smile before she shakes her head. "Thanks, Jesse. But I'm not ruling you out just yet. I think you have potential. For someone else."

There's only one person I want.

"Anyway," she continues. "Thank you for your help. Facing Ashley and Jonah was a lot easier with you there."

I thin my lips and nod. "No problem. See you at work."

Pippa's face drops as I abruptly end the conversation, but she recovers quickly, waving as she walks back to the elevator, stepping in as the guy with my takeout steps out. Her eyes flash to mine just before the doors close and she nods, leaving me with a tightness in my chest.

That wasn't fun. At all.

It almost felt like we were *truly* breaking up, and maybe that's because our friendship seems as though it might be over.

I don't hear from security after Pippa leaves, so I assume she found her car, and when ten p.m. comes around and I've cleaned up after dinner, I force myself to try and sleep.

But like last night, it fails me.

If it's not stress, it's worry, and if it's not worry, it's nightmares. And it all comes back to the same thing...*the past I tried to forget.*

But what's worse is that I have no idea when it's all going to catch up with me, only that I'm no longer able to run.

4
Willow

One Month Later

Twisting my fingers together, I sit straight in the chair and take a deep breath. My therapist, Gretchen, watches me carefully but doesn't speak, waiting for me to go first.

"I want to try hypnotherapy," I state plainly, my voice devoid of the nervous waver I assumed would come considering I'm terrified by the prospect.

It's been almost a month since I found out the truth about Jesse, and I've been trying to process everything that happened between us—on the mountain and in the week leading up to it—but I'm still at a loss. Especially now I know we share a past and I can't remember any of it. No matter how hard I try.

Jesse's called a few times too. And sent messages. But other than his message about Tate, I mostly ignore him, only sending the occasional "when I'm ready" text here and there. Because while I desperately want to know what happened twelve years ago, I'm not ready to face him. And I want to find out as much as I can on my own. In case he lies to me again.

I am grateful for one thing, though. He was right to think that Tate was on my mind. I hate that I know he was involved, but have no details on the how or why. So, the fact that he's not around does put me at ease, just not fully settled.

Which leads me back here. Searching for answers.

I haven't been to regular therapy sessions for years, but after everything I went through recently, I felt myself spiraling again, and couldn't let the darkness take over. I haven't yet broached the topic of why I'm really here. *What I know*. But I told Gretchen about Lucia naming her daughter *Jade*, and how the mention of her name still affects me all these years later, and that seems to be reason enough. It's not a lie—while Lucia has had someone take over running her shop in the short term, I still see her and Jade around town on occasion and it hurts. It's just not the *main* reason for needing these sessions.

But everyone keeps things from their therapists, right?

"I've mentioned hypnotherapy in most of our sessions," Gretchen says, her pen poised at her notebook, ready to write down her secret observations. "Can I ask why today? Has something changed between when I last saw you and this moment?"

Of course, she can't get straight to the hypnosis. I should have preplanned a response.

"Nothing's changed," I say, and it's not exactly a lie. I still don't remember. "I just need answers and nothing else seems to be working."

"*Okay.* I do need to let you know, as I've said before, there are no guarantees that this will work. The longer a patient goes without regaining their memories, the lower the chances they ever will."

"I know."

"Perfect. Let's get started then."

She motions for me to move to the couch, and a shiver runs through me. I've always preferred the chair over the couch. I never lie down in our sessions. But I guess it's a must with hypnotherapy.

When I'm settled on the long burgundy chaise, Gretchen dims the lights. "Now close your eyes and breathe slowly," she says softly. "In through your nose, out through your mouth."

I do as she asks and wriggle slightly until I'm comfortable, a nervous energy running through me.

"I want you to listen to my voice, and my voice alone. Focus on that; block everything else from your thoughts. From your mind. And breathe."

I breathe in deeply and listen to her calm, rhythmic tone, praying for this to work.

It has to work.

The alternative is to visit Jesse for answers, and despite my parting words to him up on the mountain, I don't want to do that. At least, not yet.

***

Even after the forewarning, I'm still disappointed when the hypnotherapy doesn't work, telling me just how much I was relying on it to save me.

Gretchen schedules a few more sessions, but it does nothing to ease my mind. I wanted to remember something. I'm desperate to. Even the smallest little detail, just to prove to myself that it's not gone. It can't be. I spent years thinking all was lost, and that I'd never know.

But now that I'm finally trying... What if I was right?

I'm tired for work the next day, but unlike in the past when I would have tried to hide it, I own it, even yawning as I greet my store neighbor, Debbie, on my arrival. Instead of my usual cheery hello, I smile, but I don't mind that it doesn't reach my eyes. I'm allowed to be tired. Everyone's tired.

When it gets to ten and I've only had one customer, I find myself scrolling the online news to pass the time. And an idea hits me.

I quickly register for their news archives and search for Jade's accident, along with any other news from the following week, hoping something will stand out.

Anything.

But after a good hour, it's safe to assume that like everything else, it's useless.

I'm hunched over, my eyes wide as I stare at the screen, when Sara appears.

"Whatcha doing?" she asks from behind me, making me jump up, almost knocking her over.

"Jesus," I screech as my hand flies to my chest. "You almost gave me a heart attack."

Sara raises an eyebrow but doesn't otherwise react. Instead, she crosses her arms over her chest and stares. "Well?" she asks again.

"You can clearly see what I'm doing," I note but hate that I was busted when I told everyone—including her—I was moving on. *I'm not. I just needed everyone to back off.* None of them know I've been talking with my therapist, that I'm back to square one. I'm not ashamed. I'm just not ready for the questions. And that's okay. I feel good about my decision.

"Why don't you call him and ask for the truth?" Sara suggests, like it's a new idea and not something I've been stewing over every single day since he left. Or more accurately, since I sent him away.

"I know you only met him for a few minutes," I say. "But he's not very forthcoming." A nice way of saying he's likely to spin some bullshit answer.

After I was sent home from the hospital, I broke down and told Sara everything about Jesse and me, including what I knew about the accident. Which I guess means she officially knows more than my therapist. I needed someone in my corner. Someone that wasn't family, since my family is too close to this entire situation.

And then I told her I was fine. I was moving on.

43

"Believe it or not,"—Sara giggles—"I actually got that impression of Jesse during our short exchange," she says. "Especially when he ran off to find you without any explanation. We could have helped."

"I'm assuming he didn't want the help. He obviously doesn't want me to remember what happened. And if I *had* remembered, he probably didn't want anyone around."

Sara frowns. "I'm sorry you've been through all of this, and that it had to be Jesse."

"Me too. Thank you for not telling me to go to the police." I may be pissed at him right now, but I'd never report him.

Sara's hands lift to her hips and she frowns. "As I said when you first told me, you should tell the police. You *absolutely* should, but I do understand why you want to hold off."

"Oh yeah?"

"You care about him." She smiles warmly as I roll my eyes.

"I had a crush and it's over," I lie...to her and myself.

Sara's eyes widen before she playfully shakes her head. "If you say so."

I gape. "God, you sound like Pippa sometimes."

Sara laughs, bumping her shoulder into mine. "While she's away, I'm your replacement big sister."

"What about Ashley?" I ask, biting back a smile.

"I'm going to pretend you didn't just compare me to Ashley. I know how you feel about her."

"You're nothing like her," I say, pulling her into a hug as my tablet screen fades to black, drawing my attention.

Sara looks between me and the screen, her brow furrowed as she worries her bottom lip. "Did it help at all?" she asks after a beat.

"Not yet. It's hard when my parents kept my name out of everything. I can't search for Willow Sanders and see it all pop up." I frown, bringing the screen back to life before punching in the password. "I know I—"

"Wait!" Sara exclaims, grabbing my shoulders to spin me around. "I can't believe I forgot."

"Forgot what?"

"The password."

"What password?"

"Robin Hood."

I cringe because even I knew it was a strange choice. It just popped into my head one day, with no meaning behind it, and it definitely had the potential to be forgotten. "Sorry." I step back, out of her hold. "There's no exciting story behind it. I have no idea where it came from." Sara bounces up and down like she's bursting to speak, but lets me finish up before she does. "Anyway, I'll change it soon. I promise."

"I know where it came from," she blurts the second I'm done.

"What?" I chuckle. This should be good. "Don't tell me there's a Robin Hood poster somewhere or a new movie coming out and I subconsciously saw the trailer."

"Nope." She shakes her head comically.

"Okay, fill me in."

"You remembered." Her eyes bore into mine as the smallest smile plays on her lips.

"I, what?"

"You remembered it. Your parents asked me for your password to try and track your phone. When I gave it to them, Jesse was there, and he kind of freaked out before saying 'I've got to go' and running off."

Jesus.

"I didn't think much of it at the time," she continues. "I was too wrapped up in finding you. But I should have put it together when you told me the story. I'm sorry."

I'm still a little confused about what she's trying to say, and she must notice something in my expression, because she steps forward and grabs my arms again, looking me in the eye.

"You said that he knew where to find you. And that he admitted he was there that day. Well, he ran to look for you the second I mentioned the password. What if you remembered Robin Hood? What if that's significant?"

"Why would that be significant? Because it took place in a forest?"

"No." She laughs. "Maybe you spoke about the movie. You love talking movies."

Robin Hood, Robin Hood, Robin Hood. I repeat the name over and over in my head, hoping it will trigger something more, but it doesn't. All I get are images of the actors that played the character over the years... Kevin Costner, Russell Crowe, Cary Elwes...

"I did love *Men in Tights*," I say with a smile. "But if I was with Jesse long enough to have a discussion about movies, wouldn't I remember that?"

"Didn't you say the entire event was missing from your memory?"

"Yes, but I just assumed it was all traumatic." I shrug.

Sara's face drops as I speak about it so easily, like it's nothing. But it's hard to have feelings toward something when I don't know what that something is. Ask me about my time in the hospital—about waking up with a tube wedged down my throat, about staring at my parents as they explained what they knew, and me having no recollection of any of it. Ask me about losing my best friend. Ask me about the pain I felt when I learned I'd never see Jade again. *That* is agony for me. *That* hurts. But ask me about what happened on that mountain and I'm numb.

Which is almost harder to take.

"I hate all of this," Sara says, her voice barely above a whisper, making me want to comfort her.

"Me too."

"Can I help?" she asks, a hint of hope back in her tone.

"Help?"

"Yes. I'd like to help you search for answers."

My bottom lip quivers as I try to smile through my emotions. "Other than the archives, I've got nothing. But help would be great."

Sara pats my back before reaching for my tablet. "I love watching *Cold Case*, and this feels like that. The answers are out there. We just have to find them." Her response makes me chuckle, and the smallest weight lifts until she adds, "What about the other guy?"

Does she mean Tate? Or Alex? I'm about to ask, when our new front door chime interrupts us. We should have changed the damn bell years ago; I much prefer the soft angelic sound of the replacement.

Sara and I fall silent as we wait for our customer to come into view but when he does, Sara quietly gasps while I stiffen.

"Alex?"

5
Willow

"Hi Willow." Alex smiles shyly, and it's a complete contradiction to the man I knew last month. "I'm sorry to interrupt you at work, but I'm wondering if you have a moment?"

If that sentence doesn't make me nervous, I don't know what else will. He's sorry to interrupt me at work? Since when?

"Sure, we can talk out back."

I point in the direction of our back room and wait for him to approach before leading the way.

"Willow. Can you quickly double-check this order so I can send it off?" Sara calls out after I've taken a few steps, confirming she's just as weirded out as I am—we have no orders.

"Of course. Alex, I'll be there in a moment."

When I get back to the desk, Sara has a piece of paper waiting for me to review.

Don't close the door and stay on the right so I can see you.

So dramatic. I bite back a laugh, but nod. "That all looks perfect," I say out loud before whispering, "Will do."

Alex is leaning against the left wall when I enter, making me giggle internally as I stand on the right. He moves to shut the door, but I stop him. "Sorry, I need to be able to hear if Sara needs me. She sometimes has to rush off for her son."

"Ah. Sure. Okay."

"Thanks. So how can I help?" I ask, trying to project a confidence I only half feel.

Alex runs a hand through his hair and focuses his gaze away from me, looking down at the floor, drawing my eyes in the same direction. "I thought it was time I told you the truth."

"What?" My gaze flashes to his so quickly it's almost comical. "What truth?"

He takes a deep breath before finally looking my way, and the emotion in his eyes shocks me. "I knew Jade," he rasps slowly before pausing, most likely waiting for my reaction.

But I have none because... *He what?*

"She and I were...something. I don't know, we never labeled it," he continues after a beat, causing me even more confusion. "We were something and then she was just *gone*. And I had no idea what happened. No one knew about us, so there was no one to tell me. Until I heard the news."

He pauses again and looks away before running his hands down his face. I know it's my turn to speak, and

God knows I should have a million questions, but I can't compute what he's saying.

"I'm sorry." He huffs out a laugh as he looks my way. "This is a lot. But I couldn't keep quiet anymore. Not if there was a chance you remembered..."

"You knew Jade?" I whisper, hoping that if I say it out loud it will make sense.

Alex laughs again, but it's full of sadness. "I did."

"Then why..." I trail off because I was going to ask why he was pursuing me, but that's not the first thing I should be addressing. I should be saying... "It's been twelve years."

"Trust me, I know."

"Why now?" I ask, my brain finally firing.

"It's a long story and—"

"So, shorten it," I cut in because I'm not letting him leave until he tells me. Jade never mentioned him. She never mentioned anyone except the occasional boy at school. "I need to know."

Alex nods and leans back into the wall, his expression pinched. "As I've told you before, I met Tate in jail and we became friends. One night, I jokingly told him I'd forgotten a few years of my life, and he told me about you. The girl from his school. The girl who couldn't remember."

"Okay." My heart pounds in my chest even though that part isn't new information for me. I'm more worried about what's coming.

"When I asked him if you were still living there...here, he couldn't tell me. Said it had been years since he'd seen you, and that you'd most likely moved away. End of story."

I huff out a laugh because I wish that was true, but Alex doesn't see the funny side. Instead his face drops as he continues his story.

"Sometime later, I can't remember how long, he got that invite to your dad's thing and told me to come along. I wasn't going to because what was the point... You didn't have the answers I needed. I'd already resigned myself to the fact that I'd never know. But then he got wasted and started mumbling about how he thought you might remember...how it was only a matter of time...and I changed my mind."

"I don't understand."

"Willow, if there was even the slightest chance you remembered... I had to find out." His voice shakes as he speaks, the emotion in his tone bleeding through. But it doesn't add up.

"Why didn't you ever come and see me? Or just tell me the truth when you first came back? Why pretend to be interested?"

And why the hell does everyone I know feel the need to lie to me?

"I wasn't pretending," he says, and I roll my eyes. "When I first asked you to dance, I did it to get to know you. For answers. But then I felt this connection and I couldn't stay away."

"But—"

Alex raises his hand to tell me he's not done and continues on. "The reason I never came to see you sooner is because I thought it would hurt too much. To know you had all the answers I wanted but couldn't access them."

Ouch. That's all I need...more reasons to feel guilty.

"This *is* a lot," I repeat his words back to him. "Why are you telling me now?"

"I felt bad after convincing you to go up the mountain."

"It's been a month." *All of that was about him. Not me. Him. Ugh. I'm an idiot.* "If you're here to ask if I know anything, I don't." I cross my arms over my chest as the lie easily leaves my lips. "It didn't work."

"I'm not here for that. I just came to apologize."

"Oh. Okay." *I didn't expect that.* "Thank you. I guess."

He takes a step closer, but when I shake my head he steps back again. "I'm sorry. I should have told you when you were in the hospital."

"Or before that?"

"Yeah." He chuckles. "I should have told you from the start."

"You should have. But it's too late. You can, however, tell me about you and Jade."

"I can. And I will. Can I take you to dinner?"

What? "I don't think that's a good idea. We can talk here."

Alex's eyes widen, but he nods, gripping the back of his neck. "I cared about her deeply, but she didn't think anyone would approve of me."

My stomach swirls with more guilt, but I don't want to believe him. We told each other everything. Jade would have said *something*.

"She begged me to keep it a secret," he continues, "and I reluctantly agreed. I would have done anything for her."

"Do her parents know?" I ask, my brow furrowed. "I mean, did you talk to them after?"

"No. There was no point." His face drops again and my heart clenches. If he's telling the truth, I can't imagine what he went through. Actually, I can...it's the same thing I went through. We both lost someone we cared for and have no idea why.

"I wish I could tell you what happened," I say quietly. "I wish I had the answers."

"Me too."

The front door chimes and we both fall silent. Though, even if we hadn't been interrupted, I don't think there's much more to say. I feel completely blindsided by what he's told me, but Jade's gone. Hearing more now isn't going to change that.

When Alex and I walk out, Grant's moving down the aisle, his gaze locked over his shoulder, back toward the front windows. "Sara, you forgot your lunch," he says absentmindedly. "I knew you were doing a full day so... Oh, hi Willow." His voice raises as he finally turns and spots me, his frown morphing to a smile.

"Everything okay?" I ask as he gets closer, reaching for Sara when he comes to a stop. A sharp sting hits me in the chest, making my mood shift. I want that.

What they've got. I *really* want that. And I hate that the person who made me finally realize I wanted more from life is the same person who made me so against it in the first place. And I never even knew why.

I glance at Sara, thinking about her offer, as my two life choices come to mind. The way I see it, I need to choose *one* path. I can take Sara's offer and do everything in my power to find out exactly what happened that day. I can keep working with my therapist and actually face Jesse, forcing him to talk. *Or* I can forget it all, use what little information I *do* have to start fresh, and move forward as though *that* Willow never existed.

Jesse may very well have been the cause of my heartache, but he also helped me find myself again. He helped me to question my life. Maybe I need to take that blessing and run with it. Truly move on from my past.

Grant's frown appears again, pulling me from my thoughts, and my eyes flash to Sara's in concern.

"There's a guy hanging around out front. It's probably nothing. It's just..." He trails off and shakes his head while Alex stiffens beside me, and a nervous feeling settles in my stomach.

"Forget it," Grant continues before I can say anything. "He was probably just looking at your new window display."

Sara looks toward the window at the same time I do, but there's no one there.

"I'll have a look on my way out," Alex says, nodding toward the door. "But I'm sure he's right." He points to Grant before walking away, only turning back at the last second to wave goodbye.

Goose bumps spread across my body, telling me I should be worried, but why? Who could it be? Unless it's Tate? But Jesse told me not to be worried about him. *God, I'm paranoid again. And short of discovering everything, I'm not sure how I'm going to shake it.*

My gaze moves to my tablet in Sara's hands and I inwardly curse. *I've been kidding myself.* There's no way I can move on without knowing the truth. I hate that there are people out there that know more about me than I do. I hate feeling like I'm not in control of my own life. And I need to fix that.

Plus, I remembered something...

"I'm going to San Francisco," I say out of nowhere, making Sara smile.

She walks forward and pulls me in for a quick hug. "I think that's a great idea. But first, what the hell happened with Alex?"

After telling Sara about Alex, I'm more determined than ever to discover the truth, but it doesn't last long. Yes, I pack a bag as soon as I get home from work, but beyond that, I make no plans to actually leave, suddenly aware of how big a deal it is. I've never even been past the border of the next town. The hospital is the farthest place I've visited, and now I want to go to San Francisco. To the city. To chase something that might not even be there.

I head off for a walk, testing my ankle a few times with a slow jog, thankful that my injury wasn't as bad as I first thought. When I reach the sign for the lookout, like always, I pause. My heart lodges in my throat as I fight to keep my emotions in check. Over the years, my fear of going back kept me grounded, but I always felt like that mountain held all the answers. Now I know the truth. All I found was more pain. More questions. More heartbreak. And most of that came from Jesse.

A stick crunches under my foot as I step off the path and into the brush, my legs guiding me forward without my permission. Millions of images flash through my mind of all the times I came here with Jade, but none of them link to the one memory I desperately need.

I remember the twelve-year-old versions of us, dressed up in what we considered appropriate hiking wear, packing a lunch for our very first journey. I remember seeing the view for the first time, the way the air left my lungs at the beauty of it all. I remember the scratches, the falls, the laughter, the tears.

And I remember standing in this very spot, time and time again, willing my legs to walk but being frozen in place, unable to move forward without my best friend, my world.

The hardest thing to take is that it wasn't a rarity for Jade and me to be up there. It was *our* escape. When I wanted to be alone, I went to the next town over, but when Jade and I needed to get away, that's where we went.

But never with anyone else.

We even avoided times when it was likely to be busy. Like summer.

Yet Jesse was there...and Tate. But Tate never told Alex about it. Why? Was it him? *God, I just need to know.*

Did we interrupt them doing something illegal?

Or did they follow us?

Did Jade invite them?

God, did they know Jade beforehand?

When I was questioned by the police, they asked me if Jade had been spending time with any new people or if her personality had changed in the lead-up to her death. I'd always said no. But I lied. Something about her was different. I just couldn't quite remember what that was. And now I know. It was Alex. She didn't want to tell me about Alex. But if he's looking for answers then he wasn't involved. And Jesse would have told me if he was...

A thought hits me suddenly as a sharp pain radiates in my chest.

Was it me?

Did I invite Jesse and block it out?

No, that can't be right. If I knew Jesse before the mountain, I would have remembered him.

Right? *Right?*

The sound of a car driving past breaks me from my madness, and I startle before making my way back to the road. Even if I wanted to go up there again, I know not to go by myself.

When I set off toward home, I notice a truck stopped on the side of the road ahead of me, but it pulls away before I can register any details. A shiver runs through me and I have to laugh. I'm once again imagining things, letting my mind run away from me, and it has to end.

My packed bag haunts me from the doorway when I get home, telling me that enough is enough. I can't spend the rest of my life wondering. I'm supposed to be stronger; I need to stop being so indecisive.

Without giving it any more thought, I slide down the wall and call Pippa. If I tell her I'm coming, it will be harder to back out.

The call connects, and the first thing I hear is the deafening background noise, before Pippa calls out through the chaos. "Willow, hi. I'm just walking through—" Everything goes quiet as though she hung up, but the noise starts up again before I've had a chance to check my screen. "Sorry, cell service goes in and out here," she yells in my ear. "Can I call you back?"

"Of course. Talk soon."

I hang up without waiting for her to respond because the only thing that call achieved was to freak me out even more. Reminding me of how different our worlds are. *What am I getting myself into? Where do I even start?*

It's another hour before I hear from Pippa, and in that time, I achieved absolutely nothing. I haven't even moved from my position on the floor, my legs curled up as though I'm in my own tight little bubble.

"Sorry again. This is much better."

The only background noise I hear now is the distant sound of a TV, and the relief I feel is a little bit worrying. "Thanks for calling me back. I..." *Shit. What do I even say?* "I'm coming to San Francisco." *That's a good start.*

Pippa's dead silent, and if the TV wasn't still playing, I'd think we got disconnected again. "Pippa?"

"I'm sorry. Of course, you can come. I'd love for you to visit. I've got a spare room and a car you can use. I can even pick you up from the airport, or at least, I can send someone if I'm working. When are you coming?"

"As soon as I can?"

Pippa sighs but I know she doesn't mean for me to hear it. "Is there any chance you're going to tell me what's going on?"

Now it's my turn to sigh. "Yeah, I can do that. But I don't know that much more than you do."

"I just want to help, and also, it would be nice to know why I'm annoyed at Jesse."

I bark out a quick laugh. "You're annoyed at him?"

"Of course I am. But as I said, if he ever asks me why, I can't really answer."

"Thank you." I *think*. "Do I need to explain now or when I get there?"

Pippa laughs. "It's been a month. I can wait. Book a flight and let me know the details. I'll be here."

My heart clenches as it all gets a little bit more real. Confronting Jesse is going to be hard enough, but add the flying, the city, plus the fact that I'll be completely out of my comfort zone, and it's tenfold.

After saying goodbye, I stare at the phone for a good five minutes before pulling myself up off the carpet and texting Mom. I've learned my lesson about doing things without informing her.

Willow: I'm going to visit Pippa. I'll be gone for a few days. I'll call you when I get settled.

Mom doesn't reply, but I don't expect her to. She's not a texter. Instead, she calls. Immediately.

"What do you mean you're visiting Pippa?"

"Hi Mom."

"Hi. Now, please tell me it's a joke."

Closing my eyes, I take a deep breath and hold it, before releasing it slowly so she can't hear my sigh. "It's not a joke. I'm about to book my flight."

"No."

"Excuse me?"

"I don't think it's a good idea."

"I'm just visiting Pippa. Taking a vacation if you will. I'm doing something for myself."

"What about the shop? You have responsibilities."

I roll my eyes, and for once, I wish that she could see me. "Sara's looking after the shop. I've got it covered. I'm not looking for your permission. This is a courtesy. I'll see you when I get back."

"Willow?"

"I love you, Mom."

With that I hang up and drop back onto the couch, throwing a hand over my face with a sigh. Why can't she ever just support my decisions? She's happy about the shop now, but even that was a challenge until Sara came on board. I didn't even realize how much she was holding me back until I got older. Maybe we really do get wiser as we age.

I book a flight for the next day, and by five in the afternoon I'm touching down on California soil. *California.* I'm in California. I made it.

My lips pull into a smile without my permission before I actually giggle out loud. I left Hepburn Falls and the world didn't end. I feel invincible.

The seatbelt sign switches off, and it's like a race to see who can get off the plane first. I take my time, watching everyone rush around, and it's not until the last of the passengers exit, I grab my carry-on and smile as I leave, thanking everyone I see. After collecting my bag, I search for Pippa, but she's nowhere to be seen. She said she'd be here. Even though she joked about sending a car.

Fifteen minutes later, I almost give up and call an Uber when I see her come running through the doors, looking frazzled. She brushes her blonde hair away from her face and throws her huge bag over her shoulder, her eyes frantically scanning her surroundings, her panic only subsiding when she spots me.

"Sorry I'm late. I've been through hell to get here." Her phone rings, and when she checks the screen, she curses under her breath before smiling back at me. "But that doesn't matter. It's not for you to worry about," she adds, grabbing the handle of my suitcase. "Let's get you home."

I can't say how many times I grip the door as Pippa zips around the streets, weaving in and out of traffic. But it's a lot. *How do people live like this?* Seriously, they need to *slow down.* And I don't just mean the driving. I mean life in general. The trip from the airport seems to take forever, but I'm told that's because I decided to land during rush hour. I didn't even think about that when booking. I just went for the next available flight. *God, I feel so out of touch.*

And don't even get me started on the hills. I live in a mountain town yet our land is flatter.

Pippa slows as we approach an eclectic looking apartment building, a smile lighting up her face. "We're here," she sings. "This is—goddammit!"

My eyes flash to hers before following her gaze out the window. Goddammit, all right. Jesse's leaning against the wall with his arms folded over his chest and his usual scowl in place, looking like he's waiting for someone.

And when his eyes meet mine, it's no surprise to discover...that someone is me.

6
Jesse

"Alright men, good practice today. We're just over a week away from our first preseason game, and I can already feel the difference. You're bonding in a way you haven't before."

The guys all cheer before Coach raises a hand to silence them. "But...you've been known to get cocky in the past. Don't fuck this up. You're onto a good thing. Let's show them what's coming for them this year."

Cheers ring out again until we're silenced for a second time.

"Hastings and Blakey," our forward coach calls out, drawing everyone's attention. "My office after you're dressed."

"Shit," Ryan curses under his breath while I skate off the ice, barely acknowledging his existence. And perhaps that's the problem.

The past month has been hell. Never in my life did I expect I'd find someone who completely consumed me. For the first few months after I left Mossman Hills, all those years ago, I was a shell of a human. I couldn't sleep; I barely ate. My life essentially ended that fateful day. The day she forgot.

But my new foster family slowly brought me back to life the best way they knew how...hockey. Bit by bit the cold and brutal sport thawed me out, broke through my walls, and allowed me to breathe again. To feel something more than the numbness that had taken over.

Hockey gave me back my life.

But back then, I thought leaving her was the best thing I could do for her.

This time around, I'm worried leaving made things worse.

Other than a few random, emotionless responses to my calls and texts, I have no idea how she is. Pippa won't talk to me about her, and Ryan says he doesn't know anything. There's no news headlines to keep me informed this time, no hearsay filtering back.

All I'm getting is silence.

And I guess I can see the justice in that.

For years, I kept quiet. Even after I found her again, I bit my tongue. It's about time I had the favor returned.

But it fucking sucks.

I'm fighting an uphill battle. And this time, hockey isn't helping.

I need to see Willow.

She's all that matters.

When I get to Coach's office, Ryan's already there, sitting like a school kid on his first day, with his eyes focused ahead of him, ever the teacher's pet.

I'd probably chuckle if it hadn't been weeks since I found anything worth laughing about.

"Why am I getting calls about the two of you feuding?" Coach says as soon as I enter the room, his gaze locked on his laptop screen in front of him. I quickly glance toward Ryan as Coach continues. "If this has anything to do with Pip—"

"It doesn't," I say, cutting him off. "And we're not feuding." I may be pissed off with Pippa at the moment, but I'm not about to throw her or Ryan under a bus.

"I've noticed some tension and—"

"You don't really buy into gossip, do you?" I ask, realizing immediately that it wasn't my smartest move.

"Watch it, Jesse. Now's the time for you to be on your best behavior, isn't it?" He doesn't have to say it for me to know what he's referring to. I'm still unsigned after this season. "You're a great player," he continues on. "One of our best. And if we want to win and keep winning in the next few years, we'll probably need you. But we'll never tolerate players with an attitude problem." He pauses, but it's obvious he's not finished, so for the sake of my job, I stay quiet. "We've let a lot slide over the years when it comes to you. But that's because we'd all avoid the media if we could, and it isn't hurting anyone. But if you bring that same disrespect to me, other staff, or the team, you're out."

Jesus. I think we got him on a bad day. He's usually the nicest of the coaches.

"As for you," he says, turning to Ryan. "Next time something happens with a member of our staff, have the balls to tell us yourself. I shouldn't have to hear it from your girlfriend, like she's briefing me on a fucking publicity issue."

Ryan nods as I internally cringe for him.

"And if this one's giving you a hard time," he adds, pointing to me, "tell him to fuck off. Don't let it affect your game."

Damn.

"Will do," Ryan says, sitting up even straighter, something I didn't think was possible.

"Good, whatever it is, or isn't, sort it out. We've got a cup to win this season."

That we do.

Especially if I'm not getting a new contract.

I'm walking a few paces behind Ryan as we both make our way back to the locker rooms, and when he rounds the corner before me, Pippa's voice has me coming to a stop.

"Willow's coming late afternoon tomorrow and I have to..." She pauses and I lean forward, desperate to hear what she has to say.

What, Pippa? What? My heart thumps in my chest as a million thoughts run through my head. Just the mention of Willow's name has me completely spiraling, and now she's coming *here*. To San Francisco.

Within seconds, the angel and devil that have attached themselves to my shoulder go to war. The angel tells me to leave Willow be. To wait for her to make the first move. To give her peace. Like she wanted. But the devil says *fuck that*, if she's coming here, she knows exactly what she's doing, and it's time to talk. Of course, the devil is going to win—Willow wouldn't expect otherwise—but it kills me to know that talking to her is only going to make things worse. If she hates me now, that's nothing compared to how she'll feel when she knows the truth.

"We should talk about this later," Ryan says, cutting into my thoughts as he stops Pippa from saying any more, knowing I'm going to round the corner any second.

Pippa's silent for a beat before I hear her shuffle around. "Um, okay, sorry. I'll leave you alone."

Typical Pippa, she doesn't even wait to hear him out.

"Pip."

I don't have to look to know she's shaking her head as she backs away. "It's fine. See you later."

I could cut in and get him out of the bind, but if I want information from Pippa, I need to wait. If she knows I heard about Willow, she'll avoid me more than she already does. And I can't have that. I need to see Willow and for that, I need Pippa.

When she's gone, I wander around the corner to find Ryan waiting for me, his hands over his face. When I clear my throat, he drops his arms.

"Dammit!" he says before mumbling something to himself.

"What's the matter, Blakey?" I ask, playing the part of an innocent man, my spirits suddenly lifting.

Ryan shakes his head before I've even finished speaking, a look of shock on his face. "You're smiling. You don't *ever* smile."

I *am*. I hadn't even noticed. But now that I think of it, I know why. I'm fucking proud of Buttercup. She may despise the very sight of me, but she's taking a huge step, getting her life back. And that little part of this entire fucked-up situation makes me happy.

"Busted." I shrug, even though I no longer recognize myself.

"I don't know the details, man. But please don't cause trouble."

My brows rise as I stare him down, trying hard not to tell him to mind his own goddamn business. Instead, I shake my head. "I don't know what you're referring to. Keep quiet, and all will be fine."

The next day, I lean against the wall opposite Pippa's office, with my arms folded over my chest, waiting for my moment. She said Willow would be arriving late afternoon, so I'm here for details. I want in. I want to be there.

Something crashes behind her closed door before she releases a string of curses and the door flies open.

After lifting her bag to her shoulder, she checks her phone and curses again before finally looking my way, jumping at the sight of me. "*Jesus!*"

"Nope. I am definitely not holy."

"What do you want, Jesse?"

I push off the wall and take a step toward her. "I want to cash in on *my* favor," I say, the idea only now popping into my head. And fuck, it's a good one.

Pippa eyes me in confusion, her brow furrowed until a light bulb goes off and I see the moment everything registers. "Goddammit. How'd you find out?"

I bark out a laugh as she completely deflates in front of me. "I overheard you telling Ryan. He knew I'd be coming soon so he was trying to get you to stop talking."

"Again. Goddammit. The answer is no. No matter what the question is."

"Pippa. Pippa. Pippa. You owe me."

"Yes, but this isn't about me. I've got to go."

She pushes past and rushes down the hall, assuming that's the end of it. I admire her for holding strong, but I can't let this go. I'm a desperate man. I don't know when I turned into that guy, but Willow fucking owns me. And I just need to make sure she's okay.

"Let me come with you," I say, stopping short of demanding.

"No."

"Pippa, *please*."

She pauses her steps and spins around, her expression softening. "I'm sorry, Jesse. I can't. But if it makes you feel better, I'm ninety-nine percent sure she's coming here for you, not me, so you won't have to wait long."

I've already waited a goddamn month. Not to mention the twelve years before that. I'm no fucking saint. I have no patience left.

"I *need* to see her."

"I know but I have to go. *Alone*. I'm sure it won't be long."

She picks up her pace and frantically presses the elevator button, probably thinking I'm going to follow her and force my way into her car. I'm not. I may be an asshole, but I'm not that bad, really...

I'll meet them at her apartment instead.

7
Jesse

T welve Years Ago – Age Sixteen

We easily catch up to the girls and skirt around them, blocking their path as we stop.

"Jade," I hesitate, my hands held out in front of me like she's a wild animal. "I need you to calm down so we can work this out."

Jade's panicked gaze flits between me and Buttercup, before she squeezes Buttercup's wrist tighter and steps back. "Just let us go. I'm not going to say anything. You've got my money. Do your job."

"T...Captain America will give the money back. You can walk away as though this never happened. Start fresh."

"What the fu—" Tate starts, but Jade cuts him off. "No."

From the way her hands shake and the utter terror in her expression, I take a chance on the fact that this is her first time and try to make her see sense. "You picked the right guy to contact; he won't punish you if

73

you change your mind. I can see you don't want to do this."

I feel Tate's stare boring a hole in the side of my head, but I ignore it and focus on the girls.

Jade steps back again, shaking her head as she does, her nerves on full display. Buttercup, on the other hand, looks angry. "What's he talking about?" she yells, ripping her arm from Jade's grasp. "What money? What are you trying to buy?"

Jade's eyes widen as she continues to shake her head. "It's nothing," she tells Buttercup before turning to me. "Please just let us leave."

I really wish I could do that.

8
Jesse

C lenching my fists, I shake off my thoughts and curse under my breath. What's taking them so long? Did Pippa drive back to Hepburn Falls to pick Willow up?

Being alone with my thoughts is dangerous.

Every time I let myself think about the incident, I feel physically sick. None of it should have happened. But that damn drug deal set off a domino effect that no one saw coming. And now it's coming back to haunt me, while I'm waiting patiently for the madness to arrive. *Or not so patiently.*

I feel like a dickhead stalking the front of Pippa's building, but she just doesn't get it...desperate times call for desperate measures. And fuck, I'm a desperate man.

Another few minutes pass before Pippa's Mercedes finally pulls up, and I'm so fucking tense I could snap. But when I glance up and lock eyes with Willow for the first time in weeks, the tension fades.

She turns away seconds after our gazes meet, but it doesn't matter. The relief I feel, just having her here, is indescribable.

The gate rises for Pippa to drive through, and I follow behind them as she makes her way into the parking garage. As soon as she's switched off the engine, Pippa's out of her car, her eyes ablaze with anger.

"Are you kidding me right now?"

"Apparently not," I say, because honestly, if someone had told me I'd be doing something like this, I would have thought they were joking.

"Jesse, you can't be here."

"I just need to see her. I won't even say a word."

Pippa ducks down so she can see Willow in the car, and a silent conversation takes place. I know I've won when her shoulders drop and she releases a sigh of frustration. "Not one word," she seethes as she turns toward me.

I draw a cross over my heart and nod, causing Pippa to roll her eyes. I'm about to verbally agree when Willow's door opens and my world stills.

She steps out in one quick movement but doesn't look my way, her eyes trained on the ground. While I couldn't look away if I tried.

As she gathers her hair into her hands, I focus on her every move, watching as her fingers glide through the thick waves, trying to tame the wild strands as she goes. When she's done, she brushes the strays behind her ears before finally lifting her gaze, her piercing green eyes staring through to my soul.

With all her usual warmth gone.

I hold strong, refusing to break our connection. I want to show her that I can take anything she throws at me as long as she's okay. And as long as she's fighting. But the more I stare, the more I see just how broken she is.

And *that's* what destroys me in the end.

I told her she'd ruin me. I just didn't think it would be like this.

My insides twist as I try hard not to project my feelings. But when I can't take it anymore, I look away, focusing my attention on her body instead of her lost gaze. Assessing her for any damage that she might have done to herself in the month since I saw her.

She's wearing black Chuck Taylor sneakers, so I can't see her ankle under the high-top style, but that should have healed by now. *I hope.* As I survey the rest of her, my gaze gets stuck on her toned legs. They've always been a weakness for me, and today's no exception. Especially considering she's wearing frayed white denim short shorts, showing off almost as much leg as the night she walked into the kitchen half-naked.

"You've seen me now," Willow says, snapping me out of my memory, her voice wavering as she speaks for the first time.

I open my mouth to respond, wanting to tell her she's beautiful, to tell her I'm sorry, to tell her how messed up I am, but she cuts me off.

"No, Jesse," she says, stopping me from breaking my promise not to speak. "You shouldn't be here. I deserve the right to decide when and where I want to talk. You owe me that much."

She's right, I do. But I can't bring myself to walk away.

"Please, just give me ten minutes."

"Jess—"

"I'll leave you alone after that... Until you're ready."

Willow pauses and I'm actually shocked she's considering my request. I'm not even sure what I want to say; all I know is that my heart finally feels like it's beating again now that she's here.

"Five minutes," she says before turning to Pippa, asking another silent question.

"How about you sit in the car for privacy. I'll wait by the elevator."

Willow nods before her eyes settle back on mine. "Works for me."

I take my time walking to the car, trying to decide what the hell I could possibly say in five minutes that won't make her despise the very sight of me. More than she does now. But the second I'm inside, sitting so close I could touch her, the words flow naturally.

"I'm sorry. I'm so fucking sorry for everything I've put you through. I never planned it. I never expected to see you again, or to *feel* things again. For you or anyone. And it kind of messed me up. I'm not going to sit here and make excuses, though I've got plenty. I just needed to see for myself that you were okay. I needed to know. Because Willow, it's been driving me crazy."

I pause for a second as I swallow back the emotions threatening to clog my throat, all while Willow stares at me with her head held high and her arms folded over her chest, trying to appear unaffected. She gave me five minutes, and if I've learned anything about her, it's that *five minutes* is all I'll get.

"I should have known you'd be okay," I say, suppressing my smile. "You're strong. So strong. Within a few minutes of meeting you, I knew you wouldn't be the type of girl to hold back. And I was right. You weren't back then, and you're not now. While I truly believe that you're better off not knowing what happened on that mountain, I admire you for wanting to find out. And I love that you're finally taking a stand."

Taking a deep breath, I try *not* to focus on the fact that deep down, my strong Willow is struggling beside me, and I definitely don't want to think about the fact that I'm the reason she's not okay. Instead, I say the one thing I should have been saying all along.

"I love you, Willow. And I wish things had been different between us. That we'd met at a different time. That we could fix this."

But I know there's little chance of that happening.

When I look up again, Willow's staring at me with wide, watery eyes as she squeezes her fingers in a tight grip. With the color they're turning, I'm nervous she's going to break them, so I reach forward to set them free. Only for her to jerk away so quickly, you'd think I was the one hurting her.

"I'm sorry, it's just..." I motion to her red hand as she shakes out the other, her lip trembling between her teeth.

"I can't do this, Jesse," she says, her tone pleading with me to stop, to take it all back.

"I'm sorry."

"I appreciate that, but you lied to me. That entire time, you lied!" Her voice raises as the tears start to well. "That beautiful speech means nothing when it's tainted."

"Willow, you don't understand."

"Of course I don't. Because I don't freaking remember. And you do. You know *everything* and you expect me to...to what? Forgive you and move on? To fix this? You haven't even told me what happened."

"Willow, I need—"

"I don't want to hear it now. I said I needed a second to breathe."

I close my eyes and draw in a breath. Staying silent. Because I'm not ready to tell her.

"I always thought I was a smart woman," she says after a beat, bringing my attention back to her face. "I even thought I'd figured out your secret. I laughed about it. *Jesse and Pippa are fake dating while he really wants me.* I thought I had the upper hand, but I was dead wrong. You played me like a fool. How the hell do you expect me to deal with that? I mean, what did you think was going to happen if we got together? That I'd just never find out?"

"I—"

"No. Time's up. You've had your five minutes."

She reaches for the door handle and my chest tightens. "Willow, wait." I want to touch her more than I want to breathe, but I don't. I keep my hands locked tightly in my lap. Now's not the time to get any closer; it's likely to do more damage to *me* than *her*. Especially when she looks at me with pleading eyes and a frown.

"Please," she whispers. "I can't do this now. Just leave me alone."

I bang my head against the headrest when she gets out of the car, unable to move.

While that definitely could have gone worse, I wish it had gone better. The thing is, I don't know how to tell her everything without breaking her heart. For a number of reasons. For one, she had no idea Jade was there for drugs. To this day, I have never forgotten the expression on her face when she realized. The complete and utter devastation displayed there. As though everything she thought she knew was stolen in a heartbeat.

Kind of like what I did to her after our week together. Jesus.

I can see how much my silence is destroying her, but I'm really fucking terrified that her knowing the truth will be so much worse.

And I don't know if I'm strong enough to watch her go through that.

9
Willow

Emotions are high as I step out of the car, slam the door, and walk toward Pippa. She takes one look at me and nods before heading in the direction I just came from. To Jesse.

I press the button for the elevator and keep my eyes locked on the doors, waiting for them to open.

Waiting for my chance to escape.

I'm hurt, I'm confused, I'm angry.

But I'm not just angry at Jesse. I'm angry at myself.

I should have demanded that he tell me everything then and there, but I couldn't. The tightness in my chest wouldn't allow me to get the words out. For as much as I want to know, I'm also freaking terrified. I'm not ready to hate Jesse when he tells me what he did. And I'm not ready to relive losing Jade all over again. But I'll need to...soon.

The elevator doors open and I practically jump inside, holding my hand out to wait for Pippa. The second she steps in and the doors close, my entire body deflates, finally allowing me to breathe.

"Are you ready to tell me what happened?" Pippa asks almost immediately, and I can tell from her weary expression that wasn't easy for her to see.

"I'm ready to tell you what I know. But in comparison to what happened, it's not a lot."

She nods as she busies herself getting her key out of her bag. "That looked intense back there," she says with a frown. "Jesse seems pretty messed up."

He's not the only one. "He needed more from me, but I couldn't give it to him."

"You don't owe anyone anything, Willow. Ever. It's about time you started putting yourself first. I know I'm guilty of taking advantage of your kindness and generosity, but it ends now. I'm sorry. I wish I'd noticed how much you were struggling. It took seeing your real smile for me to realize how unhappy you were."

"My real smile?"

Pippa huffs out a laugh. "Yeah, I'm sorry it took me so long to notice the difference. But something made you happy."

Someone. Jesse. If only he wasn't currently making me sad.

After Pippa shows me around her apartment and orders takeout, we curl up on opposite ends of the couch, ready for me to talk.

Other than Sara, I haven't told anyone about my connection to Jesse, and honestly, if I wasn't staying here and expecting Pippa to help me, I probably wouldn't tell her either. It feels strange talking about it when Jesse and I haven't even had a real conversation. Almost like I'm betraying his trust.

The irony.

"I don't really know where to start, but I should probably tell you that Jesse and I were together more than once when you both visited. But nothing happened until *after* I found out it was fake between the two of you. I would never—"

"*Willow*," she says, cutting me off as she sits up. "Even if you'd acted on it beforehand, it wouldn't have been the same."

"Actually, it would have, because we all believed Jesse was your boyfriend and—"

"Did you? Did you for a second actually believe it? Even I could see we weren't fooling everyone. If just one person had questioned it out loud, *the town* would have been talking about it."

"Still." *That's not the point.* Regardless of the fact that Jesse flinched when they touched or that they spent most of their time apart, we were *told* they were together.

KATHERINE JAY

"Don't beat yourself up about it. The point is, you *didn't* act on it. You're not Ashley. Or me. And this has no relevance to your story."

We lock eyes for a beat, without saying anything, as I try to determine whether she's really unaffected by what I did.

"Come on already." She laughs. "Get to the important stuff."

I roll my eyes but allow the smallest of smiles to shine through, until I remember what I'm about to say. "Okay. Here goes." I release a slow breath and tuck my hands into my lap. "The night before I disappeared, Alex came to visit me at the shop. And by visit, I mean, he snuck in while I was closing up."

"What the hell? Why wouldn't you have told anyone that? Did he do anything? I *knew* Jesse was right—"

"He made me uncomfortable, but he didn't do anything. I'm still not convinced he's a *bad* person." *Especially after his confession.* "But I'm also not sure that he's good. If that makes sense?"

"Not even a little." She grimaces, making me huff out a laugh.

"I just mean that I don't think he's as bad as Jesse thinks he is. Misunderstood maybe?"

"Okay, gotcha." She doesn't get it, but I move on.

"Anyway, that night he asked me out again, and to try and convince me to say yes, he told me he *knew* things...and that he could help me find out what happened to Jade."

Pippa's jaw drops as her posture stiffens. "Jesus! Was he there?"

Her door buzzes and she jumps at the intrusion but rushes to get it. "Hold that thought. Goddammit."

I can't help but giggle as I wait for her. *What a moment for the food to arrive.*

"Okay," she says when she gets back, puffing as though she's run a marathon. "I'm ready."

"Did you go down to the lobby to get it?"

"No," she says with a chuckle. "But I ran to the elevator and impatiently jogged on the spot as I waited for them to arrive. Now. Tell. Me."

"Alex wasn't there," I blurt, putting her out of her misery.

"Oh, thank God." She relaxes, throwing the bags of takeout onto the coffee table before sitting back down with her arms folded over her legs, food forgotten.

"But he suggested he could find out who it was."

"Oh-kay." Pippa's brow furrows before she tilts her head in question, clearly confused. "And you don't think he's as bad as Jesse says he is? Sounds like a manipulative little asshole to me."

"Maybe, or maybe he saw how messed up I was and thought it was time I knew the truth?" *For both our sakes.*

"Nope." She shakes her head. "I don't believe that. Why wasn't he with you? Why didn't he help?"

"Because I told him I wasn't interested in knowing. I told him I was moving on. I lied. And then I decided I was going to find out for myself."

"So, you went back up the mountain."

"I went back up the mountain," I repeat, now knowing how bad an idea it was.

"And you didn't think to tell anyone?"

"Honestly, no. Because I knew I'd either be talked out of it, or you'd want to come with me. And I needed to do it alone."

Pippa nods but stays silent.

"And...you know the rest. I rolled my ankle and got stuck there with no cell service."

"Until Jesse and Tate found you."

"Actually, it was just Jesse at first."

"Okay."

"But they both knew *exactly* where I was."

I swallow a lump in my throat because that's the part that always gets me emotional, whenever I think about it. They both knew. When Tate walked into that clearing, Jesse was shocked to see him. They hadn't been searching together. Yet they both knew.

Pippa blinks a few times, trying to piece together what I've just said. It may be a small town, but it's a huge mountain. I could have been anywhere. *They knew.*

She gasps suddenly, and I know she's figured it out. "Nooo," she says, shaking her head almost violently. "No. Nooo. And Jesse *knows* Tate. I was with him when they ran into each other before Dad's dinner.

I questioned him but he said he knew him from when they both lived in Seattle. What the actual fuck?"

Jesus. I wish I'd known that piece of information, although, it probably wouldn't have meant anything to me at the time.

"Yep, they were both there."

"Then why the hell are you here? And why the hell didn't you tell any of us that you knew what happened?"

"Because I don't know what happened!" I half yell before covering my mouth.

"What?"

"I'm here to find out the truth. All I know is that Jesse and Tate found me, and Jesse admitted that he was there the day Jade died." *And that he had either killed someone, committed an unforgivable crime, or worse.*

"And you didn't think to ask him for more details?"

"Of course I did!" *Sort of.* "He wouldn't tell me."

"*Jesus.* I just left you alone with him. What if he'd done something to silence you?"

"He's not a murderer, Pippa." That much I'm certain. He may have been involved in Jade's death, but I don't think it was intentional. Mind you, many serial killers don't seem like the type to murder people and still do it. No. *That's not Jesse.*

"And before you ask, I have no intention of telling our parents *or* the police."

Pippa cringes with a comedic expression, like the idea makes her sick. "I wouldn't be telling them either.

But God, do I want words with Jesse. I'm glad I didn't know before today."

When she says that, a thought hits me. After Jesse left the hospital, no one questioned me about why he was there and why he was so desperate to see me. Except Sara. "What did you *think* happened?" I ask, wondering if that might explain things.

"I assumed the asshole had saved you and then told you he didn't want any strings or that his life was too 'complicated.'" She uses finger quotes as though that's an exact excuse he's used before, making my insides squirm. "I'll admit, I was confused when Tate called to tell me where you were, but I figured Jesse had run into him and asked for help."

Makes sense. I would have believed that too if I hadn't seen Jesse's expression when he arrived.

"Please don't mention any of this to Jesse. Not yet," I ask, looking her in the eye to show her I'm serious, but to my surprise she easily agrees.

"I won't. As much as I'd like to, it's not my place."

"Thank you."

Pippa kicks her leg out and pokes me in the knee with her toe, her attempt at affection without having to move. She smiles for a moment until a flash of pain crosses her face. "So, even after being up there with Jesse and discovering he was there *that day*, you still don't remember anything?"

"Not a thing," I say, running a hand down my face because it's so freaking frustrating. "I've been working with Gretchen again, but still...nothing."

"God, I'm sorry. That must be frustrating."

"It is." I laugh to myself after thinking the same thing. "Although Sara mentioned my password, Robin Hood, and she thought that maybe I remem—"

Pippa gasps as her hand flies to her mouth. "It's Jesse's nickname."

What? I stare at her blankly as my mind fights to process what she just said.

"Tate calls Jesse *Robin*. I laughed about it. And when Sara told us your password, and Jesse was shocked, my first thought was that you'd spoken to Tate. Which was strange because I knew he always made you uncomfortable. God, now we know why." She shivers. "I never once considered you only knew it because Jesse was there on the mountain. But Sara's right. You must have remembered that. How else would you know?"

"Maybe I overheard it?" I shrug. I can't fathom the idea that after all this time, I just randomly remembered something. There must be an explanation.

"You may have. But what if you didn't? What if you've also remembered other things but they seem so insignificant that you pushed them out of your mind?"

"Like what?" I ask, but instantly regret it. *How would she know?*

Pippa laughs, reading my inner thoughts, before she frowns. "God, I wish I could tell you. I don't even know how to find out."

We both fall silent after that, staring into space. I spend the time trying not to spiral, trying to figure out how the hell I knew about Robin Hood, as Pippa presumably tries to come up with ideas.

"God, I loved that *Robin Hood* actor," she says suddenly, out of nowhere. "You know, the one that was in *The Princess Bride.*"

Or she's daydreaming about Hollywood men.

"Did you ever watch it?" she asks, but she's so lost in a memory that I doubt she'd hear my response even if I gave one. The answer being no. I know of *The Princess Bride*, but I've never seen it. "Ah the memories," she says wistfully as though we weren't just talking about something important. I'm about to make her snap out of it when she adds, "Westley and his Buttercup."

"What?!" I bark out in shock, and then cover my mouth. I *knew* the name Buttercup was in *The Princess Bride*. Well, at least, I knew it was in a movie. But I never made that connection when Jesse was calling *me* Buttercup. He said it was about the flower.

Pippa grimaces before her expression turns apologetic. "God, I'm sorry. Now's not the time to be-"

"No." I cut her off even though I'm not sure I want to tell her about my name. It may have started as something negative, but as time went on, it grew on me. And now it feels like a secret between Jesse and me. But talking about it may help me remember.

"Jesse calls me Buttercup," I say shyly, refusing to look Pippa in the eye.

"He what?" she asks, clearly confused considering she doesn't realize the degree of our relationship.

"Do you think it's related?" I ask, without answering what I know she's actually asking me.

"What do you mean?"

"I don't know, maybe I'm wrong, but...you said Robin Hood was the same actor and... It's just a strange coincidence. Or maybe it's not."

Maybe I'm crazy. It's highly possible. I could just be so desperate for answers, I'm seeing connections that aren't even there. Yet another thing Jesse's unlikely to give me a straight answer on.

"It doesn't matter," I say with a shrug before shifting the conversation away from my personal life and onto Pippa's work. I'm too mentally drained to continue, and thankfully Pippa lets me move on. We finally start eating while we talk, and when we're finished, I head off to bed.

My chest remains tight as I try to fall asleep, but I expect I'll still be lying here staring at the ceiling in a few hours. Only when I still my mind and focus on the noise of the outside world—the traffic, the sirens, the wind—before I know it, I'm out. Not at all ready for the next day.

10
Willow

"What are you thinking over there?" Jesse asks as he takes a sip of his beer.

I eye him curiously, trying to decide whether I trust him or not, while Jade chats to Tate, not a care in the world.

Jesse smiles when I don't immediately answer, and I hate to admit that he makes me feel giddy. His eyes do this thing where they look past the surface, seeing things I thought I'd kept hidden, seeing past my faults. And while it should make me feel uncomfortable, I like it. It makes me feel seen.

"I'm thinking about the weather," I lie, causing Jesse to chuckle as he runs his fingers through his unkempt hair.

"Are you worried it's going to turn?" he asks, playing along.

"Not really. I was just thinking it's uncharacteristically warm for this time of day."

"Is it the weather warming you up, or the heat radiating from these two?" He points toward Jade as she moves closer to Tate.

I can't hold back my eye roll as I watch them. Do
they even know each other? I didn't think they did,
but now I'm wondering.

Tate laughs at something Jade says before pulling
a cigarette from his pocket and lighting it up,
instantly ruining the moment.

In one swift movement, Jade jumps up and moves
away, a look of disgust on her face.

She's got a thing about smoking, so this is not
going to end well.

Since I don't really mind what someone does to
their own body, I plan to stay quiet, but when his
expression turns dark and he starts arguing with
Jade, I change my mind.

And unfortunately for him, I've never been one to
hold back.

"Hey!"

I startle awake, my pulse racing as I'm woken
from my dream. *God, that felt real.* I've had
nightmares before, but that was different. I'm
sure of it. More than just the fact that I've never
dreamed about Jesse or Tate before.

And with the way my stomach swirls with a
nervous energy, I know I'm onto something. I just
can't figure out how I know that.

The words, "*I've never been one to hold back,*" pop
into my mind and my breath hitches. *Didn't Jesse*
say something like that yesterday?

And if he did, am I just mirroring his words, morphing them into my dream? Or did he trigger a memory?

My eyes glaze over as I stare straight ahead, a chill running down my spine.

"*Let's just go?*" I hear Jade say, clear as day, like she's speaking directly into my mind.

Oh hell! It's real. After all these years, I still remember her voice.

Leaping out of bed, I grab my phone to call my therapist's emergency number, but pause. It's five in the morning. And this isn't the type of emergency she was referring to.

After deciding to call her office at a more reasonable hour, I contemplate going for a slow jog. But considering everything about this place is foreign to me, I think better of it, and instead pull the sheet up again, attempting some more much-needed sleep.

When I wake sometime later, I can hear Pippa buzzing around. She's talking on the phone, a million miles an hour, while cooking something on the stove.

"Can you get Masters and Jacobs? I need them at the stadium by ten... No, Hernandez is resting this morning... Yes, I know that. It's not my call."

I walk toward the kitchen and find her hunched over with her fingers massaging her temples.

"I know what she said, but it's not happening," she grates out, before noticing me in the doorway. A small smirk pulls at her lips as she nods my way. "Tell them they can have Hastings. He doesn't have any plans today."

With that she hangs up while I gape.

"What?" she asks, biting back a smile.

"He's going to hate you for that."

"He already does." She shrugs. "And I did it to make sure he left you alone."

I huff out a laugh as a smile pulls at my lips. "As much as I appreciate that, I need to talk to him."

Now it's her turn to gape. "Didn't you basically tell him to fuck off last night?"

"I did."

"But now you want to talk to him?" She shakes her head as she goes about finishing her breakfast.

"I remembered more," I tell her, because I'm now almost certain my dream last night was real. And I think Jesse is my answer.

Pippa drops the spatula she's holding into the sink and spins around, her eyes widening almost comically. "What?"

"Last night, I had a dream. But when I woke, it felt real, and then Jade spoke to me. I don't think it was a dream, Pip. I think it was a memory."

Pippa stares at me like I'm talking in riddles, her eyes wide, unblinking.

"Okay, enough of that," I say, waving my hand in front of her face. "You're freaking me out."

"Sorry." She snaps out of it. "I was processing. When you say 'Jade spoke to you'?" She says the last part hesitantly as though she's genuinely worried about me.

"I mean that I had a vivid memory of something she said that day."

"Okay." She physically relaxes. "So not like a ghost-of-best-friends past situation."

"No." I laugh. "Not like that."

"I'm guessing you think that if Jesse tells you what happened, it will help you remember?"

"I do." Although I planned to talk to him anyway.

"Are you sure he's even going to talk?"

"He has to. If I ask directly, he can't continue to remain silent." *Can he?*

Pippa drops onto a kitchen stool and frowns. "I don't know about this. It doesn't seem very scientific. You lost your memory because of a head trauma, it's been years, and—"

"I'm going to call Gretchen," I interrupt, talking about my therapist. "She's told me over and over that it's possible I still have the memories, I just can't access them. I never believed her because they just weren't there. Nothing was. Even the hypnosis didn't work. Now I'm wondering..." *If Jesse can help.* I trail off thinking about the possibilities. How incredibly freeing it will be to finally know the truth. No, not to know it, to *remember* it.

"She also told you it's possible they're gone, right?"

Way to bring my mood down, Pippa.

"She did. It's not common for dissociative amnesia to last this long and not be permanent. But it's not unheard of."

Pippa's silent for a beat before she slowly nods. "Memory or not, you should talk to Jesse. You need to know what happened."

I open my mouth to respond but she cuts me off.

"*After* you've spoken to Gretchen. Take today to rest and explore this beautiful city. I've blocked out my calendar for sister time this afternoon, so we can have some fun. Book an appointment with your therapist, talk things through, and see what she says."

I almost gasp because Pippa's usually the first to choose the out-there idea route—*fake dating, anyone*—but this time, she's making a sensible suggestion.

Disappointment fills me but I nod with a fake smile. "Yeah, I guess I can do that."

***

I manage to get an after-hours therapy appointment for that evening instead of waiting the two days for my scheduled one, because it turns out, the fact I remembered something is actually a big deal.

So, after spending the morning on Pippa's balcony, watching the world frantically go by, I'm ready to check out her life, knowing there's nothing else I can do before tonight.

"Where should we go first?" Pippa asks as she reapplies her blush. "We've got the wharf, the bridge, Alcatraz..." She trails off when she looks my way and laughs at my confused expression.

"What's that look for? What did you expect me to do? Take you shopping?"

"Honestly, yes. I thought you'd take me to your favorite shops, favorite restaurant for dinner, maybe even your favorite bar." *And I'm not sure I'm in the mood for any of those things.*

Pippa laughs again. "Oh, I definitely have plans for all that. *After* we get the touristy things out of the way. This is your first time in a big city. I want you to see the sights."

"Okay." I smile genuinely. Distraction can't hurt. "I've always been intrigued by Alcatraz."

"Perfect. I've actually never been there."

"What?" I gawk, completely baffled.

"I never really got around to doing that stuff."

My head tilts to the side as I think that through. But rather than asking any questions, I just go with it. Pippa and I are very different individuals. I shouldn't be surprised that she skipped all those things for herself. I should be grateful she's suggesting them now, even though it's of no interest to her.

So, after a quick thank you, we plan our day and off we go. *Please let this work.*

We're all smiles as we step off the boat, but we're both a little frazzled. Alcatraz was an experience. I wasn't really sure what to expect, but what I got wasn't it. What I do know is there's no chance I'd go back there at night; it's definitely haunted.

But it did help to take my mind off things.

When we arrive at the pier, though, I'm happy that it's exactly how I pictured it based on the images I've seen, and I absolutely love it.

I feel like I'm in the middle of a film set, a romantic movie, about to meet the love of my life. At least, I do until a group of kids run past and almost knock me over on their way to the arcade area. It makes me wonder if San Francisco residents visit here, or if all these people are outsiders like me.

It makes me think about my life.

One day it would be nice to find my place, to finally belong, and I hate that I don't even feel that way in the only place I've ever called home.

"What about taffy? I can't remember if you've tried it or like it," Pippa says, interrupting my thoughts as we walk.

"Huh?" My face scrunches.

"Taffy? Do you want some taffy?"

"Oh, yes." I smile. "I'd love some."

Pippa wanders off in the direction of the store, as I stare out at the view. Of all the things I've seen, and all the things I've yet to see, I know this will remain my favorite, right here. *The bay.* Hearing the waves crash against the beams of the pier, watching the sun's reflection glistening on the water. It gives me a feeling of hope. And while I'd usually think that's dangerous, it doesn't seem so out of reach anymore.

I'm calm as we take our time chatting and wandering the pier, but when Pippa mentions we better get going, the call with my therapist comes to mind and I fall quiet.

To Pippa's credit, she notices. "How about we skip the restaurant and have takeout instead?"

I open my mouth to argue, knowing she wants to go out, but she cuts me off.

"It's already decided. But tell me, are you more worried about the possibility you're not actually getting your memory back, or what you might discover if you do?" she asks, her face racked with concern.

Up until now I thought that was an easy question. But hearing it out loud gives me pause. Before she asked it, I was only concerned about *not* getting my memories back, but now that it's out there, my stomach twists with nerves as to what might happen if I do.

"Both," I say honestly. "But I need to know one way or the other."

11
Jesse

I'm on edge when I don't hear from Willow after our talk. I know she came to San Francisco for answers, so I hate to think that when I showed up at Pippa's, I somehow altered her course.

My phone buzzes with a text as I watch late night talk shows on the couch, instead of being where I should be...bed. We only have a few more days before our first preseason game, and I can't be tired. I need to show them I'm still at peak performance.

After finding Willow on the mountain, and with everything that's happened—or hasn't happened—since, I haven't been able to get my blood pressure back down. While my levels aren't considered dangerous day-to-day, once I'm on the ice, that's a different story.

I play a high-risk sport and my levels have *never* been high. My heart's always been stone. I honestly thought it was broken.

But now, everything's changing. And I have no idea what to do about that. On some level it's a good thing, but right now, it could end my career.

Case in point, as my chest tightens just from checking my fucking phone and seeing that it's not Willow. It's Seth reminding me of my doctor's appointment tomorrow. Like it's *not* one of only three things on my mind right now.

I finally drift off to sleep sometime before the sun rises and drag myself to the stadium when I wake. Doc's there waiting for me with a hesitant smile on his face and his hands resting on the table. The picture of a man who's about to deliver bad news.

"I haven't even been tested yet, but that look on your face tells me you're about to end my career."

"I only have to look at *your* face to know you're still stressed. But that doesn't mean it's over. It just means we'll need to make everyone aware of it so they can adjust accordingly."

"Meaning what exactly?" My voice rises an octave. This conversation is doing nothing to help bring the stress down.

"I don't know. I'm not a coach. It might affect your time on the ice or the way you practice before a game."

My shoulders drop, but it could be worse. I can handle that.

"Anyway, before we panic, let's get you checked out."

"Sooooo?" Seth says as he meets me in the hallway, a hesitant expression on his face.

"Don't you have other clients to annoy?" I snap, walking straight past him toward the locker room. The last thing I want to do right now is talk about my shitty test results.

"I do," Seth says, easily catching up beside me. "But none of them have issues like you do," he adds.

I keep walking, not even bothering to dignify that with an answer, and Seth laughs.

"Okay, lots of them have issues, but none of them need me at this very moment."

"I don't need you."

I can feel Seth's "bullshit" expression without looking his way, so I wave my hand in the air, letting him get it over with. "Say what you've got to say, but understand, I'm not in the mood."

"You need me because your results weren't good, and the woman causing your stress is somewhere in San Francisco."

What? I come to a halt, making Seth stumble. "Dammit, Pippa."

"It wasn't Pippa."

"Fucking Ryan," I mumble. I don't know which is worse. Guess it doesn't matter. Neither of them can keep their mouths shut and they're together. We're all fucked.

"He thought you might need a friend." Seth shrugs.

"So..." I drag out, waiting for what that means.

"So, you're wondering why he told me, instead of telling a friend?" Seth cuts in, trying to make a joke. "I wondered that myself."

"Fuck off." I shake my head. "He told the right person. You are the right person. You're just annoying sometimes, like now. As I said, I am not in the mood."

"Good, glad we got that straightened out. I can sleep easily now. But that tells me nothing about your results. Am I about to lose my big paycheck?"

I flip him the finger as I roll my eyes. "You know it's not too late for me to fire your ass and negotiate on my own."

"Ha!" Seth claps to himself as he laughs. "We both know that's never going to happen, so just answer me."

He's right; it's not. I can't be bothered dealing with that. "Doc says my levels are still high compared to my past levels, but have dropped closer to reasonable athlete level. He's required to tell the coaching staff, but his recommendation is that I can still play." *For now. I still don't see it as good news.*

"Thank God," Seth says, slapping me on the back. And while I definitely flinch, it seems more out of shock than anything else.

Is that progress?

We part ways when I reach the locker room, but not before Seth tells me to calm down, making me more pissed than I was before. And when I get to practice, it becomes so much worse.

Word gets back to the coaches faster than small-town gossip, and I can instantly tell that they're worried. Even the guys on the team can see that I'm not being pushed as hard as usual. I honestly thought they'd ignore the information completely, but since there have been a few players with heart issues arising midgame recently, I can only guess they don't want to risk it.

Thankfully, no one questions me about the strange energy in the air, and when practice is over, I rush off the ice, determined to continue that luck. *The last thing I need is for whispers to start.*

I've just stepped onto solid ground when Seth pops up from his seat, making me jump.

"Jesus, what are you doing?" I say, gripping my chest.

"I thought you saw me," he says, raising his hands in the air. "Trust me, I am *not* trying to mess with your heart."

KATHERINE JAY

"Fine. But why are you still here?" I drop down beside him and pull off my skates, only turning his way when I realize he's been quiet for too long.

"I have some news," he admits and I groan.

Goddammit. "They're not ready to start negotiations yet, are they?"

"Not yet, no."

"Fuck. *Fuck!*" I try to whisper yell, but I'm apparently bad at it because several heads turn my way. "Shit."

I storm off to the locker room, ignoring Seth as he calls out from behind me. Today is not my day, and I'm done with it.

Since I was the first one off the ice, I'm alone when I get inside. And after slamming the door shut, I rip my practice jersey over my head and throw it to the ground before taking off my protective gear and dropping onto the bench for a breather.

Just when I thought things might finally start working out for me... I should have known better.

I'm still lost in a fog as the door bangs open again and my teammates file in, their chatter working to drown out my thoughts.

But when someone squeezes my bare shoulders before running his fingers up my neck and ruffling my hair, all sounds turn to static, as a violent shiver runs through me.

"Don't fucking touch me," I yell, throwing my elbow back as I stand, connecting with my teammate Rick's face. He cries out as he rears back and then yells in anger, shoving me against the lockers in retaliation.

And I see red.

I'm strong, one of the strongest on our team, and even more so if someone pushes me. Like now. I'm not holding back.

"What's the matter, Hastings?" Rick—who is one of our injured reserves—goads me as I shove him backward, scrunching his jersey between my fingers. "Scared I'm going to hurt you?"

I lift my free hand and clench my fist, ready to slam it into his face, when Ryan steps between us, at the same time another teammate pulls Rick back.

"Stay the hell away from me," I yell to anyone that will listen, and surprisingly they all do. Even Ryan.

I tensely finish getting dressed, trying to block out Rick's complaining, but can't help noticing no one seems to be taking his side. Not that they're taking mine either.

As soon as I'm covered up, my muscles relax, but the nausea doesn't fade.

I've had small flinching moments throughout my career, but no one has ever grabbed me like that, at least never when I was without clothes.

I swallow back the bile in my throat and shake off my thoughts before slamming my locker closed.

Grabbing my things, I bolt out of the room and rush through the halls until I know I'm alone and out of sight.

After falling back against the wall, I run my hand down my face and close my eyes, trying to calm my breathing.

I lost it back there because I feel like I'm losing at life. Like everything that's ever made me happy is about to slip from my grasp, and there's nothing I can do to stop it.

Willow hates me. My career's up in the air. And I'm once again out of control when it comes to my body. I thought I was better. I thought I was finally moving on.

But the reality is, it's all falling apart.

I never should have allowed myself to think otherwise. I don't deserve it. I *never* deserved it.

Voices filter through the empty halls, so I start walking, determined to get as far away from here as possible, maybe even drown my sorrows at a bar.

But when I walk across the parking lot and spot my truck, Willow's waiting for me, instantly changing my course. She's a beautiful sight and exactly what I need right now. The only thing I need, period.

12
Jesse

Twelve Years Ago – Age Sixteen

The punch connects with my chest again, and I wince as the air's knocked out of my lungs. It's been a while since he hit me this hard, but I can't react or it will only make things worse. When he's done, he sighs as he runs the tips of his fingers over my bruises, causing my stomach to swirl as bile rises in my throat.

This is the part I can't handle.

"Don't," I say between gritted teeth, making him laugh before he stands up and kicks me in the gut. Speaking always gets me another beating, but I'll take that over these rare moments when he tries to soothe the pain he's caused. When his guilt kicks in. And that's been happening more often lately.

After one last kick, he stumbles away as my body heaves. It takes a minute but I manage to lift myself up before shaking uncontrollably. Another one down. God knows how many to go.

And two years left to survive it.

13

Jesse

"**I**'m ready to talk," Willow says as I reach her. Her voice lacks all emotion, and considering what she's asking, it messes with my head. "Actually," she continues, standing a little taller, "I guess I'm ready to *listen*, since I have no reason to talk."

Jesus.

"Want to go for a drive?" I ask, knowing I can't avoid this any longer, and wanting to do anything I can to be in her presence.

Maintaining her blank expression, Willow steps closer to my truck and opens the front door before getting inside. "Works for me." She shrugs, repeating her words from the other day, like it's no big deal, when in reality what happens next could change both our lives.

I inhale deeply to prepare myself, then walk around to my side, catching Seth as he waves his phone in the air, telling me to check mine. I consider ignoring him, but take a peek at the last second.

Seth: Don't let the contract stuff distract you. Concentrate on Willow.

115

I almost laugh because now that Willow's in front of me, I couldn't care less about any of that. But I give him a wave anyway, hoping to ease his mind.

When I'm settled in my truck, I don't waste any time, grabbing Willow's headrest and turning to look out the rear window, catching sight of her body stiffening. I hate that my close proximity does that to her now, instead of making her melt. If only we could go back to that place.

We travel in complete silence until I pull into the parking lot of a quiet beach I often visit. As expected, there are no other cars here, so I park as close as possible to the sand, ensuring Willow gets a good view of the waves.

While this spot has become a sort of sanctuary for me of late, this time, I came for her, knowing she's probably never spent time listening to the sounds of the ocean.

Willow gasps when she looks up from staring at her hands, and her eyes light up before she jumps out of the truck, walking straight to the sand.

"Wow," she whispers, completely lost in the moment as I reach her, causing my chest to tighten. This is how we should be spending our time together. I should be showing Willow around, introducing her to my life. Not bringing her here to essentially end any chance I have with her.

"It's beautiful, isn't it?" I say, referring to both our views.

"It is. Pippa took me to the pier yesterday, but this is magic."

Not magic enough to fix things, I'll bet.

And here goes.

"I didn't know you were coming that day," I say quickly as the air rushes from my lungs. "Tate told me he was meeting some girl, and I was just there so he didn't get bored while waiting."

Willow's eyes flash to mine, and any hint of happiness she had disappears in an instant.

Her loose-fitting tee blows around in the wind, causing the neck to fall from her shoulder and my gaze to lock on her bare skin as I swallow a lump in my throat.

"I'd seen you around town before," I add, clenching my fist so I don't reach out and touch her. "I didn't know who you were, only that you weren't from Mossman Hills. I'd guessed that you were probably from Hepburn, and it turns out, I was right."

"I don't need all the minor details," Willow says like I'm boring her, even though her throat bobs. *I see everything, Willow. You can't hide.*

"Got it." I nod. "To the point." *I can do this.* "On the mountain, we spent a bit of time together while Tate and Jade chatted, but then they had some kind of argument." Willow's eyes widen but she blinks quickly to hide it, letting me continue without a word. "Jade grabbed you and ran. She was so frantic that I took off after you, with Tate following close behind me." I pause for a second, knowing I now have a decision to make—either give her the full truth, or leave her with enough for closure, minus the heartbreak—and it only takes one look in her eyes to decide on the latter.

"When we caught up, you and Jade were in a heated discussion. It looked like you were trying to step away, but she wasn't letting you go."

Willow's brow furrows as her gaze drops to her hands, once again squeezing her fingers together.

My stomach knots to an uncomfortable level, but I keep going, because she deserves to know more.

"Tate called out and I rushed to stop her, but as I did, she—"

"She fell," Willow says, cutting me off. "We both did. And you could only catch me."

I nod, taking the easy way out, letting her believe her own words even though that's not exactly what happened.

Willow shakes her head, finally allowing her feelings to come to the surface. "I knew you hadn't done anything on purpose, but I just couldn't figure out how we ended up close enough to the edge to fall." She pauses before her eyes meet mine. "Why not come forward if it was an accident?" she asks, and it's a valid question, but one that I can't give an honest answer to. "Why make it look like you weren't even there? What if I'd remembered all along?"

"We had planned to come forward," I say, and it's not exactly a lie. At least, I was prepared to after I thought things through. We wouldn't have had a choice if Willow had spoken to the police. "But since you couldn't remember anything, we left it alone."

Willow shakes her head again, this time with a frown as she looks to the sand. "That doesn't make any sense."

Of course it doesn't, because there's more to it.

She looks up again and my eyes lock with hers, the hurt in her expression breaking me. But what's worse is that I know the whole truth will likely shatter her beyond repair...and I can't bring myself to do that to her.

Because it wasn't me that caused Jade to fall that day. And it's going to destroy her when she finds out the truth.

14
Willow

Thirteen Years Ago – Age Fourteen

My bedroom door flies open and Jade comes running in, her eyes lit up with excitement. "Are you ready to go? Mom said we can sleep outside if the weather holds out."

"With Luca?" I say, jumping up as I picture her new golden retriever puppy.

Jade frowns, shaking her head. "He's not allowed outside yet, but we can play with him before sunset."

"Sounds perfect. My bag is at the door." I throw the book I was reading onto my desk and roughly remake the bed—just enough so I don't get told off about it when I get home—and then follow Jade into the kitchen.

"Have you finished your reading?" Mom asks the second she sees me.

"Yes."

"What about your—"

"All my homework is done. It's on my desk if you want to check it." I stop short of telling her she can grade it if she wants. She's always checking it over so carefully.

"What about—"

"Let her go," Dad says, interrupting her as he gives me a wink. "If she hasn't finished, she'll have time tomorrow night."

"Yes. You're right." Mom pulls me into a hug and presses a kiss to my head. "Then take care, Sweetie. Tell Heather I'll pick you up around two."

"Two?" I whine.

"Yes, two. I'm making a roast for dinner and need to be home in the afternoon."

Ugh. I roll my eyes but only Dad sees it and chuckles as Mom turns away. She's said her piece and now she's moved on. "Bye, Mom," I say, only walking away after she raises her hand in a wave.

"Bye, love," Dad says, following us down the hall on the way to his bedroom. "Have fun."

I give Dad a quick hug before racing after Jade.

"Two is still good," she says as I reach her, always trying to be positive. We live at opposite ends of town, and Jade lives on a ranch so it's not easy to walk to each other's houses. It drives me crazy having to rely on our parents, but Jade's much more accepting. Probably because her parents would pick her up at three a.m. if she asked. God, I love them.

"Two is good," I agree with a smile just as we pass by Ashley and Pippa in a standoff in front of the TV. Jade giggles before we sneak away. My sisters love bringing other people into their arguments, and Jade and I have been caught in the middle way too often.

After grabbing my bag, we've just made it out the door when they start screaming at each other, making us both burst out laughing.

"Some days I wish I had a sister," Jade says as she peers back through the window. "Other days I really, really don't."

I laugh even harder, curling my arm around her shoulder. "I've told you time and time again, I'll move in any day. Just say the word."

Jade leans her head into mine and smiles. "Sisters forever?"

"Sisters forever," I repeat easily because that's one thing that's never going to change between us. She's the sister I choose. The one I need.

15
Willow

I'm barely holding on to my sanity as I process everything Jesse said. None of this feels real. None of what he's saying makes any sense, nor does it trigger a feeling of déjà vu like I was sure it would.

When I'd hung up from my therapist, I'd been full of hope. While she couldn't explicitly say I was getting my memories back, she was optimistic, and considering what I knew, I was happy with that answer.

And determined.

Really freaking determined.

But as I stand here, in this beautiful setting, listening to Jesse tell me the ugly truth, it all sounds like fiction. Like something straight out of a movie. One of those shitty movies that either don't give you a happy ending or cut to credits before you're ready to let go, leaving you hanging.

And I hate it.

I hate not knowing.

More than I hate anything else.

Jesse's silent as he stares into my eyes like he's looking for something. But God knows what he's seeking because I feel completely dead inside.

Jade's death was an accident, and he ran, potentially leaving us both to die, while— *Wait, what?*

"You left," I say quietly as thoughts swirl in my mind. *Oh God.* "You left!" I say louder this time, anger taking over the emptiness. "I was lucky to be alive. What if no one had found me? Did you even stop to check on Jade?"

Jesse's eyes widen before I see a hint of his own anger. "Do you really think I'd do that?" He pauses as his head drops back, running his hands down his face. "Tate went down to check on Jade while I carried you to the fucking road," he says through his fingers. "I waited with you in my arms, your blood soaking my clothes, checking your pulse every other second. I *stayed* until someone came to help."

"*The driver who found you saw someone else as he was approaching, but he didn't give a good description.*"

A memory of one of the many police interviews comes rushing back, and I draw in a breath. I knew that. I even used it in an argument with my mom.

That someone was Jesse.

"Walking away from you was one of the hardest things I've ever done in my life. I had every intention of finding you again and making sure you were okay, but..."

"But?"

I knew there was more. There had to be more. Why would he leave?

"Tate was known by the police. He was on his last chance. He couldn't be there. So, when he texted me to say Jade was dead, I told him to run."

I cringe, but I guess I'd do the same for a friend. "Okay, that's his excuse. What about yours?"

Jesse sighs, but it's not out of frustration—he's defeated. "I couldn't get dragged into it either."

My heart jolts, like it knows something I don't, and a tightness fills my chest. I'm the one who should be hurting, yet I'm breaking for him. *Why?*

We both fall silent until I can't take it any longer. I don't know how much more I can process tonight, and I also get the feeling Jesse's not giving any more away.

"Take me back to Pippa's, please," I say softly, my voice coming out raspier than I would have liked.

I don't wait for an answer before walking back to Jesse's truck. When we're both settled inside, Jesse's hands clench around his thighs before he grips the steering wheel, his eyes locked on the water.

"I'm sorry, Willow. I really am." His gaze briefly flashes my way, and his expression displays his honesty. He is sorry. But for which part—the accident or the fact I found out?

Without another word, Jesse takes in a deep breath and puts the truck into gear. As he turns his head to reverse, he grabs the back of my seat, and just like when we left the hockey stadium earlier, I have to bite my tongue so I don't react. So I don't look at the bulging muscles in his arm, or lean forward to smell his familiar cologne. It's hard to stay angry when my entire body warms around him.

It was one week, Willow. Get a grip.

We're quiet on the drive, with me staring out the window as I replay our conversation over and over in my mind, watching the world go by but never actually seeing it.

Jesse said he'd seen me before but I don't remember him.

We hung out on the mountain.

Jade and Tate argued.

Jade and I had a heated discussion.

Jade. And I. Fought?

That's the part I'm struggling with the most. Jade and I never fought. *Ever.* She was my rock. I was hers.

There's something Jesse's not telling me, either that or he's completely fabricated the entire story. I'm not sure which is worse. Because if Jesse really is the man I thought I was getting to know, and he's holding something back, then I can only imagine it's heartbreaking.

But if he's lying... *God.* The thought alone makes my chest ache.

"What were Jade and I arguing about?" I ask, turning in my seat so I can see Jesse's expression.

"What?" he says, lost in thought, although I don't miss the way he tightens his grip on the steering wheel.

Beams of sunlight flash across my face, making it difficult to focus, but I refuse to close my eyes, raising my hand as a shield instead. "You said we were having a heated discussion. What was it about?"

"How would I know?" he scoffs, but the tone of his voice seems off.

"You were there." I blink a few times. "In the middle of it. You *know*."

His body tenses as he continues to focus on the road, his height protecting him from the glare. "I didn't get the—"

"Don't bullshit me, Jesse. I can see the veins in your hands." Made even more glaringly obvious in the bright sunshine.

"So?" he says, trying to relax his fingers.

"So...you're really freaking tense. What was it? Did we both want the same guy?" *And was it you?* "Did one of us want to stay and the other go? Or was it bigger than that? We never fought. What was it?"

Jesse swerves onto a side street, narrowly missing the curb before slamming on the brakes and turning my way with an expression of rage.

"You really want to know? Are you sure you're ready to shatter both our hearts?"

"What?" Said heart clenches as I stare at him in shock. "Yes," I whisper almost apologetically. "I need to know." *I'm all in now.*

Jesse sighs, dropping his head into his hands while mumbling something to himself. I only manage to catch the words "sorry" and "forgive" before he slowly looks up to face me, only opening his eyes at the last second, his expression completely obliterating my anger.

I have never seen another human so broken in my life, even when I look in the mirror.

A sheen of water coats his usually expressive eyes as he stares through me, his vacant expression tearing me apart. With his jaw locked tight, he remains silent for a beat, and I feel so uncomfortable, I have to fill the void.

"Jesse, I..." I trail off because I'm not sure what I want to say. I know he needs me to take it all back. To tell him I don't want to know. But I can't do that.

"Jade was there to meet Tate," he says, his voice somewhat robotic. "She'd found his details from someone on your side of the mountain and asked him to meet her."

"Okay." I nod even though I'm pretty sure he can't see me. He may be staring into my eyes, but he's not here. He's up on that mountain, experiencing his pain all over again.

"Tate was..." He pauses and I instinctively move closer, knowing his next words are going to be vital. "Tate was selling drugs on behalf of my foster father." He pauses again while I scrunch my face in disgust...until he adds, "Jade was there to buy."

What? "Excuse me?" *There's no way.* "You expect me to believe that." My voice rises, cutting into Jesse's trance, making him sigh.

"It's the truth," he rasps. "I'm sorry."

Again, what? I shake my head and finally look away. *I can't. That can't be.* "That makes no sense. She'd never tried drugs in her life."

"I know," Jesse says, his voice softening while mine rises.

"You know!"

"What I mean is, I could tell. I didn't know what was happening in the beginning because Tate promised he'd only ever sell to regulars, to those that would've gone directly to the source if not to him." He takes a deep breath and I can see how much this pains him. "We were talking, you and I, and they started arguing. As soon as I figured out what was going on, I told Jade to take the money back and that we'd forget all about it. But she refused. I found out later that the argument started when Tate began asking her intrusive questions."

"How... When..." I'm completely at a loss for words as I try to imagine the story playing out. *Jade buying drugs?* How did she even know what to ask for?

I clench my fist so hard that my nails press into the skin of my palm. *How is this even possible?* No wonder we were arguing. I would have been livid once I figured that out. Pippa had just been sent away to boarding school because she came home high from a party. My heart was breaking because of drugs. No, it's not possible. She'd never, and yet...

"I can't even fathom that," I say honestly, refusing to meet Jesse's gaze. *God, I hate this.* I don't want to feel this negatively toward Jade. She was my everything and I lost her. *But what was going on. She... Unless it was Alex? Shit. Was she changing for him?*

Jesse grabs my hand out of nowhere, cutting into my thoughts, and I flinch away, just like he normally would. "Don't," I say, shaking my hand, ridding myself of his touch. But he ignores me and reaches out again, prying my fingers open.

"You're bleeding," he grates when I try to pull away again. "Let me look."

Ignoring his request, I hold my hand out of reach and unclench, stretching out my palm. The second I see what he's referring to, my eyes widen, the puncture marks from my nails clear as day. *Jesus.* I don't even feel pain. I don't feel anything. Except a little nauseous.

"Was there more?" I ask, pressing my palms together to stop the bleeding or, at least, hide it away.

"I told you what happened after that," he whispers, his eyes glued to my hands while he tries to keep his own hands busy.

He told me. We were arguing, Jade wouldn't let go of me, something about Tate, Jesse stepped forward, Jade fell, but... "You didn't tell me," I say, my brow furrowing as I play out our conversation. "You were telling me what happened but I cut you off. I was the one that said Jade fell."

A small grin starts to form—I'm proud of myself for figuring that out, for remembering—but when I see Jesse suck in a deep breath, my light dims.

"What happened?"

"Please, Willow."

Huh? "Please, Willow, what?"

"I can't." His voice cracks as he struggles to get the words out. Every part of me wants to reach forward and comfort him, except for one—the part of me that's still trapped on that mountain waiting for the answers that will set me free.

"Please, Jesse. If there's something else, I have to know."

He's completely still for a beat until he gives me the smallest nod, closing his eyes as his face contorts.

"You were arguing when Tate and I caught up," he says, opening his eyes to look at me. I swallow back the emotions clogging my throat and nod for him to continue. "Jade wouldn't let go as you questioned her over and over about the drugs, desperately trying to pull away. She got the upper hand and pulled you into her, stepping back at the same time. While her expression was menacing, she was clearly terrified. If I hadn't known otherwise, I would have thought she was on drugs in that moment."

Tears well in my eyes but I can't speak or even acknowledge that I'm understanding him. All I can do is stare, hopeful that he continues. And he does.

"Tate and I tried to get you to stop, but neither of you were listening. And at one point Jade's grip must have tightened because you started begging her to let go, telling her she was hurting you, as you tried to push her back. I couldn't take it anymore; I couldn't just watch you suffer."

Jesse sucks in another breath and closes his eyes before releasing it slowly. "So that's when I moved closer," he says, opening his eyes again, piercing me with a look of utter devastation. "That's when I decided to intervene...but I was too late."

A solo tear slides down my cheek and I quickly wipe it away, not wanting anything to stop him from finishing his story, even though it's breaking my heart.

Jesse blinks at my sudden movement, seemingly snapped out of his daze, but instead of stopping, he rubs his eyes and continues on.

"It all happened so fast. One second you'd pulled yourself free and then Jade was reaching for you again." He pauses and shakes his head. "She was frantic and wouldn't listen to anyone. And she was *hurting* you."

God, what did he do?

"When she wouldn't give up, there was no other option. So, with both hands on her chest, you shoved her away. Hard." He pauses and it feels like forever. "And she pulled you down with her."

What? It was me?

Someone gasps, and it takes me a second to realize it came from my mouth. Bile rises in my throat as tears blur my vision, my entire body shaking uncontrollably while I cry out in silence.

I did it.

I killed Jade.

"No. No. No. No." *This can't be happening.* "No."

Digging my palms into my eyes, I try to stop the tears as pain rips through me, my chest tightening to unbearable levels.

"You didn't know," Jesse says, breaking into my madness, his voice quivering, as though fighting his own tears. "You just wanted her to stop," he continues, and I don't know if he's whispering, or if I'm so messed up, I can't hear him properly anymore. "There was long grass. We didn't even notice you were standing on the edge."

"Oh God. I can't. I killed her. I killed Jade."

"No, you didn't. Willow, listen to me. You both fell. The only difference is that you fell to the side and hit your head against a rock. It was an accident. You could have died too."

Huh?

"Why didn't I die? I should have died. It should have been me."

"You did nothing wrong. I should have done more. I couldn't save you both. I wasn't fast enough. I only managed to grab you at the last second because the rock delayed your fall, but—"

"God, what is he saying? *I killed Jade.*"

"No! You didn't kill Jade."

What? Did I say that out loud? "I have to go," I announce suddenly, conscious of my words this time.

"What? No. Willow..."

I finally glance his way to see he has one hand on my shoulder, while the other squeezes my leg. And yet, I hadn't felt his touch.

"I can't do this," I say with more urgency, my pulse racing inside me, trying to ignore his glistening eyes. "I need to be alone."

Rushing to unbuckle my seat belt, I shake him off and grab my bag from the floor, opening the door to get out. But when I try to exit, I'm pulled back.

My first instinct is to yell at Jesse, but when I see the strap of my bag stuck on something, I burst into tears once more.

I frantically try to pull it free, but it won't budge, and with my throat clogged with so much emotion, I'm struggling to breathe. "Come. On," I cry out, wasting what precious air I have left. "Please."

I vaguely hear my name being called but it can't be Jesse; it sounds too distant. I contemplate leaving my bag and running without it, but at the very last second it springs free, propelling me toward the open door.

Jesse springs forward and catches me before I fall out, like he always does, but rather than thank him, I leap from his truck the second I'm steady and back away with my hands out in front of me. "Please leave me alone," I beg, but he shakes his head, reaching for the door handle behind him.

"Stop," I add quickly. "It hurts too much. I'm *begging* you. *Please.*"

His eyes fill with so much hurt that I feel my heart shatter.

"I can't just let you go," he whispers, his voice choked with pain. "Please don't make me do that again."

A million thoughts and feelings rush through me, but I push them away as fast as they arrive, blocking everything out so I don't feel this agony anymore. I can't go back there. I can't go back to the dark place I was in when I first woke up and realized Jade was gone. *I won't.*

Bit by bit, I lock everything away until I'm left with nothing but an empty feeling and a fractured soul.

I'm done.

16
Jesse

Twelve Years Ago – Age Sixteen

Buttercup cries out and I take a step forward, only stopping when Jade's eyes widen with fear. "Let her go," I say slowly, hoping to keep the panic from my voice. Something's seriously wrong for her to be so frantic. "Let's talk. It's going to be okay."

Jade's eyes flash to mine as she shakes her head, tightening her hold on Buttercup's wrist. "Just go! Do your job. Go!"

Fuck.

"Please, Jade," Buttercup pleads. "You're hurting me. I won't say a word either. Please just let go." She cries out again, but when her pleading doesn't work, she fights back, thrashing about to get the upper hand. "I said... Let. Go."

Instead of pulling away this time, Buttercup steps forward, forcing Jade to stumble backward into the long grass as she's caught off guard, releasing Buttercup in the process.

Jade reaches for her again just as I notice how close they are to the edge. "Wait. You're going to-" I yell as I race forward, Tate's loud footsteps behind me. But they're not listening. We're too late.

I'm only a few steps away when Buttercup pushes Jade backward using all her strength, silencing my words as they both start to fall. "No!"

17
Jesse

Willow stares through me as some kind of war rages inside her. I can see all the emotions playing across her features, but when she finally focuses again, it's all gone. As though she's been stripped bare. Like her soul's been sucked from her body and all that's left behind is a shell of the girl I was finally getting to know. I'm not even sure she's hearing me anymore.

"Willow, please, I just need to..." I trail off because what I really need, I have no right to ask for. I need to comfort her; I need to hold her in my arms until I know that she's okay. That she's going to *be* okay.

She shakes her head but even that lacks energy. "I've survived this before. I can do it again," she says in monotone, making my heart clench. "I don't need this in my life. I don't need you."

Fuck. I want to tell her she's wrong; she must be. I thought she felt the same way I did, and I need her like *oxygen.*

"Willow, I—"

"I only came here to learn the truth," she cuts in. "And now that I know, I can move on."

The stilted way she speaks feels like a stab to the chest with every word, but I let her finish. She's hurting. She's not in her right mind. She just needs time. *She just needs time.*

After taking in a breath, she squares her shoulders and stands tall before sucking her lips into her mouth. Tears prick the back of her eyes, and for a split second, it looks like she's coming back to me, but she blinks them away, and in an instant, she's back to being broken.

"Goodbye, Jesse," she says with a nod. "Thank you."

She turns and walks away, moving toward the main road, knowing that since I pulled into a one-way street, I can't follow her. Although, maybe she's not even thinking about that.

Jumping from my truck, I prepare to chase her on foot as I call out her name. But she doesn't even flinch. She doesn't even react when I call her Buttercup. "*I don't need this in my life. I don't need you.*"

"*Fuck!*" I cry out, eliciting some dirty looks from those passing by. But I don't care. Nothing means anything right now except for Willow's pain. I *caused that.*

Tate and I agreed to take *two* things to the grave, and that was one of them. If Willow never remembered, we vowed *never to tell her.* No one deserves that kind of anguish.

And I fucking told her.

I went against every instinct I had. Everything I'd been fighting for so long. Why the hell couldn't I have stayed away? Or lied more convincingly? I can handle her hating me because she thinks I killed Jade. I *can't* handle her hating herself.

I continue to watch her until she reaches Pippa's building, only a block and a half away. My stomach twists in knots and my heart beats so hard that it causes a dull ache in my chest.

Willow disappears out of sight, and a fresh wave of emotions hit as water fills my eyes. *Tears* fill my eyes. And before long, an emptiness consumes me. She's gone.

When my phone rings sometime later, I realize I'm back in my truck, with no recollection of how I got here. Pippa's name lights up the screen, causing a mix of dread and relief to take over.

"Hello," I rasp, my free hand clenched in a fist, waiting for her onslaught or whatever hurt she's about to inflict.

"Hi," she says softly before shocking me with her question. "Are you okay?"

"Is Willow?" I counter because my pain is very much deserved.

"What do you mean?" She pauses, her question making my heart race as her panic rises. "I'm still at work. Did something happen?"

Everything happened, but I'm not sure what Willow wants to tell her.

143

"We just had a chat and she needed to be alone. Why are you asking if I'm okay?" I question, dropping my head back to the headrest.

"I heard the rumors."

"What rumors?" I sit up so quickly, I almost hit the roof.

"That the coaches went easy on you today. Some of the players think you might have a health issue that's holding you back. Are you okay? Are you worried about your contract?"

What the actual fuck? I really don't need this right now. Rumors my ass.

"Tell Ryan to get all the information straight before you worry next time. I'm fine." *I'm not.* "My contract's fine." *It's not.* "And it's all going to be okay." *I really hope I'm correct about that one, because fuck, things feel hopeless right now. And that has nothing to do with hockey.*

"Okay. Well, I'll start packing up so I can go home and check on Willow."

"Thank you," I say but it does nothing to calm my concern. *Willow's home alone.* I assumed Pippa would be there, but now that I know she's not, I can't just leave her. Pippa could be an hour getting home.

After convincing Pippa's doorman to let me in, it takes a minute of me pounding on the door before I hear movement and Willow finally opens up.

"No," she snaps, immediately starting to shut the door in my face. "I can't do this now," she rushes out as she disappears from my view.

"Willow, wait. Please." I stick my foot out just in time, cringing when the pain hits.

"Go away, Jesse. I want to be alone. I deserve that."

"You're right. You do. But I need to know you're okay. Well, as okay as you can be."

The door slowly opens and Willow stands before me with another blank expression. "As you can see, I'm fine. I'm just processing. I wanted the truth. I've got it. But I need you to leave."

"Willow—"

"Go." Her voice raises slightly but she maintains her composure, refusing to let me see her pain.

"Okay," I say reluctantly, knowing I'm not going to change her mind. "I'll go, but I don't like it."

"Thank you," she says, releasing a slow breath of relief, her lips pulling into a forced smile.

Against all better judgment, I walk away. Again. But as I near the elevator, I stop, needing to plead with her one last time.

I've just reached Pippa's apartment again when I hear a thud from inside and then Willow's gut-wrenching cries fill the air. Without thinking of what she might want, I push open the door, thankful she left it unlocked, and rush in, dropping to the floor beside her. I expect her to push me away, but she curls into me, sobbing against my chest as her entire body shakes.

Completely obliterating my soul.

I remain silent, letting her take what she needs, knowing that if I speak, I'm likely to break this moment of truce.

We stay like that for God knows how long, with me rubbing her back, until her tears dry up and she moves away.

"Thank you," she whispers, her voice croaky. "But I..."

"I know," I say, so she doesn't have to say it again. "You still need me to go."

She nods as a lone tear slides down her cheek. "Please."

I'm once again stuck between a rock and a hard place. I want to do right by Willow, but leaving her when she's just broken down in front of me isn't fucking easy.

"Please," she repeats before standing up and dusting herself off. "I can't."

My heart clenches, but I stand up next to her, my eyes bouncing around her face, unable to look away from the pain. "I'm sorry. And I know I don't deserve it, but please don't disappear on me. I couldn't handle it if you did."

Willow doesn't say anything, but her eyes well with fresh tears as she moves to open the door.

"Goodbye, Willow," I say when I really want to say, "See you soon."

"Goodbye," she whispers as the door clicks shut.

When I get back to my truck, I can't move. Instead, I sit and stare at the steering wheel with Willow's cries on repeat in my mind. My chest aches. My muscles are tense. And I'm struggling to get air. I know I need to move, but I have no idea where to go. If I leave, even a foot, I'm too far away from Willow, but staying here isn't going to work either.

I stew on my options, not caring how much time slowly passes, until two texts answer for me.

Pippa: I'm home.

Seth: Where are you? We still need to talk.

Seth's waiting by his car in my visitor space when I pull into my parking garage, a smirk locked in place as he talks on the phone. As I step out of my truck, he ends the call and pushes off his car, walking toward me. "Do you offer this service to all your women?" he says but then scrunches his nose like the words taste sour. "Sorry, you know I joke at inappropriate times."

"It's fine. But to clarify, I don't have women at my apartment. Ever." *And I'm not in the mood.*

"Good to know." He nods before following me to the elevator. "How are you holding up?"

My brow furrows as I contemplate his question and realize my contract worries are far from my mind. "To be honest, I'm not really concerned about the contract. I—"

"That's not what I meant," he says, his mouth set in a slight frown. "How's Willow?"

"What do you mean?"

"She didn't look too good when I saw her waiting by your truck. I almost stopped to ask her, but figured it was between the two of you."

Shit. And here I thought she was good at hiding her true feelings.

"So, is she okay?" he asks again when I don't answer.

She's not okay. Far from it. And I don't know what to do. I don't know how to fix something so broken it's likely beyond repair.

"She's taking things day by day," I offer as the only answer that's not a lie, while also giving nothing away.

Seth nods again, though I'm fairly certain he has no idea what I mean. "Is it okay if we chat about your contract now? I know you've got a lot on your mind, but I need to know how you want me to proceed."

"Tell them yes. Whatever it is, it's a yes."

"What if they want to trade you?"

"No, fuck that."

He chuckles lightly. "That's what I thought. So how about we go inside and you hear me out."

"Yeah, I guess I can do that."

"So, the short of it is, they want me on the team, but they're not willing to sign a new contract this early on, because of my age."

"You're a forward, and you're not exactly a cautious player. Plus, there's the blood pressure."

"Fuck. It's normal."

"It's not normal for *you*. It's not normal for athletes. That's what they're comparing. They're not looking at your levels based on what the normal levels are; they're looking based on your *past* levels."

I sigh because I don't need the lecture. I know all of this, but it's not helpful. For so long I thought I was invincible. I've survived things in the past that would have broken others. Not only do I have a strong exterior, but inside I'm stone. No, I *was* stone. Now I'm not. Now I feel things I haven't felt for over a decade, and it's completely fucking me up. I thought I was immune, and that my body was built accordingly. Guess I thought wrong.

"Things are messed up at the moment." *I'm facing stress I thought I'd long escaped.* "It's not going to be an issue."

Seth raises an eyebrow in question, silently checking if I'm sure.

"It's *not* an issue," I repeat with more conviction, and it seems to work because he sighs in relief.

"Good. *Good.* I know you're worried about Willow, but she's got Pippa, she's got family, and she's got friends. We need to get your focus back where it belongs."

Huh? "You know that's a fucked-up request, right?"

"Is it? Because not too long ago, hockey was your *only* priority."

I shake my head. That may be true, but I'm not going to pretend nothing's changed. "It's still a priority, and I'm trying here. But if you think I'm going to pretend Willow doesn't exist, you're dead wrong."

Seth smiles. "Okay. I just wanted to make sure I knew where you stood. I like this new loved-up version of Jesse. Even if he is risking my commission."

"Asshole."

"Maybe so, but I'm *your* asshole." He bounces his eyebrows while I roll my eyes.

"How does Amber put up with you? And God help Bailey when she's old enough to find you annoying."

"Oh, she's almost there, don't worry."

"Ten's the new thirteen, right?"

"She's been a teen for years if you go by her personality. But of course, we love her."

"Of course." My lips curl into a grin and it shocks me a little. I didn't think I'd be smiling today.

"Is it time for a beer yet?" Seth asks, ending our discussion. "I want you to fill me in on what's going on with Willow."

"That's not going to happen."

"Just a beer then?" He smiles expectantly while I glare.

"Only 'cause you said please," I say sarcastically, moving toward the fridge.

"He jokes! How am I the only one that heard that?"

"Do you want this beer or not?"

Seth laughs. "Noted. I'm shutting up."

"Good."

Seth didn't shut up. He pried several more times before I gave up and told him Willow and I had an argument and I fucked up. It's all I was willing to say about the situation, and thankfully he was satisfied.

When he finally leaves, it's late, and the second the door shuts, my stomach rumbles, making me realize I haven't eaten since before practice. Not that I can even think about food. All I care about is Willow.

I send off a text to Pippa asking if Willow's okay, and then stare at my phone waiting for it to go off.

I'm actually going crazy. I'm a teen all over again and have just seen my mystery girl for the first time.

The girl who changed my entire world without even realizing it.

At fourteen, I was on the same self-destructive path as Tate. I'd been living in Mossman Hills for six months, and my life was falling apart. Our foster father was an abusive asshole, and the only way to stop him was to peddle his drugs.

It started off small, just dealing to peers, but the fucker got greedy.

No one gave a shit about me. No one saw past the young kid with no chance of a future.

Until Willow...Buttercup.

I'll never forget the first time we crossed paths. The start of my obsession. Long before we ever spoke again.

It was such an insignificant moment for her. All she did was smile and tell a boy who was having a particularly rough day to hold his *chin up* because things would get better. That I *could make them better.*

The point is she saw me.

While the rest of the town ignored my existence, *she saw me.* And then she was gone.

Even if I never saw her again, I realized she was right. I couldn't continue on that path; I didn't want to. I refused to be the one fucking up my own life. It was *my* choice. And I was going to take a stand.

So, from that day on, I took the beatings. I watched Tate sell drugs during the day, while I was beaten at night. If Tate had a good day, sometimes I'd be lucky too, but mostly, I just zoned out and let it happen.

I closed myself off to the pain.

Getting small glimpses of Willow during that time gave me hope that I'd one day find a better life, and because of her, I kept going. Hoping I'd be able to talk to her. Hoping I'd be the type of guy that deserved to talk to her.

But by the time we officially met, that fateful day on the mountain, I was nearing my limit. I'd been pushed as far as I could go, and the events of that day sent me over the edge.

Because of that, I had to stay away. She deserved better.

But now that she's back in my life, now that she's under my skin, it's a struggle to do the right thing anymore.

When it comes to Willow, all rational thought goes out the window. Everything I've fought so hard to protect gets obliterated.

She's my undoing, and I have a feeling she's going to run before I become hers.

And I don't blame her.

She should. But God, I hope that she doesn't.

An hour passes without a word from Pippa, increasing my concern as Willow's cries flood my mind. But when she finally texts me back, I don't feel any better. Instead, my heart sinks because I hate being right.

Pippa: She's on her way home.

18
Willow

I smile brightly at my customer even though it pains me. "Of course, I'll package that up for you now. Was it just this one or were you after anything else?" I ask, but regret it instantly.

She muses over my question. She's been in the shop for about twenty minutes, so you'd assume she'd have it figured out by now. But here we are.

"You really don't sell the necklace from that image?" she asks with a shy smile while I try really hard to keep mine in place.

"Not yet," I tell her. Just like Sara did a few minutes ago. "I'm sorry." *Freaking Jesse.*

"That's okay. Do you know if he recommends any of the other scents?"

Apparently calling every few days to check up on me wasn't enough for Jesse—he had to go and do a social media post about my store. And he *never* posts.

To make matters worse, he didn't just post about the store in general. He singled out my oils, specifically the Fresh New Love oil that Pippa shared, *and* my jewelry. *That's not even for sale yet.*

155

"I saw him buying the Fight for Love essence," Sara says from behind me. "And he may have even bought the Whatever it Takes one," she lies, and I almost spin around to cover her mouth.

"She's kidding; they don't actually exist. It was just this one."

The girl grows pink in the cheeks, so I plaster a smile back on my face and offer her some matching bath salts, free of charge. "Thank you for visiting. Hopefully we'll see you again soon," I say as she walks out the door, instantly turning to Sara when she's gone.

"What the hell was that?"

"That was me trying to get a reaction."

"A reaction to what?"

"Jesse."

"I have nothing to say about Jesse. I'm—"

"Fine. I know. You keep reminding me. But you can't tell me that hearing his name over and over doesn't affect you."

"Of course, I can't. Because it *does* affect me, but not how you're thinking. I'm doing a great job of moving on. I *want* to move on. But he keeps popping up as a constant reminder of why I hate myself. And why I *need* him out of my life. For my own sanity."

"Willow—"

"Nope. Moving on, remember?"

Sara gives me a "you're kidding me" look before nodding. "Yep, I remember. You're doing a great job," she says with a smile, not even bothering to hide the sarcasm in her tone.

I'm about to respond when my phone rings, breaking the tension in the room. Though I'm still in a mood when I answer.

"Audrey's Gifts and Homeware, can I help you?" I say with a slight edge, less upbeat than usual.

"Hi...hi. I'm calling from Raven's Boutique in California, and we'd love to talk to you about your products."

Dammit, Jesse. "One moment, I'll pass you on to the right person."

After pressing mute, I turn to Sara with what I'm sure is a deranged grin. "I need you to deal with this. She says she's from a shop in California. This is definitely Jesse's doing, and I don't want to bite her head off."

"He's just trying to make amends."

"Why are you on his side? He *lied.*"

"To *protect* you. I kind of admire him for that. Plus, he loves you and you clearly lo...like him."

"If I felt anything for him, it's past tense. I can't be with him if I want to get through this."

"Okay, fine. Give me the phone."

I hand it over and walk away so I don't have to listen to their conversation. I don't want to know. I can't. Hearing his name is breaking me.

I spend time tidying up our shelves and rearranging the displays until Sara comes running over, almost bursting with excitement as she interrupts my thoughts.

"They want to stock your jewelry," she blurts, her eyes flashing to the necklace I have around my neck, the very necklace that Jesse posted about. "They want you to create designs to put in all of their stores."

"What?" She's talking so quickly I'm momentarily confused. "Who does?"

"Raven's Boutique. They're in locations all over California. Their flagship store in Los Angeles just won some big award, and they're talking about opening a store in New York. This is huge, Willow. Huge."

"That seems like a scam. I don't even have any of my designs for sale."

"It's not a scam. I looked them up while she was talking, and—"

"Still, there'll be some kind of catch. Like they'll pay me for the designs but take all profit from the sales."

"Again, no. She said she'll pay upfront for the designs, plus an advance, and then you'll get a percentage of sales once they hit the stores based on an agreed sale price."

"I don't know—"

"Willow! Stop being stubborn and think about this. If she was calling because she'd been visiting and saw the jewelry we had on display, you wouldn't be questioning it."

"*Exactly*. I wouldn't be questioning it because it would mean we had pieces to sell and she genuinely liked my designs. But she's going by a stupid social media post by hockey's hottest player."

Sara's lips pull into a smirk but she tries to hide it. "Hottest player, huh? What about Cam Hardy?"

Okay, she got me. Everyone in the US knows Boston's center is a god, even if they have no clue about hockey, like me. But Jesse...

"Point is, this has nothing to do with us or our products and everything to do with him. It's a no."

I walk away so she can't question me any further, but immediately feel bad. It's not just my decision to make. While yes, technically, we're talking about my designs, everything I do is only possible because of Sara's encouragement and financial support.

"Sorry," I say, spinning around. "Let's talk to them about it. Maybe see if someone will come here to discuss it all in person."

Sara smiles but shakes her head. "No, you're right. They're taking a huge risk on something they've never seen. I'm sure there's some minor disclaimer that I'm missing."

My stomach twists. God, I'm a horrible person. "No, Sara. That's not what I meant."

"Hear me out."

"Okay."

"What about if we use this opportunity to look into expanding. Maybe we could start with an online store?"

"That could work, only shipping from here wouldn't exactly be easy. It's definitely something we can look into."

"Great." She smiles, but it doesn't meet her eyes.

Ugh. "How about we still find out what the boutique has to say, just in case," I say, watching Sara's smile grow.

"Okay, let's do that. Let's at least hear them out." She tries to hide her new bout of enthusiasm, but it doesn't work, and while I try to smile back, the idea of being a part of something that big makes my stomach swirl, and I'm not sure if it's nerves or elation. If this is a real offer, and not just something Jesse conjured up, then it could be my answer to leaving this place, something I'm still working toward. I just want to do it on my own terms.

"We'll work it out together," Sara says, and I know with no uncertainty that she'll back me one hundred percent, no matter what.

But what the hell do I want?

19

Jesse

The team sits quietly as our head coach finishes his spiel before dismissing us from our official duties for the day. Once again, we nailed practice. Everything ran smoothly, like a well-oiled machine. If I was a superstitious man, like some guys on the team, I'd probably be nervous.

Our goalie, Knuckles, believes that if he successfully stops every puck in a practice shootout, then he'll miss when it really counts, but if he misses one in practice, he'll be fine. We've told him many times over the years to miss on purpose, but it doesn't work that way.

My linemate, Ace, on the other hand, believes that it all comes down to the flavor of his toothpaste. When he was in the juniors, his team hadn't won a game in a few years. One day, when he was getting ready, he noticed that his new roommate had replaced his regular toothpaste with a strawberry flavor because he was allergic to mint. Ace thought nothing of it, even said it tasted delicious, but then his team won. He claims he headed straight to the store after the game and bought ten tubes of the stuff in case he couldn't find it again. And he still swears by it today, even when we lose.

I could never afford to be superstitious. I had to pool all my energy into my game. I had to believe I was the only one in control of my destiny. The only way for me to play well was to shut everything else out and focus on the game alone. Because if I were to ever let outside influences in, I'd likely buckle. And that in itself became my ritual.

It's the reason I avoid the media, it's the reason I don't have many friends, and it's the reason I've never even tried to let anyone into my life. Willow being the exception. Willow being *every* exception.

It's now been three weeks since I last saw her. Three *fucking* weeks. And while every second without her is destroying me from the inside, I can't even be angry about it. It's my goddamn fault.

And I wouldn't even change it, given the chance. If she hadn't pushed me on it, I would have continued to take the blame for Jade's death. I deserved that. It should have been me forced to live with the guilt because God only knows I don't feel guilty about other things I've done.

But now that Willow knows the truth, it kills me that she pushed me away. She won't take my calls; she only occasionally responds to my texts—she's just gone. Sticking to her "I don't need you in my life" notion.

Not even caring that I might need her.

That for me, it's only ever been her.

I'm lost in thought as we all collect our things to head home, but aware enough to hear a few of the guys organizing to meet up for a beer, while others complain about an early morning photoshoot they've been roped into. Quickly throwing my bag over my shoulder, I sneak out the door, not wanting to be pulled into either of those conversations.

But I'm not quick enough.

"How is it that you and Pippa are barely speaking and she *still* gets you out of media commitments?" my teammate Clayton asks as he moves into step beside me.

"Just lucky, I guess." I shrug, but it's the truth. After Pippa volunteered me for a magazine photoshoot last month—when Willow was in San Francisco—I assumed that was the end of my run. That she'd be putting my name forward for everything, or at the very least, no longer giving me any special treatment. But I was wrong. Other than the barely speaking part, nothing's changed, and I'm still not sure if that's a good thing or a bad thing. Is she doing it to keep the peace, or does she feel sorry for me? After all, her sister pretty much ghosted me after I left Pippa's apartment, yet I can't stop thinking about her.

"Your luck can't last forever," he says before walking in the opposite direction. And if that's not a statement of my life, I don't know what is. I'm constantly waiting for the other shoe to drop. For shit to get real. For my luck to run out. Every time I see a police officer walking toward me, my heart stops. Every time I get a call from my foster parents, I hold my breath until I hear the smiles in their voices. From the day I left that hospital in Oregon, I've had luck on my side. But I've used so much, I must be nearing the bottom of the barrel. And I have a feeling it's all about to end.

As if summoned by our conversation, Pippa appears in front of me with a folder in her hand and a frown.

And so, it begins...

"Pippa?"

"I've managed to reschedule your clinic in Oregon."

"What?" My chest lightens as my lips pull into the smallest smile. I wasn't expecting that.

"I've had it all cleared, so we can go this Tuesday and Wednesday. We'll fly on Tuesday night, host the clinic Wednesday morning and fly home Wednesday night." She's direct and to the point. A lot more businesslike than she'd normally be.

"Okay."

"Good. And we'll have a film crew with us for some extra exposure."

Goddammit. "Are you kidding me? Why?" I should have known there would be a catch. Pippa hasn't spoken about the clinic at all since we got back to San Francisco.

"I'm not kidding. That was the trade-off."

"Who asked who?"

"What?"

"Which one is the trade-off?" I'll bet my life savings that Pippa was approached about increasing our profile ahead of the season opener, and the trade-off is my clinic.

"The clinic. It's a team thing now. There'll be a few players there."

Great. I guarantee one of them is Ryan. I never had anything against the kid before all this started, but now, he's getting on my nerves.

"Fine. I'll be ready." At least it brings me closer to Willow. I just have to decide what to do when I'm there.

Considering I have nothing going on in my life except hockey, the next few days strangely fly by, and before I know it, I'm sitting on the plane waiting for takeoff.

Ace sits down beside me, lifting his leg onto his knee as he leans back. "I don't think I'll ever get used to traveling like this," he says, presumably talking about our luxury seats. "I hear you're the one we have to thank for this little adventure," he adds, making me huff out a laugh.

"Don't thank me. I wanted to do this alone. And if it was up to me, I would be."

"Well, thanks anyway. I'm looking forward to it. It's nice to be able to give back. I still feel like an impostor here. Like any day now, the coach is going to call my name and tell me there's been a mistake, and there's another guy out there with the same name who's really the guy they wanted."

"With the name Ace Lockier?" I ask, suppressing a small smirk.

"Yeah." He laughs. "You never know."

Ace started with us three years ago, and last year was his first year on the playing roster and on my line. He's an absolute gun. There is no way in hell they picked the wrong guy. At twenty-two, he's already shaping up to be one of the best. But I guess it shows how much we all doubt ourselves.

"Ace, this may not mean much, but I can assure you, they got the right guy. You're going places."

Ace's jaw drops to his chest as he stares at me in shock, his eyes boring into mine, unblinking.

"Ah...are you okay there, buddy?"

He shakes his head and chuckles to himself. "Yeah. Yeah. It's just...since when do you offer compliments and reassurance? I've been your linemate for a year and the most you've said to me, outside of play, is hi. I mean, you're nice enough to answer questions when asked. Sometimes you answer with a grunt but it's still a response. This, however, is new."

"What can I say; you caught me on a good day."

"Nah, it's more than that. You're going soft in your old age." I'm about to laugh but he jumps up and takes a step back, making me frown instead. "Just making sure you don't deck me," he says with his hands raised in the air.

"Yeah, yeah. I'm an asshole. I get it."

"Not anymore, apparently."

"Quit while you're ahead," I say, shooting him a glare.

"Will do." He smiles with a grimace before sitting back down and pulling a Jack Reacher novel from his bag, opening it to halfway. When he notices me checking it out, he lifts it in the air. "Book six. I'm hooked," he says, immediately diving into his reading, leaving me to fall back into my own head. Probably not the best place to be.

I usually bring something to read myself, but lately, my mind's been so full of the complicated mess I've found myself in, that I can't relax enough to concentrate on the story.

Flashbacks of my past have been threatening to come to the surface, memories I buried so deep, I almost let myself believe they never happened. But they did. And after everything that transpired with Willow and *that* day, I'm starting to lose the control I once had.

But I have to hold strong. Even allowing myself to think of that time could mentally ruin me.

Yet another reason I should leave Willow alone. *Should.* That and the fact she made it clear that she didn't need me. I have to respect that. Don't I?

Don't I?

Nah, fuck that.

She may not *need* me but I know that she *feels something* for me, and it's time I tried to win her back. It's time for me to remind her of our connection, to show her how I feel, and to kiss the sense back into her.

I messed up. I lied. But I did it for *her*. And I'm prepared to work to get her back.

Because Ace was wrong. I'm not going soft in my old age. Instead, I finally know what's important. And I'm not going down without a fight.

20

Jesse

My alarm goes off at five a.m., but it wasn't necessary. I've been watching the clock since two, trying to stop myself from getting out of bed, to at least allow my body to rest. Being this close to Willow is a new kind of torture. One I hadn't even considered. It was hard enough being in the same town as her and trying to push my feelings away. But now that I've tasted her lips, now that I've completely fallen for her, I'm fucked.

She said she couldn't be with me, but that's bullshit. I know how she feels, even if she's never explicitly said it, and I've been the good guy. I've given her space but now I'm done.

I want to be there to help her heal.

This could end badly. I could lose her forever, but I have to take the chance, because doing nothing isn't going to work for me. I've been doing nothing for too long. It's time I got her back.

I'm the first one at the rink to set up for the clinic—shout out to the janitor that recognized me and let me in—and I've got most of the equipment ready before the organizers arrive.

"Jesse Hastings," one of the local coaches says, a big smile on his face.

"That's me."

He chuckles to himself as his eyes flash to the woman beside him. "Pippa wasn't kidding when she said this was your idea. We didn't expect you to set it up."

"I don't mind at all. I couldn't sleep."

"Uncomfortable bed?" His face pinches in apology, as though it's his fault, and I almost laugh.

"Yeah, something like that."

"Well, we're grateful to have you here. I'm Pete, and this is Leena."

I nod as I continue getting ready. "Nice to meet you both."

"The kids should be arriving within the hour. What about the others on your team?"

"Any minute—"

The doors bang open, cutting off my words. "Dalton's in the house!" one of our defenders hollers as the team enters.

"Now," I finish, huffing out a laugh.

Pete watches the guys as they try to trip each other, his expression a little hesitant. "Not all as professional as you, I see," he says nervously.

I'm going to guess they had a big night. "They're good guys; they'll be professional when it counts."

I hope.

Thankfully, I'm right, and my teammates all are on their best behavior when the families arrive, smiling, shaking hands, playing the parts of the professionals I know they can be. The camera crew may have something to do with that, but I'll give them the benefit of the doubt.

In fact, we're all in high spirits until the kids line up in front of us and it's a struggle to maintain our happy expressions, seeing just how bad some of them have it. Their clothes are too big, or too small. Some of the kids are covered in bruises, while others are too terrified to even be here. These kids are the ones that can't afford to be part of the local club or don't have the opportunity to play. Whether it's because they can't get here or aren't allowed...this is a one-off for them. At least, that's all they know it to be.

I smile and greet everyone as the clinic begins, but while the local coaches are speaking, I sneak away.

"How do I go about funding the club to allow for scholarships or something?" I ask Pippa quietly.

Pippa offers me a sympathetic smile but shakes her head. "You don't. You can't fund them all, and it wouldn't look good for you to be playing favorites."

"That's bullshit and you know it. Plenty of sports stars make donations to their junior clubs."

"Yes, but you're not talking about *your* junior or youth club. You're talking about *this* club. You don't have a connection here."

"I do now. I can't unsee this."

"It's happening all over the country. There are disadvantaged children everywhere."

"Oh, I fucking know that. And if I could help them all, I would. But anything is better than nothing."

"Let's talk about it when we get home. For now, just concentrate on what you can give them today."

I bite back my smile as an idea pops into my head. "Good advice, Pippa. I will."

Pippa calls out as I head back to the group, undoubtedly having figured out what I'm going to do. If I can't donate to a team, I can at least donate to those standing before me. So, when it's our turn to speak, that's exactly what I do.

"Along with the skills workshop, everyone here will be getting a grant that can be used for anything youth hockey related, whether that's personal equipment or transport to and from the field. I'll be talking with officials here to work out the details. And…" I trail off before turning to the parents, "funds will *only* be made available for ice hockey. You won't be able to access the funds yourself."

I have no idea how the hell I'm going to make that happen—and judging by Pippa's groan behind me, it's not an easy task—but I will make it work.

Little faces light up all around me, while some parents smile and others frown. When I turn around,

THE SOUND OF FOREVER

my teammates are a mixed bag of emotions, with half of them nodding their heads in agreement and the others staring at me like I'm a complete stranger. Which pisses me off, because I have always been generous with my money. I've always given back. I just don't do it so publicly.

Once the excitement's out of the way, we divide everyone into groups and begin the workshop.

The talent in this arena blows my mind; these kids are incredible. No matter how apprehensive they were when they first got here, all that changed the second they got a stick in their hands. It stems from their passion. I can tell hockey is something that keeps them going, keeps the light in their life. And while it's beautiful to see, it's also heartbreaking.

For a while in my life, *I was that kid.* Running around the yard using a broken tree branch for a stick and an old tennis ball for a puck. Cheering myself on. Dreaming.

These are the players we need in the league, the ones that bleed hockey. It's their world, their everything.

We spend a lot of our time on solid ground, running through the skills part of the workshop. But once they've proven themselves, we move into the rink and split off into teams, giving them a chance to play a real game.

A few of the kids struggle, and it's clear they haven't spent much time on the ice, but the harder they try, and the more we encourage, the more their confidence grows. So much so, that I'm pleased to say it's a competitive game in the end.

"Congratulations! Well done to all of you. Your natural talent, enthusiasm, and passion is unrivaled," I say when the game ends, needing them to know how awed we all are. "Since it was a draw, you'll all be getting medals." *We were prepared.* "And a ticket to one of our games in San Francisco, with travel." Again, I have to figure out the logistics of that, but I know it's possible. "On behalf of all of us on the team, I want to thank you. You've shown us what it's like to truly love the game, and I think I speak for everyone when I say we'll never forget today. So, use your grants, come and join the team here in Grovedale, and hopefully we'll see you in the big leagues one day."

The stadium fills with cheers as the kids all exit the ice with smiling faces. And I get it—I can't keep mine away either. Knowing we've given them an opportunity of a lifetime is everything.

So, after accomplishing one positive thing today, I'm ready for the next.

"Thank you for today, and for the grants. We need fresh blood in our competition here, and these kids were incredible," Pete says, a grateful smile on his face.

"They were amazing. I'll be in touch to work out the details, or someone will, hopefully by the end of the week." *I wonder if Seth can help.*

"Thanks, Jesse. Thanks for picking our league. I have no doubt we'll be getting a lot more interest once word spreads that some of the San Francisco team have been here."

"My pleasure. I wish I could stick around but..."

"Of course, go. We'll pack up."

I grab the rental keys from the bench, along with my bag, and wave to the guys.

When I spot Pippa across the rink, I call out, signaling to the door. "I'm taking the car, Pip. I'll be back to pick you up in a few hours." Her eyes widen and she frantically shakes her head, but I keep walking. Or at least, I try to.

"Jesse, stop!" she yells and I surprisingly do as she asked. "We're leaving at four on the dot," she calls out as I turn around. "With or without you," she adds, driving her point home.

She's obviously not happy about what I'm doing, but the fact that she didn't stop me suggests she's not completely against the idea. And that means one of two things—either Willow's struggling and she thinks my presence will help, or Willow is thriving and she wants me to see it.

I don't care which it is as long as I get to find out for myself.

The drive is easy enough, but as I arrive in Hepburn Falls, the car slows the closer I get to town. *To Willow.* It's not until my chest tightens that I realize I made it happen. I slowed down. For all my bravado and talk of fighting, I'm not quite ready for what I might find.

But I came here for a reason, and it's better that I know one way or another.

I give myself a little pep talk—one that involves telling myself to snap the fuck out of it—and by the time I'm pulling into a parking space across from her store, I'm set, jumping from the car before I start questioning things again. I've already wasted too much time.

After learning my lesson when I was last here, I check for the one car that might be driving by, before crossing. I've just taken a step when the world stills.

Willow rushes from a neighboring store with a large box in her hands and a genuine smile lighting up her face. She says something to Sara as she holds open the door, and they both burst out laughing before moving inside.

A heavy weight settles on my chest as I watch her. She's happy. I'm fucking miserable and she's *happy*.

While the thought of her living life without me is soul crushing, seeing Willow's smile means everything to me.

God, should I leave?

I reach for the door handle behind my back, contemplating my decision as I stare at her now empty doorway. If I leave, I'll never know, but if I stay, will it stunt her progress?

I'm stuck, unsure what to do, as the girls walk back out, making my decision for me. Sara's the first to see me, her smile fading as she flicks her curly brown hair out of her face, pinning me with a look I can only describe as apprehensive. When Willow sees her expression, she spins my way and gasps, her unforgettable eyes boring into mine.

She whispers something and then takes a few tentative steps toward me, hesitating when she reaches the road. "What are you doing here?" she asks, her tone less accusatory than I expected.

Letting go of the handle, I move forward but stay on my side of the road. "I just finished running a clinic in Grovedale. We have to head home in a few hours."

"Okay." She nods slowly. "But why are you *here*? Almost an hour from there."

"I thought that would be obvious," I say honestly. "I'm here for you."

Willow quietly stares at me, her brows raised in defiance, refusing to give.

"I'm not leaving until you talk to me," I say, standing my ground, my gaze unwavering.

She huffs, and her body deflates before she rolls her eyes, as if my presence is bothering her. "Fine, you can help me with more boxes. Come on."

21
Jesse

I jog across the road, quickly falling into step beside Willow, following her into a clothing store I hadn't even noticed the last time I was here.

"What do you need to collect?" I ask, looking around the space.

"There was a mix-up with our deliveries this morning. Those boxes over there are meant for us."

"Wow, that's a lot of new stock," I say as a tightness pulls at the pit of my stomach. It looks like they're expanding the store, which means she has no intention of leaving, even after telling me she'd love to spread her wings.

"It is. It's double our usual order."

"That's great. Have sales increased?" I'm careful not to mention my potential part in those sales. We both know what I did; there is no need to discuss it.

Willow's lips pull into a smile, sending my heart racing. She opens her mouth to say something, but laughs instead. "You could say that. It's amazing what a little bit of promotion will do."

"I've heard that usually helps." I wink, and for the briefest of seconds, her eyes light up with a spark, before it's gone.

Conversation over, we collect as many boxes as we can and take them to the shop. Sara opens the door and guides us to their back room so we don't knock anything over along the way, her smile friendly but cautious.

"Nice to see you again, Sara," I say with a nod. "Willow tells me the store's doing well."

"Did she?" Sara says, raising an eyebrow as she turns to Willow. "I didn't think—" Willow shakes her head, cutting Sara off, and the pang in my stomach worsens. I feel more like an outsider *now* than I did the first time I was here, when I barely knew her. I feel like I'm a voyeur in her life, only here to watch and see how well she has it. At least, now I know why Pippa didn't stop me from coming here. She's definitely thinking it will help me move on. And it probably should.

When the boxes are all spread out, Sara excuses herself, leaving Willow and me alone. The air shifts as the tension rises, quickly becoming uncomfortable as a foreign feeling takes over.

"Why are you really here?" Willow asks the second the door shuts. She busies herself searching the contents of the first box while I watch her from behind.

"I came to see you. To apologize again."

"I don't need the apology. We said everything we needed to say when I was in San Francisco."

"*You* may have said everything, but I never really got the chance to explain."

Willow spins to face me. "It doesn't matter. Nothing will change the outcome. You still lied. Even after seeing me again."

Her words hit me like a punch, bruising my soul as she connects over and over. Just like when my asshole foster father used to beat the shit out of me. Only this hurts so much more.

"I just wanted to protect you," I state, my voice a little more abrupt than I mean it to be, desperate for the words to sink in. For her to understand.

"I didn't need you to protect me, Jesse. I just wanted the truth. I just wanted you to want me. To care for me. To be in this *with me*."

"I was. I am."

"It doesn't fix things."

"You keep saying that without telling me what *will*. You've got to understand that I never wanted to hurt you. Everything I did was about keeping the pain away."

"I know."

"Do you?"

"Yes, I get it. I know why you did it. Doesn't mean I think it's right."

She knows. She gets it. But it changes nothing.

Willow closes her eyes and lets her head drop back, a new tension crossing over her. "I can't do this. Please," she whispers, her genuine happiness replaced by an ache that breaks me.

"Pushing me away isn't going to fix anything, Willow. I know you feel something for me. Doesn't that count for anything?"

"I can love someone and still choose not to be with them," she blurts out, her voice higher than before. "You hurt me, Jesse. And now I need to let you go. No, now I *want* to let you go." Her voice cracks but she holds strong in her expression, while I shatter.

What do I say to that? She can love someone but choose not to be with them. *Me.* She can love and leave me.

"I'm sorry," I whisper since there's not much more I can do. I've hurt her enough. It's time to stop. "I didn't come to mess up your life again. I just wanted to see you. To try and win you back."

"You're a great guy, Jesse. I just—"

"Yeah, yeah," I say sarcastically. "One day I'll make someone else really happy. *I'll* be really happy."

"Hell no, I don't want that. I want you to be miserable," she jokes, and it confirms just how happy she is. This is the real Willow—she's confident, strong, knows her worth, and she's happy. What more could I want?

"Do you ever wish you could go back?" she says suddenly, making my smile fade. "To do one thing differently."

"Every. Fucking. Day," I say honestly because I've never thought about anything more.

Except maybe her.

Willow nods in understanding, but she has no fucking clue.

"I'd have spoken to you the first day I saw you," I cut in before she has a chance to speak, stepping forward to close the space between us. "*Years* before we officially met," I add. "Or I'd have spoken to you one of the many times I saw you after that. I would have gotten to know you. Told you I thought you were cute. Maybe even asked you out." I tentatively lift my hand to her face before tucking her hair behind her ear, letting my fingers linger when she doesn't back away. "The first words I spoke to you would not have been on that mountain. If I'd have spoken to you at any moment before that day, *that* day would never have happened. So yes, I wish I could go back."

Willow gapes, shell-shocked until she seemingly decides she shouldn't be acting that way and snaps out of it, blinking a few times before finally moving back, out of my reach. "What if you couldn't go back *that* far, you couldn't stop Jade's death. Is there anything else you would change after it?"

I internally wince because she's not going to like my answer. "I wouldn't go back and tell you the truth, if that's what you're asking. That's not something I can change."

"I know you can't change it. I'm asking if you would?"

"No."

"No?"

"I wouldn't."

Willow recoils as if she's been slapped before shaking her head. "Even after knowing what I went through?"

"Even so, yes."

Her lips curl as she shoots me a look of disappointment, but it doesn't affect me. I knew it was coming.

I've thought about this very question often since I left her by the road. And while I'd change pretty much everything in the lead-up to that point. I wouldn't change much after. Because while I may constantly regret the way I fucked up Willow's life, I can't regret my part in protecting her from the truth, and I'll never regret the fact that my coming back made her stronger, helped her take her life back. Even if it is giving her the courage to kick me out of it now.

"Do you want to know what I'd change?" she says after a moment of quiet.

Not if you're about to tell me you wish we'd never met. "Yes."

"I'd have turned around the second I realized Jade and I weren't alone up there." She points in the direction of the mountain, making my stomach churn. *Close enough.* Holding her hardened gaze, her eyes lock on mine, making me feel her pain. And then she smiles. She *smiles.* "After that, I'm sure I would have recognized you the next time I was in town, and maybe I would have said hello. Maybe we would have met under different circumstances."

The tightness subsides, making way for longing. Until I remember that if things had played out differently, I wouldn't be here. She would never want the man I was set to become. And I wouldn't have let her even if she did.

"That's a nice dream," I say with a forced grin. "The perfect fantasy."

"It is," she whispers. "But that's all it can ever be."

I nod and suck in a breath, knowing I have to say goodbye. "This doesn't feel right. I can't just walk away."

Willow's breath hitches but she covers it by clearing her throat, and when her eyes water, she blinks back the tears, standing tall as she takes a step closer.

"It's the right thing for me," she says, breaking my heart even more. "I wish you nothing but happiness, despite what I said earlier."

I pull her into a hug to buy myself some time, and breathe her in, memorizing her scent, the feel of her pressed against me, her warmth. Making sure to lock it all away in case I never get to do it again.

But God, I hope that's not the case.

"How does this work?" I whisper into her hair before pulling back. "Am I meant to just go on with life as though you don't exist?"

"I don't know. Maybe... Yes. That's probably best, for now."

"For now." She said, *"For now."* I'll take that.

"I'm sorry." I nod, before cupping her face in my hands and staring into her beautiful eyes. "I promise, I'll stop making this harder on you." I gently press my lips to her forehead and squeeze my eyes shut.

My heart aches, but I manage to step back, keeping my promise to walk away. "Goodbye, Willow," I say, trying hard not to look at her so I don't change my mind. She just needs more time. That's all, and I can wait. She's worth the wait.

I make it safely to the rental car and start it up before I even have my seatbelt fastened. I'm back on the road within an hour of arriving, yet I feel like I just lost years of my life.

Pippa's glaring at me when I pull up in Grovedale, but I have thirty seconds to spare, so I ignore her, checking my phone while I wait for her and the guys to jump in.

I honestly thought I'd end that conversation with Willow in my arms, making her mine, though I should have known better. My luck was never going to last forever, but God, this hurts.

As we drive to the airport, I think back to her questions about changing things, and wonder what would have happened if I'd given her a better answer. Told her what she wanted to hear, even if it was a lie.

Because I would have been lying. I meant every word I'd said. I wouldn't change it.

She was fifteen when Jade died. She couldn't have survived the truth, and that was made even more apparent by how she reacted in her twenties.

On top of that, if I had stayed by her side, told her *and* the police what had happened, the rest of my night would have played out very differently, and I wouldn't be where I am today.

I wouldn't have broken free.

I wouldn't be the man she loved.

Because Jade wasn't the only person to die that day. And that second death was my savior.

22
Willow

As soon as Jesse walks away, I shut the door and break down in tears. Just like I did the last time I saw him, only this time I'm silent and he's not here to comfort me.

I don't want him here.

I pushed him away because it's too much. I can't handle it. My *heart* can't handle it.

I've barely had time to think when Sara knocks on the door, forcing me to pull myself together.

"I'll be out in a minute," I rush out so she doesn't come in, frantically wiping my face to hide the evidence of my feelings. Trying to hide the pain.

When I join her, Sara's busying herself with some paperwork. Her eyes meet mine, but she doesn't acknowledge what we both know is there. She knows I'd prefer to let it go.

"Do you want me to stay?" she asks, because she's due to pick up Benji.

I shake my head. "No. I'm good. I promise. You head off and I'll see you in the morning."

It will make it easier for me to mope around for the rest of the day.

Taking a deep breath, I close my eyes and let the sun warm my face, the picturesque view in front of me still at the forefront of my mind despite no longer looking at it. It's hard to forget; it's the reason we come up here. That, and the peace.

I hear Jade huff behind me and I can't help but laugh.

"Tell me again why you decided to bring your bag with you? Are you hiding something in there?" I chuckle again until Jade's face pales slightly.

"What's going on?"

"It's nothing. I just brought some aspirin and extra water. I've had a headache since breakfast."

Shit! "Are you okay? Why don't we call it a day? We've made it here. We don't have to do it all. Come on, we'll come back next weekend."

I turn to leave but Jade grabs my tee, pulling me to a stop. "No."

"No?" My brow furrows as I spin to face her, but she has her usual warm smile plastered on her face.

"I'll be fine. I promise. You need this today after your week."

She's right. This week has been one of my worst with Pippa being sent away, and the family arguments. I *could really use this moment of respite.* "As long as you're sure."

Jade pulls me into a side hug, but it feels a little shaky. "I'm sure. Have you heard from Pippa at all?" *she asks, changing the subject so I don't continue making a fuss.*

"Not yet," *I say, watching her closely.* "But I guess it hasn't been that long, and I don't know how strict they are with phones at her new school."

"I can't believe that happened. That they'd just send her away like that."

"Me either, but she's been spiraling for weeks now. I just didn't think they'd go through with their boarding school threats."

"I'm sorry, Willow."

"I know. At least I have you."

"You will always have me."

My head's groggy when I wake, but fragments of my dream float to the surface.

"What's going on?"
Jade's shaky voice.
"You will always have me."

Jesus! I don't think that was a dream. And if it was a memory, that means I saw the signs back then, and I missed them. I let Jade continue on up that mountain knowing something was wrong. I failed her as a friend more than once.

My heart lodges in my throat as I bite back the tears threatening to fall. I have to be strong. I love Jade but I was better. I was living. At least, I was surviving. I can't go back to the darkness again. I won't let myself.

Since the sun's up, I set off for a run with music blasting in my ears. I usually use this time to think, but today I want the opposite. Instead, I work hard to focus on the beat, to listen to the lyrics, and find meaning in each song. Surprisingly, it works...until one of the songs reminds me of Jade, and I'm right back where I started.

By the time I get home, I'm lost in a familiar haze. A fog I promised myself I'd never go back to.

I told Jesse I was fine. I *was* fine. At least I thought I was. But he made me realize, I'm barely keeping myself afloat. It's all just another show. But this one's not for others. This one's for me, and it's called the-lies-we-tell-ourselves-to-survive.

Taking my time to get ready, I somehow still make it to work with two minutes to spare, unlocking the door just as my delivery guy arrives.

If he notices my somber expression, he doesn't mention it, but I can guarantee he'll be telling someone before the day is through.

Willow always smiles, what's happened?

Have you noticed Willow hasn't been as friendly lately?

They think I don't hear the whispers, but I do, and it's all bullshit. I'm still just as friendly, but I don't hide when I'm having a rough day. And I'm allowed to have rough days. I shouldn't be made to feel guilty because I don't smile all the time.

It pains me that I didn't wake up to that sooner.

The more I have time to think, the more I spiral, and by ten a.m., I find myself slumped over the counter, my eyes falling closed as I wish the day away.

Jade picks up speed until I'm forced to almost jog to catch up to her, my eyes locked on my feet as I dodge the uneven terrain, careful not to fall and piss her off even more. Something is definitely wrong.

"Jade!"

"Jesus, you look like shit," Sara says out of nowhere, making me jump. I blink a few times as my eyes adjust, and when I finally focus, I realize I'm leaning against the wall. *When did I stand up?*

"Um, wow. Tell me how you really feel." I try to joke but it falls flat, my lackluster tone giving the game away.

"What's going on?" she asks, her motherly voice kicking in.

"It depends," I say honestly. "How long were you there?"

Sara laughs but it's one of those laughs that means this is anything but funny. "I just arrived, but from that comment, I'm guessing you've been out of it all morning."

"Not *all* morning. I smiled when Mrs. Jones stopped by to ask for her usual bouquet."

A soft smile tugs at Sara's lips. Mrs. Jones is always so busy she never takes the time to focus on what shop she's walked into before asking for an order. She once asked the butcher for one of our Christmas scents. We'd be worried if she didn't have three kids in tow, a bunch of bags, and a sleep-deprived expression.

"I guess that's something, but you really do look unwell."

"I'm fine," I lie.

"Of course you are. Silly me. How could I have possibly thought otherwise."

"Sara."

"Nope. I thought you said Jesse leaving was a good thing. I even pretended not to see the signs that you'd been crying after he left, but—"

"It is!" I cut her off. "That's not why I look and feel like shit. Well, I guess he's a part of it. But this time, it's not him. Him leaving was the right thing."

"Oh-kay." Sara drags out her vowels as she scrunches her face in confusion.

"I had another memory, or dream. No, it was a memory. I know it was."

Sara's eyes light up. "That's good, right?"

194

"No, it's not. I've recently come to terms with my memory loss. And while I feel like a broken record in saying this, I'm moving on."

"I thought you were working with your therapist to try and figure it all out?"

"I was. But after finding out the truth from Jesse, I changed my mind. I don't want the memories back. Last night I remembered Jade and how I missed the signs that something was off. I *missed* it."

"Oh, Willow. No. You can't blame yourself for anything that happened that day. You—"

"It's my fault!" I yell, and then softly add. "I pushed her."

Taking a tentative step forward, Sara pulls me into a hug and gives me a squeeze. I'd told her about Jesse's big reveal the day I came back. I didn't really have a choice. I was so shattered, I needed someone to pick up the pieces.

"It's not your fault," Sara says, as she steps back. "If Jesse's story is true then it was a freak accident. You can't let the past get to you."

I open my mouth to speak but she covers it with her hand. "I thought you were moving on." She raises a brow.

Dammit. "I was, but it's hard when it's all I can think about."

Sara frowns, seemingly lost in thought. "Why today?" she asks after a beat, making me frown too.

"What do you mean?"

"You've had two of these *memory dreams*, right?" She holds up two fingers.

"Two and a half."

"Okay. What's the common denominator?"

"What?"

"Jesse. You were with Jesse before both dreams."

"Not the half one."

Sara glares at me, making sure I know it doesn't change her point.

"Okay, what are you trying to say?"

"Maybe you need to spend time with him to see if he triggers something else."

What?! "I just told you I don't want to remember anymore." *It hurts too much.*

"But maybe you *need* to. For closure." Ugh, I hate that I also came to this conclusion the last time I remembered something. Only now, it's not the same.

"That seems a little backward for moving forward. We just said our goodbyes. Seeing Jesse is the last thing I want to do."

"Willow, you and I both know that's not the end of you and Jesse."

"We do?" I ask, folding my arms over my chest before staring her down. I'm trying to be confident, but Sara sees right through it for what it is—protection—a shield against the feelings I don't want to let in.

"I'm not going to use the L word, but you care about him. You may be angry with him right now. But you care. A lot."

"I don't even know if I'm angry. I'm just tired. And hurt by all the lies."

"That's totally expected. No one is saying you can't feel that way. Or that your feelings aren't valid. But you can't pretend that this distance between you is forever. It's not going to help you heal."

"I can, and I will."

"God, there's that stubbornness again."

"This is me." I point to my chest. "This is who I truly am. I was just playing the part of someone else for a while."

"It's funny because I became friends with the 'pretend' you," Sara says, using quote fingers. "The person you became," she adds, and the guilt hits me, knowing I was partially fake with her too.

"God, Sara. I—"

"I like this version of you," she says, cutting me off. "Even more... and I kind of feel like we're closer."

She smiles and it's so infectious that I smile back, my first for the day. Because she's right. "I'm glad you like this *me* more, because you're stuck with her. I need you."

"I'm not going anywhere," she says, hugging me again as her smile widens.

I smile back, but something painfully tugs at my heart because... *That's what Jade always said.*

A few days pass without another memory, so I start to relax again, but it's never far from my mind. Jesse's never far from my mind. Probably because everyone keeps inadvertently bringing him up when they talk about a certain social media post. Not that I can complain about the sales.

I'm once again restocking the scent Jesse promoted when Mom's friend Maeve enters, a smile on her face.

"Willow, Sara. How are you both on this fine morning?" she asks cheerily.

"Wonderful, thank you, Maeve," Sara responds as I make my way back to the counter. "How about you?"

"I'm alive. What's not to be happy about?"

Maeve often speaks as though she's close to dying. We'd probably gasp if she hadn't been speaking like that since I was a kid.

"I just popped in for one of your ceramic vases. The damn cat broke my last one this morning, and I've had my eye on your pink floral vase for weeks. I guess I should call it fate."

"Of course. I'll just grab it for you."

Sara wanders off, leaving Maeve and me alone. I smile politely but when her smile drops, I know I'm in for a lecture. She's not just here for a vase. "Let me have it."

"It's been two weeks since you stopped by your parents' place. Two weeks! Your mom's going crazy with worry and your dad's tired from having to placate her. We've all seen the change in you, Willow, and I thought it was a good thing but—"

"Here it is," Sara announces loudly, giving me a sympathetic smile before Maeve looks her way. It's amazing how quickly a town can turn on you when you stop being the broken "yes girl."

"Oh. Thank you, Sara. It's perfect."

My phone buzzes with a text, and since it's on loud, I use it as an excuse to leave.

"Sara will ring that up," I say, already walking away. "I've got to check this."

I bang my head against the wall as soon as I'm out of sight, and that's where Sara finds me a few minutes later. "Well, that was nosy," she says as she falls against the wall beside me. "Sometimes I wonder who these people think they are."

"Very different from suburban life, huh?"

"It is."

"Do you miss it?"

"Only the anonymity. I love our ranch. I love the vast landscapes. I love you. But sometimes it would be nice to live somewhere where not everyone knew my name."

"Yep, that's the part I hate the most, and I've never known anything different."

Sara's lips purse. "Maybe you need to get out of here for a while. Spend more time in the city."

"You mean more time with Jesse."

"Of course not. I meant Pippa."

"Isn't it the same?"

"Not at all. I'm sure they don't see each other *that* often."

"Uh, I—"

The sound of the store phone cuts into our conversation, which I'm not exactly complaining about. "Better get that." I shrug, before backing out of the room with an apologetic grin.

"You're not sorry at all," Sara calls out as I round the corner with a fake pout. "Don't even pretend you are."

I'm laughing to myself as I answer the phone, so my tone comes across much lighter than it's been lately. "Hello, Audrey's, how can I help you?"

"Willow, it's Kim from Raven's Boutique." *And there goes the lightness.* I'd assumed they'd forgotten about us.

"Hi. How are you?"

"Good. Good. Thanks for asking. I'm sorry for the delay in getting back to you. I was so grateful to hear that you'd called."

"We haven't made any decisions. We just wanted a few more details before—"

"Oh, I know. God, I've barely given you any information. I'm actually calling because my boss wants to invite you to a dinner we're having in LA on Friday night. You and Sara."

"Ah, what kind of dinner?" I hesitate, not even hiding the nerves in my voice.

"It's a sponsorship dinner. We do a lot of collaborations like yours, so it would be a chance for you to see all the happy clients we work with while giving us time to chat."

Smooth. I can't help but laugh.

"Let me talk to Sara about it. Can you email me all the details?"

"Yes, of course. I'll send you the official invite. We'd love to have you there. And it's always a good night."

"Great, we appreciate you thinking of us."

"Willow, you're our priority right now. Please don't doubt how much we want to work with you."

"Ah, okay. Thank you."

I hang up with a furrowed brow and mindlessly check the message I received earlier while gathering my thoughts. None of this makes any sense. *If we're a priority, why did it take a week to return my call?* We're a small-town store, not some up-and-coming designers. *Why us?*

Unknown: Don't go anywhere. I'm coming to visit. We need to talk.

I ignore the obvious wrong number as Jesse's face comes to mind and my chest burns. If I find out he's behind the Raven's stuff, I am kicking his ass. Literally. With a stiletto heel. *That is not cool.*

But why would he do it? He may not have known me for long, but he knows me well enough to realize it's not a good idea. Something deep down tells me this isn't him.

So, if this boutique offer is real, could it be my ticket to another life?

23

Willow

"I hate that you're not here," I whine to Sara as she laughs. "What if they convince me to sign something without you?"

"They're not going to make you sign *anything*. We haven't even had a proper conversation with them. Plus, you've got Pippa."

Ugh. "I know. She's very excited. Apparently, this brand just designed *the* dress of the season. Whatever that means."

"I'm still trying to figure out why a clothing brand that sells no jewelry is suddenly looking to buy yours," Sara questions, her tone a little quieter than before, as though she's talking to herself. "I don't mean that in a bad way, but—"

"You and I both, Sara," I cut her off. "Maybe I can find that out tonight. Or maybe I'll get Pippa to do it. She'll know what to say."

"Ooh yes!" she squeals in excitement. "Do that, then report back in the morning. I'm so jealous."

"No, you're not."

Sara laughs. "Okay, I'm jealous of the luxury accommodation and a night in Los Angeles. Not the event itself."

Los Angeles. I'm in Los Angeles. "I can't believe I've now been to two new cities in the space of a month. Who am I?"

"You're Willow Sanders, and you're amazing. Don't ever forget that."

My heart clenches as emotion clogs my throat. Time to end this conversation. I can't let myself get emotional tonight. "Thank you. I better go. Pippa has a bunch of dresses for me to try on."

"A bunch?"

"I wish that was an exaggeration."

"Have fun." Sara laughs again as I groan before hanging up the phone. *What am I doing?*

A few hours later, Pippa slows as we near a multistory parking garage, glancing my way. "How are you doing? Do you need a pep talk?"

"No, I'll be fine. I'll just picture everyone in the room naked. That's what I'm supposed to do, right?"

Pippa laughs at my expense. "Yeah, if you're doing a speech. I'm not sure it's necessary if you're just a guest at a party."

"A party? Kim said it was a *dinner*."

Pippa grimaces. "Dinner...party. Same thing." She shrugs.

My jaw drops before I recover. "It's not the same thing. At all. Do you know something I don't?"

"No," she protests with a hand in the air. "I just heard about it through the grapevine, and they were calling it a party."

"Goddammit." I suck in a breath, suddenly struggling to get air. I don't know why the idea of a party feels so much worse, but it does. *Breathe, Willow.*

"Willow, it's going to be okay. You've got me. I promise not to leave your side."

Why does that *not* fill me with confidence? "I'll be okay. I'll just do what I do best and blend into the background."

Pippa slams on her brakes, and I'm not sure if it's because of what I said or the fact that she found a free parking space. But when she turns my way with a stern look, I have my answer. "You are *not* a blend-into-the-background girl. This brand is *huge* and they want *your* designs. This is an amazing opportunity, Willow. Be the shining star you used to be."

"I used to shine?"

"Always." A horn blares behind us and Pippa flips them off before driving into the parking spot, a megawatt smile on her face, making me laugh.

"You enjoyed that, didn't you?"

"I did. But only because I think I recognize the car, and the driver's a bitch."

With wide eyes, I try to catch a glimpse through the side mirror, but I can't see her. I'd love to know the story behind that reaction though. "Care to share?"

Pippa laughs. "Of course. Come on, let's go. I'll tell you on the way."

Even with Pippa's gossip-filled story to distract me, my confidence drains as we walk toward the gala room, and the closer we get the more I regret my decision. *What was I thinking?* I don't fit in here. A dinner I can handle. I'd get to know the people seated next to me, make some small talk. But a party...nope.

And, other than Dad's retirement, it's been years since I wore something this fancy. And *that* dress was at least one I picked out for myself, not an item from Pippa's wardrobe. *Again, what was I thinking?* I pull at the hem of the fitted silk dress—*Pippa's* fitted silk dress—as if I can make it longer. I can't. Add to it that it dips lower in the front than I would have liked, and I'm a hot mess.

Nope, I'm not doing this.

I turn to go back to the car when Pippa grabs my hand and pulls me back around, her eyes trained on the beautiful event in front of us. Two security guards stand by the door, and behind them it's like nothing I've ever seen before. *I was definitely right to freak out.*

Through the gap in the doorway, I can see crystal chandeliers, flower bouquets that I'm sure stand taller than I am, and models. So many models. Or maybe they're just really beautiful people in designer wear that fits perfectly, displaying their confidence like a badge of honor. Either way, they're not me.

"It's go time," Pippa says, and my gaze flashes to hers.

My heart races as my eyes bounce between her and the entry. "Actually, I'm having second thoughts. I don't think—" Words escape me as the one person I never expected to see steps into view, freezing in front of me, his eyes wide with shock. Jesse. *What in the world?*

My cheeks heat as my skin undoubtedly turns a light shade of pink, his stare so intense, I feel naked in front of him. Pippa says something but I don't hear her, as all sounds blend into one while I try to make sense of what I'm seeing. Jesse's at an event. Jesse's here.

His lips pull up into a small smile until he does a double take and frowns. I mentally question what he's thinking until his gaze lowers, and he rakes his eyes over my body, starting his visual assault at my legs until he settles on my neck, bringing back memories of our intimate moments together.

A tingling sensation runs through me as I remember the warmth of his touch and the way he set my soul on fire. *God, Sara's right.* Things with Jesse are far from over. I've never felt like this before. I've never needed someone so badly that I want to spend every spare second touching them even when

I'm mad. And right now, all I can think about is touching Jesse. Him touching me.

I bite down on my lip as his gaze lingers, trying hard to focus. A metallic taste hits my tongue but I ignore it, looking away to break whatever spell he has me under. Only when I look back and see Kim standing a few feet behind him, everything clicks into place and I'm fuming.

"Oh fuck," Pippa says with a nervous laugh, while a rage burns inside me. "Did you know he'd be here?"

"No, I didn't." But I had a bad feeling about all this, and him being here confirms it.

Jesse, what did you do?

I smile politely as we wait to get our names checked off at the door, but the second I'm inside, my smile fades and I beeline straight for Jesse.

I open my mouth to give him a piece of my mind, but he presses a finger to my lips, before grabbing my hand and pulling me away from prying eyes.

"Jesse. I—"

"Are you trying to kill me?" he says painfully between clenched teeth, running a hand through his neatly styled hair.

His question throws me, making me pause because I'm the one that's supposed to be angry. Not him. "Excuse me? What do you have to be pissed about?"

Jesse groans. "You told me to go...and you expect me to pretend you don't exist. *For now.* How am I supposed to do that if you show up here, looking like that?" He waves his hands at my dress, circling them close to my chest, and my blush darkens. But this isn't on *me*.

Stepping forward, I get in his face, making him stumble back until he hits the wall behind him. "Unlike *you*," I snap, "I had *no* idea you would be here. I didn't dress like this to hurt you." I poke him in the chest. "I thought I was here for *me*."

I pause, letting my finger linger for a beat too long and Jesse notices.

"So, seeing me here doesn't affect you at all?" he asks, his voice softer than I expected.

"No," I lie, swallowing a lump in my throat. "Unless you count the fact that I'm mad about it."

Jesse's brow furrows but he shakes off his thoughts, spinning me around before closing in on me to whisper. "Well for me, seeing you here, *now*, is torture. You look fucking incredible, Willow. But it's not just that. It's you in general. If you want me to forget you, I need more time. I need *forever*."

My breath hitches as my heart pounds in my chest. I know what he means; it will take a lifetime to get over him too, but that doesn't change the facts.

If only he didn't also look incredible, and smell incredible, and... No. I'm pissed off. I need to focus on that.

When I don't say anything, Jesse steps away, shaking his head. But I don't let him get far before reaching for him, curling my fingers into his shirt, ready to unleash my wrath. "Wait!"

He stares down at my hand before glaring up at me. "What, Willow? What? Why are you so angry? Tell me what you're feeling."

His gaze is so intense, so heartbreaking, that I lose all train of thought for a second and my mind turns to static. "I'm—"

Without letting me say a word, Jesse grabs my face and leans forward, his lips hovering dangerously close, as he stares into my eyes.

His touch warms my soul, even though it shouldn't, and I bite down on my lip, nervously pulling it into my mouth.

Jesse sucks in a breath, and my heart stops as everything around me stills.

Don't kiss me. Don't kiss me... Kiss me.

He lets out a whispered groan and steps back, shaking his head as the word "sorry" leaves his lips on a breath. "This just doesn't feel over. And that's not going to change until you tell me it's over. For good."

My stomach twists in knots and guilt hits me. Because I can't tell him it's over but I also can't tell him it's not. And right now, I shouldn't be focused on any of that. I should be focused on why I'm here.

"Jesse," I begin, taking in a long breath, trying to still my rapid heartbeat.

Jesse shakes his head as if to tell me no, then changes the subject. "Why are you here?" he rasps, his voice so pained that I almost forget I'm mad at him. Almost. Until it all comes back to me.

"You know exactly why," I rush out, my voice shaky. "Tricking me into coming tonight, even if you had good intentions, is still tricking me. And I won't stand for it."

"What are you talking about? I didn't know you'd be here," he says, his confusion so genuine that I second-guess myself. *Am I wrong?*

"Why are *you* here?" I ask, changing tack, trying unsuccessfully to keep the accusation out of my tone.

Jesse stares at me before answering cautiously. "They want me as a client. For me to wear their clothes. This is nothing but a schmoozing session."

My face drops, the fire gone. "Oh. That's nice of them." *I'm right.* This is Jesse's doing, only he probably has no idea that he's done it.

"What's that face for?" he asks. "What's wrong?"

"They want to sell my jewelry designs in their stores," I admit, watching as a warm smile lights up his face.

"That's amazing, Willow. I'm so—"

I shake my head. "Stop. It's all bullshit. They're doing it to get to *you.*"

"What? That's ridiculous. No one knows about us."

"You freaking posted about me on your socials. You mentioned my jewelry designs, and guess what they want to buy."

His eyes widen for the briefest of seconds before he recovers. "It wouldn't be that. It's you. It's not—"

"It's the only thing that makes sense," I cut him off again. "Why else would they want me? *You* did this."

"I didn't do this. You're so fucking talented, Willow. Why can't you see that?"

I huff out a laugh before scrunching my face, trying to hide my growing anger. "Even if I was, it doesn't change the facts. I'm here because of you. Was it part of your deal?"

"Of course not."

"Jesse—"

"No. I didn't do this. I hate seeing you upset." *You mean livid.* "Let's talk to Hailey and find out the truth."

"I don't even know a Hailey," I snap before realizing I'm getting angry at the wrong person, because if Jesse didn't orchestrate this, I know who did.

"Fuck this," I seethe, spinning on my heel to find Kim. I'm done doing the right thing. I'm done letting people treat me like I'm nothing. Like I don't have a voice. Because I do have a voice. A loud one. And I'm going to make some noise.

24
Jesse

I curse quietly before following after Willow, my heart lodged in my throat, wondering where I went wrong but also questioning... Was she going to kiss me? And if I hadn't pulled away, would she have let me kiss *her*?

I can't even believe that she's here. Willow's here and looking like the devil sent her to tempt me. I didn't want to come tonight. Despised the very idea of it, but I had no choice. I'm supposed to be thinking of my future. And now...fuck, am I'm glad that I came.

I don't usually give any weight to the idea of fate, but I was definitely meant to be here. If only it was under different circumstances, and Willow wasn't so mad.

"Willow, wait!" I call out as she rushes past guest after guest, only stopping when she reaches a few people I recognize from Raven's, pulling a dark-haired woman away from the group.

The woman frowns, but follows Willow until they're out of earshot of everyone but me. All while I stand hopelessly watching, wondering what the hell is going on.

"I'm so glad you made it, but is everything okay?" the woman asks, her eyes flashing to mine.

"This is Jesse," Willow says, skipping the niceties. "But you already know that, don't you?"

The woman's eyes widen but she shakes her head, instantly denying it. Since I don't recognize her, she might be telling the truth. "I'm afraid I don't. What's going on?"

"You may not personally know him, but someone in your company does. So, I'm here to tell you that I have no sway when it comes to his decisions. Having my designs in your store is not going to entice him into signing with you. In fact, it's likely to do the opposite. You might want to rethink your strategy."

Her jaw drops as she clearly freaks out. "Willow, I don't know what you're talking about. Where did this come from? Is that what Mr. Hastings is saying, that we're using you to get to him?"

Shit. Mr. Hastings? She said she didn't know me. Willow stiffens and I have to fight not to react, because I think she's right.

"Okay, Kim. Whether this is a misunderstanding or not, I'm out. Thanks for having me here, but I'm going to go."

She doesn't wait for a response before walking away. Actually, storming away is the appropriate word. *Go Willow!*

My eyes flash toward Kim's shocked expression as I consider giving her a piece of my own mind, but I can't stay here while Willow's getting away. She's my priority.

Chasing after her again, I easily catch up as she steps out the door. "Willow, stop. I promise I had no idea."

She doesn't stop, and a little part of me knew she wouldn't. She's pissed. Understandably. I just have to make sure she knows I had nothing to do with it.

"Willow. Come on." While I could quite easily get in front of her and make her stop, I move at a slower pace and stay behind her, letting her power walk her frustrations out. But when she turns toward the parking lot, I have to stop myself from reaching for her. Because I have a feeling she's about to realize she doesn't have a car. There's no way she drove in LA.

"Dammit," she mumbles as the first car comes into view.

"No car?" I ask, trying not to smile. "Come on, let me help."

"I have a car. But no key. I'll wait for Pippa."

"You'll wait?" I ask incredulously. "You haven't even told her you're leaving. Let me help."

"I'm fine."

God. "You're being stubborn."

Willow's eyes flash to mine, narrowing instantly. "I'm not being stubborn. Why does everyone keep saying that? I'm choosing my own path."

Damn. That's obviously a sore point, and I'm supposed to be making her *less* mad.

Willow continues walking until she reaches a black rental. "Okay, I'm sorry. Let me call Pippa. I'll ask her to come out and—"

"No," she cuts me off, her body sagging against the door, her arms folded over her chest.

"Willow. *Please* let me help. With Pippa *or* Raven's. I promise I didn't know anything about this. I don't even know the woman you were speaking to."

"As you can see, I handled that fine on my own. And I can call Pippa. You've done enough."

"I didn't do *anything*."

"That's right," Willow yells. "You didn't do anything. You left us!" Her eyes widen as the words leave her mouth. Meanwhile, my heart fractures into a million pieces. *She's never going to forgive me.*

"I'm sorry, Willow. I—"

"Don't. I didn't mean to say that. I'm just pissed off. I shouldn't have taken it out on you."

"Yeah, you should have. I'd much rather you got everything out in the open."

"I told you; I've moved on."

While a little part of me wishes that were true—for her sake—a big part of me hopes that's not the case.

"I haven't," I whisper, my heart picking up speed when her eyes flash my way.

"Jesse..." she whispers back, her quiet tone full of emotion. "I don't know what you want me to say or do."

"I want you to be honest with me, and yourself. Did seeing me tonight do anything to you?" I repeat my earlier question.

"Of course it did. I care for you, but it hurts too much."

"How can I fix things? I need to fix things." I take a tentative step forward and wait to see her reaction. When she doesn't move away, I step even closer until I can reach out and palm her face. "You may not understand it, but these feelings I have are not going away. Ever. I can't just move on. I'll never move on." *I know this, because I tried.*

Willow gasps as her eyes fall closed.

"I remembered something," she whispers, opening her eyes again as she steps back, watching my hand fall from her cheek before her gaze meets mine. "I don't know how, but something you've said or done has triggered a dream for me that I'm certain is real."

My eyes widen before the confusion sets in. *She remembered?* "You think it was me?"

"I do."

"But you never remembered anything the week we were together." At least I assume that because she didn't know who I was.

"No, I didn't. And I can't tell you what the difference is, just that it's happening."

"Wow. That's good, right? You want your memories back. What did you remember?"

Willow falls silent and her cheeks flush pink. *Fuck, is she remembering our kiss?*

"Just us hanging out and a moment between Jade and me."

"Jesus." My lips pull into a smile. "That's great progress and..." I trail off when Willow frowns. "Isn't it?"

"I don't know. It's definitely not helping me move on."

"I'm not sure this is something you move on from. For me, it was something I learned to live with."

Willow nods. "That may be true, but I can't decide if it's a good thing or not."

She sounds terrified of either prospect and it breaks me. All this time I've been trying to hide the truth, worried about hurting her, while she's been stuck in this limbo. I still think she was better off not knowing, but now that she does, the rest should be up to her.

Running my hands down my face, I contemplate what I'm about to offer but easily decide it's the right thing.

"Let me help you."

Her beautiful face scrunches as her brow furrows. "What?" she asks and it takes a lot of willpower for me not to reach out and smooth the worry lines.

"I want to help. In whatever way I can. If that means giving you more time, I'll do it, but I think you might need the opposite."

Willow's shoulders drop and she mumbles something I can't understand. "You think spending time with you might bring my memory back?" she asks with some sass to her tone that wasn't there before. "So did Sara."

Hope swells within me but I don't show it.

"As friends?" she asks, and my face drops. I knew that's where this was going, but hearing it out loud sucks.

"Nothing has changed, Jesse," she says as she studies my expression. "I'm still not ready to forgive and forget. I'm not even sure I'll ever be."

"I don't want you to forget. But someday, I want you to see that I did it for you."

"I do—"

"No," I cut her off. "I want you to truly understand why I did it. Because hurting you is the last thing I ever want to do. And that hasn't changed since I was sixteen."

Willow's breath hitches as she bites her quivering lip. "Okay."

"Okay?"

"I want to try."

"Try to get back to us? Or just try to remember?"

"I'm not sure yet. Everything between us happened so quickly, and your feelings are so strong...and I...I'm just trying to process it all."

"And that's okay. You don't need to know yet. One step at a time." *I'll take it. It's good enough for now.*

"What do we do?" Willow asks, a shyness coming over her.

"What do you mean?"

"I...um...don't really have many friends. I don't really know the protocol. Sara and I spend time together at work and just kind of make plans naturally. Do we make plans ahead of time?"

Jesus. My chest aches. *I did that. Jade's accident and her not knowing did that.* "We can make a plan," I say, hoping to ease her mind. "How about tomorrow? Could I take you to lunch?"

"Yes, great. Lunch is easy. Perfect."

"Perfect," I repeat because as hard as being her friend will be, spending any time with Willow is better than nothing.

"Should we go back and find Pippa?" she asks, making me laugh.

"Yeah, we probably should."

25
Willow

What the hell did I do?

I've been back at the hotel for two hours, and I'm still trying to process it all.

I can't even blame it on alcohol because I was stone-cold sober. The "I'm taking back my life" outburst was all me. It was time for me to stop holding back and finally take a stand, make some noise. At least, sticking up for myself with Kim was, but with Jesse...

Actually, I blame Sara.

She put the idea back in my head and when Jesse suggested it, I went for it. But I'm still not sure that spending time with him is a good thing. Every time I think about his lies, my heart aches, but then when he's close, it drifts away, like he's the answer to all of life's problems, rather than a contributor to the cause. And that's not how I want to live.

I want to move on; I want to find that place where I'm happy, where I no longer feel like my life is in the hands of other people...but right now, I can't see that. I can't fathom a way for that to happen.

On the flip side of that, when I'm not thinking of Jesse—for the very brief moments that I'm able to push him far from my mind—I feel nothing. No pain, no darkness, no fear. And while that means I'm also missing out on the good feelings, I'll take feeling *nothing* over the torment of knowing that the first person I ever fell for shattered my soul. That the person I thought was going to make me whole again had already ripped me to pieces. He may not have killed Jade or put me in that hospital, but he let me die. Physically I survived that day, but inside...that's a different story.

And, I couldn't even tell him it was over. Even when he asked me to. Because deep down I know that it's not.

But I need to take it slowly so I don't break us both.

My phone vibrates on the bedside table, waking me from a dream the next morning. A dream about beaches and sunshine, nothing to do with my life.

My senses awaken as I bring myself out of the fog. Yellow light dances across the comforter, a horn blares in the distance, and the aroma of fresh coffee permeates the air.

Life feels normal. Whatever normal is.

My phone buzzes again, and I remember what woke me. Checking the time, I note that it's just after eleven. That explains why it's so bright, but...eleven? *Shit!*

I jump out of bed so fast my head spins, and I have to physically still myself until it passes. A nauseous feeling settles in my stomach, but I power on, rummaging around to find my phone.

When I finally have it in hand, I lie back down and check the screen, my heart lodged in my throat as I imagine seeing Jesse's name.

But it's Sara.

"Hey," I answer groggily, feeling hungover even though I didn't drink.

"Big night?" Sara says with a laugh. "Did you just wake up?"

"No and yes. I actually left early—well, almost immediately—but I didn't sleep very well."

"Oh no. What happened?"

Taking a deep breath, I prepare myself for the disappointment in her voice and tell her the truth. "They only wanted us to get to Jesse."

"Jesse?"

"Yep. He was there last night. They're trying to sign him to their brand."

"Shit."

"It is."

"That doesn't mean..." she trails off and I know what's coming next. "Fuck."

My jaw drops before I burst out laughing. Okay, I didn't know what was coming next, because I didn't expect that. I just knew she was going to realize I was right.

"Did you just say fuck?" I ask between giggles.

"I did. Your new attitude is rubbing off on me. I used to swear a lot before Benji came along."

"Sorry about that."

"Don't be. I said it last night and Grant happened to love it. He—"

"Ahh, stop right there." I bite back a smile so she doesn't hear it in my voice. "I do not need any more details."

"Wait, I don't mean—"

"Nope. Moving on."

Sara giggles and the sound comforts me. God, I'm lucky to have her. She's always been a godsend, but in the last few months, she's become my rock. My sounding board. The only person I truly feel like I can trust.

"Thank you," I say out of nowhere, stopping her laughter.

"For what?" she asks.

"For always being there for me."

"I said I would be."

"I know. But I still want to say thank you."

"You're welcome. But please remember you love me after our next conversation."

My heart jolts at her words. That's never a good way to start something. "Okay," I hesitate.

Sara sighs. "I called for a reason."

"Okay," I say again, my nerves increasing.

"Tate stopped by."

"What?" My pulse spikes as a strange nervousness flows through me. One that's beyond my control. Like it's coming from a place I haven't explored. Jesse told me everything. I know what Tate did and I know he had nothing to do with Jade's fall. But something still feels off. Jesse didn't seem concerned but... God, who do I trust? "What happened?"

"He stopped by yesterday to talk to you. Said it was fairly urgent. At first, he was pleasant, charming even. But when I said you weren't here, he didn't believe me. It was weird."

"Shit. Are you okay?"

"I'm fine. He wasn't threatening or anything. Just...I don't know. Like I said. It was weird. Thankfully, Neil came in to buy his wife an anniversary present, and Tate left. I've been here for a couple of hours this morning, and he hasn't come back. I'm hoping that's the end of it. But seeing him made me remember he'd called last week too."

Jesus. What the hell does he want? He never once spoke to me when we were in school. Why now? Has he spoken to Jesse? Does he think I'm going to go to the police? After all these years?

Thank God for Neil. He runs the local hardware store and hardly ever visits us, unless it's for his anniversary or his wife's birthday. I shouldn't be worried. Tate has never done anything untoward, but for some reason, I'm still grateful that Neil was there. Something's not sitting right.

"I'm sorry you had to deal with that. I'll be home tomorrow."

"I know. And don't worry, I didn't tell him anything. He rubbed me the wrong way."

I bark out a laugh and vow to give her the biggest hug when I get back.

"So, tell me." She moves on. "What are your plans for today? Sightseeing?"

"I definitely want to see Rodeo Drive and the Hollywood Walk of Fame. But first I have lunch with Jesse." I mumble the last part, but of course she picks up on it.

"I'm sorry, what?" She fake gasps, but I can hear the smile in her voice.

"I want to see Rodeo Drive and—"

"Don't mess with me... Jesse?"

"As I said, he was there last night and we had a few...ah...confrontations, and it ended with him asking me to lunch."

"And you said yes?"

"I did. Because I can't seem to think clearly when it comes to him."

"This is good. You're making my day," she says, trying to hold the excitement out of her tone. "But I'm curious...what kind of confrontations?"

My face contorts into an uncomfortable grimace. "Mm...maybe confrontations was the wrong term."

"Okay, what's the right one?"

"I yelled at him and we almost kissed." *I would have kissed him back if he hadn't pulled away.* "Then I realized I was only there because Raven's wanted him, and I confronted Kim about it."

"Jesus. That's a lot."

"It is. Thank you for not gushing."

"Why would I gush?"

"The almost kiss."

"Oh, don't worry. I'm excited about that, but I'm not going to throw it in your face when there's other things to talk about. Like your epiphany."

"What epiphany?"

"You agreed to spend time with Jesse, so you must have figured something out."

"I guess. But I don't really think it was an epiphany."

"So, I can gush?" her voice rises.

"No. No gushing. I'm still hurt. It's just lunch." *For now.*

"Oh-kay."

"Shut up." I smile.

"I didn't say anything," she protests.

"You didn't have to. It was all in the tone."

"I love you."

"I know. But I better go. He's picking me up in thirty minutes."

"Oooh, what are you wearing?" So much for not getting gushy.

"Something boring," I deadpan, rolling my eyes even though she can't see them. "Goodbye, Sara."

"Bye." She laughs.

When I hang up, I have a message from an unknown number, but with only twenty minutes before Jesse's arrival, I ignore it and rush to get ready. Trying hard not to care about how I look but also knowing that I do care. A lot. Basically, I'm trying to convince myself more than Sara.

Jesse texts as I'm putting on a coat of mascara, and when I read his message, telling me he's in the lobby, I see the one from before, and it's the same number that texted a little while back.

Unknown: You're not home. You're always home.

What the hell? I thought it was a mistake the first time, but was it Tate? I never gave him my number. I mean, it's not hard to find—it's on our store website—but still, if it's him it feels like an invasion of privacy.

I text Jesse to say I'm coming and ignore what I now assume is Tate's text. For all I know it could still just be a wrong number. And while I'm here and he's in Oregon, there's nothing I can do anyway.

But why is he looking for me?

And why is my skin crawling?

***

Jesse smiles when I step out of the elevator, but I can tell that it's forced. Doing this as "friends" isn't easy on him. But it's hard on me too. Especially when he's looking like God's gift to women as he leans against a pillar wearing a navy blazer over a fitted tee and his hair mussed just enough to make you want to run your fingers through it. Maybe pull on the strands a little or... *Dammit!*

His smile turns to a smirk, and I know he's busted me ogling him. But I challenge anyone not to stare at him like he's a piece of meat, because he's freaking mouthwatering.

"Thank you for picking me up," I say with a polite smile.

He nods and gestures to the glass doors ahead of us. "Thank you for checking me out," he whispers as I walk past. *Again, dammit.* Ignoring him, I pick up the pace, walking toward the rental he pointed out, my head held high. What was I thinking with this? *It's going to be a long lunch.*

Jesse puts some music on when we're seated, so we spend the drive mostly in peace. But when "The Sound of Silence" by Simon and Garfunkel comes on, Jesse starts singing to himself and I almost gape. *Jesse sings?* I mean it's not amazing, but I never imagined his broody ass would actually enjoy music.

"I love this song," I say when he stops singing at a light. Apparently, he can only sing when we're moving.

"Me too, although I prefer the Disturbed version."

I do too, but I keep that quiet. "What about the Anna Kendrick one? That seems more like your style," I joke, but it falls flat when he has no idea what I'm talking about.

"Who?"

"Poppy from *Trolls*."

"Again, who?"

Where's Sara when you need her? She would have laughed.

"Never mind. Where are we going?"

"A restaurant closer to the touristy part of town. I thought you might want to see the Walk of Fame." He shrugs like it's no big deal, while my traitorous heart skips a beat.

"Thank you," I say, giving nothing else away. So what if I was just thinking the exact same thing. It doesn't mean he knows me. It just means he's being thoughtful. Like he would with anyone new to town.

Jesse doesn't do thoughtful for anyone. Except me.

Pushing my inner musings from my mind, I smile politely as we pull into a parking space. Jesse laughs to himself, and I'm sure it's because he can see right through my fake attempt at being fine. He always can.

When we reach the door to the restaurant, he darts around me to hold it open, eliciting a feeling of déjà vu. Last time he held a door open for me, our roles were reversed. He was the one trying to pretend, and now it's me. Because as much as I tell myself I'm okay, just being in Jesse's presence proves that I'm wrong.

My chest tightens again as I plaster on a tight smile, trying hard not to give the game away. It's just lunch. I can do this. And if I don't remember anything else, then at least we tried. *But if I do?* I'll cross that bridge when we get there.

26

Jesse

Willow tries to make small talk for the first half of our meal.

"How's hockey going?"

"What do you think of this strange weather?"

"Are there any famous people in this restaurant?" She asks that last one in case there's someone she doesn't recognize. And at one point she even asks my views on climate change.

But when she asks me what it feels like to ice skate, I freeze as excitement fills my chest. This could get interesting.

"You've never been on the ice before?" I ask, trying to keep the shock out of my voice.

Willow rests back against her chair and glares my way, folding her arms across her chest. "Why is that so hard to believe? Did you see anywhere to skate in Hepburn? We can ski, but there's no skating."

"True, but I ran a clinic in a hockey rink less than an hour from your town. You never went there?"

She laughs like I'm crazy, but I fail to see why it's not a valid point.

"No, I never went to the *ice skating rink* in the next town," she says, putting extra emphasis on "ice skating" instead of hockey, making me chuckle. "Like I said, I've never been."

"Well, we can't have that, can we. I'll take you out before I have to leave tomorrow. You'll be skating in no time."

Willow's jaw drops before she panics. "What? Noooo. Not happening. I'm content to have missed out on that particular activity. Plus, I'm heading home in the morning."

"What?" *This is all I get? I need more time.* "Ah okay, of course. Are you planning to visit Pippa any time soon?"

"I honestly don't know. I can't just keep playing hooky from my responsibilities, but I'm not backpedaling. We'll find time to hang out."

Hang out. Goddammit. This woman...

"Okay, sure. Have you finished? I promised you some touristy shit," I grumble, unable to keep the disappointment out of my voice. I feel like I'm losing her all over again.

"I love the enthusiasm." Willow smiles and it actually looks real until she adds, "Technically, you didn't promise me anything, so you don't have to."

Oh, I have to, otherwise who knows when I'll see her again.

"We're going." I grunt, finishing off the last of my drink. "Come on."

Willow neatly folds her napkin, placing it on her plate before standing up at the same time I do, a smile on her face.

"I'm going to the bathroom," she says quietly, so I sit back down. "I'll be back."

As she walks away, I swear she whispers something about "grumpy Jesse being back" but I ignore her and focus on getting the attention of our server.

Of course, that Jesse's back. You're leaving!

It's busy, so the server doesn't arrive until Willow's on her way back, and when she sees him, she rushes over. Since I know what's coming, I cut her off before she speaks. "I'm paying! No arguments."

The server raises his eyebrows as I hand him my card, and I swear I see a spark of something in his eyes. *Weird.* And when I turn to Willow, she's trying to hide the same look. I clench my fist thinking they're having a moment, until the server mumbles, "That was hot," as he walks away, making me wonder if Willow was thinking the same. I can be that grumpy guy if she needs me to be.

God, who am I? This woman drives me crazy.

Ignoring my thoughts, I set off with Willow following behind me. Hollywood Boulevard is only a short distance from the restaurant, so we leave the car and make our way by foot.

We're both silent as Willow checks out the Walk of Fame before slowing down at the hands and footprints, spending extra time on some celebrities, skipping over others. As for me, I couldn't tell you any of the names. I'm more focused on her. Watching her small smile when she recognizes someone, taking in her giggles at the size of the hands, measuring them against her own.

It makes me want to do the same thing, to grab *her* hand and check the difference, before curling our fingers together and never letting go.

We've been wandering around for about thirty minutes when her phone buzzes, and she stiffens before reaching into her purse. She sees the screen and her body relaxes before she smiles my way. "All good, it's just Pippa. I'll get back to her later."

It may be *all good*, but I don't like the way she reacted to getting a text. *Is something going on?*

I try not to overthink it as we continue on, but it's only a few minutes later when *my* phone rings and Seth's name pops up. I wince and show Willow my screen. "I hate to say that you're right, but I'm going to guess Raven's called him." *Maybe that's who she was expecting.*

I'm about to answer when she stops me. "Don't turn them down because of me," she rushes out, guessing my intentions. "They make beautiful clothes and... just think about it properly."

"I will. I'm not one to make rash decisions," I lie, feeling a little guilty when Willow relaxes.

"Seth, my man. How are you?" I answer with a little too much enthusiasm, and Willow sees right through it, fuming beside me.

"Who are you and what have you done with Jesse Hastings?"

"Will that joke ever get old?"

"Never. Listen, I have to be quick, but Raven's called and they're desperate to sign you."

"I bet they are." I scoff.

"What does that mean? Did something happen last night?"

"Last night was great, but I've decided to go with someone else."

Willow gasps as Seth curses. "*Shit.*"

I bite back a smile as I watch Willow, my anger softening at her bulging eyes and pursed lips, along with the invisible steam coming out of her ears.

"I thought you liked them."

"I did, but I changed my mind. In fact, they can go f—" Willow pushes my chest and I cut myself off.

"Jesse this is a big deal. Raven's is—"

"I know, but I'm not interested," I say firmly. I'm done with them. "I'll explain everything later."

"Whatever you say."

When he hangs up, I expect Willow to yell at me, but instead she just stares, her face tight with anger. "You," she huffs out. "*Ugh.*" She turns and storms away, throwing her hands in the air. I chuckle to myself before walking after her, but she stops suddenly and spins back around.

"Why would you do that? I could hear Seth. It's a big deal."

"Not to me."

"You're...you're incorrigible."

"Not true at all. I'd say that was me being the opposite of incorrigible."

"Frustrating then. Annoying. Really hard to live with. But also, really hard to—" She cuts herself off, and every part of me wants to answer for her. I'm hard to stay away from.

"I wouldn't be any of those things if you didn't care about me."

Her anger subsides. "We've been through this. I'm not denying that. But..."

"You're not ready."

"I'm not."

"And you don't know if you'll ever be."

She says that, but we both know that's not true. She will be ready. It's the time that's in question. When we're together, the pull is strong and it's easy to forget. It feels like we're progressing, moving in the right direction, when in reality, this could just be an experiment for her. Nothing's changed.

Yet.

Willow looks at a few more stars on the Walk of Fame before calling it a day. "You've seen one, you've seen them all," she says, even though her beautiful face lit up every time. Once again, I've let her down. She's pissed off at the Raven's situation and annoyed that I rejected them when she told me not to.

We quietly listen to music on the drive back to her hotel, but this time I don't sing. I hardly ever sing. It only really happens when I'm truly happy, and just being around Willow usually brings that out in me. Even when I know nothing is happening between us.

"What time is your flight tomorrow?" I ask when we arrive. "If you remember something overnight, maybe we can see each other early, before you go? To try again." I shrug.

Willow smiles but I can see the rejection coming. "It's not until eleven, but since I woke up at eleven today, I'm not sure I can make an early meet-up."

My chest tightens with more proof that she's not okay. My five a.m. riser is sleeping until eleven. *God, this is all really messing with her.* And my selfish ass keeps thinking that the more time we spend together, the better chance I've got of winning her back, when I should just be focused on helping her truly get through this. Even if there's a chance she doesn't want me after it's done.

"Can you call me tomorrow? Or even text?" I ask, reaching forward to rub the little frown lines from her brow. "Just so I know whether it worked or not?"

Willow steps back out of my reach but relaxes a little. "I can text."

"Thank you." It might not be much but I'll take it.

Maybe there's a way I can do both—win her back and help with her memories. It's not like she's going to remember anything that makes her hate me.

Though there is something I have to talk to her about. I just need her to trust me first.

27
Willow

I t didn't work. Sure, my dreams—all three of them—were full of Jesse, but he was very much the Jesse I know now, *not* a sixteen-year-old boy.

Even though I swore to myself that I'd see this through, I'm torn over it. Do I try again? Or give up after the first go?

Yesterday was nice, but it felt like two almost strangers walking around on eggshells. At least, I felt like that. We weren't ourselves. Things were stilted and maybe that made all the difference. We may not have been in a happy place the last two times I had a memory, but Jesse was still optimistic. Yesterday was different. I could tell that he was holding back, even if he didn't notice it himself.

As promised, I text him to let him know, and he replies within seconds, as though he was waiting by his phone.

Jesse: We can try again. Maybe I just didn't say the right things.

My heart aches for him. He's trying to help. Really trying and I keep pushing him away. It's not because I don't want him in my life. I just don't want to give him false hope in case I never get over this. When I see him, there are times when I forget. Times when I'm able to convince myself it will all be okay. That we can be Willow and Jesse, the same couple that stole private moments away from the spotlight, the couple that didn't share a past, only the promise of a future.

But that's not us, and when reality hits, it hits hard, and I feel worse than I did before I saw him.

I wish there was a happy medium. Some way I could coexist in both worlds, but as of right now, I haven't found that.

I don't respond to his text as I continue to mull over whether or not I'm going to test the theory again. I can see positives to both options, but it's the negatives that worry me.

I'm still completely lost in my thoughts as I board the plane, but when I see another text from Jesse just as the captain says we're ready for takeoff...it all clears up.

Jesse: I don't ever want to make things harder on you but I need you to know... I'm not giving up...on you...or on us. I'll be here in any capacity you need me, but I will always be here. I can't let you go. I won't. I've tried. And it sucked.

Tears prick my eyes as we depart, knowing I'm taking myself further away from Jesse. And just like when he drove away from me after our first night together, I feel a cord snap, the tether keeping us together unable to take the force. And it breaks my heart with it.

A million things flash through my mind in an instant. Jesse's breathtaking smile, his warmth, the way he seems to put me ahead of everything else. The way he's still fighting, even though I've given him nothing in return. I owe it to both of us to see what happens when we try to be ourselves again, even if in the end, it doesn't work out. This connection is so much more than just our short time together. I can feel it. I just wish I understood it.

For the entire flight, I think of nothing but Jesse, and by the time we land, I've made the decision to go back. So, as soon as I turn my phone on, I send him a text, a small smile on my lips.

Willow: Maybe it's time I learned to ice skate.

Another week passes, but every time I try to book a flight, I think of the money I'm spending. Money I could be reinvesting in the business. Mine and Sara's business. Sara, who I've forced to pick up my slack. She's a godsend but she deserves better.

I know I promised myself I'd try, but I can't justify it.

Not that Sara gives me a chance to say no.

When an airline ticket arrives in my email inbox for the following Friday, Sara makes my decision for me.

"You can't say no to that," she says, trying to be stern. "Especially with the big "NONREFUNDABLE" Jesse put in the subject line."

"But…"

"You need to do this," she tells me again, her arms crossed over her chest. "And if you don't go, I'm going to fire your ass so I'll have to run this place solo anyway."

I bark out a laugh, because she technically can't do that, but I reluctantly agree, with a promise to look after her little one so she can have a night out with Grant. I hate that I'm once again leaving her to run the shop, but I push my guilt down exactly as asked.

I land in San Francisco Friday morning and automatically head toward the doors, ready to call an Uber, but before I get there, Pippa calls my name, flowers in one hand and a pissed-off expression on her face.

"Apparently I work for Jesse now," she says, handing me the flowers as I put my bag down.

"You said you had to work." I frown. We definitely had this conversation.

"I *do* have to work. But that man can be very persuasive when he needs to be."

"Do I want to know?"

"All you need to know is that he's got some embarrassing stories on me, and he was more than happy to spill them."

"Asshole," I say, biting back a smile. Though, I'm pretty sure that's a lie.

"He is. But in all seriousness, you're my sister; I should have said yes to begin with."

"It's fine. You're not even happy about this idea."

Pippa frowns, before wrapping me in a hug. "It's not that; I'm just worried about you getting hurt again. Willow, if it had been me, and you'd seen me the way I saw you after your talk with Jesse that day, you'd have never let me out of your sight. You'd be monitoring me twenty-four seven to make sure I didn't start drinking again. That's how bad you looked."

My face scrunches as my stomach fills with bees. Not butterflies, bees. Same fluttery feeling, but with bite.

"I'm sorry."

"No. I didn't mean for you to feel bad. I'm just worried. You may not have an addiction that you could fall back on, but it's almost like you're addicted to each other. I'm just wary."

"That makes us sound toxic." *I don't think we're toxic.*

"Trust me, it's not that. If you two didn't have a past, you'd be perfect for each other. But you do, and I'm concerned about how that will play into things."

"We're just catching up, that's all." I don't tell her about the memories, and I'm surprised to find I have no guilt about it. Until I know more, it's best to keep it quiet. I don't think she'd approve of me spending time with Jesse under these circumstances, even though there's more to it.

"So, the flowers?" I ask, as I smell them when we're seated in her car.

"As much as I love you, they're from Jesse. Picked them out himself and shoved them in my hands to deliver them. Well, *shoved them delicately*, because I was told to protect them with my life."

It's a beautiful bouquet, full of flowers I can't name. But on closer inspection, I recognize one and my chest tightens.

He added buttercups.

While he never really explained if the name Buttercup had more meaning, I know that it does. I can feel it. I'd ask, but I'm secretly hoping that it comes up in one of my memories.

Pippa drives me straight to the stadium, and I stare at it in awe, especially when we come face-to-face with Jesse, or at least, his broody expression on a banner the size of Hepburn's tallest building.

"He's bigger than big, isn't he?" I mumble, mostly to myself.

Pippa bursts out laughing. "What are you referring to there, Willow?" she asks, with a sassy smile and a spark in her eye.

"Not that," I shriek with mock offense. *Though he's definitely not average.* "I mean that he's famous. People whisper about him back home, and he's talked about on television. But seeing all this. He's not just a guy, he's... I don't even know."

"Don't put him on a pedestal, Willow. He'd hate that. He only wants you to see him as Jesse. As the guy you fell in love with."

I turn to Pippa with a raised eyebrow. "I'm not in love. I can't be. And what happened to your worry and concern? That sounds a lot like you're rooting for us."

Pippa raises an eyebrow. "I want you to be happy. And if Jesse's that guy, then of course I'll be rooting for the two of you. But that doesn't mean I'll stop wanting to knee him in the balls."

"That's fair." I laugh. "I wouldn't stop you."

"Good to know."

By the time we walk into the building, Jesse's dressed and waiting for us. "You'll be pleased to know she delivered the flowers, and me, in one piece," I say when I reach him, smelling the flowers again.

"At least we know she's good at something," he jokes and Pippa lifts her knee, silently asking if she can get it over with now. I shake my head, thankful that Jesse is none the wiser.

"Are you ready to go?" he asks, a hesitant smile on his face.

"Go?" I say, pausing until Pippa's out of earshot. "I thought you were teaching me to skate?"

Jesse laughs. "I am, but we can't just carve up the ice here. I rented out the public rink."

"Oh. Of course." My chest heats; I really know nothing about hockey. Or ice skating. Or ice. Would we really carve up the ice while learning? *Shit! Am I going to fall?*

Jesse tentatively steps forward, his hand lifted in the air, his finger curled as though he's about to brush hair away from my face. The world stops, and I feel every heartbeat in my chest, the pounding so loud there's no way he can't hear it. Our eyes meet just as his hand drops, making my heart sink along with it.

"What's going on in that head of yours?" he asks with a chuckle.

I almost laugh at myself, except it's not funny. My mind is a pretty messed up place to be. "Just nervous," I say, because that's what I was originally thinking. "I don't want to embarrass myself."

"You won't. We all have to start somewhere. Plus, it's just you and me. And I promise I won't let you fall."

The intensity of his gaze has my breath hitching as his words settle between us. He may have lied in the past, but he's shown me time and time again that when it comes to falling, he will always catch me. I can always rely on that truth.

28
Willow

I feel like I could be in one of those memes where it shows how someone thinks they look compared to how they actually do—for instance, right now I'm gliding gracefully around the rink, hair perfectly windswept, arms in the air like I'm flying, my footwork...perfection. When in reality my arms are wide because I'm wobbling uncontrollably, my hair's windswept, but only as I'm falling to the ground, and I'm flushed red. As promised, Jesse doesn't let me hit the ice, and I'm grateful, but I'm still unstable.

"Why can't I do this?" I laugh when Jesse catches me. Again.

"It takes time. We all have our talents. There's no way these big hands could make fine jewelry." He holds up one hand, the other holding on tightly to my waist.

He's been doing that since we got here, giving me subtle compliments so I don't feel embarrassed, and it's working well to distract me. Only this time, I don't think it's his words. I'm more focused on the big hands he mentioned, and remembering them curled into my hair, pulling my head back as his lips meet mine.

"*Willow*?"

"Huh?"

"Do you want to try again?" Jesse asks with a slightly furrowed brow.

"Oh yes, definitely. I'm determined to skate by myself before we leave here today."

Jesse looks at his watch. "Better get moving. I've only got the ice for another hour."

Shit.

With all the patience in the world, Jesse continues to guide me. "That's it," he encourages with a huge smile when I finally grasp the ability to stand. "Now, I'm going to take you around," he says when I've been standing on my own for a moment. "And all you have to do is hold on."

That sounds easy enough, but I'll bet it's not. "Hold on. Okay. Got it."

I hold on for dear life, one arm curled tightly around his with the other out to my side for extra balance. I can do this.

Jesse moves, and by some miracle, I actually stay up. "Okay, this is happening," I say, eliciting a soft chuckle from beside me.

"You're a natural," he jokes and I huff out a laugh.

"You've already used up your quota of lies, remember?" I expect Jesse to laugh again, but he's obviously not ready for that joke. "God, I'm sorry. That sucked."

248

"Nah, it's okay. I just..." he trails off but I get it. I shouldn't have brought the mood down.

We skate in silence for half a song and then I get the crazy idea to try it alone. I've been slowly moving my feet rather than letting Jesse drag me along, and I genuinely think I've got it.

"I'm ready to fly," I say before loosening my hold slightly, while Jesse's eyes flash to mine, his brows rising.

"For real?"

"For real."

"Okay, I'll let go on three. But I'll be right here beside you. You've got this." My chest fills with warmth, and it's his words that give me confidence, managing to glide the second he lets go. I actually glide.

"Am I really doing this?" I ask, my eyes focused on my feet, hoping Jesse hears me.

"You really are," he says with a smile in his voice. "I'm proud of you, Buttercup."

My gaze shoots to his and I wobble slightly. Jesse reaches forward but I shake my head, trying to right myself. "It's been a while since you called me that."

"I know."

"Was that my nickname before?" I ask hesitantly, giving up the idea of figuring it out for myself.

Jesse smiles, and it lights up his entire face. "It was. I gave you that name the first day I saw you. When I was fourteen."

"*Fourteen?*" I half shriek.

"Yep," he chuckles, sounding embarrassed. "That's when it all started." He shrugs while I bite back a gasp. He mentioned seeing me before, but I never really thought about it.

"And the nickname?" I ask, now even more desperate to know.

"I'd love to say it was because of the long blonde hair, the fact that you were forbidden, destined for someone on your own side of the mountain, while I was nothing. You know, like *The Princess Bride*. But the reality is, it's because the first words you ever spoke to me, way before we met on that mountain, were 'Chin up,' and I remembered that saying, 'Chin up, Buttercup.'"

We spoke? And he remembered my words? He only ever mentioned *seeing* me. My eyes widen as my chest fills with butterflies. The good kind.

"So, it's not because I was a damsel in distress?" *I've looked the movie up since realizing where the name came from.*

"Hell no. You had this spark, and every time I saw you..." he trails off as I stare at him confused. "It wasn't the damsel thing at all. That thought never occurred to me. All I ever saw was strength."

I think on that for a moment. "I like that. Thank you for sharing."

"Yeah, well, you asked," he says, clearly embarrassed by the story he just told.

"Jesse—"

"You know you haven't looked at your feet in a good two minutes, and you're still skating," he points out, changing the subject.

But he's right. "I'm a natural." I wink, picking up the pace...a tiny bit.

We skate side by side for another few songs, and when Katy Perry's "Firework" comes on, I decide I really want to soar.

"I'm ready to lose the safety net," I announce, much to Jesse's confusion.

"What safety net?"

"You."

"But I'm not touching you."

"I know, but you're *here*. It's time for *you* to sit on the bench for once."

"I actually sit on the bench a lot, it's—"

"Stop." I raise a hand in front of his face. "Please don't point out my lack of hockey knowledge."

Jesse sucks his lips into his mouth, biting back a smile as he nods.

"Thank you. Now please show me how good you are at sitting."

"Oh, I'm a pro."

"I'm sure."

I watch him as he skates gracefully over the ice, showing me how it's really done, even doing this fancy spinning thing before he reaches the edge. I roll my eyes but otherwise ignore him, focusing on my solo skate as though it's my redemption. My way of proving I can do anything.

I skate hesitantly for a bit, but when "Chandelier" by Sia plays, I sing along and my confidence grows.

I'm so lost in the music that I don't notice Jesse back on the ice until he's right in front of me, moving closer until I can't avoid him. *Not that I want to.* He wraps his arms around my waist and spins me, allowing me to throw my arms back, tilting my head to the ceiling, completely letting go. Trusting Jesse's hold on me. Knowing with every fiber of my being that he won't let go.

The song ends and he pulls me to a stop, releasing his grip only enough for me to stand comfortably.

A moment passes between us as we stare into each other's eyes, and an overwhelming feeling hits me. I want to kiss him. I want to feel that connection again. To remember.

As if hearing my silent words, Jesse palms my cheek and lowers his forehead to mine, releasing a soft groan. "You are amazing, Buttercup. I'm trying to do the right thing. I'm trying to hold back. But God, I need you."

My heart thumps in my chest as a sea of emotion floods me. "If you didn't have to think about right or wrong...what would you do?"

Jesse's lips pull into a smirk as he leans back. "Oh Buttercup, you are not ready for that."

I huff out a nervous laugh. "Sorry," I whisper before biting my lip. I really shouldn't have said that.

Jesse's eyes drop to my mouth before he groans again. And just when I think he's going to move away, he does the opposite, telling me he's sorry again before pressing his lips to mine.

He freezes when we touch, and my heart restricts as my body breaks out in goose bumps. I'm sure he's expecting me to break the kiss, but I don't. Not yet.

He's still for another beat, waiting, until I softly caress his bottom lip, making him hum against my mouth. His hands slide into my hair next, gripping the strands to tilt my head, making my mouth open in a gasp.

And instead of panicking, I feel like I belong here.

Like I've always belonged here.

I love the possessive hold he has on me, and I want more.

Our kiss turns frantic and raw, with Jesse holding on for dear life while I fight to stay afloat. Fully aware that I could easily drown in him and forget everything I've been working on... *me*.

When he subtly tugs my hair again, I moan, loving the feel of him as his tongue caresses mine.

My entire body heats and I internally curse myself. I'm not supposed to want this. Not yet. But right now, it's everything.

He continues to explore my mouth for another minute before breaking the kiss and leaning back, his eyes wide. "*Jesus*. I'm sorry. I didn't mean to do that," he rushes out, running a hand down his face as the other continues to hold me.

And I believe him.

"It's okay." I shake my head before looking away, my mind a mess of wild thoughts and feelings. I totally forgot we were on the ice.

"No," Jesse rushes out, grabbing my waist when I wobble slightly. "I wanted to let you set the pace," he whispers, "but seeing you so free...and... God, this is hard." He pauses, shaking his head. "You're breathtaking, Willow," he rasps. "What I wouldn't give for you to always be that carefree."

"No one's that carefree." I laugh. "I was picturing myself as the dancer from the video clip." I *was picturing myself finally living in the moment.* "She's young. She's got her whole life ahead of her. At least, she did back when the song was released."

"You shouldn't have to be someone else."

"Maybe not. But it's fun sometimes." I laugh it off, encouraging Jesse to do the same thing, but while he doesn't laugh, he at least smiles.

"Our time is almost up," he says, changing the subject. "Ready for one more skate together?"

I'm not. At all. I need more time, especially after that kiss, but instead I put a smile on my face and agree. "Let's do it."

We move slowly at first, but I get a little overconfident and try to skate faster, keeping in time with the upbeat song. When it hits the chorus, I raise my hands in the air, throwing myself off-balance, letting out a high-pitched squeal as Jesse barely catches me in time.

"Always my hero," I say, safely tucked into his arms.

"I will *always* be what you need me to be," he says, reiterating what he said in his text. "Even if I don't like it. Even if I want more."

He's not referring to catching me. He's referring to the role he's playing right now. The dutiful friend who's helping me get my memories back. The guy expected to spend endless time with me but who may never get anything in return. The selfless guy showing me exactly what I mean to him, without him even realizing it. The guy willing to walk away if that's what I want. What I need.

The man that has always loved me.

Jesus. What am I doing?

Jesse loves me, and while I've been trying hard not to admit it, I've been falling for him. Above all else we've got that.

A line from *Moulin Rouge* slaps me in the face as I remember promising my younger self that I'd live by it, before fate dealt me a rough hand. A line about the greatest thing being to love and feel love in return.

It's corny but it's true. For me anyway. I'm stronger because of Jesse. I'm here because of Jesse. I constantly say he left me to die, but if he hadn't reached for me, I could have fallen with Jade. And while I'm reluctant to admit this, even to myself, I'm also ninety percent sure that if I'd discovered the truth about Jade *before* meeting Jesse again, I never would have survived it. I was beyond broken, and he put me back together, showed me that he cared, and that he needed me as much as I needed him.

I may never get over what happened. There may always be a part of me that hurts, but can I really walk away from the one person that makes the rest of me happy?

"Jesse, I—"

Buzz.

An obnoxious sound cuts me off, making me jump as Jesse laughs beside me.

"And our time is up. What were you going to say?"

"I–"

A crackling starts before a voice comes over the speaker. "We've got a crowd hovering, Mr. Hastings. You might want to sneak out the back exit."

Laughter filters into the space and an urgency fills the air. "It's not important," I say. "Sounds like we better go."

Jesse waves a hand in thanks, but when I look around, I can't see who he's waving at.

We pack up our things, and I hand back my skates before we sneak out the back door. The second we're outside, another buzzer goes off and the crowd enters. They're so loud that I can hear them from the parking lot. *Did we take away some of their usual opening hours?*

I hold off telling Jesse what I was going to say because the moment's gone, and I need a night to think about it. But one thing I know for certain is that I want to try and move forward, with him rather than without.

And that's a pretty big realization.

29

Jesse

I don't think I'll ever get the sight of Willow floating around the ice out of my mind. Nor do I want to. I've never seen her so comfortable, so beautifully serene.

I could tell she wanted to talk about us before we were interrupted, but I wasn't going to push it. And she hasn't brought it up again.

"Pippa mentioned you've got a few big days ahead," she says as we arrive at Pippa's building. "That starts tomorrow, right?"

"It does. Wednesday's our first game of the season, so tomorrow's a biggish day."

"Wow, your first game? I thought she mentioned you'd already been playing?"

Her nose scrunches and I can't help but laugh at her puzzled expression. Hockey can be a lot.

"We have been playing, but they were preseason games. This is the real deal."

"Right, okay. Great. I shouldn't be distracting you then."

257

"You're never a distraction. But I might have less time now. No, that's wrong; I will *definitely* have less time. Our schedule is pretty hectic."

Willow smiles and shakes her head, trying to hide the disappointment that's clearly displayed on her face. "I get it. No problem. This is your life. I can give you some space until—"

"No." I cut her off abruptly, a wave of panic rushing through me. "It's hectic but I'll find time. Players have families, wives, girlfriends, friends. It's not a solitary life." I probably didn't have to protest that much, but I needed to drive my point home.

And it works, because this time when she smiles, I can see it in her eyes.

"Let me know. Maybe we can just catch up over the phone or FaceTime," she says, trying to keep it casual, even though we passed casual months ago, maybe even years ago for me.

This woman is the only one I've ever had feelings for, and making time for her is the easiest thing in the world. It's winning her back that I'm struggling with.

"We'll work something out. But for now..." I grimace and point out the window to where Pippa's standing like she's ready to scold Willow for being late. "Your mom's waiting," I joke, making Willow groan when she sees what I mean.

"I'm sorry."

"I get it. She still doesn't quite trust me. I wouldn't let my daughter anywhere near a guy like me," I joke again, but a strange feeling passes through me.

"That may be true, but she's my sister, not my mom. She's supposed to support my decisions."

"She's just looking out for you."

"Literally."

We both stare at Pippa and laugh when she raises her hands to her hips.

"I probably should go," Willow says between giggles.

"Yep, you should. I get the feeling she's about to pull a baseball bat from somewhere and assault my truck."

Willow bites back a smile. "It's possible. I'm sure she's still pissed about you making her pick me up."

"I didn't *make* her. I guilted her. There's a difference."

"Either way, I'm getting out so I can keep you safe."

"Aww, you care."

"I do. This is a beautiful truck."

She bounces her eyebrows as she departs, and I relax even more. It's nice seeing playful Willow again. I need to do more to bring it out of her.

I'm anxious the next morning waiting for Willow's text, wondering if I did enough to jog her memory yesterday, or if I should be dropping more hints.

She said I can't tell her anything, because that would be defeating the purpose as she wouldn't know what was real or not. But she also mentioned that special words or phrases seemed to trigger her, so maybe I need to think about that? Or maybe just being around me helps. Or our kiss.

The fucking kiss. I'm not sure if that was a good or bad thing, but God, she breathed air back into my lungs. And I didn't realize how much I was struggling. *I need her.*

She still hasn't texted by the time I head to the stadium, and it pains me to leave my phone unattended. I almost ask Seth to come down and keep an eye on it for me, but that's more trouble than it's worth. Willow wouldn't be expecting an immediate response; it's not life or death.

Pushing everything from my mind, I focus on hockey, powering through our practice session, paying extra attention as we watch tapes of our opposition, mentally taking notes, making sure I'm ready for anything they might throw our way.

It's a big day, so I'm exhausted when I get back to my locker, but when I see Willow's text, I relax, breathing a sigh of relief. Until I read it.

Willow: Radio silence last night. Hope you're having a nice day.

Goddammit. I feel useless. I have no idea how to help. Short of sitting her down and making her listen to every last detail of that day, I'm at a loss. But she doesn't want that. She wants to remember, and I'm really worried that I'm not the answer, when she desperately wants me to be.

I text back asking her to call me, but by nine p.m., I still haven't heard a peep.

Pretending I'm fine, I take a long shower before jumping into bed, and then stare at the ceiling instead of closing my eyes. I can't let any of this get to me. I need to be one hundred percent focused on the game tomorrow. What good is fighting for Willow if I fail the other parts of my life and hate myself for it? If Willow and I are going to work, we both need to be in a good place.

This could be a history-making year. True, we've said that before, but we came close last season. We've got a taste for the finals, and now we're out to win. We're the strongest, fastest, most experienced team we'll probably ever be, so it's now or never. And I'm going to be a part of that.

I'm going to win.

So...focus!

My internal pep talk must have worked because the next thing I know it's morning, and I actually had a decent sleep. I'm refreshed and ready to go. Ready to win the game, and then get my girl.

Though when I still haven't heard from her, except for a short "I'm okay," text, I'm not sure whether to be worried or pissed off. Has she changed her mind again? Decided that since I didn't spark a memory for her, I'm not worth her time? Or is spending time with me really getting her down? Maybe I royally messed up when I kissed her.

"Alright, boys! Let's do this," our center, Jax, calls out before we all start stamping our feet, a ritual we do before every game. "Leave your baggage in your locker, tense those beautiful abs, and let's go!"

Jax throws out the baggage part of the line before every game, but loves to mix up what comes next. I don't usually pay attention because I've never had anything to offload. The second I pull on my game day suit, I'm in the zone, and all else fades away. But today, it feels like he's directing his spiel to me, and I needed to hear it.

Throwing my phone into my locker, I bury it under my socks—like that will make all the difference—then push all outside forces from my mind, leaving nothing behind except hockey. A weight lifts instantly, and it's completely freeing.

But when our first warm-up song blasts through the stadium, and the crowd roars, a strange energy comes over me, something I've never felt before.

Something that runs through my blood.

I skate out with my usual enthusiasm, but for the first time, I'm smiling. I'm happy. And it only takes a second on the ice for me to see why. Like I'm instantly drawn to her.

Willow's here.

At my game.

Staring at me from the team seats, making my heart soar with the tiniest smile on her face. A smile just for me.

A warmth coats my skin, and a peace settles in my chest. For the first time ever, I'm playing for someone I love.

And fuck, is that a good feeling.

30
Willow

"Are you sure it's okay to sit here?" I ask Pippa with a subtle glance at all the die-hard fans surrounding me. All of them are dressed head to toe in gear, while I sit in one of the best seats in the stadium, wearing a pair of faded jeans and a long-sleeved tee, not even close to the team colors.

If I'm honest with myself, my nerves have nothing to do with what I'm wearing and everything to do with the man I'm here to see, and yet when Pippa asks if I want a jersey, I'm blurting, "God, yes!" so fast her eyes widen. "I mean, yes, please. If you have one."

Pippa laughs as she gets up from her seat. "Believe it or not, I have a few. There's a spare in my car. I'll run and get it."

She spins on her stiletto heel, but I grab the back of the jersey she's wearing, pulling her to a stop. "It better not have Ryan's name on the back."

"Would you prefer Jesse's?" she says as she laughs out loud, shaking her head.

Not yet. One step at a time. "I'd prefer it was blank."

"Well, it's your lucky day."

She walks away, leaving me alone and completely out of my element. It's safe to say I have never been in the presence of this many people in my life, and I'm not at all comfortable with it. The only thing keeping me sane is knowing that Jesse is somewhere in the building, and God, do I need to see him, even if he doesn't see me.

It took everything in my power not to call him last night or today, but with the messed-up way my head was, I didn't want to bring him down before the game. I wanted to send him a longer text, but I knew he'd read more into anything I wrote, and would likely show up at Pippa's to talk to me. Being vague was better in the long run, even if it ended with him annoyed at me. A pissed-off Jesse is better for the team than a tired, emotional one.

As I wait for Pippa, I do all I can to pass the time without drawing attention to myself. The last thing I need is someone discovering I'm a fraud. That I have absolutely no idea how this game is played. That I've never even watched a second of ice hockey in my life—even though my dad loves it—and that I'm here because Jesse and I have something going on. What that something is right now, I'm not sure.

My body tenses as someone taps my shoulder, but when I turn to look, I'm relieved to see it's a young girl, maybe around ten, rather than an angry supporter.

Her bright smile instantly calms me until the first words leave her mouth. "Are you one of the WAGs?"

"Bailey!" a woman gasps from beside her, pulling her back down onto her seat. "I'm sorry. She was just being friendly."

"Oh, it's okay." I smile back. "I don't mind. But no, I'm not." A pang hits me low in the gut. God, my life's complicated these days.

The young girl, Bailey, frowns. "Dad always told me the wives sat here, and I wanted to meet one."

"Does your dad play?" *Why else would she be in the team seats? Or am I the last of those seats? Pippa said these were team seats, right?*

Bailey laughs. "He wishes he could play hockey."

The woman—who I'm going to assume is Bailey's mom based on the fact that they have very similar features—laughs along with her before leaning forward to talk to me. "My husband's an agent. We don't usually come to the games, but this year *someone* wouldn't give up until her dad said yes." She points to Bailey and I laugh.

"I'm hoping to get on TV," she says with a shrug as she straightens in her seat.

My stomach churns, and I pretend to sneeze in case it's noticeable. The thought that I might be on TV never even occurred to me. *Why the hell did I think it was a good idea to come here?*

"You look perfect," I hear from beside me, turning with a furrowed brow.

"Sorry?"

"You started fixing your hair after I mentioned TV, so I wanted to tell you, it's perfect."

Jesus. Tears prick the back of my eyes, but I bite my cheek to stave them off. I never used to be a crier. This sucks, and I hadn't even noticed I was doing that, making myself presentable. Yes, my confidence has grown since Jesse walked into my life. Or *back* into my life, I should say. But there are moments where I'm still the girl that everyone stared at. The girl with the dead best friend. The girl that forgot.

No one knows me here. Even if I *was* on TV, no one would bat an eye. I'm a nobody, and I'm okay with that. I'd rather be a nobody than somebody people pity. But I'd still prefer not to be seen.

"Thank you. That's really kind of you to say."

"All that's missing is a jersey."

"Got it!" Pippa exclaims as she pushes through the crowd, making everyone stand as she passes by. "Sorry, I have three bags in the car and I wasn't sure which one held this." She hands me the jersey with a smile, and I have to stop myself from smelling it. *How long has it been in her car? Do I really want to wear this?*

"I'm staying at Ryan's for a few nights, remember? I only packed it yesterday." She laughs, as if reading my mind.

"So, you're definitely not a WAG then?" Bailey says, her face scrunched in disappointment.

"I'm really not. This is my sister. She works for the team. That's why I'm here."

"Oh. Hi," she says, looking at Pippa with a frown, making me smile.

"Hi there," Pippa says, "I'm Pippa. And while I do work for the team, I'm also technically a WAG."

Oops. I forgot about that. I quickly pull the jersey over my head as my cheeks heat, hoping to hide the pink tinge.

Bailey's eyes light up while her mother frowns.

Pippa and Bailey lean forward in their seats to start talking about Ryan, and I take the moment to just breathe. Despite my reservations, I can tell why people love it here. The atmosphere, the vibe. I imagine it could get very addictive.

When I get this strange sensation as though I'm being watched, I subtly glance to my left to find Bailey's mom quickly turning away before shaking her head.

Well, that was weird.

I'm lost in thought again when a techno beat permeates the air and the stadium erupts in cheers as the players skate onto the ice. My chest tightens in anticipation, wondering if he'll see me. Wondering if like me, he can sense when I'm in the room.

And I get my answer immediately. It takes Jesse about three seconds to realize I'm in the crowd, and I have to bite back a laugh. I'm kidding myself for thinking this isn't something big between us. Because this messed-up connection isn't going away, and after our kiss... I don't think I want it to. I may have freaked out at the time, but after really thinking things through, I know I need to try.

Jesse lifts his glove in a wave, and I subtly wave back, giving him a soft smile. He keeps a relatively straight face, but there's something about his expression that has the butterflies inside me turning to nerves. But no matter how nervous I am, seeing Jesse just now confirmed that being here is the right thing to do. It means everything to him and, in turn, means everything to me.

Despite having no idea of the rules, we're five minutes into the second period, and I'm on the edge of my seat. This game is brutal, but it's also really freaking amazing. I'm hooked.

Especially watching Jesse.

He has this air about him. Or presence, maybe it's presence. Either way, it's like he owns the ice and the puck, and I want in on that. His strength, his power, his aura. It's everything about him. It's not that he's a different person, because I've seen those parts of him before. There's just something bigger.

I can't keep my eyes off him.

And even though he's constantly distracting me, I somehow seem to be keeping up with the game. Or at least, I've figured out the general idea. In short, they need to score goals and stop the other team from doing the same. By any means possible. Any means within the rules, though from the looks of it, the rules allow for a lot.

I'm once again mesmerized by Jesse when Pippa leaps into the air, drawing my gaze to Ryan as he passes the puck to his teammate. My heart lodges in my chest as I watch his teammate glide toward the goal, moving so fast that it looks like he's flying. This is their chance. San Francisco is only up by a point and... "No!" I cry out as an opposing player steals the puck, sending it racing in the other direction. "Dammit." Also... *who am I?*

I sink back into my seat as the disappointment hits me like these are my boys, like I've been supporting this team all my life. Yet they barely react as the play continues on.

How do people do this?

Running my hands down my face, I expel a deep breath. I never expected to get this emotional over a game, but I love it.

"So, you're Willow?" Bailey's mom asks out of nowhere, making me jump. My eyes widen as I try to remember if I introduced myself by name or if she somehow knows me.

"I am," I hesitate, giving her a soft smile, one that she returns easily.

"I'm sorry, that question came out of the blue. I was going to ask earlier but held off for some reason. I'm Amber, Seth's wife."

"Seth?" *Jesse's agent?* I smile to cover my nerves. At least that explains why she knows me. *But how much does she know?*

"I shouldn't have said anything." She winces apologetically. "You look worried. I didn't mean to worry you."

"No, no. It's okay." *Cue the guilt.* "I just assumed I was invisible here," I say with a shy shrug.

"Unfortunately, no one's invisible in these seats, but you're doing a great job of blending in. You even appear to know what's going on. No one would guess that you don't."

What? "Then how do you know that I don't?"

"The way your face pinches whenever the players crash into each other, or fight, or fall."

"Damn."

"It's okay, I don't think anyone else has noticed. It's just because I'm sitting so close."

"Fingers crossed. Blending in is usually my specialty. I—"

Bang!

A body slams into the glass in front of me making me spring into the air, proving the exact opposite. There's no way I'm invisible now.

The player from the opposing team laughs at my reaction, before bouncing his eyebrows. I glance behind me to see who he's looking at and he laughs again, pointing at me with a wink before skating away.

"That was weird," I say to my new friend as she stares at the departing player.

"Do you know him?" she asks, and I don't even have to think about it.

"I've never seen him in my life."

"Huh." She shrugs. "Strange."

We go back to watching, with Amber relaxed and smiling, while I'm tense with pursed lips. *Again, how do people do this?*

Jesse comes back on the ice and steals the puck in his first few seconds, sending my pulse skyrocketing once more, while my heart lodges in my throat. I swear I'm going to need to lie down after this.

Without missing a beat, he passes to his teammate before racing forward to secure the puck again. It all happens so fast that if you'd blinked you would have guessed it had never left his possession.

We barely get a second to be impressed before he takes a shot at the goal, the puck gliding perfectly into position. Actually, I'm not sure "gliding" is the correct term considering the force with which it hits the back of the net.

He did it!

I jump in the air, cheering proudly as a pump-up song blares through the speakers. A song Pippa tells me is specifically for Jesse. I smile wide as I stare at him across the ice, and I'm so lost in the moment, watching his celebration, that it takes me a beat to realize he's staring back at me, a bright smile on his face and warmth in his eyes. He mouths something, but from this distance I can't make it out, though I think I understand and it makes my heart happy.

I'm here. Watching in this moment. I'm with him.

The second period ends almost as quickly as it started, and before I know it, we're ten minutes into the third.

I've finally managed to get my heart to settle down when the player from earlier pounds on the glass again, pointing directly at me. My brow furrows. I'm pretty certain I don't know him or any other players apart from Ryan and Jesse, and it's creeping me out.

Before I've had the chance to look away, the guy licks his lips suggestively, making me squirm, then laughs as he turns around, clearly happy to have rattled me. He glances back over his shoulder to wink, mouthing something I don't understand, though it doesn't take much to guess it wasn't pleasant. He smirks again when he notices my unease until a large body crushes him into the wall, wiping the smile from his face. I squeal as I jump in shock.

Jesus! This sport.

At first, I assume it's part of the game, but when I realize it's Jesse, my heart jolts.

A fight begins and within seconds, Jesse's punching the guy like an untrained boxer, laying into him with full force. The guy punches back and Jesse loses his helmet at the same time someone screams. Me. I'm freaking screaming. I don't want this. He's doing this for me.

The referees all stand close by but no one seems to be doing anything. I want to yell out, demand that they stop it, but it's no use—no one would hear me over the excited crowd. A few players take charge, trying to join in, but they're held back, kept away from the action until another fight breaks out.

Pippa groans beside me, drawing my attention, and I gasp when I see it's Ryan, now in the thick of it.

My face tenses as I struggle between wanting to look away and needing to know what happens, but as soon as Jesse has the guy on the ground, banging his helmet against the ice, the refs step in, putting an end to the madness.

Jesse and the creepy guy are immediately sent to the bench, along with Ryan and whoever he was fighting.

The crowd continues to cheer while I just stare at the penalty box, watching Jesse, my lungs finally filling with air after holding my breath the entire time.

"What the hell just happened?" I ask anyone who'll listen. This wasn't the first fight for the night, but it was definitely the most intense.

Pippa laughs. "That was Jesse staking his claim after some douchebag tried to get your attention."

"What?"

"You heard me."

I did, but what? "What a dick."

"I know. They do it to mess with the players' heads. If you're sitting here, it's usually assumed that you know or belong to someone on the team. And no one would have missed Jesse smiling your way. No one."

My chest tightens. "First, I don't belong to *anyone*. And second, I didn't mean him. I meant *Jesse*." I laugh incredulously. "Why would he risk a penalty for that, or an injury?"

And why does a little part of me find it so goddamn attractive?

Pippa playfully rolls her eyes as she pats me on the back. "You really need to watch more games. That fight was pretty tame compared to some that I've seen."

"Still." I shrug. "He didn't need to do it."

My eyes flash to Jesse's again to see him staring back at me. And when Pippa's gaze follows mine, she giggles. "Yeah, he did."

31
Willow

The game ends with San Francisco winning by a point, only just managing to hold their lead in the final seconds.

If I thought the supporters were loud before, it's nothing compared to now. The sound is deafening, but I love every second.

When the celebrations die down, Jesse skates over to the window and mouths "don't move," with a scowl on his face.

Pippa bites back a smile as she glances my way, bouncing her eyebrows as Jesse skates off. "I think he liked the jersey," she says, and I burst out laughing, my giggles more out of nerves than anything else.

The stadium clears out much faster than I would have expected, but I do as I'm told, sitting patiently as I wait for Jesse to arrive.

I'm not sure how long it's been when Pippa pops back with a smirk on her face, shaking her head when she sees me. "You're not seriously going to wait for him, are you? You don't even know how long he'll be."

"I've made him wait months. It's the least I can do."

Pippa frowns, her expression telling me her thoughts without the words that follow. "You're really going to give it a shot."

"I'm going to try. I'd rather see how it plays out then never know if I walked away from a great love."

"Ugh, when did you become a romantic?"

"When I was about twelve." I smile. "But I lost it at fifteen. I'm just starting to get it back."

Pippa laughs but there's a sadness to it. "Then you better go get your man."

"That's why I'm here."

"Are you okay to find your own way home then? If you even go back there." She grins and I roll my eyes.

"Yes, I've got your key. Thanks for letting me stay. I'll lock up when I leave tomorrow."

Pippa nods, but mumbles something as she walks away.

The second she's gone, I glance back to the rink, replaying Jesse's fight. I should be mad about it, but I can't bring myself to feel that way when all I can think of is how hot it is that he laid claim to me like that. That his actions told everyone to back off... I'm his. *His.*

Jesse arrives when I'm still lost in thought, his scowl now replaced by a frown. "Are you here for me or did Pippa force you?" he asks without a hello.

"You. Obviously," I snap, though I don't know why I'm pissed off.

"How is that obvious? You never called me, and you only responded to *one* text." His voice holds an edge to it that should make me madder, but it actually does the opposite. I know that fight on the ice affected him. I could see it in his expression when his eyes met mine. Not to mention the fact that I've been putting him through hell. Not letting him in but also not letting him go.

"I know." I sigh. "I was processing."

"Processing what?"

"*Everything.*"

I stand up and take a step toward him in the aisle, ready to tell him how I feel.

"Jesse, I'm here because I can't let you go. I tried, for both our sakes, because I don't know if I'll ever completely be over what happened, but I'm done fighting it. We can't be friends. We'll never be friends; it's so much more than that. I—"

Jesse's eyes widen and without a word he grabs my hand, guiding me through a maze of seats and aisles until we're in some kind of tunnel. I stay silent, fully prepared to follow his lead, but when he picks up the pace and I have to jog to keep up, I'm done. "Enough! Where are we going?" I demand breathlessly, making him groan as he comes to a halt, listening to my request.

"I *was* taking you somewhere to talk, but I can't wait."

He glances left and right looking for something and then shrugs, all while I stare at him completely confused.

"And we can't talk here?" I sass, watching as some kind of wicked idea pops into his head, before he stalks toward me, lifting me up in one swift movement. I instinctively wrap my legs around him as he walks, partly for safety, partly because I need him close. And when he whispers, "hold tight," a shiver runs through me, not at all a feeling I should get for a talk.

"Jesse, I—"

He stops again suddenly, silencing my words before moving us behind a Zamboni and out of sight. He spins me around, making me gasp until I'm once again silenced when he slams me against the wall, pressing his lips to mine.

We both groan as I melt into him, not realizing I needed this more than I needed air. Like I always do with him.

Our mouths mold perfectly, and I completely lose myself in the moment, unable to focus on anything other than the caress of his tongue as he seeks entry, or the way his hand grips my ass where he's supporting my weight, his fingers biting into my skin.

As the kiss heats, his hold starts to loosen and I push back, wanting my feet on the floor.

Jesse lowers me slowly without breaking our connection, before running his hands up my body, sliding one into my hair while the other continues its exploration.

I pant and moan, but it's all drowned out by his lips, his bruising kiss keeping me quiet.

But when his hand slips under my jersey and tee, and he cups my breast, I can't stop myself from crying out.

"Jesse."

"Fuck, I could get used to seeing you in my jersey," he murmurs against my lips, his hips grinding against me, creating a friction I didn't even know I needed. My heart pounds in my chest as his tongue clashes with mine before he pulls away again, his dark eyes burning into me. "The only thing it needs is my name on the back. In fact, I think all your clothes should say that."

Oh God.

He pops the button on my jeans next, and his hand moves under the waistband, making me clench in anticipation as need pools at my center. I tried so hard to tell myself I could live without him, but after one touch, I'm melting, desperate for more, needing more than anything to feel him inside me.

After running the tip of his finger through my heat, Jesse consumes me in another intoxicating kiss, smothering my moans as I whimper at his touch.

"Please," I whisper, though I'm not sure what I'm asking. All I know is that I need more. Of anything. I'll take whatever he's willing to give me.

Hearing my pleas, he slips a finger inside me and I almost thank him. *God, yes.* The more he pumps, the more I forget my own name, my mind and body completely his. I ride his fingers, rocking against him with abandon, until I hear a loud laugh from

KATHERINE JAY

somewhere nearby and I freeze, the sound bringing me back to earth as I remember where we are.

"God, Jesse. We can't do this here."

Jesse groans as his head falls to my shoulder, his fingers continuing their pursuit. "Fuck, Willow. You make me feral," he utters softly, his voice slightly pained. "You've got me fighting over you. *Obsessing* over you. It's you. All the fucking time. And I can't hold back anymore."

My breath hitches and I try to focus on the outside world, but his words run on repeat in my mind, making it hard to think of anything else. And as he curls a finger inside me, while massaging my most sensitive area with his thumb, I'm done for.

I cry out, but it's once again cut off by his kiss and everything else fades away. I'm so close to the edge that every nerve ending fires, as desire pools at my core. "*Jesse.*"

The sound of voices gets closer, and it's Jesse who stops this time, pausing with his fingers still inside me as he scans the area. "We're well hidden, but do you still want to stop?"

His chest heaves as my heart thumps in my chest, and a new energy takes over me. We should stop, we definitely should, but I find myself saying no before the rational part of my brain can respond.

"*Jesus.*"

I rub Jesse over his pants but he shakes his head in protest. "Stop. You've got to stop. Let me finish you

282

and then we'll go somewhere more private. I need to be inside you."

All I can do is nod as my core clenches, because God, I need that too. I lean forward to kiss him again, as he scissors his fingers, hitting a spot I've never felt before, sending me flying over the edge. *Oh God. Oh God.*

My head falls back against the wall, and I bite my lips to silence myself as my body convulses against his touch, a wave of ecstasy running through me.

Jesse softly kisses my collarbone, then my neck, making his way up until he reaches my ear. "You are so goddamn beautiful, Willow," he whispers. "God, I love you."

My heart stops as I melt in his arms. It's not the first time he's told me he loves me, but it's the first time I've heard it without the element of pain. And I love the sound.

I'm just not quite ready to say it back.

32

Jesse

I probably shouldn't have done that there, but as soon as she told me she was done fighting, I kind of lost my mind. Just like I did when I saw that asshole harassing her on the ice. In fact, it's safe to say, I'm a fucking mess when it comes to Willow.

But like always, all I see is her.

When I'd pushed her against the wall, I'd only planned to kiss her, but all good intentions went out the window the second she moaned my name. And now I need more.

After her breathing returns to normal, I help her tidy up and then we're off again, beelining straight for the parking lot.

"Can you take me home?" Willow says when we reach my truck, and I freeze, wondering if I did the wrong thing.

"Yeah, ah...sure. You're at Pippa's, right?"

Willow giggles and steps closer, curling her arms around my waist as she rests her chin on my chest. She looks up at me through her thick lashes, her mesmerizing eyes locking with mine as the smallest of smiles tugs at her lips. "I meant *your* home," she says, briefly biting her lip, something she does when she's nervous. "I want us to be together, and I don't just mean tonight."

I bite back a triumphant grin as I slide my hands into her hair, pressing my mouth to hers in a slow and explorative kiss. Willow moans when I suck her lip, and I feel it in my chest. We've kissed before, but this one holds a feeling of promise—of a future—and I've never felt anything like it.

After a moment, I reluctantly pull back, because if I don't, I'm likely to take it too far, and we're not protected by a wall and ice resurfacer here. "Let's get you home," I whisper against her lips, her answering smile making me chuckle.

It's only a short drive to my apartment, but long enough for me to absentmindedly start singing again. Willow smiles beside me, waiting until I'm finished before she speaks. "Do you do that often?" she asks, with her finger resting against her bottom lip, drawing my eyes there.

"Only when I'm happy."

"So, yes?" she questions with a nervous laugh, looking away.

I consider saying yes to ease her mind, but if we're even going to work as a couple, I can't hold back like I usually do. She should know every part of me. The good, the bad, and the darkness. "Actually no, hardly ever," I say honestly, briefly glancing her way.

She nods, but I can see that she's lost in thought, her bottom lip bearing the brunt of her worry as she bites down.

"Will you tell me about it?" she asks hesitantly, squeezing one hand with the other, something else she does when she's uncomfortable. While I'm sure she suspects I've got a story to tell, she couldn't possibly imagine how dark it is, and I'm terrified of how she'll react. But I have to tell her. No more secrets.

"Of course," I whisper, untangling her fingers so I can hold her hand, hoping to stop the pain she's about to inflict on herself. "I want to tell you everything."

But there's so much to say and I have so little time with her. While we've thankfully got our next game in San Francisco, after that I'm traveling for a week. Willow lives in Oregon, nowhere near any of my games. It's going to be hard to make this work in the coming months, but God, am I going to try.

"The first thing I need to tell you is that my life for the next six months is going to be hectic. I've got three to four games a week from now until April and then we hope to make the playoffs. I want us to be together, but in an effort at full transparency, I'm going to be an absent boyfriend for a while."

Willow covers her mouth as she tries to hide her expression, and at first I think she's upset until her smiling eyes look up at me. "Did you just say you're my boyfriend? Did that really just escape the lips of renowned playboy Jesse Hastings?" *Jesus, it did.* But the sass on her.

I roll my eyes and squeeze her hand. "I take it all back. I forgot how annoying you are."

"Shut up, you love me." She jokes but it's true.

"I do." I smile. "So, back to the serious stuff."

"I know you've got a life, Jesse. I didn't come here to try and railroad that, or change you. I live in another state. I run a business. I know this is going to be hard, but if you're happy to try, I want to make it work. Somehow. Lucky we have phones."

She waves her phone in the air just as it beeps with a text. "Lucky indeed."

Willow flinches before her eyes flash to the screen and she relaxes. Just like she did when we were in LA.

"Willow—"

"It's just Pippa," she says, cutting me off. "I didn't really tell her I was leaving."

"She knows, but who—"

"How?" she cuts me off.

"I saw her before I came to meet you. I told her we needed to talk."

"And we talked goood," she says, dragging out the word, making me laugh, distracting me from my worry.

"We're having a conversation now. That counts."

"Very true. Let's get going then so we can finish it."

On the drive home, the tension builds inside me. And by the time we're walking to my door, my heart is racing. If we want to make a go of this, I need to tell her everything, and I need to do it sooner rather than later.

"There's something I have to tell you," I say as I open the door, signaling for Willow to step through.

She walks past quietly without giving me a response, but the second the door clinks shut she launches herself at me, leaping into my arms as hers wrap around me.

I easily catch her, despite the shock, and we both fall back against the door. "Didn't you hear me?" I rasp against her hair as she snuggles into me.

"I did, and we'll get to our talk. But for now... I just need you close."

"How close?"

"Inside me."

Jesus. How can I argue with that?

I waste no time carrying her down the hallway. We can talk later, tomorrow even. I'm not letting her leave tonight.

She giggles as we move, and like always, I relish in the sound as it makes every part of me lighter, temporarily blocking the darkness from my mind.

When we reach the bedroom, Willow stops moving, her eyes scrutinizing the space in front of her.

"Well, this is boring," she says after a beat, sliding from my body before moving to the bed. "Could you not afford any artwork?"

"Ha ha," I deadpan, though it's a good question. Why don't I have any artwork?

"I've never really bothered with personal effects," I say honestly, even though it's not something I really talk about. "It probably stems from bouncing from home to home as a kid."

Willow nods in understanding as she reaches back, curling her fingers around mine.

"You don't need much," she says, her lips pursed in thought. "Maybe just—"

"Artwork?" I say quickly, making her laugh, though she hides it behind her hand.

"Ha ha," she deadpans instead, mocking me. "Yes, artwork. But I was actually thinking you could put up one of your jerseys. Do players do that?" She drops my hand and points to the blank wall between my two windows.

"For cup jerseys, sure."

"So where do you keep yours?" she asks with a spark in her eyes, making me cringe dramatically.

"You wound me," I say with a bit of an accent, acting defeated with my eyes on the floor, laughing when Willow gasps.

"Did you just quote *Bridgerton*?"

"What? Hell no. I've seen the ads, but that is not my scene. I quoted *Game of Thrones. Obviously.*"

"Obviously." She rolls her eyes. "Either way, I learned something new."

"What's that?"

"Actually, two things. You enjoy a little bit of TV watching."

"Doesn't everyone? What's number two?"

"You really like me." She sucks her bottom lip into her mouth, nibbling on it with her teeth as she hides her smile. But she's so pleased with herself that it shines through.

"Wrong. I *despise* you," I lie, taking a step toward her. "You're stubborn." Another step. "Sassy." Another step. "You're under my skin." Step. "In my head." Step. "You're everywhere." My last step brings my body flush to hers, allowing me to hear *and* feel her rapid breathing. "Now get on the bed."

She's dead silent, so I contemplate telling her I was joking, until she does as I asked, crawling onto the mattress before kneeling in front of me, her eyes ablaze with desire.

I swallow back a groan, watching, as in one swift movement she strips the jersey and her tee over her head, before releasing the clasp of her bra. I bite down on my bottom lip, but only get a glimpse of her body before she pulls the jersey back on, wearing nothing underneath.

My heart thuds as all my blood heads south, my cock instantly throbbing. All while she stares at me in challenge.

"Jesus, Willow. What was that?"

"That was me enjoying the asshole version of you. It reminds me of when we first met. It takes me back to that feeling." She blushes briefly but recovers quickly, with her confidence back in place. "Your turn."

My turn? I raise an eyebrow and wait, interested to see how this plays out. Does she mean it's my turn to strip or is she gonna sass me?

"Oh, I'm sorry. Did I forget to say please?"

Sassing it is.

"Get over here," I say, jumping on the bed to grab her around the waist, flipping her easily onto her back. She squeals in protest, but the fire in her eyes gives her away. She loves this.

After removing her jeans and panties, I cover her up with the jersey and stare down at her, my heart constricting with how much this moment means to me, even if I am joking around.

When she smiles up at me, her sass dissolves, leaving behind nothing but lust. And as I start to remove my clothes, bit by bit, agonizingly slow, she groans impatiently before dropping her hand between her legs.

And... Goddamn.

I was not prepared for that.

My cock springs to attention as I watch her dip a finger into her heat, her head dropping back as a moan escapes her. "Please don't make me do this alone, Jesse," she rasps. "I can't wait."

Noted! I'm naked in record time, spreading her legs so I can taste her, smacking her hand away to run my tongue through her heat.

I lie down as Willow moans, making my length harden even more as it painfully presses against the bed.

Ignoring my own needs, I spread her with my fingers and alternate between licking and sucking until she's a writhing mess, using her cries of pleasure to guide my moves, torturously edging her, knowing what she likes after our little time together.

Moving one hand under her ass, I lift her off the bed, giving myself better access and an amazing view. Her eyes widen as she stares down at me, watching as I circle my tongue, licking her until she groans.

When her breathing quickens, I gently insert a finger, curling it inside her as I continue my pursuit. Her walls tighten and she cries out again, grabbing my hair to still me.

"Wait. Stop," she rasps breathlessly, making me pause.

"Now?" I ask, confused. *I almost have her.*

"Yes. I want you inside me, remember?"

Fuck yes. How could I forget?

Jumping up, I reach for my wallet and grab a condom, sheathing myself as she watches. My cock twitches with the attention, and Willow laughs before crawling up the bed and kneeling, motioning for me to do the same, a heat in her eyes that I've never seen before.

I follow her lead and kneel on the bed in front of her, brushing her hair behind her ears as I wait to see what she does next. Only once I'm there, her confidence falters.

"What do you need, Buttercup?" I whisper, as she turns her head away.

When she doesn't respond, I grab her chin to bring her back around, willing her to face me. "It's just me. Just us."

She nods and grabs my shoulders, pulling herself higher to press her lips to my ear. "I want to be on top," she says on a breath. "But I need you close."

I know exactly what she wants. And yes, I want that too.

Moving Willow to the side, I sit with my back against the headboard and pull her closer, positioning her to straddle my lap. We both watch as she hovers above me, waiting until I line up my length, positioning it at her core.

Sinking down slowly, she takes me inch by inch, and we simultaneously cry out, the connection something we both missed, both needed.

Willow stills, closing her eyes as I fill her to the hilt. And I understand why. She's so tight that her walls squeeze me, but God, it feels good. With my hands on her hips, I wait patiently for her to get comfortable, staring at her beautiful face, drinking her all in. When she finally opens her eyes, she hits me with so much love that I feel it inside my chest. She doesn't need to say it for me to know.

Releasing a slow breath, I let her set the pace and wait until she starts to move. We're quick to find our perfect rhythm, but when she gets close and I feel her body trembling, I lose all my control, at the exact moment she loses hers.

"Faster," she gasps, picking up speed, bouncing on top of me while I slam up into her, our eyes locked the entire time, the intensity almost too much to take.

"Yes, that," she rasps. "Don't stop."

"Never, Buttercup. Never."

Releasing one hand, I slide it between us and massage her core, giving her a little extra to push her over the edge.

She throws her head back as her bucking continues, the new angle mixed with the friction, sending a tingle right through me.

"Fuck, Willow. This."

"I know."

Leaning forward, I lift the jersey and bite down on her nipple, groaning when she cries out, her body spasming as she flies over the edge. "God, yes."

I never really got the team jersey thing, but watching Willow come apart, while in mine, is fucking heaven.

I continue to pump into her as her walls tighten again, and my orgasm hits me just as she falls in a heap, burying her face in my neck, my own body folding over hers as I catch my breath.

After we've been still for a few minutes, Willow straightens up, pressing her palm to my chest just like she did when we first kissed in her store. I hold my breath as emotion hits me. Emotion I wasn't prepared for. A few months ago, I couldn't even handle someone touching my shoulder, and now Willow's touching my heart, my soul.

I gently brush my finger down her cheek until I reach her chin, tilting her head to face me before curling my hand into her hair. "You're my everything, Willow. Thank you for making me whole again."

Her breath hitches, her eyes searching mine before she smiles shyly, making me chuckle. I pull her closer until our foreheads touch, and cup her neck with my spare hand. We stay like that for a beat, relishing in the connection until Willow's hand drops and she leans back.

"Tell me about your tattoo," she says hesitantly. "I've been curious since I first saw it."

I swallow a lump in my throat and nod, not really sure how she's going to take this.

"It's a song," I whisper. "Bitter Sweet Symphony."

Willow's eyes light up. "That's one of my favorites." *I know.* "What are the chances?"

"Pretty high." I chuckle lightly, making her laugh nervously, cutting in before I finish.

"Of course, it's a popular song." She leans forward, squinting as she tries to read it. "Is that taken from something? Like an album cover? It's hard to read."

I'm silent as I watch her running her fingers over the script, taking me back to the fifteen-year-old Willow doing the same thing in the dirt. "It's taken from you," I whisper softly, smiling when her eyes flash to mine.

"Me?"

"You scribbled it in the dirt. That day. And it stuck with me."

Willow bites her lip and glances back to my chest, running her thumbs across the lettering. She hums the song until something hits her and her eyes widen. "Wait. You got this for *me*?" She gapes.

"I did." I nod with a chuckle. "No matter how much I tried to push you out of my mind, you never left. Not even for a second. I eventually gave in, and got this when I was twenty. It kind of acted as both a positive and negative reminder."

"I wish I felt the same connection you do," she says, her voice choked with emotion. "Maybe I will when I remember more."

Grabbing her face in my hands, I force her to look at me, to see what I see. "Don't rush it. You feel more than you realize." *And I've had longer to fall.*

As Willow drifts off to sleep, I brush my fingers across her naked back and stare at the woman who's become my everything. No, the woman that's *always* been my everything. And when her breathing evens out, I roll over and get out of bed, double-checking I locked the front door.

I take my time getting a glass of water for each of us, and a shirt for Willow in case she wakes up and wants something clean to wear.

By the time I get back, she's spread out on the bed, a peaceful smile on her face. If I was truly a good guy, I would probably try and squeeze in beside her, but if my plans work out, she'll be around for a long time, so I need to establish sides now.

I jump onto the mattress and lift her into my arms, putting her down on the left side, farthest from the door, before lying still behind her, my arms hovering as I consider whether or not I could hold her and still sleep.

Willow stirs as my mind races, and a beautiful little mewl escapes her. "What are you doing?" she rasps.

"Getting comfortable. Sorry for waking you."

"That's okay," she says, reaching back to grab my arm, securing it tightly around her.

I still for a second, until she kisses my hand and wriggles into my hold. "Is this okay?" she whispers. "I don't want to make you uncomfortable. Or take over."

I consider her question and the answer shocks me. "This is perfect. I like you in my space."

"Good."

"Good."

"Goodnight, Jesse," she whispers through a yawn, kissing my hand again.

"Night, Willow."

33

Jesse

When I wake early the next morning, after a great night's sleep, Willow's no longer in my arms. Instead, I find her hunched over on the edge of the bed, her hands resting near her lips as she stares ahead, unmoving.

My stomach drops and a tense feeling runs through me. "What happened?" I ask, my voice coming out croaky until I clear my throat.

"Willow?"

She doesn't answer. She doesn't even move, and if she wasn't so close, I'd assume she couldn't hear me.

"Willow," I say again, a little louder, and she jumps, spinning around with a fake smile in place.

"Good morning. Sorry if I woke you. I was up early. I'm still getting used to the loud morning sounds of the city."

Well, that's a lie. She was always an early riser. Has she forgotten I know that?

"What happened?" I repeat, sitting up to pull her back into my arms.

She stares at me for a brief moment before tears well in her eyes and she shakes her head.

"I still don't remember," she whispers in a daze, and a sense of failure consumes me.

I'm letting her down. She thought being here would help her and it's not. I'm at a loss as to what else I can do.

"I'm sure these things take time," I say, but it's a cop-out. I don't know the right words.

"I'm sure they do," she says with another fake grin. "But...what if I never remember anything else? What if that was just my brain giving me a glimpse of possibility before ripping it away again?"

I think about that for a second, wondering if she remembers certain things that stood out for a reason. Maybe she's remembering the moments that caused her less pain. "Have you spoken to anyone about it? The dreams, or rather the memories?"

Willow nods as she sniffles. "I have. There's no guarantees but..."

"Why don't you tell me what you remember?" I say, an idea coming to mind. "It might trigger something else," I add, though I have no clue.

Willow turns to face me, her eyes red, her skin blotchy, and yet, she's still the most beautiful human I've ever seen. "Do you think that might work?"

"I don't know," I say honestly. "But it's worth a try."

She moves away and repositions herself opposite me on the bed, pulling her legs to her chest, before wrapping her arms around them. Securing herself in her hold.

With a small shiver, she shares her memories like she's telling me a story, and my heart breaks for her. They're *dreams*. The memories she's been so caught up in are dreams. I mean, the part with Jade might be real, but the vision of us, sitting around as a group chatting, definitely isn't. And I have no idea how to break that to her.

When she's finished, she shrugs, once again trying to appear less affected than she truly is, and I struggle with words.

Emotion threatens to overcome me, but I bite my tongue to stave them off—now's not the time.

"Willow…" I trail off because I'm breaking inside. I'm about to take away her hope. Her one shot of moving on and I hate that I'm the one hurting her again.

I take a deep breath to calm my nerves, but it's shaky. "While I can't speak about the moment with you and Jade…" I pause. "I know that we never sat together as a group." I pause again, swallowing back my emotions as I watch her process hers. "And there was no beer."

"What?" Willow's brow furrows and she shakes her head back and forth. "No, no. I distinctly remember that."

God, this stings. "I'm sorry," I rasp, my voice almost inaudible.

"It wasn't real?" she chokes out, a single tear cascading down her face.

I shake my head because I'm not sure I can speak without getting choked up myself.

"None of it was real?"

Squeezing my eyes shut, I block out everything I'm feeling and focus on her because she needs to hear it. "I don't think so," I whisper. "I think they're still dreams."

"Nightmares," she corrects, running her hands down her face as her body shakes. "They're nightmares."

"I'm so sorry, Willow. So fucking sorry." My voice breaks, drawing her attention, and for a brief second I think my fear's about to come true; she's going to comfort me. She's going to push her own feelings aside and care for me. Just like she's always done in the past with everyone else she knows. But when I swallow back my emotion and stare her directly in the eyes, she falters, her tears welling once more.

"I didn't even want to remember," she whispers, her gaze locked on her hands. "I decided I didn't want to, until you and Sara put the idea back in my head. I wanted to move on. Forget that part of my life ever happened. Forget *you*. But now it's all that I think of. I'm missing something. A part of me is missing. And I try so hard to fill the void by pretending I'm okay. But I'm not, Jesse. I'm not okay."

She stops for a breath before the tears really fall. "I just wanted to take charge of my life," she whispers, her voice cracking, and I can't stay back anymore. I can't let her crumble without being close. *I will always catch you when you fall.*

"Why can't I remember?" she questions as I move forward, pulling her into my arms, cocooning myself around her. "And why did it feel so real?"

She shakes uncontrollably as silent tears continue to fall.

A pressure builds inside me as I fight to maintain my composure, when the truth is she's tearing me apart. Bit by bit, I want to break off pieces of myself, giving her everything I have until she feels whole again. Do anything I can to take her pain away. I'd gladly carry it all for her.

"I don't know how to help, Willow. I wish I could. I wish I could fix everything for you. I'd change the world if I had the means. But I don't know how to get your memories back. All I can do is share mine. Give you a play-by-play of everything I remember. Every. Little. Detail." *Because I remember it all.* "From the yellow scrunchie you had around your wrist, to the ugly green boots Tate insisted on wearing because someone once said they looked cool."

Willow huffs out the tiniest laugh, but is otherwise stone, so I continue.

"I could tell you what Jade and Tate talked about—because he told me—or the way my heart raced to dangerous levels when I saw you fall. I could tell you that we spoke about your loathing of bells above doors, and that the mere sound of them triggers me now. I could describe the trees, the atmosphere, the smells, the sounds. If I could give you every single memory of that day, I would. But I truly believe it would only make things worse. You don't want the darkness I have floating around in my head. It causes nothing but agony. It's not a savior; it's more like a curse." I finally pause before adding. "Let me be the keeper of that burden."

Willow tilts her head back and stares through me, her mind whirring. I'm about to say more when I see a little light creeping back into her eyes. "You're right," she whispers. "Maybe it's better this way."

"No." I can't let her hide. "Please don't say what you think you should say. Tell me what you *feel*."

"I'm *scared*," she rasps, immediately responding. "I'm scared that I'll never remember, but I'm also scared of what I forgot. I know my type of amnesia is caused by trauma, so I'm aware they're not going to be good memories. But what if I'm never truly happy because I'm never fully whole?"

If any part of me was still intact, Willow just smashed through it. "I can't answer that for you," I say with my broken heart lodged in my throat. "But I can spend every day trying to ensure that you are. I'll work hard to make you happy."

I brush a stray hair behind her ear before wiping the tears from under her eyes, all while she stares at me, her gaze full of regret.

"You do." She smiles softly. "You do make me happy." She pauses, blinking a few times before she whispers. "Tell me something real. Something about us."

"You were my first kiss," I blurt and then grimace. "It was only brief. The lightest touch. But you were my first. And my only."

"Wait," she says, her brow furrowed in confusion. "You mean back then?"

"I do."

"We kissed?" she asks with softness to her tone, almost like she doesn't believe me.

"We did." I bite back a smile.

"So, Jack wasn't my first?" she muses. "Wow."

"Fuck no, he wasn't. Who's Jack? Do I need to kick someone's ass?" I'm joking but I'm not going to lie, I'm a little jealous. She remembers *Jack's* kiss.

Willow giggles. "No, he was awful. I feel better knowing it was you."

"Good. Your first *and* last."

"My last? That's very presumptuous."

"No, it's not. It's foreshadowing."

Willow giggles again until her expression turns serious. "Will you show me?"

"Show you what?" I ask with a frown.

"The kiss."

Now that's something I can do. I will never forget that kiss for as long as I live.

Leaning forward, I slowly brush my lips against hers, caressing her mouth as my heart pounds in my chest, just like it did back then. I pull away after only a few seconds, sinking my hand into her hair to lift her face, but when she opens her mouth in anticipation,

I don't kiss her again. That was our kiss, our brief moment.

"That's all we got before..." I trail off. We don't need to talk about what happened next.

Willow lifts her fingers to her lips, her eyes softening. "Thank you."

"Thank you?"

"That was perfect, and exactly what I needed."

I smile and nod, letting her have this time without ruining it with words, and after a beat, she looks at me with wide eyes before shaking her head. "No, it's more than what I needed," she says, her gaze locking with mine as she reaches up to hold my hand still in her hair. "You're my missing piece."

My body chills. While that sounds like such a huge responsibility, it's one I'd happily take on. "You're my everything," I say for the second time because it's true. "I'm so sorry I hurt you, but I can say with absolute certainty that I will never hurt you again."

"I think that's a part of what I was struggling with. Knowing you walked away."

"God, Willow. I know. I know I fucked up back then, but I was young and stupid and really fucking scared. They're not great excuses, but I can assure you, I know it was wrong. I'm sorry."

"I know. I wouldn't be here if I hadn't moved past that. I'm sorry for bringing it up."

"Never be sorry for that. I will always want to know how you feel, and I'll always help where I can."

Willow leans forward to kiss me again, and while it starts off slow and gentle, it quickly turns frantic. We fall back onto the bed, and before long I'm ripping open a condom packet and sliding into her. My home.

"Fuck, Willow. Why is this so different?" I whisper, slowly thrusting into her again, watching as she stares up at me, her breath picking up speed. "Why is everything with you so different? So amazing. So perfect."

"Because we fit," she rasps. "Because this is meant to be. And I know we'll get through anything."

When Willow returns from the bathroom, I'm the one hunched over on the edge of the bed, waiting for her. We're supposed to be in a post-sex haze, but all I can think about is what comes next. What I have to tell her.

She smiles when she sees me, but when I pat the bed for her to sit, her smile drops.

"Now you're scaring *me*. Is this payback?"

I huff out a chuckle but it's clearly forced. I'm about to tell her something I've never told another soul. Something only three people know, and one of them is dead. "Before we go any further in this relationship, you deserve to know everything about me."

"Oh-kay," she says hesitantly, her eyes full of a wary look, as though she's ready to put up her guard any minute.

"There's another reason I tried to push you away back in Hepburn Falls," I begin. "I would never knowingly hurt you, Willow, but I'm not a good person."

Willow turns around, her gaze locked on the side of my face, but I can't look at her. Not while I say this. I can't bear to see her expression.

"I killed my foster dad. And I don't even regret it."

34

Jesse

T welve Years Ago – Age Sixteen

I slam the bathroom door shut just in time to expel the contents of my stomach, not even caring that some of it misses the toilet bowl. Sweat pours down my back and chest, the scent mixing with the smell of blood as they both coat my skin. I jump up to wash my hands but no matter how hard I scrub, the stains remain, like they'll forever be tattooed on my body, a constant reminder of what happened. Of what I did.

Fuck, I need to shower.

I race to undress, knowing I don't have much time, but the blood-soaked tee sticks to my body as I desperately try to peel it off, frantically thrashing about as the smell permeates my nose, a smell I guarantee I'll never forget. My insides squirm again as I finally rip it over my head, throwing it to the floor with a wet thud.

I left her.

She was bleeding and unconscious and I left her. What kind of fucked-up person does that? I don't even

311

know if the guy who picked her up actually took her to the hospital. I put complete faith in the fact that he was gentle when he moved her into his car. But what if he hurt her?

God. I hurt her. Walking away hurt her and I'll never forgive myself for that.

I hover over the toilet as more vomit threatens to come up, making my mouth water as sweat drips into my eyes. I blink rapidly trying to see, but for what? What do I want to look at? Her blood on my skin, the pain in my eyes, the bruises?

Turning the shower to scalding hot, I strip off the rest of my clothes and step in, not even bothering to check how it feels, my mind stuck on that mountain. On Buttercup. And on Lily...Jade. I should think of her as Jade. After all, that's what they'll write on her gravestone. Lily didn't exist, but Jade fucking died, and I have to live with that knowledge.

I could have saved her. If I knew what was going on, I could have helped. If I'd just been two steps closer...

I don't even know where to go from here. Do I go to the police? Alone? We're lucky if we get the night before they come calling, asking for answers on why we left the scene. Left them. Left Buttercup. God, I don't even know anything about her.

And she doesn't know us.

The water turns a light shade of red as I wash the blood from my body, scrubbing so hard, the cloth mars my skin. But I can't stop. I deserve it. I deserve so much worse.

What the fuck did we do?

As I watch the tainted water swirl down the drain, my head flashes with perfectly clear images of what I'm sure will become my torment. If I even make it out of this in one piece.

Her best friend is dead, and all I managed to say was, "It's okay. I've got you."

And even that was a lie. I don't have her. I don't even know if she's okay. I don't even know her real fucking name.

The sound of their screams fills my mind next, and it takes everything in my power not to scream louder, not to try anything I can to drown it out.

Instead, I grip my head and remain silent. I have no choice. I've got more than one nightmare to contend with.

Considering the blood caked to my body, I'm in and out of the shower in barely a few minutes. I can't risk staying here any longer.

I can't let him see.

I switch off the tap and still before stepping out, listening carefully for any indication that I might not be alone. But when the house remains quiet, I move, quickly drying off so I can clean up the mess.

The mess? It's more than just what I see here. More than just blood and tears. And I'm in the middle of it.

I pause again, letting my head hit the wall as I run my hands down my face. I'm so fucked.

This is so fucked.

I've just opened my eyes when the door crashes open, making me jump as fresh bile rises in my throat.

"What the hell is going on?" my foster father yells, his eyes raking over my naked body, lingering where they shouldn't.

"Get the fuck out," I bite back, standing my ground, before adding, "I'll be out in a minute." Letting him know he's free to beat the shit out of me when I'm done.

He sways slightly before turning around, and a feeling of weightlessness flows through me as every part of me relaxes. I've taken beatings before; I can survive this. But not naked. I need to maintain some dignity, some control.

The door clicks shut as I switch on the tap and I audibly sigh, grateful for small mercies. But when I look up in the mirror, the blood drains from my body and I pray to God for the very first time.

35
Willow

Tears fall down my cheeks, but I frantically wipe them away, not wanting to add to Jesse's pain as he continues on.

"He came at me with his fists held high, and for the first time since it started, I pushed back. It wasn't hard, but it was firm. I couldn't let him touch me."

He pauses, swallowing back the emotions he's trying hard to keep buried, while he clenches his fists so tightly they're turning red.

"You don't have to say any more," I whisper, terrified of where this story is going, while also feeling like I know.

Jesse clears his throat and shakes his head before continuing. "When he tried *other* things," he says, moving past the detail. "When he *tried*... I snapped. After everything that happened that day, I was already so shattered, I wasn't about to add more to my madness. A manic scream filled the air and at the time, I didn't realize it was mine until Tate came bursting into the room. I should have left. But I was done. I couldn't handle it any longer."

He falls silent again with his body hunched over as I wait patiently, not sure if he wants to go on. But when his shoulders start to shake, I know that he's finished.

"God, Jesse."

I crawl on to the bed behind him and wrap my legs around his waist, resting my head on his back. As tears fall, I curl my arms around him, holding my palm over his heart.

A few minutes pass before Jesse sniffs and clears his throat again, straightening his back. "I killed him, Willow," he says, his voice devoid of emotion. "I killed him and I felt nothing. No remorse. No regret. Nothing. If anything, I felt relieved."

When Jesse pauses this time, I try to think of the right words, but I'm at a complete loss. If I thought my heart was broken before, the pain I felt then is nothing compared to what I feel now. The pain of knowing what he went through and finally understanding why he never wanted to be touched, why he hated intimacy.

After a quiet moment, Jesse huffs out a laugh. "And that's my story."

I hug him tightly, my head still resting on his back, thinking about everything he's been through. But something doesn't add up. *How could he get away with murder?*

"When you say you killed him?" I ask, trailing off. It may not be appropriate, but I feel like it's something that needs to be said aloud because I think there's more to it. It has to be more complicated than "I killed him."

"You don't need the details," Jesse begins. "But when I saw Tate, I lost my mind. I needed to get him out of there. It had been over a year since he'd been hit, but that day felt different. We got to the back door, and with Tate outside, I prepared to fight. To give him a taste of his own medicine. But then he came at me, and he..." He shakes his head. "Something came over me. A strength I'd never felt before, and I grabbed ahold of him before throwing him down the concrete stairs."

I gasp before covering my mouth. "That sounds like an accident. You—"

"It wasn't," he states plainly. "I knew what I was doing."

Jesus. Surely that's still self-defense.

"I stayed by his bedside, waiting for him to die. Hearing that flatline was like music. In one day, I witnessed two deaths and lost you. It's safe to say, I was pretty fucked-up after that."

"Jesse, he hurt you. All you did was save yourself. Save Tate."

Jesse laughs again but it's full of sadness. "I didn't *save* Tate."

"Jesse—"

"After my dear ole 'dad' died, we were questioned, but it was ruled as a drunken fall. I was fostered by the local doctor's brother. I got to move to Seattle, while Tate went to another family in the area. One that still treated him like shit, only differently. They never hurt him, never made him do anything illegal, and apparently even sent him to a good school." He huffs out a laugh. "But they didn't care about his existence; it was all about the payment. They were just keeping up appearances."

God, Tate. I feel for them both. And yet... I don't know if I can trust him.

"I went back for him," Jesse continues, and I sit straighter, reaching out to blindly take his hand, silently promising I'll never let him go. "After I'd been gone about six months, I went back. Caught the train overnight, and then hitchhiked my way to Mossman. I thought I was being stealthy, that I was smart. But my foster dad knew, and he let me go, sensing it was something I needed to do."

Tears well in my eyes as I try to reconcile the man Jesse's speaking about with the teen from my school and the man that's desperate to speak with me now. He was popular, he was loved, but...

"I found him throwing rocks across the lake out of town, something we used to do together to pass the time. I'm not sure what I expected to happen, but I didn't expect what did. He came running toward me with so much anger, you'd think I was the one that hurt him, and right after his fist connected with my jaw, he told me to fuck off to my sweet life and never come back again. He didn't need me. He didn't want me. We were done."

I gasp again, because that's almost word for word what I said, but I was lying, and so was Tate. "Jesse," I whisper, giving his hand another squeeze.

"I know. I see it now. I know he said those things *for* me. Just like I pushed you away. I get it. But it took me too long to realize. It took me right up until the week of your dad's celebration, right around the time that I was looking for you and saw the panic in his eyes. But then he freaked out."

"What?"

"I think he was just worried about what would happen if you knew the truth. If you told anyone. Because if the police looked too closely, who knows what they'd discover."

Taking a deep breath, I decide to be honest. To see what he thinks about Tate getting in touch. "He stopped by the shop when we were in LA," I say hesitantly. "Sara said he was quite panicked, asking to see me."

"He what?" Jesse's head rears back to look at me as his eyes widen.

"Have you spoken to him? Does he know that I know?"

"No. I haven't said a word. *Fuck*."

"Don't panic. I'm sure it's nothing. I shouldn't have brought it up. Not now. We were talking about you. I don't even know how you're functioning."

"Willow—"

"No, I'm fine. It's you I'm worried about."

319

"I'm fine. I was surviving," Jesse says, a little distractedly. "We were all just surviving. You included. I escaped into hockey, Tate escaped into drinking, and you eventually found your business. But deep down none of us were happy."

I can see his mind ticking over, and I have no doubt he's still worried about Tate. So to help, I try to distract him.

"And now?" I ask, a lightness suddenly filling my chest as I finally feel the answer myself—I *can* live without remembering, because I'm happy. Jesse makes me happy.

"Now, I've never been better. I've never felt more alive and it's all thanks to you. I enjoy hockey—it was my dream and it became my life—but you, you bring me peace, and you gave me something I never thought I'd have, I never thought I wanted. You helped me *love*. Before you, I locked my emotions away. Nothing mattered. I put everything into hockey and pushed everything else out. I didn't think I had the capacity to love. But then you happened and well...you know. And I'll always be grateful for that, even if you walk away now that you know my truth, my dark past, my story."

"Why would I walk away?" I ask seriously. *Does he really think I would?*

"Because I'm not a good person. No matter how much light you bring to my life, it's still full of darkness. I still did something unforgivable."

"Have you ever killed someone, committed an unforgivable crime, or worse?" He'd already told me the truth. I just hadn't listened.

I twist around him until I'm positioned in his lap, straddling his legs, then tentatively cup his face, running my thumb gently across his cheek. "I'm here, Jesse. I'm not going anywhere." I pause because that's not exactly true. "I mean, I'm physically going to leave, but I'll always return. You have my heart and I don't want it back."

Jesse finally smiles, and while it doesn't completely reach his eyes, it's breathtaking. "I love you so much, Willow. And I'll never lie to you again."

"Or hold back the truth."

"Or hold back the truth," he repeats with a laugh.

36
Jesse

Long-distance relationships suck. Hard. You'd think I'd be too busy to notice, but oh, I notice. Especially when I have the threat of Tate constantly running through my mind. I played it down for Willow's sake, but I honestly have no idea why he'd be so desperate to talk to her, and he won't answer my calls.

This entire situation is messed up.

Willow and I went through this big emotional, potentially life-changing moment, and then she was gone. Back to her hometown like she'd never even been here. While I headed off in the opposite direction. Worried about her. Unable to protect her.

And it's really fucking hard.

I'm exhausted by the time we land after our second away game, and desperate for my bed. I'm normally on a high after back-to-back wins, but as I drive home slowly, my eyes threaten to close, and I realize it's the emotional exertion finally taking a toll on me.

What it really boils down to is that I miss Willow.

She may have said we were okay, but how can anyone possibly be okay after having a truth like that dropped on them?

I killed someone. I killed my foster dad and never even felt an ounce of remorse. I felt nothing but relief. I saw life leave his eyes, I watched as the blood drained from his body, I was there when his heart took its final beat, and I still *felt nothing.*

I may have vowed never to speak about that night... Hell, I vowed never to even think about it. But I also never expected to fall in love. It wasn't something I sought out, and it definitely wasn't something I deserved.

I couldn't imagine a scenario where I'd ever need to speak my truth, unless, of course, I was caught. But since so much time had passed, it was safe to assume I'd gotten away with it. And why would anyone question it when he was known as an alcoholic... and after his death, a drug dealer.

But Willow deserved the truth. All of it.

She had to know what she was getting herself into. I couldn't go on another day without telling her everything, even if I lost her.

And if I'm being honest with myself, I expected her to leave. Telling her now was my way of saving myself from future heartbreak, because it was inevitable. I couldn't hide my secret forever, and it's better to have her walk away while this is still new than when I'm ready to drop down on one knee.

I chuckle as I turn into my parking lot, laughing at the guy I've become. The guy that thinks about marriage. If Seth was here now, I'm pretty sure he'd be paralyzed by shock. *Who am I? What has Willow done to me?*

When I wake the next morning, I'm still groggy.

I have no issues getting myself in the zone before games. It's something I've always been good at. But if I've got the day off, sleep seems to evade me, and that's not a good place to be.

Like most mornings, I text Willow hello before spending the day catching up on my basic needs like food shopping—or at least, ordering it online—and laundry. Every time I throw a load in the machine, I tell myself I should be paying someone to do this, and then as soon as I've pressed start, I forget.

It's hard to justify spending money on something I can do myself when there are so many people out there who go without.

Like the kids from the clinic.

To my surprise, Pippa actually helped me with all the minor details of my grand proclamation, and when their season started, all twenty kids had a grant

KATHERINE JAY

available if they wanted it. Any money left over would stay with the club, to be used however they see fit.

The feeling I got when I transferred the funds was like a new kind of fulfillment. It made me consider setting up my own charity after retirement, doing this on a regular basis. With help from someone who can be the face and main point of contact, I'm happy to plan things and spend some cash, but I'd rather not deal with people.

Despite not being a busy day, I'm exhausted by the time I get to bed, and practically fall in a heap on the mattress.

I run through my plans for the next day, and like always, my mind clears, only retaining what I need for hockey.

Closing my eyes, I try to drift off to the sound of the rain on my window, but before I've fallen into a deep sleep, a wave of irrational panic hits me, and I have no idea where it came from. My heart races as I listen out for the threat, but when I'm met with silence, I consider the possibility it's not me in trouble, but someone else.

Grabbing my phone, I text Willow to make sure she's okay, and it's not until she responds that I actually relax.

Willow: All good here, just missing my man.

Her man. After our big talk about my past, that's exactly what I needed to hear. She's always exactly what I need.

The feeling subsides quickly after that so I can focus on what needs to be done. It's time to kick some rival ass. Tomorrow's another day.

After a grueling practice the next morning, we watch some tapes, get ready for our game, and then head home to rest. At least the other players do. I head off to my doctor's appointment.

"How many more of these do you think we have to do?" I ask, holding back a groan. While we all have regular checkups, having one the day before every game is getting old.

"That all depends on how today goes," Doc says with a shrug. "But it was looking better when I last saw you so...any day now."

"Thank God."

Doc laughs before putting on a fake frown. "It's a shame you haven't enjoyed our time as much as I have," he says and I bark out a laugh.

"Sorry, Doc. It's been fun," I lie, laughing again when he rolls his eyes.

Are doctors allowed to be funny?

"Unlike you, I'm not actually talking bullshit," he says. "It's been nice seeing a change in you. You used to give me nothing but attitude. I was just another person getting in the way of the only thing you cared about—hockey. But now I have a feeling you care about more than that. And it suits you."

Fuck, I hate perceptive people. Okay, I don't hate them, but it's annoying.

"I'm not going to answer that, Doc. You never know when someone's going to spill to the media."

I shoot him a wink as he shakes his head.

"I've got to earn my millions somehow," he jokes back and I chuckle. I really have changed. And I don't hate it as much as I would have thought.

We get down to business and when Doc frowns, for real this time, I know it's not going to be good.

"It's not as high as it was," he says with a grimace. "But not as low as last time. Let's check it again tomorrow before the game. If it's back down, then I don't have to mention this visit."

"Fuck. You're a good man, Doc. But I really hope I don't have to see you for much longer."

Doc's lips pull into a lopsided grin and he nods. "I get it. Let's see how tomorrow goes. In the meantime, go home and watch TV or read a book, something light. Just relax and try not to think about whatever else you have going on."

"Thanks, Doc." *I'll try.*

37
Willow

I'm rushing around to get ready when my phone rings. Sara will kill me if I don't open the shop on time, but I can't seem to get my shit together today. She's been keeping us afloat while I've been galivanting around, and I owe it to her to show some interest, even though my love for the store is slowly drifting away.

While I may never get my memories back, I'm still managing to find myself. And the more I discover, the more distant I feel from my life here. This wasn't supposed to be my future. I wasn't supposed to stay here and raise the next generation, like Ashley. I was supposed to break free and see the world, like Pippa. If I was going to have a family, I was going to raise them where I wanted, not where I was told I should be.

I answer the phone at the last second, my shoe half on as I bounce around on one foot, wedging the phone between my shoulder and ear.

"*Hello*," I rush out, a little louder than necessary.

"Willow, it's Tate."

Tate?

I drop my shoe as I grab the phone, slowly lowering myself to the bed. "Hi. Uh. How are you?" *And why are you calling?* I don't even know how to talk to him. We've *never* spoken.

"I've been better," he says before releasing a long sigh. "God, I don't even know how to say this. Do you think we could meet in person?"

What? "No! I mean, I've got a lot going on. I'm not sure when I'll have time to meet, but I'm free to talk now," I lie. I'm so late, but I don't want him here.

Tate huffs out a laugh. "Yeah, that's what this is about."

"What is?" I rush out, cursing myself for not hiding my nerves.

"I saw you've been hanging out with Jesse and..." he trails off.

"And..."

My hands shake, clenched too tightly from the tension building up inside me.

"We both did. There are photos of the two of you."

"Both?"

"I'm kind of hoping I'm wrong, but Alex saw the photos when I did and started searching for information on Jesse."

My chest tightens, but I try not to freak out. Not yet. "What do you mean?"

"He asked me how well I knew him. Even looked him up online. Not that he knows I saw that but it happened."

"Okay."

"There's more... When you were in the hospital for your ankle, he wanted to visit, but I told him to stay away. He completely flipped out and said I needed to stay out of his business."

While that should be concerning, I know what that was about so I'm not worried. But the Jesse stuff has me on edge.

"So, you think he's after Jesse?" I ask, though I'm not sure why he would be... *unless he knows?*

Tate huffs. "No, I'm worried he's after *you!*" *What?* "I don't know if it's an obsession or a game...or it could be nothing... I just think you should be wary of him. Has he been by or called?"

"No, not for a while." *You're the only one that's been sending strange messages and—* "Wait. How did you get my number?"

"Your website."

"When?" I ask, my voice coming out in a whisper.

"This morning."

Oh God. Oh God. The messages were from Alex? Not Tate. Does he know?

"How worried do I need to be?" I ask, trying to keep the panic out of my tone.

"I don't know. Maybe he's just pissed that you rejected him and now you're with Jesse."

God, I wish that was it, but I know that it's not. Only thing is, I'm not sure if I trust Tate enough to tell him that. This could still be a ploy to see if I remember or to find out if Jesse's told me.

"Okay. Thank you for letting me know," I say with an unwavering voice.

"I'm sorry, Willow. I really hope it's nothing."

"Thanks. Me too."

With that, he hangs up and I'm left reeling. *What the hell is going on? I have no idea what to believe.*

I'm staring into space, my mind racing with too much information, when my alarm goes off, telling me I'm late. *Shit.* Slipping into my shoes, I grab my bag and race out of the house, only remembering halfway there that I left my lunch on the counter.

The work phone's ringing as I unlock the door, and after dropping everything and running, I manage to pick it up just in time.

"Audrey's Gifts and Homeware. This is Willow."

"You made it," Sara says with a light chuckle.

"Are you checking up on me?" I huff out, catching my breath.

"I'm not, but I just passed your mom on her way to you and wanted to give you the heads-up."

My shoulders drop as my head falls back with a groan. That's all I need right now. I should be calling Jesse. "Thank you. It's always better to be prepared when it comes to my Mom," I say, pushing the Tate issue out of my mind until I have more time to process it.

"At the risk of pissing you off... Can you cut her a little bit of slack?"

"What?"

"She thought she lost you. Twice. I know she's been overprotective and—"

"A bitch. She's been a bitch."

"Okay, yes. She hasn't been particularly nice to you. But she's stressed. She's about to become a grandmother—"

"What's that got to do with anything?"

"I don't know. Maybe she's feeling older all of a sudden. Or nervous for Ashley. I know my pregnancy was stressful, and the only person that knew, other than Grant, was my mom."

"Okay."

"I'm not making excuses, just...be nice if she's there to make amends."

The chime at the door rings, and Mom's voice filters through the building. "Willow?"

"She's here. I better go, and I will."

"Thank you."

"I'm here," I call out as I hang up the phone, waiting for Mom to reach the counter. Sometimes, I hate having a long, skinny shop, but then an image of Jesse pushing me against the back wall hits my mind and my heart races. Maybe it's not so bad having a blind spot.

I hear Mom mumbling to herself and I roll my eyes. By the time she reaches me, she has a hesitant smile. "It's nice to see you actually working," she says, her lips pursing. "Poor Sara's been worked to the bone."

Of course, she'd point out my flaws. She was always hard on me, but there was a time when we had a great relationship. I'm not even sure what went wrong. "I already feel the guilt; I don't need you adding to it. Hi, by the way."

"Hi to you too. I didn't think we said 'hi' anymore. You practically bowled me over last week without even acknowledging it."

Jesus. "I did? Mom, I promise, I didn't see you."

"Oh, I know. You're busy, busy," she mocks. "You must love spending time with Pippa, since you're always there."

"She's my sister. Of course, I love it."

"What else do you love about the city?"

"A few things, but I don't love it all. I'm sorry, did you come by for something?"

"Yes! I came by to see my daughter. The daughter of mine that seems to have disappeared off the radar."

"You told me not to visit until I had an attitude change." *Yep, that happened.*

"Well, then you should have had an attitude change!"

What the... "This is me, Mom. This person is *me*." I point to my chest, pissed off that I have to—once again—explain myself. "I can't go back to pretending. Please don't make me do that."

"It's him, isn't it?" *God, what's with today?* I really need to see the photos that are out there. First Tate and Alex saw them, now I'm guessing my Mom has.

"What's wrong? Why do you look pale?"

"I'm just tired. I didn't sleep well last night." In fact, I haven't slept well for weeks. Months even.

"Maybe you need to stay put for a while. All that traveling can't be good. And I hear that the altitude isn't good for your skin. It brings on premature aging."

I can't help but laugh. "I'll keep that in mind. But I can't stop. Not yet. I need to do this. For me."

"What changed? What happened on that mountain that changed you?" she asks, mentioning the mountain for the first time in years.

"I don't know. Have you forgotten that I can't remember?"

"I don't mean back then. I mean now...the other month."

Oh.

"It just made me realize I've been a slave to my circumstance for too long. I decided I needed to live a little. So that's what I'm doing."

"Did it have to change your personality? People have noticed. You're not as friendly anymore. Or helpful. Debbie said she asked if you could watch her shop for an hour and you refused."

"I was on the way to the airport. I would have missed my flight. A flight I didn't pay for."

"This is what I mean. You need to stop. And who's buying your tickets? Pippa?"

"It doesn't matter. I can't change who I am just because the townspeople don't like the person I've become. For *years* they walked all over me." I say "they" rather than "you" because I know she won't take kindly to being included in that group, even though she should be there. She's no better.

Mom huffs anyway. "Honestly, Willow, I just don't know how to deal with you anymore."

My jaw drops because *what the hell?* She doesn't know how to *deal* with me?

"I'm sorry, Mom. I am. I wish I wasn't such a disappointment."

I turn to walk into the back room but Mom stops me. "You're not. I just..." She trails off.

"Just?"

"It's too much."

"Okay, Mom."

She walks away without another word, and I realize she never gave me a reason for her visit. Did she seriously just stop by to attack me?

I'm angry when I hear the door shut, and I use that anger to deal with the Tate and Alex situation. I need to talk to Jesse. I need to know why he wanted me to stay away from Alex.

I'm calling him before I've even decided what to say, and when he answers right away, I sigh in relief, his voice instantly putting me at ease.

"Hi, Jesse. I know I shouldn't be calling on game day, but do you have a minute?"

"First, you can call me anytime you like. Day or night. And if I'm on the ice, and it's urgent, call Seth. Please don't ever hesitate."

I release a slow breath. "Okay. Thank you."

"And second, I have exactly one minute. I'm about to see the team doctor."

My back stiffens as I silently panic. "Why? Everything good?" I ask casually. *It's no big deal.*

Jesse chuckles. "Are you worried about me, Buttercup?"

"No, of course not. But..."

"It's nothing. I've just got to get my blood pressure checked before my games."

That's not nothing. "Like a formality. Do you all do that?" *Please, please be a hockey thing?*

Jesse's silent, giving me my answer without any words. "No more lies."

"I know, but I don't want you to think this is more than it is."

"What is it?"

"It's just stress-related. I've spent my life pushing my emotions down and now I've set them free. Apparently, it's stressful. So my blood pressure is a *little* high."

"How high?"

"They're still letting me play, so doctors aren't worried."

"But high enough to get it checked."

"I'll be fine. The stress is gone. I've got you. We're happy. It should drop any day now."

Unless I tell you about the call from Tate. I saw his reaction last time I mentioned it. He played it down, but I know he was worried. And if I add Alex to the mix... I can't.

"Okay, that's good. I'm glad it's getting better, but I'm sorry for my part in that."

Jesse growls, making me laugh. "You're not allowed to blame yourself for this, Willow. Only for the good."

"If you say so."

"I fucking do."

Damn him. That gruff tone gets me every time.

"Shit. They're waving me in. We didn't get to talk about what you needed."

"Just wanted to hear your voice," I lie, even though we said we wouldn't.

Jesse laughs. "Which voice?"

"Definitely the growly one."

"Figures. I'm finally nice to someone and she doesn't want it."

"Shut up," I snap.

"Mmm...yeah, I see the appeal."

I burst out laughing until I remember why I really called and my smile fades. "I better let you go do your thing," I say, keeping my voice light. "See you soon?"

"Definitely."

I try unsuccessfully to push Tate out of my head, but he's freaking wedged himself there, like a song that gets stuck on repeat in your mind. An annoying one. One that makes you want to scream.

I'm not good at staying silent. I know how it feels to be on the other end, and it pains me to do it. But I can't tell Jesse now. He's mentioned his contract concerns. Surely, a high blood pressure reading isn't good for that.

I'm antsy all morning, moving around, cleaning things that have already been cleaned, rearranging things that don't have to be changed, but none of it helps. I need to tell someone.

I grab my phone to call Sara but stop myself before I dial. The last thing I need is more people worrying about me. I'm sure it's nothing. It will be fine. I'll be fine. There's nothing I can do but wait.

38
Willow

Even though I'm desperate to see Jesse, and would love to disappear again to annoy my mom, I stay home, giving Sara some time off.

It kills me not seeing him, but at the same time, I'm nervous that if I do, he'll be able to tell something's wrong. And I don't even know if I need to be worried. It's been a week and nothing. I've been here and Alex hasn't shown or called. Maybe Tate's wrong. Or lying. *Or they're both just messing around?* If I tell Jesse, I'm potentially stressing him out for no reason. And I can't risk that. I just have to go on with my life. Yet again, pretending I'm fine.

Jesse calls the night before every game, and every time I ask him the same question. "How's your blood pressure?"

I'm like a broken record and he pretends to hate it, but deep down I know he likes that I care.

When he tells me it's almost back to normal, his normal anyway, I take that as a sign that I did the right thing. Telling him about Tate would have only caused unnecessary stress since Alex has been silent. They both have.

But I still feel guilty about it.

After spending another week apart, Jesse calls me late at night, as I'm getting into bed. His tired face lights up my screen, and a sharp pang hits me, making me feel homesick.

I'm in my own bed, in my own house, and I feel homesick. Something has to change.

"Hey you," he says with a grin, running his hand through his hair as he lies down, holding the phone in the air. "I miss you."

"God, I miss you too. But you should be sleeping."

"I know. But I just got to the point where I couldn't do this anymore and needed to lock something down."

I start nodding before he's even finished because I like this plan. I just have to hope Sara doesn't mind. "Yes, please," I say quickly. "I need to see you. And not through a screen."

Jesse's face lights up as though there was a chance I'd say no and he smiles. "Good, I have a proposal for you," he says and then grimaces. "I mean, not a proposal, proposal. I wouldn't do that over the phone. Maybe proposition is the right word?"

I bark out a laugh so he realizes that's not much better, but instead of continuing he just stares at me until I stop.

"God, you're beautiful," he whispers. "And fuck, I wish I was there," he says louder, making me laugh again.

"Come on." I move on because of my inability to take compliments. "Tell me your idea—it doesn't matter what you call it."

"Okay. Okay. I'm playing in New York next week and have a day off after the game. I want you to come with me. As my girlfriend."

"To New York?" Butterflies attack my chest. *New York. Girlfriend.* I'm not sure which one I'm more afraid of or excited about.

"Yes, New York. We'd have to meet there, but I want you to come to my game and then I want to show you around the city. I've been a couple of times, so while I'm no expert, I'm sure I can cover the basics—Eiffel Tower, Statue of Liberty, Buckingham Palace."

Laughter bursts out of me. The contrast between this Jesse and the one I first met is astounding. "You know only one of those things is in the US, right?"

"What?" he mocks horror as I shake my head, biting back another grin.

"You know, I kind of like this version of Jesse too. Feel free to alternate between both."

Jesse smirks, and I know what's coming. "Willow, my love. I'm inviting you on an adventure with me," he says sweetly before his face morphs into something a little Alpha. "And I am not taking no for an answer."

"That'll do it. When and where?"

Jesse laughs but it's softer than I would have expected. "Not soon enough."

Guilt hits me like a gut punch and I frown. "I'm sorry, I should have visited sooner. I just—"

"Nope," Jesse says sternly, cutting me off, his expression telling me he's serious. "We knew what this was when we started. It's going to be hard, and I'm going to be constantly whining about it, but I'm never upset at you. Just the situation."

"We've never talked about it," I say, the realization only just hitting me.

"You're right, but that's because I didn't think there was much we could change right now."

"Right now?"

"You've got your business, and I've got hockey. But I can come to you during the offseason, and I'll be retiring in a few years, *if* they re-contract me. It's not forever."

"When you say you'll be retiring, you mean...?"

"I won't be playing anymore, so I can come to you."

My jaw drops so low, I almost have to lift it off the floor.

Jesse chuckles. "Why is that so hard to believe?"

"Because you hate this town and everything it reminds you of."

"Wrong. I hate Mossman Hills and *almost* everything it reminds me of. Anyway, this has only just begun. Who knows where life will take us."

My stupid eyes water, and I scrunch my face to hide them. But fail.

Jesse smiles sympathetically. "I mean together," he says reassuringly. "Who knows where life will take us *together*."

"I knew that," I lie.

"How did this become a sad conversation? We're supposed to be talking about New! York! City!" He punctuates each word with a hand gesture, making me smile again.

"You're right, and I'd love to come. I can't wait."

Having a set date to see Jesse is almost worse than not knowing when I'll next see him. The anticipation kills me, and by the time the day arrives, I'm a nervous wreck. Especially considering the Tate and Alex issue I have hanging over my head.

"You all set?" Jesse asks as I wait to board my flight from Seattle, after a short layover.

"I am," I half lie. I'm definitely ready to see him, but I'm not sure I'm ready for all that it entails. "I can't believe you're taking me to New York," I add with a smile. "I didn't think I'd go there in my lifetime."

"Technically I'm not *taking* you to New York, and I hate that. But I've arranged a car for you when you get here, and Pippa will meet you at the game."

"Thank you. It's a shame Pippa won't be able to actually sit and watch with me," I say softly. "She said she'd be working."

"She is, but the other wives are lovely, and—"

"Yes, of course." I cut him off, trying to keep the worry out of my voice. "I can't wait."

Flight 348 to New York City is now boarding. Please make your way to gate 12.

"They've just called my flight to board. I better go."

"Wait! Ah, before you go. I have a jersey for you. Two, actually. One with my name, one without. They're both yours and," he trails off and I picture him running a hand through his hair, "you can wear either. I know having my name on the back is a big deal and—"

"Jesse?" I cut him off, ending his concern. "I'll wear your name. I want to." *In fact, I'm feeling kind of giddy about it.*

"Okay," he says quietly, unable to hide his happiness. "Thank you. I'll see you soon."

Who knew the jersey thing was such a big deal.

When I finally arrive, I push open the door to our room and freeze at the sight. I've never seen anything so opulent. Smaller than the room I had in Los Angeles but so much grander. The floor-to-ceiling windows light the elegant but eclectic space, brightening the red and making the gold sparkle. The bed looks like it could fit an extra two people, and there's even a small Jacuzzi under the side window. Something that has me both nervous and excited.

In fact, this room has everything, except Jesse. There's no presence of him at all. I assumed we'd be spending the night together, but maybe he has to stay with the team? I didn't even ask. I really need to learn more about hockey.

When I walk into Madison Square Garden later that afternoon, Pippa's waiting for me exactly as planned. "I only have ten minutes to get you to your seat," she says, waving her hand in the direction we need to walk. "But I'll introduce you around and check on you during the game."

I nod as my stomach fills with butterflies, despite this being the least of my worries right now. *I can do this.* No one knows me here, and I'm not the same broken girl anymore. *I can do this.*

After finishing her duties and introducing me to the women sitting on either side of me, Pippa rushes off, and something doesn't feel right. She didn't even smile, and her voice lacked any kind of feeling.

I peer over my shoulder to check on her, and find her running back down the steps, calling my name as she goes. "I almost forgot. Your jersey."

She throws me a jersey and it unfolds as I catch it, the name Hastings in bold letters across the back. My stomach churns as my nerves worsen, but the second I put it on, everything changes. My *energy* changes, and a proud feeling comes over me as my worries float away. I'm Jesse's girl. He's mine. And he wants me to wear this. I *can* do this. I will.

Nothing else matters while I'm here. In this stadium, supporting my man.

I can't talk to Pippa. Tate isn't here. I haven't heard from Alex. I can focus on all of that later. Right now, it's about hockey.

By the time the game ends, I'm a shattered mess. Not because I'm uncomfortable being here, but because of the game itself. Jesse's team won, but they won during something called a shootout, and *my God*, was that nerve-racking.

"I wish I could tell you you'll get used to that," the goalie's wife, Lauren, says from beside me. While we didn't speak much during the game, she's been warm and welcoming when we have.

"I don't even know if I could go through that again. I don't think I've ever held my breath for that long."

"It feels like you're a part of it, doesn't it?" she asks with a genuine smile.

"It does." I grimace. "Is that weird? All I did was cheer him on, but I feel like I won with them."

Lauren laughs. "Not at all. We all feel the same and the guys love it."

I smile back at her until her face drops as she glances over my shoulder. "This is the first time you're going public, right?"

"What do you mean?" I ask, puzzled.

"I mean, until today, Jesse was single. Apart from the rumors. This is the confirmation that he's not."

"Oh." *God, I didn't even think of that. Is that bad?* "Yes, I guess that's correct. Did I do something wrong?"

Lauren gasps as she reaches out for my arm, giving me a comforting squeeze. "No, of course not. You just have a few not-so-happy admirers glaring at you."

"I what?" I spin around without thinking, and sure enough, there is a group of girls staring at me with scowls on their faces, talking behind their hands, undoubtedly asking "why her?" or worse.

"Block it out. If you and Jesse are serious, that's never going away."

"*Block it out.*" That's something I'm kind of an expert on. I plaster a smile on my face and turn back to the women, giving them a wave.

Lauren bursts out laughing. "Jesse did good. I have a feeling I'm going to be seeing you around for years to come."

My skin heats and I feel my cheeks turning pink. "Thank you. I'm out of my comfort zone for all of this," I comment, gesturing toward the ice. "But that?" I say, referring to the women. "That's nothing new."

A frown dampens Lauren's smiley features but she recovers quickly. "That really sucks, but at least you're prepared. Maybe you won't break down and almost run away like I did." She smiles and stands up, brushing her hands over her tailored pants. She's dressed beautifully. In fact, they all are. I need to rethink my hockey wardrobe.

"I'm heading to the Wives' room," Lauren tells me as we both stand. "Do you want to come? You're allowed in if I invite you," she adds, pointing behind us. *Wives' room?* God, what is this life? The thought of mingling has my body shivering, so I politely decline, opting to wait for Pippa to come and collect me.

I'm not sure I'll ever get used to this, but I don't hate it either.

And God, is my man like fire on the ice. I definitely want more of that.

Just like I knew she would, Pippa arrives as the crowd starts to clear, her somber mood still in place. "Come on, I'll take you to see Jesse," she says, turning away without a hello, making me pull her to a stop.

"What's going on? Are you okay?"

Pippa stares at me for a second before a smile lights up her face. "Of course, I'm fine. You know me."

"I do know you, and you're not fine. Sit down. Talk to me."

I sit down, but Pippa stays standing. "You don't have time for this. Come on."

"Sit! I know I've been stuck in the middle of my own problems lately—or I guess for years if I'm being honest—but I'm still here for you."

"I'm freaking out," she says, dropping into the seat next to me. "I don't know what I'm doing with Ryan. I'm not good at relationships. I'm selfish. I don't think sometimes. It won't be long before he figures that out and leaves."

Oh God. "Has something happened?"

"No, not yet. I'm waiting."

My heart aches. This is Pippa. When things get too serious, or hard, she runs, and no one has ever stopped her. No one has even been on her side. It started back with Jonah. She thinks no one knows, but I know. I saw it. She broke up with him to protect her heart. She could see he had feelings for Ashley. And like she's saying now, it was only a matter of time.

That's why I can't stand him. He's been bad news since he first came into our lives.

But Ryan's different. At least I hope he is. He just needs to prove it.

"Have you told Ryan how you feel?"

"I've done that with past relationships. It never works."

"Pippa—"

"Nope, I'm just being silly. I guess I'm not as strong as you. I'll be fine." She jumps up again, but I grab her wrist to still her.

"I'm not strong, Pippa. I'm terrified. Every single day. But Jesse knows that, and he's helping me. You need to talk to Ryan. Please."

"Maybe. Come on."

She pulls me along without another word, and when we meet up with the guys, she hugs Ryan like she's just as fine as she says she is, only it's obvious something's off. And from the look on Ryan's face, even he notices.

But as Jesse pulls me into his arms, I let it go. I've got too much on my mind right now. And it's time I focused on me.

39

Jesse

Willow's waiting for me after the game, and it shocks me how much it hits me in the gut. Game after game, I've seen the wives, girlfriends, and kids waiting for their men, and I've never wanted it for myself. There's been no longing, no jealousy. I was happy with my solitary life. But as Willow stands hesitantly, her arms clasped in front of her, unsure of how to act in this very new situation, it hits me.

I want this.

I want someone to come home to, someone to care for, someone to love. I want a family. My first family. And I don't mean I suddenly want two point five kids and a golden retriever. I want Willow as my family. But God, that's fast moving.

I need to slow down before I scare her away.

I've been thinking about her since I was fourteen, but to her, it's only been months. I need to take my time.

"If it isn't my good luck charm," I say when I reach her, wrapping my arms around her waist.

She lifts to her toes, before palming my chest as she leans back to look in my eyes. "And how did you come to that conclusion? You've won plenty of games without me."

"Yes, but I scored three times."

Her nose scrunches as she tries to remember the third goal. "The third one's tonight," I say like a corny motherfucker, making her laugh.

"Seriously, who are you?"

"Apparently, this is what happy Jesse looks like."

"Quite a contrast to the guy I just watched slamming grown men into the wall."

Now it's my turn to chuckle. "There's definitely two of me."

"And I happen to like them both," she says, wrapping her arms around me before running her fingers through the hair at the base of my neck, making me shiver. "What happens now?"

I almost say bed, because I'm wrecked, and just the sight of her has my pants tightening, but I promised her New York, so I'm going to deliver.

"We'll drop off my bags and then I'm taking you to a late dinner."

"Don't you need sleep?"

"We'll get there. I've got plans for you before then."

Her eyes darken as she bites her lips, and I have to close my eyes to block it out. *Dinner, Jesse.* She needs a New York meal.

Willow giggles, undoubtedly sensing my inner musings, and I give up. "What about a quick dinner? We can play tourist tomorrow."

"Deal."

As we walk away, her eyes flash back to the players still hovering behind us before she looks around in all directions, her brow furrowing.

"Is everything okay?" I ask, pulling her gaze back to mine, concern settling in my chest.

"Yeah. Yes. It's just Pippa. I'll tell you about it another time."

I nod in understanding. It's time to focus on us right now. Still, I make a note to check in later.

After being wined and dined at one of New York's famous Italian restaurants, I'm not in as much of a rush to get to the room as I thought I'd be. "Do you want to walk back? We could detour through Times Square."

Willow's face lights up and I know the answer before the breathless "yes" leaves her lips.

After linking our fingers, I stare down at the connection, huffing out a small laugh. It wasn't long ago that this would have made my skin crawl, but now it gives me a different feeling, a feeling of warmth.

"Is this okay?" Willow asks, when she notices my gaze.

I lift our joined hand to my lips and kiss her fingers, smiling against her skin. "With you it is. It's better than okay."

"Do you think..." she trails off, nibbling her lip, hesitating.

"What? You can say anything. No holding back, remember?" She stares up at me with wide eyes and my chest tightens. "What is it?"

"I...I was just going to ask about the touch thing."

A nervous chuckle escapes me. For some reason I expected worse. For as good as this all feels, I'm still expecting something to fuck it up. I can't be this lucky after everything I've done.

"Go ahead. I'll tell you anything you want to know."

"I know now why you don't like it. But I guess, I'm wondering...are you cured?" She shakes her head with a grimace. "No, that's not the right word. God, I'm sorry." She disconnects our hands and covers her face, trying to hide away.

"Willow," I say, pulling her hands from her face. "I know what you're asking. It's okay." She smiles but it's forced. "Nope, you're not allowed fake smiles anymore, remember?"

"Yeah, about that..." she trails off and I raise an eyebrow. "Don't worry, I'm not about to tell you I've been faking this whole time."

"Oh, I know." I chuckle. "I've always known the difference."

"That you have." She frowns, and if I didn't know her better, I'd think that was a bad thing, but I'm sure she's just thinking about everything we've been through, and the fact that I've known her longer than she's known me. I can't even imagine how she feels.

"Anyway." She shakes her head and smiles. "I'm not retiring the fake smile; I'm keeping it in my pocket so I can bring it out whenever I have to deal with your fans."

"My fans?" My brow furrows until realization hits. "What the hell happened? Did someone say something?"

Willow laughs, pulling me into a hug. "Easy there. No one said anything. I just realized that people aren't going to be happy about you being off the market. With me."

Fuck. I didn't even think about that. I'm such an asshole. "Willow..."

"Honestly, I'm fine. I've been talked about behind my back for half my life. I've got a tough skin."

"No, you don't. You pretend to have a tough skin. But it's soft, smooth, and beautiful, and I don't want anyone to mess with it." I press a kiss to her forehead, letting my lips linger as I speak. "If you don't want to come to games anymore, I understand. It's just another hurdle for us to get through, but I know we can handle anything."

"I'm coming to more games. It's kind of addicting. And I like knowing that they're jealous, because you're mine."

"Good." I smile. "Because seeing you there in my jersey did something to me." I bite my fist as I groan, making Willow burst out laughing.

"Best we get back to the room then. And fast."

"You don't have to ask me twice."

***

While at first, we hurry, when we reach Times Square, we slow back down, drinking in the atmosphere, getting lost in the crowd. At midnight, Times Square still looks like rush hour. There are kids running around, friends gathering or heading out for the night, and noise. So much noise.

"This is incredible," Willow gushes. "A little overwhelming, but incredible. You'd think it was the middle of the day," she adds, her eyes wide with wonder as she spins around, taking it all in. "Thank you. For giving me this moment. I never would have experienced it without you."

I smile as I watch her, not wanting to interrupt, and it's then that I vow to show her the world. She deserves every bit of happiness, and I'm going to give it to her.

"The hotel's not too far, right?" she asks, moving beside me. "We should go."

"Take all the time you want, Willow." *We've got forever.*

"I'm ready," she says, linking our fingers. "I'm ready for bed."

I swear we act like two school kids after that, laughing as we power walk to the hotel, dodging people like it's some kind of emergency. Although maybe it is.

When we reach the elevator we pause, trying to maintain our composure, but as soon as we're in and the doors close, Willow jumps into my arms, slamming her lips to mine. She kisses me with such fervor that I have to fight not to press the stop button. I need her and I need her now.

The door dings and she springs back, standing as far away from me as physically possible, her gaze locked on the floor, not realizing it's our level.

Clearing my throat, I burst out laughing and grab her hand, pulling her through the doors in the direction of our room. "My innocent little Buttercup," I say as she laughs, covering her face in her hands.

"I thought someone was about to get on."

"Oh, I know. Come on, we're here."

As soon as we're inside, Willow's embarrassment subsides with both of us frantically stripping, wordlessly heading in the same direction—the Jacuzzi.

Left in nothing but a thong, Willow leans over to start the water, and the sight she leaves me with is so breathtaking that I can't help myself. I drop down behind her, running my tongue through her heat.

She gasps at the sensation but lowers her chest to the tub, holding on tightly as she opens herself up, giving me a better angle.

The perfect angle. *And fuck...the view.*

After dragging her thong down her legs, I circle my tongue around her core and roll her hips, doubling the pleasure as my stubble rubs against her. She cries out and takes over the movement, rocking back and forth on her own, taking what she needs.

I release a guttural groan as precum pools at my tip, and a tightness fills my chest. Everything about this woman makes me want her even more. Love her even more. And I will never get enough.

By the time the Jacuzzi's full, Willow's screaming my name, wriggling against my face as her orgasm rips from within her.

She catches her breath while I lean over her to switch off the tap, before helping her stand, her legs unstable after my attack.

"Fuck, you're glorious when you come apart like that...with your flushed cheeks and beautiful smile." I bite back another groan as I stare into her eyes.

Instead of shying away from the compliment, a wicked grin lights up her face and she drops to her knees, grabbing my cock before I've had a chance to register it. She wraps her lips around me in one swift movement, and then, in a move reminiscent of when she wanted me to admit my feelings, she grabs my ass and holds me still, swallowing my length until I hit the back of her throat, choking back her tears.

"Fuck, Willow," I rush out, my voice breathless. "You...you don't have to do this."

She pulls away with a pop, glancing up at me as her tongue flattens against my tip. "What if I want to?" she whispers, making my cock jump as I nod, no longer able to form words.

With one hand wrapped around my base, she works me until my legs start shaking, her eyes locked on mine, making sure I know she's in control. Her expression alone has my balls tightening, but when she circles my tip with her tongue, while squeezing my length, I'm done for.

"Willow, I—"

She sucks me again until I cry out her name, filling her mouth as she moans.

Goddammit. "Willow."

Dropping down beside her, I wrap her in my arms and pull her on top of me, pressing a kiss to her head.

"God, you're amazing," I whisper against her hair, smiling when she starts to giggle.

"Is it bad that I love that?" she asks with a slight flinch. "I love watching you lose control, knowing I'm the one that's doing it."

I bark out a laugh and shake my head. "I mean, it makes me nervous, but it's not completely *bad.*"

She sits up and shoves at my chest. "You better be ready; I am going to control *everything.*" Her lips pull into a smirk before she loses it and laughs, making me chuckle with her.

"It feels so easy here and now. With you," she says, turning serious. "We have such a messed-up past, but it just feels... I don't know."

"Right?" I ask.

"Yes, right. But so much more than that."

She snuggles into me again and we stay like that for a moment, both lost in thought, curled up on the cold tiles, the Jacuzzi abandoned.

When she starts to shiver, I lift her up and take her to bed, positioning her so she's resting on top of me.

She breathes out a contented sigh, and I smile against her hair. She's right. *This is so much more than that.* And I want to share everything with her.

"I didn't get to answer you before," I whisper, running my hand through her hair as her fingers glide over my naked chest.

"Mmm," she mumbles, leaning back to glance up at me through her lashes, her messy hair dancing across her face.

"I'm not cured." I pause, brushing her hair to the side, my eyes focused on the strands instead of her face. "I still don't like people touching me," I admit. "It still sends shivers through my body and has my chest tightening. But with you, and to a point with those that I trust, it's different."

"Why do you think that is? Why was it different with me?"

I take a deep breath, ready to say my theory out loud for the first time. "Because you were there before."

"What?" She sits up with a pinched expression on her face.

"When I was bruised or aching, I hated people getting close to me because I didn't want them to see me flinch or question my reaction. And to prove my point, I flinched the first time you touched me. It was more reactive back then. But after that night...the last time, it became a mental reaction as well as a physical one. I didn't want anyone to touch me, period." I shudder just thinking about it now.

"But Willow, I'd kissed you *before* that night. Yours was the only positive touch I'd *ever* had, ever allowed, and I guess my body never forgot that." I shrug while Willow sucks her lips into her mouth, fighting back tears.

"I may not remember what I felt back then," she whispers, running a finger down my cheek, her eyes following the movement until the next words leave her mouth. "But I know how I feel *now*. I love you, Jesse. More than I ever thought was possible. When I think of you, my heart feels so full it could burst, and I'm sorry it took me so long to say it. Because you are the only one for me. I felt it even before I knew anything about you. This connection—I knew it was real. I've just been so terrified of how big it is. But I love you. So much."

My world shifts as though something finally clicks into place, sending my heart racing.

I knew. I knew she loved me, but hearing it... *fuck*. "I'm so fucking in love with you. Come here."

Crawling into my lap, Willow sinks her hands into my hair and smiles as her eyes continue to glisten. "I'm in love with you too."

40
Willow

My shoe sinks into mud as I leap to the edge of the water, but it doesn't matter. The view on this side of the stream is worth it. There are only two places you can safely see the horizon on this part of Mt. Beauty, and this one tells me we're halfway.

Jade sighs from behind me, her patience running thin today. Not that she'll talk to me about it. "Why are you so slow?" she cries out in frustration.

"We come here all the time. Why are you in such a hurry? What's different about today?"

She ignores me and keeps walking, not even bothering to check if I'm following.

"God, what's your problem?" I grumble, mostly to myself since she's too far away to hear me. But when I catch up, she's getting a piece of my mind.

I wake with a start to find Jesse's side of the bed empty and light streaming under the bathroom door.

My heart races as I try to calm my breathing. Another nightmare, only this time I know it's not real because I never would have snapped at Jade like that.

Never. It's just my stupid conscience wanting me to feel bad now that I know the truth.

I sit up groggily and call out, but he can't hear me over the running water.

Throwing one of his tees over my head, I walk toward the room and knock on the door, cautiously entering when I don't get a response.

"Jesse," I call out again with my eyes closed. "Is it okay if I come in?" I normally wouldn't be worried about surprising him, but since a big part of his trauma took place in a bathroom, I don't want to surprise him in here.

Jesse chuckles as the shower door opens, but before I've had a chance to look, a wet arm wraps around me as he pulls me into his hold. "Whatcha doin', Buttercup?" He laughs.

"I just..." I don't know what to say, but all it takes is for him to look into my somber eyes and he knows.

"Thank you." He smiles softly. "But I'm fine. Bathrooms hold much more positive memories for me now," he says with a wink, making me blush.

"Okay. I...ah...had another dream," I say, changing the subject.

Jesse pauses with his hand in the air as he reaches for a towel. "And?"

"They're definitely nightmares. I should have known."

"I'm sorry, Willow. I really wish that hadn't been the case."

"I don't. I'm okay with it. It's just going to take a bit of getting used to. But I'm ready for New York. What are our plans?"

Jesse ponders that for a second before listing off his ideas. "Rockefeller Center. Magnolia Bakery. Central Park. Brooklyn Bridge. The High Line. Empire State Building. And...one more thing."

I bark out a laugh. "There is no way we are going to fit all that in. We only have the day."

"Care to wager on that?"

Huh? "Jesse Hastings, I didn't know you were a gambling man."

"I'm usually not." He chuckles. "But I'd love to get something from you."

"Okay, if I win, I get a full box of cupcakes at Magnolia Bakery. If we get there." I laugh.

"Come on, aim higher. You've got the world."

In that case, I think about it, and smile when an idea pops into my head.

"Fine. I want a private jet," I joke, when what I really mean is... *a way out of Hepburn Falls.* "And I want a runway near both our houses," I add, because it's true. That would make life so much easier.

A smile lights up his face and he bounces his eyebrows. "Maybe I should lose?"

I huff out a laugh and flick his ear before walking away.

"Just kidding," he calls out. "I can't wait to have some phone sex."

"You're betting that? You could have just asked."

"Would you have done it?" he questions, and I actually have to think about it. Maybe I would have. Although maybe I wouldn't.

Jesse laughs at my silence, patting my back as he walks out of the bathroom. "Come on, you've got five minutes to get ready. We have a big day ahead."

By lunchtime, I realize Jesse's going to get me on a technicality. He plays dirty. We never specified how long we'd be spending at each place, and so far, we've driven past the Empire State Building and over Brooklyn Bridge, twice. We've walked under Rockefeller Center to get cupcakes at Magnolia Bakery and now we're on our way to Central Park.

"You know, I haven't really seen any of the things you mentioned," I say as we wait at a light to cross the road. "For a star athlete, I'm surprised you condone cheating."

"Don't worry your beautiful face. You're going to have a great day."

I know he's right because I'm already having fun. *But still...technicality.*

When we finally enter Central Park, I feel like the world stops. It's so strange to think that we're still in

Manhattan, surrounded by the hustle and bustle, as I look around me, seeing the abundance of nature.

"Now it's time to slow down," Jesse says, physically slowing his walking. "I thought we could make our way to the lake and have lunch by the water," he adds, linking our hands as we go.

"Sounds perfect." I smile.

We walk in silence as I breathe it all in. I practically live in nature, but this feels different, more romantic or something. And so much bigger than I ever pictured it to be.

"Do you have a horse and carriage ride planned?" I ask as we pass by, smiling at a little girl as she beams in happiness.

"Absolutely not," Jesse says quickly, dragging me in the opposite direction, making me bark out a laugh.

"Did I just find out your weakness? Are you afraid of horses?" I will never tire of learning new things about Jesse, the good, the bad...

"Absolutely not," he repeats but shivers, giving himself away.

"It's nothing to be ashamed of. I just thought you were made of stone; nothing scares you."

He stops suddenly, his gaze turning serious. "Losing you scared the hell out of me. I may spend a lot of time on the ice, but I'm not completely frozen."

Oh my heart.

Lifting to my toes, I press a chaste kiss to his cheek before curling my arm around his waist and snuggling against his chest. Jesse doesn't react to any of it, but as we continue our stroll, he groans and I feel his head shake.

"One of the fuckers kicked me when I was a kid. They're nasty."

I burst out laughing again, and Jesse chuckles along with me. "Good to know. Best we don't visit Sara's ranch."

It takes a good thirty minutes to reach the lake, since we're not in a hurry—*only one thing left to check off Jesse's list*—but by the time I get there, I'm starving and in desperate need of some water.

"Why don't you stay here and enjoy the view? I'll see if I can get a table at the Boathouse restaurant."

"See? You didn't book?"

"I did not."

"Why don't we just order something to go and sit on the grass? That line looks massive."

"It's highly likely that's the takeout line. I'm told it's always busy around here."

"Is there a backup?" I ask, looking around for other options.

"Yeah, there's a few, or we could get food delivered."

"Delivered to Central Park?"

He shrugs and I huff out a laugh until I realize he's serious. *What is this world he lives in?*

"No, that's okay. Let's just keep moving."

"Let me at least check first. I like it here." Jesse points at the grass patch I'm standing on and kisses my head. "Don't move. I'll be back." He runs off in the direction of the Boathouse, shooting a glance over his shoulder as he reaches the door.

I consider walking closer to the lake to see if he notices, but the view here is good enough, and I'm better placed to people watch.

So that's what I do.

Jesse's gone for a while, and I'm lost in the moment when I hear my name being called. I turn toward the sound, but don't see anyone I know, making me laugh to myself. *Wishful thinking that Jesse would be done.*

As I turn back to the water, a little boy rushes past, forcing me to step back and straight onto an uneven path. Because I'm me, my good ankle rolls and I fall, hitting my arm on a nearby rock, bruising instantly.

A few people rush to my aid, but I shake them off as embarrassment coats my skin, opting to stand on my own. "Thank you. Thank you. I'm okay."

I'm waving off the last person, when a figure in the distance catches my eyes, causing the blood to drain from my face.

No, it's not him. It can't be him.

My chest tightens as I struggle to take in air. I'm overreacting. No one knows I'm here. Only Sara does. *It's okay. I'm okay. Jesse's okay.*

The guy turns to face me and I breathe out a sigh of relief. It's not Alex. Tate's made me paranoid again and I need to relax.

I've just managed to calm myself down when I receive a text that makes me sick to my core.

Unknown: I wonder what would happen to Jesse if anyone learned his dark secrets. Do you think it would ruin his career? His life? We need to talk.

The world around me fades as I stare down at the screen, hoping more than anything that it's my imagination. That the text is about to disappear. But it doesn't.

Burying the phone in my pocket, I heave a few times to get air into my lungs, but I still can't breathe. I feel like I'm choking. He can't know. Tate wouldn't have told him. Unless they're doing this together. But why? Why would Tate want to hurt Jesse after all these years?

Shit. Shit. Shit. A chill runs down my spine as I face the real possibility that one of them might be dangerous. *But what the hell do I do?*

Jesse gets back while I'm absentmindedly rubbing my arm, my thoughts focused on my nausea. But by the time I register he's there, I'm too late to hide my fear, and Jesse's eyes darken in an instant.

"What happened?" he says, dropping a bag to the ground as he gently grabs my arm, staring at my obvious bruise. "Did someone hurt you?"

He grabs my face next, his eyes bouncing between mine, and it's that panic I see that reconfirms I'm doing the right thing. If I told him about Tate, Alex, or the text, I have no doubt he'd worry, or worse, hunt Alex down.

"I'm okay. I fell. I'm just a little embarrassed."

"Are you sure?" he croaks out, emotion coating his words.

"I'm sure." I smile, covering his hands with mine. "I promise. Is that food?" I say, lighting up to distract Jesse, making him laugh.

"Yeah, there are some benefits to being famous."

"Some?" I giggle. "I bet there are many."

We move on, and I somehow manage not to think about Alex or Tate for the rest of our afternoon, and as we get closer to nightfall, I'm surprised to find we've made our way back to Rockefeller Center, just in time to watch the sunset.

"Okay, you're forgiven for cheating, though I would have liked to walk the bridge," I say on the way up to the observation deck, excitement building inside me.

Jesse chuckles. "Guess we'll have to come back then."

I smile so wide I'm sure I look funny, but that idea absolutely thrills me.

"Maybe." I shrug, playing it down, just as the elevator stops.

"Maybe?" Jesse laughs, shaking his head. "Lucky for us, this isn't our last stop. We've got the High Line and then one more surprise for tonight. Are you ready?" He waves his hand toward the pinkish sky and bounces his eyebrows.

Linking my arm through his, I step out with a smile. "Lead the way."

41

Jesse

The look on Willow's face as she watches the sunset is truly breathtaking. I can't even tell you what the view looks like, because it's been impossible to take my eyes off her. *For more than just her beauty.*

Fuck, I freaked out today. The rational part of my brain knew she wouldn't have been attacked in broad daylight, and even if she had been, she wouldn't be standing there alone. Someone would be comforting her.

But when I saw her scared expression and the bruise on her arm, all rational thought left me.

Every time I see her in some kind of pain, my mind flashes back to that mountain, to the way I felt as I raced her to safety. To my tight chest as I sat by the road, praying for someone to help her. To the panic that consumed me in the days following, waiting to hear if she'd awakened. I will never get the image of her head crashing against that rock out of my mind. And apparently, it's making me crazy.

If I thought I'd ever move on, I was dead wrong. I've learned that lesson many times. But I'm prepared to live with it forever, knowing she's safe.

"This is perfect, Jesse," Willow says softly, reaching for my hand. "Thank you. I remember why I love sunsets so much."

"When was the last time you watched the sun rise?" I ask, a little nervously. I'm not sure I want to know the answer, especially when Willow scrunches her nose.

"Since you were in town?" she whispers, breaking my heart.

She used to watch them almost every day. It kept her going and brightened her life. What keeps her going now? It's definitely not me; I barely see her.

"I just haven't had the time," she lies. "But I'll get back there."

A feeling of guilt rushes through me, but I push it away. She will get back there. I'll make sure of it. I'm certain it's because she hasn't been sleeping well.

"What's next?" she asks suddenly, changing the subject with a new energy.

"Next stop is close to our hotel, but we have one little detour before then."

After waving down a cab, we drive via the High Line and stop to let Willow step foot on it before racing off. She's right, I am playing dirty—I'm competitive. I can't help it. And I want her to see it all.

"Now it's time for Broadway," I say after the cab drops us off close to our destination, grabbing Willow's hand as we walk in the direction of the theater. The only thing I actually booked.

"We're seeing a show?" Willow gasps, her eyes widening as she once again takes in the magic of our surroundings.

"We are. And not just any show. *The Lion King*. I did some research, and apparently, it's one of your favorite movies."

Willow laughs. "You did some research?"

"Of course." I wink.

"Does this mean you and Pippa are on better terms?"

"She loves me. She's just protective of you. I get it. I feel the same."

With her lips pursed to hide her smile, Willow nods before turning away. "Which way to *The Lion King* then, tour guide?" she asks, pointing in all directions.

"This way," I chuckle, directing her down the street. "It's just around the corner."

As we walk, Willow frowns and I wonder if she's thinking about Pippa. She hasn't mentioned it again, but I can tell something's wrong. "Is everything okay with your sister?" I ask, hesitantly.

Willow's eyes narrow before she huffs out a laugh. "Are you reading minds now?"

"Only yours." I chuckle. "Want to talk about it?"

"She's worried about her relationship. For no reason. She always runs when things get tough, preferring to be on the front foot. And no one's ever stopped her. Even my parents shipped her off to boarding school when she started to rebel. They basically taught her that running away from your problems was the right thing to do. But she won't talk to Ryan about it. And I'm at a loss with how to help her."

"I know that feeling," I say and Willow laughs.

"You're doing okay, Jesse. *I'm* doing okay. Plus, you fought for me. You knew what I needed."

That may be half true but it wasn't easy.

"Do you think Ryan realizes?" I ask, trying to think back to the times I've seen them together.

"He definitely senses something," Willow says, "but I doubt he knows what exactly."

"You never know. Not all the Sanders sisters are good at hiding their feelings."

Willow laughs. "You're right. I'll try and talk to her again."

And maybe I'll talk to Ryan.

It's late by the time the show ends, so when Willow yawns, I abandon my idea to go out for dinner, and grab something on the way back to the hotel instead. We have to be up early for our flights.

"Thank you for today," Willow says, trying to undress herself when were getting ready for bed, looking so tired I almost laugh.

"Here, let me." I rush over and remove her hands, pulling her top over her head slowly, before unclasping her bra. She doesn't protest or thank me; she just watches as I guide her arms into one of my tees, careful not to bump her bruise, before dropping to my knees and removing her shoes and socks, sliding her leggings down her smooth legs.

When I'm done, I pull back the sheets and straighten the pillows before lifting her in my arms and settling her on her side of the bed, tucking her in.

"Well, that was romantic," she says with a grin, her head resting on her hands as she watches me undress.

"You look exhausted. I couldn't very well let you do it yourself. Knowing you, you'd probably fall over and bruise your other arm."

Willow laughs sarcastically as she flicks back the covers, rolling onto my side, making herself comfortable on my pillow.

"I think I might sleep here after that comment," she sasses. "I've noticed you always put me on the same side. Does it help you sleep? Is me being here a deal breaker?"

"It is. But you've got it all wrong. I don't have a side; you do. We just haven't stayed in enough beds for you to notice."

Willow's brow furrows as she stares at me in confusion. "I don't have a side."

"Yeah. You do. Your side will always be farthest from the door. *That's* what helps me sleep."

Knowing she's safe.

With glistening eyes, Willow shuffles back to her side and pats the now empty space next to her. When I crawl in, she curls her body around mine, resting her head on my chest. "I love you, Jesse. Every version of you."

I shake my head, because I know I'm over-the-top sometimes, but Willow stops me, grabbing my chin until my eyes find hers.

"I love that you want to protect me. But I need you to know that I'm also stronger because of you. You'd be surprised what I can do."

"That's where you're wrong," I say, laughing when her mouth drops open in a silent gasp. "I know you can do anything."

My alarm goes off at five a.m. so we can check out early enough to both make our flights. Willow grumbles about needing more sleep, so I leave her for a minute, letting her have the extra time while I pack our things. I wore her out on this trip—in more ways than one. I'm surprised she even stirred enough to complain. Not to mention, I felt her tossing and turning last night, but I'm trying not to be worried.

When we arrive at JFK airport, a strange feeling settles in my gut, and it's more than just having to say goodbye again. I've felt that before, but this is different. It's like something bad is coming and I have no way of stopping it.

Pushing the negativity away, I write it off as my own fears of losing her, and smile, pulling her into a hug. "I'm going to miss you so damn much," I say, not even bothering to hide my pain.

"You've got some phone sex to look forward to," she replies, bouncing her eyebrows, as I burst out laughing.

"That I do, and it's going to be amazing. But when can I see you next?"

Willow's face drops and that old feeling comes back. *Why is this so hard?*

"I don't know," she says, making me frown. "I feel bad leaving Sara, and as the weather cools, we're going to be getting busier with people visiting the slopes."

"I know. I'm sorry. I'm asking a lot."

Willow grabs my hand and intertwines her fingers with mine. "No, you're not. We will make this work. I just have to think of something."

I make a note to check out my schedule to see if I can start visiting her, but don't mention it yet, not wanting to get her hopes up. "We will think of something. It's not just on you." *I'll think of something.*

Since her flight departs first, I walk her to the gate and wait with her until boarding. But when they call her flight, I'm still not ready to let go, always needing just one more minute.

"Call me when you land in Seattle, and again when you get home," I say like an overprotective dad, hoping to make her smile. Only it doesn't work. She's feeling the same way I am.

"I hate this. Maybe I should sell the business?"

"No!" I blurt out a little too quickly, making her scrunch her nose. "What I mean is that I don't want you changing your life for me. It's not forever." And I couldn't live with myself if the decision made her unhappy.

Willow's lips lift into a smile, but it's not real, and I hate that she's walking away on a bad note.

"Let's just talk things through, look at all our options," I say, hoping to ease her mind. "Right now, you need to board a plane and I need a kiss."

"Sorry," she sasses with a fake cringe. "But I have to go."

She turns to walk away, but I grab her wrist, pulling her back against me until she crashes into my arms. "They can wait."

I steal a kiss while she pretends to protest, but the second I caress her bottom lip, she stops, relaxing into my arms.

We're forced to pull apart when we hear the final call, but I don't let her leave until our lips touch one last time.

"I'll be seeing you," she says, walking backward toward the gate, her fingers pressed to her mouth.

"Just try and stop me." I smile until she's gone, and then my heart and body sink to the ground.

The flight home feels never ending, but within an hour of landing, I'm thrown back into the thing I call life, forced to once again push everything else from my mind.

I'm struggling with fatigue after practice, but when I see Ryan moping around, I can't leave it. Not when I know what's wrong.

"Blakey," I call out. "You got time for dinner before you head home?"

Several sets of eyes flash my way, including Ryan's, but I ignore the rest. *Yeah yeah, this is new.*

Ryan nods as though he's unable to talk through his shock, and when he's done getting dressed, he tentatively walks over. "You want to get dinner? Together?" he asks, making me laugh.

"I do. But don't make this weird."

"Yeah. Sure. I won't."

We head to a local diner that the team frequents and sit down in a quiet booth, away from prying eyes.

As soon as we've ordered, I get straight down to business. I'm not good with these things, but I know how to get to the point.

"Is everything okay with Pippa?" I ask, making Ryan gape.

He eyes me suspiciously before he nods. "Yep. We're great."

"Are you really?" I push, holding my stare.

His shoulders drop under my scrutiny and he sighs. "I have no idea. One day things are going well and the next she seems like she has one foot out the door."

"That's because she does."

"What?!"

Shit. I probably shouldn't have worded it that way.

"How do I put this? You haven't done anything wrong. And I shouldn't be telling you this, but as a friend I want to help."

"We're friends?"

"Sure." *Jesus, I'm an asshole.* "Yes, we're friends. And we're likely to be seeing more of each other since we're dating sisters."

"If it lasts."

"Ryan, Pippa's scared. She's never had a lot of people in her corner. She even lost Willow for a while after her accident. She doesn't know how to deal with the fear of losing someone else. You."

"Really?"

"Yes, really." *Fuck.* "You need to fight for her. Show her you're not going anywhere. Make her see that you're in it for the long haul and that you'll always be there for her." I stop short of telling him she has good reason to be scared since he messed things up last time, but I'm sure he knows. Instead I put it in a language he understands. "Convince her that you're a *team*."

Ryan's jaw drops and I get it. I have no idea where all that came from either, but I know it's what she needs. "Got it?" I ask.

"Yes." He nods. "Thank you. I'm new to this relationship stuff, and I just assumed she was getting over me. I've tried to leave her be, but I guess that was the wrong thing to do."

"Relationships are hard, but you've got this. Just make sure she knows how you feel." I am no expert, but I've heard that said many times before.

"Yeah. I will. Thanks, man."

"You're welcome."

We talk about hockey for the remainder of our meal, and don't mention Pippa again. Yet, I have this feeling he's going to step up and be the guy that she needs. She may not have been through what Willow has, but she's been through enough, and she deserves her own piece of happiness.

When I get home, I stare at my empty apartment, my empty walls, my empty life. And for the first time ever, I contemplate retirement. I've had a great career. I've received two personal trophies for my own achievement, and I've come close to winning the cup.

I thought I had it all. I didn't know what I was really missing. And now that I do, it's hard to stay away from her.

Dropping to the couch, I call Seth, needing his always annoying, but always helpful, advice.

"Jesse. How was New York?" he says with a smile in his voice.

"It was perfect," I say quietly. "I could have stayed there forever."

"Ah fuck. Is this call what I think it is?"

I expel a slow, deep breath with a laugh. "How do you always know?"

"Know what?"

"*Everything.*"

"It's my place to know."

"No, it's not. I don't believe that for a second. This is bigger. You don't just know about my career; you know about *me.*"

I've questioned him many times before, most recently on our drive to Hepburn Falls, but for the first time, I don't want to stop until I'm satisfied with an answer.

"I know your foster dad," he says suddenly, without me having to push. "I'm only telling you this now, because I feel like you've changed since meeting Willow, and I don't think this information will affect you like it would have in the past."

Holy Fuck. "Which foster dad? I've had many."

"Cain. Your current one."

While technically I don't have a "current" foster dad since I'm out of the system, Cain and Samantha have continued to check in, and I know they'd be there for me if I ever needed them.

"Okay, so what does that mean? He asked you to look out for me?"

"Among other things."

"What other things?" I snap and then cringe. "Sorry, what things?"

Seth chuckles but I can hear the slight waver in his tone. He's nervous.

"Cain told me what happened back in Mossman Hills. At least, he told me what he *thinks* happened. Since you never spoke to anyone about it, it's only a guess."

Fuck. I feel sick. He could be referring to the abuse alone, but something tells me he's not. Call it intuition or the caution in his tone. But for all these years I thought only Tate and I knew our big secret. *How the fuck did Cain know?*

"I'm not sure what you mean?" I lie.

"Good answer. I'm happy to go on like we never had this conversation, but on the flip side, I'm around if you ever need to talk."

"Yeah. Yeah. I know." I smile through my unease because he definitely knows, and while I probably *should* talk to him about it, that's for another day. "If it puts your mind at ease, I've talked it through with Willow, and I'm good."

She's even convinced me that I should talk to a professional...soon...ish. I've only just spoken about it out loud for the first time; bringing it all up to a stranger is going to take a little while longer.

Seth sighs. "That really helps actually. It's like a weight has been lifted. You're her problem now."

"Fuck off." I laugh, but appreciate his joking. After all, he knows me, and I don't do well with serious talk.

"So, now that's out of the way, hopefully you won't mind me saying you're out of your fucking mind if you think I'm going to let you give up the contract fight when you've been so desperate for it. You will get it. You will be playing for the next few years, and you will be bringing home that cup, wearing that ring. And I'll bet I'm not the only one that feels this way. Before making any rash decisions, ask Willow what she thinks. I guarantee she won't be happy if you give up hockey for her."

"You're such an asshole," I say with absolutely no conviction.

Seth laughs. "That's why you love me."

That, and the fact that he's right, especially after I just told Willow she couldn't give up her store for me.

It's time to make this long-distance bullshit work for us.

42
Willow

"Are you sure you don't mind coming here? I don't want to mess with your routine," I say, biting down on the tip of my nail as I walk to work, holding the phone up to my face. It's only been a week but I miss him. Plus, I could use the sleep. I haven't been sleeping with thoughts of Alex and Tate running through my head. And they haven't even done anything more.

Jesse frowns. "Willow, how many times do I have to tell you? This *isn't* a one-way relationship. I don't expect you to be the only one of us making sacrifices. I've got a meeting this morning and then no game tomorrow, so the timing is perfect."

"But you admit it would be a sacrifice."

"I'm coming. I'll be there by six. I've already chartered a flight. I expect dinner on the table when I arrive." He chuckles to himself and I can't help but laugh at his proud expression. He's all about the jokes now.

"Shut up. Not happening. Also, you chartered a flight?"

"I did, otherwise who knows what time I'd get there. And you love me being an ass."

"I do, when you're here." I pout and he chuckles again.

"Tonight. I'll be there tonight."

"Okay," I whine. "I'll see you here at six. Next time, I want to come to you so I can watch another game."

Jesse smiles and it lights up his entire face. "Really?"

"Yes, really." I roll my eyes. "I'd watch them all if I could."

"I know, I'm just messing with you. Maybe if we schedule ahead of time, you can come to a few more around the US. Like New York."

Ooh, yes. I'll take all the "like New York" that I can get. That's one day—and night—I'll never forget.

"I love you, Jesse. Let's make some plans when you're here."

"Sounds great. And I will never tire of hearing that. I love you too."

By the time he hangs up, I'm at work, already missing his voice.

I've only just had a chance to switch on all the lights when someone enters the shop. I'm not expecting Sara for another hour, so I straighten up and force a smile, trying to ignore the new panic that comes over me every time I have an early or late visitor.

Ashley comes into view, and I almost do a double take. I can count on one hand how many times she's been in here, and all of them have been when she's wanted something.

"I want your crib," she says, getting straight to the point. I'd laugh except that I'm confused.

"My crib?" I ask, looking around the store to see if Sara added a doll's crib to our kids' section. She didn't.

"Mom and I were going through the baby stuff, and we came across your crib. I want it for peanut."

Why would it be *my* crib? Didn't we all use it? And if Mom and Dad bought it, isn't it theirs? "What happened to your crib?"

"Mom sold mine to buy Pippa's, and she sold Pippa's to buy yours. It really is beautiful, and Mom wants me to have it, but Dad says we have to check with you."

Again, why? "Why don't you just buy a new crib?" I ask instead of just saying yes. I didn't even know it existed; I don't need it. "You could probably find something similar."

"We've got a wedding to pay for, and Jonah's not getting as much work as he used to."

I roll my eyes when Ashley turns, but she notices it in her peripheral vision, her expression livid.

"What do you have against Jonah? I get that you took Pippa's side all those years ago, but she broke up with him. She *didn't want him*. It's not like I stole him away from her."

This conversation is a long time coming. I'm actually shocked it's only happening now. And it's about time I got it off my chest.

"Believe it or not, Ashley, but my feelings about Jonah don't stem from either of your relationships. From the day he stepped into our lives, yes, *our* lives, not just Pippa's, our dynamic changed. Maybe you didn't steal Jonah away, but you never hid your feelings for him either. Not from me, anyway. We were a close family, but one by one, he tore us all apart. You drifted when he started dating Pippa, and Pippa was sent away because of drugs. Drugs *Jonah* gave her. She was never the same after that, and neither was our relationship." I realize I'm unleashing a lot on her in one go, and it's probably not a good thing for a pregnant woman, but I'm in too deep now. I have to finish. Meanwhile, Ashley doesn't say a word.

"Mom took sides; she'll never admit it but she did. Almost immediately. And while I never understood it, I also never called her out on it, and I should have. The only person that seems to be immune to Jonah's curse is Dad, but he's not as oblivious as he acts, so I'm sure he's purposely trying to keep the peace."

Ashley continues to stare until I tell her I'm done, and then she screams, "Are you kidding me with this, Willow? You expect me to believe that you've been feeling this way for a decade and never said a thing? I suppose you blame Jonah for Pippa's drinking too?"

"Of course I do! But he's not solely to blame for that one. That was a buildup of everything—Jonah, boarding school, my accident. She wasn't coping and had no one to help her. No one." I give her a pointed look so she knows I mean her as well as everyone else, but she doesn't acknowledge it.

"You should have said something. What's the good of waiting until now?" Her words seem harsh but her tone's softer than usual. She's definitely thinking about my grand speech.

"I didn't say anything back then because I didn't think anyone would listen. Least of all you. You pretty much gave up on me after my accident."

Ashley's shoulders drop and she nods. "I had to," she whispers, shocking me, as tears well in her eyes. "I didn't know what to say. Or how to act around you. I didn't want to say the wrong thing."

Wow, that's the most vulnerable she's ever been with me. But her reasoning sucks. Everyone tiptoed around me, except Pippa. If she hadn't drifted before it happened, she would have known what I wanted. She would have known *me*.

"You can have the crib," I say, instead of getting into a deep and meaningful conversation. "I don't have any plans for it."

Ashley's eyes light up and she actually smiles. "Thank you. I'll look after it, in case you ever want to use it."

"Don't worry about it. You can keep it."

She thanks me again and then we fall into an uncomfortable silence, both of us knowing this is some kind of truce, but nothing groundbreaking.

"I better go," she says when the silence gets too much. "But I really appreciate it. I owe you."

"It's fine. I promise."

She leaves and I count down the minutes until Sara arrives, desperately needing to debrief on that weird conversation. *She had to pull back from me?* What a joke.

Just when I'm expecting Sara to arrive, she calls instead, telling me she's unwell. My guilt hits instantly... Can Jesse and I really keep doing this? Sure, he's starting to come here too, but he could be playing for another three years. I can't do that to Sara, not if I'm driving her to exhaustion.

It turns out to be a quiet day, so I listen to music as I restock the shelves, surprisingly uninterrupted other than a few waves through the window. When it hits four and I still haven't had a customer, I close up early. My heart's not in it anymore. Or maybe it never was and I'm only just realizing it. I enjoy two things about the store these days—Sara and making jewelry. Though, I've only made a few more pieces to add to the collection. Not enough to warrant putting them up for sale yet.

After tidying up around home and prepping dinner, I realize I still have an hour before Jesse arrives, and decide on a jog, needing to work out the weird energy flowing through me.

But the second I set off, I instantly hate the fact that it's the afternoon instead of morning. It feels wrong. And sounds different. I'm not greeted by my usual morning bird calls, there are no farmers about when I hit the open road, no machinery. It's eerily quiet. But it's better than nothing.

I take my usual route, and as I'm nearing the lookout, like always, I picture myself up there, the wind blowing through my hair, the warm air on my skin, the view. It's been a while since I watched the sunset in Hepburn. But today's not the day to start again.

I turn around to go back in the same direction when someone calls my name, and it's a voice I've come to recognize, a voice I haven't heard for a while.

Bile rises in my throat as I spin on my heel, my eyes locking on Alex, a smile on his face.

"I've been looking for you," he says, walking closer. "You're a hard woman to find these days."

I huff out a laugh to hide my panic, and put on a smile of my own. He doesn't know Tate called me. *I don't think.*

"It's really not that hard," I say, nonchalantly. "I'm either here, home, or the store."

"Or San Francisco," he adds for me. "Or New York." His brows rise and my skin breaks out in goose bumps.

"Yes, true. I've been with Pippa."

"Pippa or hockey man?" he asks as he reaches me, sending a shiver down my spine as a new energy fills the air. *Jesus.* Our last conversation wasn't easy, but it felt more friendly than this. Tate was right to be worried.

"Pippa," I lie before changing the subject. "You said you were looking for me?"

"I was. I came to warn you about Tate."

"Tate?" My mind whirs as confusion sets in. *Who the hell do I trust?*

"He got a little freaked out when he saw photos of you with Jesse, and it got me thinking. Why would he be worried?"

Shit. Shit. Another shiver runs through me as he shortens the space between us. "I have no idea," I say calmly. "I barely know Tate. Why do you think you need to warn me?"

"Just a hunch. Do you think he's worried you remembered something?"

Holy shit. *He knows. He knows about Tate and Jesse.* "Why would that matter to him?"

"I'm not sure. I was hoping you could tell me." He gives me a pointed look, making me even more convinced that he's somehow figured it out.

"I'm sorry I still don't know anything," I lie, taking a step back. "I don't remember. If that's what you're asking."

"You're lying."

"What?"

"Did I mumble?" he snaps, his frustration growing. "It's time we had an honest conversation. Don't you think? And it's not just you. We've both been holding back."

My chest tightens, and I feel like I'm being choked, but I push through it. "Sure. Okay. How about we go back to the diner and talk there?" I say, standing tall, shocked that I'm able to keep the fear out of my voice.

"Nope. Here is good. I'll go first. Did you consider it odd that you were never accused of Jade's death? If you were the only one there at the time, and you survived, then it's safe to assume you had something to do with it, right?"

"What? No!" My heart races as a new level of panic runs through me. *He definitely knows.*

"How come no one ever accused you?" he asks, his tone scarily even.

"Because I didn't do it. Because I couldn't remember. Because they said we weren't alone." *Shit! Shut up, Willow.*

"That's right. *You weren't alone.*" He smirks as though he's backed me into a corner. "But was that person me? Was I there?"

My head whips back as that information slaps me in the face. *Why would he ask that?*

"What? N—" I cut myself off because I'm not supposed to know that, so instead I fake a gasp. "Were you there?"

"No, I wasn't there. You know I wasn't. But Jade's parents pinned it on me anyway."

Huh? "I don't understand."

"Of course you don't." His voice rises as he moves closer. "Because you know what happened," he spits out. "Stop. Fucking. Pretending."

"I don't. I don't remember." I shake my head frantically, hoping he can't see through my lies.

"Bullshit!" he yells again, louder this time. "I was blamed for *everything*. *Everything*. 'Innocent little Willow wouldn't hurt anyone,'" he mocks, putting on a voice. "'They were best friends. She was like family.'" He shakes his head as he growls, and I use the opportunity to subtly step back.

"You said no one knew about you and Jade. Why would they blame you?" I ask, finally putting some distance between us. Not that it lasts, as he's in my face seconds later.

"It doesn't matter what I said. The point is that they found out about us and tried to pin Jade's death on me. Only they couldn't make it stick. The best they could do was try to convince the police that I'd pushed her with my actions."

What? "Jade didn't jump." *God, I need to stop talking.*

Alex laughs. "For someone that doesn't 'remember,'"—he sneers, using quote fingers—"you seem pretty certain about that. How could you possibly know?"

"I...I guess, I don't. It's just a feeling. She was happy."

"Was she? Are you sure?" *Yes! No. I was. But that was before I knew about the drugs. Oh God. The drugs. Is that what this is about?*

My heart palpitates as the rest of my body goes numb, the reality of the situation finally hitting me. I have to stop myself from breaking down as Alex eyes me suspiciously, like he's reading my mind, before laughing again.

I turn away, but he leans forward and grabs my chin, forcing me to face him. "Willow, Willow, Willow. Let's go for a walk. But first, why don't you message your boyfriend to tell him where you are. In case you end up lost like last time. I heard you talking to him earlier, so I know he's on his way. We don't want to worry him."

Jesus. "No, thank you. I'm fine." *That feels like a trap.*

"It wasn't a question," he snaps, grabbing my wrist tightly before pulling my phone from the holder around my arm. "Text him. Now."

I do as I'm told, stumbling over the keys as I rush out a text, telling him I'm near the lookout.

I hover over the send button, seriously considering holding back because I'm so terrified of what's about to happen, but Alex rips the phone from my hand, making the decision for me, before shoving it in his shirt pocket.

"You're lucky I haven't told anyone what I know about him. He's getting off easy."

Oh God. Oh God.

"What? I don't know what you're talking about?"

"Oh Willow, so many lies."

No. He can't know. He must be referring to something else? Maybe he thinks Jesse hurt Jade.

As I internally spiral, Alex grabs my arm again and drags me toward the tree line. My heart races, and I pray with every step that a car comes past. Any car. I just need someone to see me.

We reach the sign for the lookout, and I grab the pole with my spare hand, hoping Alex will loosen his grip or let go, but it doesn't work that way. Instead, he falls into me, knocking the back of my head against the metal with such a force that my entire body shakes.

I cry out as a sharp sting ripples through me but quickly bite down on my cheek, stopping the tears threatening to fall. A feeling of nausea hits next, forcing me to close my eyes and suck in a breath. *I'm okay. I'm okay.*

While I'm focused on staying upright, Alex pulls me through the trees, walking in the direction of the clearing, ruining any good memories I had there. The sound of an engine filters through the air, and I almost scream out, but it's no use; they'd never hear me.

If I'd just delayed things for another few seconds.

By the time we get to the view, I'm struggling to stay upright. My head aches and I feel a little groggy, but I don't let him see it. I can't. "Why are we here?" I ask shakily when he finally comes to a stop.

"Privacy," he responds as he types something out on his own phone.

"Why do we need privacy?"

Alex smiles at me, his gaze then traveling up the mountain. "To give you a chance to tell me the truth before I ruin your life like you ruined mine."

What? "I didn't know you. I didn't even know that Jade knew you until you told me."

"That's right. But I knew you. Jade always spoke about you. I would have come to visit sooner, but you couldn't remember. So, what good would that have done me? And now I'm glad I waited; this is going to be so much more fun."

With my mind stuck on Jade, I don't answer. *She didn't tell me about him. Why?*

"You really have nothing to say to that?" Alex demands, anger rising to the surface.

"I've got plenty to say, but I'd rather we just got this all over with," I rush out, almost breathlessly. "I still don't remember. I'm sorry Jade's parents blamed you. But I can't help you." *And God, I feel sick.*

Alex smirks again, his gaze a little unhinged. "Oh, but you can help me. Just wait and see."

All my common sense is screaming at me to stay quiet, but I can't. I hate silence. "Stop speaking in riddles and just tell me...tell me what you want or how you're going to ruin me." My voice wavers as my head throbs, but I maintain my composure, refusing to let him see that I'm weak.

"Wow. Look at you." Alex laughs. "I didn't think you had it in you."

"Alex—"

"Because of Jade's damn diary," he cuts me off, "because of her lies, I spent years behind bars. *Years.*" I stare at him blankly as he speaks, my mind struggling to keep up. I don't even know if I'm hearing him correctly because...*what?* "I was officially convicted on drug charges after my apartment was raided," he continues. "But they tried to get me for more than that; they just couldn't make it stick." My head spins as I stare his way, processing his words. *Drugs. Oh God. Did he force her?*

"I held on to a lot of anger after that, but my time behind bars pulled me out of it. I was lucky enough to meet some very influential people, and from the moment I was free, I was living the high life. I didn't need revenge."

He chuckles to himself as he wobbles slightly, but he doesn't seem drunk.

"Of course, that life didn't last long..." he continues. "And what goes up must come down, and on the way to hell, I met Tate."

I want to ask him to speed up his story because I'm not feeling so good, but I hold back.

"We had fun," he adds with another smirk. "But when I found out he knew you, it was like adding salt to an old wound. Until one day he gave me a gold mine."

What the hell?

He walks forward, swaying as he does, making my eyes go in and out of focus, watching him as the light fades even more. *Is it already sunset?*

"You look confused, but I've already told you this part. Tate mentioned you might remember. That the town was holding you back. So, I turned it into a game after that," Alex says, taking a few steps back to me. "Figuring it all out was what made it fun. Until I tried to get you to remember, and you didn't seem interested. Not that it mattered in the end. I found out the truth anyway. Because when you went up the mountain, all alone, two people knew exactly where to find you. *Exactly where.*"

Oh God. My text to Jesse. He wants Jesse *here.*

Alex stops walking when he's directly in front of me, sinking his hands into my hair. "Imagine my surprise when one of them was Tate, and the other, a big-name hockey star. It made this whole thing so much more interesting."

My vision blurs again, and I start seeing spots. *This can't be happening. Now is not the time for a panic attack.*

It's all been a game?

Alex leans forward, pressing his forehead to mine, and even though it's the softest touch, it burns, adding to the headache already threatening to take over me. "And now I'm about to win," he says, giving my hair a strong tug, sending a nauseating pain down my spine, rendering me speechless.

"Get off her!"

43
Willow

"S top!" a voice yells, and I manage to turn just enough to see Tate arriving breathlessly.

Alex laughs sardonically as he grabs my arm, spinning me around. "One down, one to go. Jesse's coming, right? I already know he's in town."

It's my fault he knows about Jesse, but how is Tate here? My head spins and I struggle to make sense of anything. Like why Tate is swaying, too. *Are they both drunk?*

"He's coming," Tate confirms, stopping in front of us. "Let Willow go so we can talk. You know she's done nothing wrong. It's me you want."

"And Jesse," Alex adds. "Don't forget about him."

"Okay, fine. I said he's on his way, and I know he'll give you anything. He—"

"I want my fucking life back!" Alex yells, releasing my arm so that he can grab Tate, scrunching his tee in his fist. "I want you *all* to suffer like I did."

"What's going on?" I ask, taking a few unbalanced steps back. No one answers, and it makes me wonder if I whispered it or only thought about speaking.

I feel sick, praying that Tate's wrong about Jesse. But I know he's not. I sent the text.

I made him come.

"You should have tried harder to warn Willow," Alex says to Tate, his voice lowering once more. "How do you think Jesse's going to feel when he finds out you could have saved her?"

Oh God. I should have listened. This is *my* fault. Not Tate's, *mine.*

Tate's eyes flash in my direction as Alex laughs hysterically. "God, this is fun," he sings out, his personality seemingly split in two. "You should have spent more time deciding who to trust, Willow. You should have paid more attention. Are you sure you can even trust Jesse?"

I'm about to tell him to fuck off when Jesse comes tearing through the darkness, moving so quickly Alex has no time to react before he's thrown against a tree, the shock of it making me stumble. "If you fucking hurt her, you're a dead man."

"She's fine," Alex wheezes with a laugh, unperturbed by the pressure Jesse has on his neck. "See for yourself," he croaks out.

Jesse turns around, and I nod to tell him I'm okay, though I'm not entirely sure that I am. My vision's a little blurry, and the pain in my head seems to be traveling.

When he continues to stare, I whisper, "I'm okay," but he sees through it, softening his hold on Alex, giving him the chance to shove back and step out of his grip.

"Now that you're all here, I'm ready to talk," Alex says, moving away from Jesse, his eyes manic as he clenches and unclenches his fists, pacing between us. "To *all* of you," he adds, his lips curling into a sneer. "I could have focused my energy on Willow, made her life hell before ending it. And at one point, I seriously considered it. But when I found out the two of you were involved, I couldn't waste the opportunity. I just had to be sure. And when Tate saw the photos of you two, his panic confirmed it. You were all there, so you all deserve to be *here*."

"It's three against one," Jesse says with a smirk of his own, ignoring Alex's speech. "How well do you think you'll fare with those numbers?"

"I'm not worried about numbers," Alex says, touching his pocket, making me gasp. "I'll be fine."

This can't be real. None of this is real.

"What do you want?" Jesse demands, only now showing his emotions. "You want the truth? The facts. Here you go." He steps forward, getting up in Alex's face, and my heart stops. "It was me. *I* was the one trying to sell Jade drugs. *I* took her money. *I* pushed her over the edge. And you know what...I've never once regretted it. How could I? Look at where it got me. Look at how great my life is."

No.

"Jesse, what—" He raises his hands to cut me off, and while I'm happy I at least got the words out, I almost yell at him for lying. Only Alex gets in first.

"You took *my* money," he screams, shoving Jesse back. "She was there to buy *my* drugs. For me. So I could sell them." He slams his fist against his chest before shaking his head. "You took everything from me!" He reaches into his pocket as he takes a step closer. "My money, my plans, *Jade*. And I don't even think you get it."

I know I don't. I don't understand anything about this, especially the drugs, and I can't keep up with Alex's mood swings. One second this is a game, and the next he's screaming about his loss. "Alex, we didn't—"

"Shut the fuck up," Alex screams again, cutting me off as he reaches into his pocket. "My life was ruined because Jade died, and I didn't even like her. She was spineless, weak, easily manipulated. I enjoyed making her life hell. I craved it. The way she obediently played all my games. But she was supposed to be my way out. She wasn't supposed to die."

Jesus, what had she been going through? What had I missed? My chest aches as I work to push that information out of my mind again while my panic increases.

"You said life got...got better," I say, trying to keep my eyes on his face when I'd rather be watching his hand. "Maybe—"

"I told you to shut the fuck up!" he yells, running his free hand through his hair, looking rattled. "The only way to fix this is for one of you to suffer like I did. To have your life changed in an instant. And I'm choosing *you* Willow. Because I get the feeling that will hurt the most."

Jesse turns toward me just as Alex pulls the gun from his pocket. But before I get the chance to panic, I lose my balance, falling into a tree as a warmth hits the back of my neck. My head stings again, and when I reach around to touch the source, my hand comes back covered in blood. Warm, fresh blood.

"I don't feel so good," I whisper before my vision goes black and the world around me spins.

"Willow!"

44

Jesse

I don't even think about Alex, or the gun, as I race toward Willow, only reaching her after she hits the dirt, causing a pain to rip through my chest. *I didn't catch her. I promised I'd always catch her.*

"Willow, baby, wake up," I whisper as I cradle her in my arms, listening to her breathing, my fingers feeling for a pulse. "We need to get you off this mountain and—"

Someone yells, cutting me off, but I don't recognize who it was. I know Alex and Tate are arguing, but I'm choosing to ignore it, with all my energy focused on Willow. Where it should be.

"Buttercup, wake up. You have to see the sunset. It's beautiful and I know you haven't seen it in a while." It's almost gone; darkness is about to fall but I'm hoping my words work.

"Willow—"

"Get the fuck off me!"

A gunshot echoes through the air, and the world stills as I throw my body over Willow, shielding her in case the gun was aimed our way. A hysterical scream shatters the silence, but it fades away as though I imagined it, replaced by a ringing in my ears.

I don't move, don't even look up, terrified that if I do, Alex will have a clear shot at her. I would rather die a thousand deaths than let that happen.

Silence fills the air again, and it hits me why Willow hated it so much. This is torture. The quiet. Not knowing. The unspoken.

I'm not sure how long I've been crouched in this position when something hits my shoulder, and I spin around so quickly, I almost knock Tate out.

"It's me," he says, holding one hand in the air while the other hangs limp by his side, blood seeping from a hole in his sleeve.

Fuck.

I move to stand, to lift Willow with me, but Tate shakes his head. "I'm okay. Stay there. Willow needs you more than I do. Is she breathing?"

"She is." I nod. "Alex?"

"No, I don't think he's breathing." He smiles but it's forced. "He met the same fate as Jade. Only his fall wasn't an accident."

Fuck. He stares straight through me as though he's not even seeing me, while I see everything. This is going to kill him. He's not like me. He's not made of stone. He feels the guilt. And it's my fault he's in this situation. I should have saved him back then.

"It's your turn to run, Jesse," he says suddenly, snapping out of his daze. "Take Willow and go. Get her help. I'll deal with this."

"Fuck off. We'll go together. Come on. I need your help to save her."

He doesn't move for a beat, maybe thinking I'm joking, but when I lift her in my arms and try holding my phone for light at the same time, he snaps out of it.

"Fine. I'll help you down, but then you need to go."

There's no way that's happening, but I don't argue. We'll cross that bridge later.

We're not too far from the clearing, but I detour, walking past the cliff edge, needing to see for myself. When I glance down, all I see is darkness, yet I know that Tate's right. The drop's more severe than the place Jade fell; no one's surviving that. I know with no uncertainty that Alex is dead, and the thought actually brings me satisfaction.

Just like with my foster father, I feel no remorse, no sadness, no guilt. I'm happy Tate did what he did. He's a hero, even if he doesn't see it that way. It seems I haven't changed as much as I thought I had.

When we reach the trees, I throw my phone at Tate and he catches it in his good hand, shining the light in front of us. After securing Willow in a tighter hold, we take off running through the darkness toward the road. All while I whisper her name over and over, begging her to wake up. Getting nothing in return.

At one point my shoulder slams into a short branch, sending pain radiating through my body, but I keep moving. Nothing is more important than getting Willow to help.

"Are you sure this is the right way?" Tate yells as the light disappears from in front of me, lighting up a path in another direction.

"I don't fucking know." I panic. "I'm just—"

"Jesse?" Willow rasps, and I almost drop to my knees as the tension leaves my body. Relief swarms me, and it's not until she says my name again that I realize I'm not only relieved that she's awake, but also relieved that she remembers me.

"Fuck, Willow." I gently kiss her head, her cheeks, her nose, every spare bit of skin I can see, as tears prick my eyes.

"She's okay," I call out to Tate when he doesn't stop. "Willow's awake."

"You're okay, baby. You're okay." I kiss her again and she giggles before wincing in pain. "Don't move, I've got you."

"Did you just call me baby?"

"No?" *Fuck, did I? It's not important.*

"What happened?" she asks next, seemingly moving on from my term of endearment. "What happened to Alex?"

"Alex is gone. You're safe. That's all you need to know for now."

"Why does my head hurt?" She winces again and my heart cracks.

"I don't know. I was hoping you could tell me that."

Her face scrunches as she stares up at me with a puzzled expression. "Was I shot?"

I cringe at her question. I was so worried about Alex and the gun, I didn't even realize Willow was hurt. "No, Buttercup. You weren't shot. Something happened before we got there and I didn't fucking notice. I didn't see it until it was too late. I should have been focused on you."

"I'm happier you were focused on Alex. I only wish you'd done more damage." She speaks softly and I know she doesn't mean that. She's not that person. Not like me. I wish I'd killed him myself. I wish I'd ended his life the second I ran into that clearing.

"We don't have to think about him anymore," I say instead of telling her how I really feel. "Let's just concentrate on you."

We continue walking again and thankfully reach the road relatively quickly. Tate's car is parked in front of us, while mine's farther away, so I automatically walk toward his, desperate to get moving, until he calls out for me to stop. "It's a manual. I can't drive a stick." He points to his arm and I feel nauseous. If we don't get him to the hospital soon, he might lose function in his hand.

"I'll drive, it's—"

"No!" he snaps, cutting me off. "You need to stay with Willow. Is yours auto?"

"It is. Let's go."

When we're settled in my rental—Tate in the front, Willow and me in the back—she snuggles into me, trying to keep the pressure off the back of her head.

"Alex knew you were there when Jade died," she says softly, but it comes out as more of a question than a statement. "Because you found me on that mountain." She suddenly sits up, her eyes flashing around the car as though she's panicked. "But how did he know that? Was it me? Or was he there?" Her breathing shallows and she struggles to take in air.

"Willow, it—"

"I don't remember seeing him," she continues breathlessly, working hard to suck in a breath. "God, maybe he overheard me telling Sara. I thought it was Tate threatening me but it wasn't. It was Alex. I didn't know at first. I should have listened. I did this."

"*Willow.*"

"Oh God, I could have put Sara in danger by telling her the truth. He could have gone after her if he knew. And Jade. What did he do to Jade? How come I didn't know?"

Tears flow as she breaks down in front of me, and it takes all of my power to keep my shit together.

Ripping off my seatbelt, I turn to face her, grabbing her face in my hands, careful not to touch her still open wound. "Block it all out, Willow," I rasp, but then clear my throat to strengthen my voice. "It's all white noise. None of it matters right now. Just focus on me. On the sound of my voice."

Willow nods but continues hyperventilating, her body shaking uncontrollably.

"You could have died; Tate could have died. Jade *did* die. I did this. I did all of this. She didn't trust me and I didn't trust you. If I'd told you someone was threatening me... I can't, Jesse. I can't."

"Listen to my voice," I repeat, staring into her eyes until she finally focuses. "I love you. We will get through this," I say slowly, making sure she hears every word. "I'm here for you, however you need me."

She nods again, but I'm still not sure she's understanding. "Willow?"

She's quiet for a beat before taking a deep breath, slowing her breathing. She takes a few more long slow breaths before she nods again. "I'm listening," she whispers.

"Good. What do you hear?" I'm hoping she repeats at least one thing that I said, but she shocks me by reaching out and squeezing my arm, pulling me closer.

"My forever," she says, resting her forehead on mine. "I hear *you*."

Fuck. I bite back the tears, as emotion clogs my throat. *We're going to be okay. We have to be.*

Because she's the only one for me.

"Let me take the blame," Willow whispers when the hospital comes into view a little while later and I almost laugh at the absurdity.

I connect our hands and pull her into me, pressing a kiss to her brow. "That's never going to happen, Buttercup. You are not to blame. None of this is your fault, and I won't let you think otherwise."

"Then whose fault is it?"

"Mine," Tate begins but I cut him off with a groan.

"*Alex*. The only one to blame here is Alex. It's been his fault from the beginning. He hurt Jade, he tried to hurt you," I say, looking at Willow, "and he shot Tate. He deserved what happened." I notice Tate's eyes on me in the rearview mirror and give him a pointed look. "As for *you*. Telling him about Willow didn't cause this. He didn't have to go after her."

"But I trusted him."

"No, you didn't," Willow chips in. "The day he came to see me when I was closing up, I saw you. You were staring through the window. Watching. I only just remembered that. God, why didn't I remember that? You never fully trusted him. Why didn't I trust *you*?"

"Why would you? I never gave you a reason to." Tate shrugs as I pull Willow closer. My little warrior. She's been through more than anyone should have to endure, but from here on out, I'm going to work hard to give her an easy life. To give her anything she dreams of.

"What do we do now?" she asks, her eyes on the road behind us, as if she can see the mountains.

"I'm making sure you're both okay, and then I'm calling the police," I say, my mind made up.

"What?" Willow gasps in shock, as Tate yells, "Like hell you are."

Tate pulls into the hospital emergency bay as if I'm going to let him just drop us both off, and then turns around to face us, but I don't let him speak.

"Don't worry. I'm not about to get myself thrown in jail. Everyone will know what happened up there. They'll just know our abridged version."

A pinched expression mars Willow's features as she undoubtedly questions if she can live with that response. But when she looks my way, she must see the determination in my eyes because she nods.

"Okay," she says. "Let's go inside."

When I turn to Tate, he holds my stare, keeping me in a standoff to see if I'll break, but when I don't, he sighs. "Okay. Fine."

Relief fills me at the same moment that Tate's body drops to the steering wheel, everything he's been holding finally releasing now that we're here.

He finds a proper parking space after that, and we slowly make our way inside, Willow in my arms, Tate beside me. And while I haven't decided exactly what to say to the police, a feeling of warmth takes over me because for the first time, it feels like it's over.

45
Jesse

A shiver runs through me as I watch Willow sleep. And even though I know she's getting better, it breaks my heart to see her back here. To know that I almost lost her. Again.

I never thought I'd come back to this place. I actually promised myself I'd avoid it at all costs. It holds nothing but darkness and pain. I lost Willow here, and I had to pretend to mourn a man I loathed for the sake of my future.

I shudder at the thought. It doesn't help that everything looks the same, from the yellowing drywall to the light blue tiles. Only there's a big difference between now and back then.

Now I've got something to look forward to. I've got Willow.

The nurses all tell me to sleep whenever they come in to check on her, but I can't. Between the uncomfortable chair and her restless mewls, I'm wide awake, needing to know she's okay more than anything else.

Seth calls me first thing in the morning, and I rush to silence it, sneaking out of the room to let Willow sleep.

"How's she doing?" he asks before he's even greeted me. "And how are you holding up?"

I texted him last night to tell him Willow was in the hospital and that I'd give him more details when I could. It's hard to explain everything that went down. It's almost unbelievable. But I guess I'll have to start telling people soon enough, especially considering I'm going to miss a few games.

"Physically she's okay. They just have her here for observation. But mentally, we'll have to wait and see."

"What happened?"

I lean back against the wall and sigh, running a hand through my messy hair. "I'm not sure you'd believe me if I told you, but it's a story that started twelve years ago."

"Fuck."

"Yep."

"I've told management you won't be back this week. Told them you'd miss the next couple of games, so you've got around five days to get home. Does that work?"

"Yeah, I'll make it happen. Somehow." As the words leave my mouth, they physically pain me, making me feel nauseous. I don't want to leave Willow. Ever. Especially now. She's my priority. But I know she's not going to let me give up. Not when she knows how hard I've been fighting, how badly I want a new contract. She even admitted that the reason she's here is because she tried to deal with the threats alone, terrified that if I knew, it would affect my game.

"Fuck, this is hard," I say honestly because it's Seth. "I'm being pulled in two different directions."

"I know, and I don't envy you."

"I better go. I want to be with her when she wakes."

"Yeah, of course. Keep me posted."

"Thanks."

I move to hang up but he continues. "And remember, you've only got a few years left of hockey. Willow's yours forever."

He disconnects the call after that, leaving me utterly confused. Does he mean that I should focus on hockey because Willow will still be there, or should I be focused on Willow because hockey's short term?

I want to believe it's the latter. After all, it wasn't long ago that he told me he once left Amber, and since they're back together and living their happily ever after, I'd say he probably regrets his decision to leave. So, will I?

Willow's still asleep when I sneak back into the room, making me sigh in relief. While she seemed okay when we arrived here, I don't know how she's going to feel when she wakes. I'm guessing part of her strength last night was adrenaline, or even the shock of everything that happened. Both of those should have worn off by now, so naturally I'm worried.

I close my eyes for a beat, the heaviness becoming too much, when she calls my name.

"Jesse?"

I jump up as my heart thuds in my chest, an invisible tension leaving my body. Willow's eyes meet mine, and when she smiles warmly, I take a deep breath, as though I'm finally able to fill my lungs. She's okay. Even after talking to her when she woke up, even knowing that she went to sleep with my name on her lips, something deep inside me was worried.

I don't deserve her, and I'm almost certain that one day that's going to come back to bite me.

"Come here?" she says, her smile dropping. "I'm okay."

"I don't know what you mean," I say, faking a smile of my own as I walk to sit on her bed.

"I'm not silly, Jesse." Willow giggles. "Or blind. I can see the worry lines all over your face."

"Hey now, just because I'm a year older than you doesn't mean you can joke about my age."

"*Jesse*," she grates, her stare telling me I need to stop. That I need to be real with her instead of playing it away with jokes.

"Fuck, I was so scared. What the hell were you thinking?" I say, giving her a piece of my mind.

She smiles, reaching for my hand to intertwine our fingers. "I just wanted to keep you safe. I wasn't thinking about anything else. I..."

"You almost died."

"I know."

"God, I can't live in a world if you're not in it. I know that's a bold statement, but Willow, it's the truth. I've done it before. And I'm not strong enough to survive it again."

Willow squeezes my hand and pulls me forward until we're face-to-face. "I'm not going anywhere, Jesse. You're stuck with me."

"Wouldn't want to be stuck with anyone else." I smile. "And you know that's the truth because I only like about five people, and only tolerate a few more. As for everyone else—"

"I know. Mr. Hockey Recluse. I know."

"Enough out of you. Can I kiss you?" I gently brush her hair away from her head, careful not to touch the bruising that's visible now that there's light. She has a dressing to stop the bleeding at the back of her head, but other than that, she's relatively wound free. At least on the outside.

"I would love nothing more. Don't hold back," she says, using the words I once said to her. "I'm still me. Don't treat me like I'm fragile."

She sits up and presses her lips to mine before I've even had a chance to process it, and I softly kiss her back. She can say what she likes about not being fragile, but with the vision of her lifeless body still very present in my mind, it's going to take me a while to truly believe that.

I expect her to protest, but instead, she matches my slow speed, and it's not until a wetness hits my lips that I notice she's crying. But when I pull back to look at her, there are no tears in *her* eyes. They're mine.

"I'm here, Jesse. I'm here," she says, folding me into a hug just as more tears fall and a guttural cry rips from my chest, the weight of the past twenty-four hours, the past twelve years, finally bearing down on me.

"I'm sorry," I rasp. "I'm so fucking sorry."

I'm sorry for not being there sooner. I'm sorry for hurting her so many times. I'm sorry for my lies. The pain I caused. My silence. But of all the things I'm sorry for... I'm sorry for not having the courage to talk to her the day she first helped me. For not asking her name and for starting a chain of events that almost killed her.

What's that saying...? The butterfly effect...a small change in the past could have a huge impact on the future? This feels like that—saying hello could have saved Jade's life, and in turn, made Willow's life better.

"Don't, Jesse," she whispers, breaking into my spiraling thoughts. "We're not allowed to focus on the past anymore, or try to take the blame. Because even you said it yourself—you wouldn't change it. Everything brought you to me. The good, the bad, the heartbreak, the love—everything led us to now, to us being together, to making us stronger, to making us the people we are. The people that love each other and share a bond so strong that no one will tear us apart."

She presses her lips to my head before smiling again and wiping away my tears. "From now on we just focus on the now. On us."

I close my eyes and attempt to do just that, but fuck, it's hard.

"Listen to me," Willow says, her voice filtering into my mind. "Focus on my voice." She repeats my words back to me, making me finally relax. "What do you hear?"

"I hear *you*," I say with a smile. "It's the sound of forever."

46
Willow

I must have fallen asleep again after my talk with Jesse, because when I next open my eyes, the sun's high in the sky and I'm alone.

My eyes drift shut again until I hear a tentative knock on the door and Tate appears. "Mind if I come in?"

Instead of the wariness and nerves I used to feel around him, a sense of guilt hits me. "Of course, yes." I signal to the chair beside me.

Tate walks forward slowly as though he's waiting for some kind of negative reaction. And he probably deserves one. But I no longer have it in me to dish it out. Life's too short to hold on to the past; it's why I need to leave it all behind.

He stops when he reaches the end of the bed and pauses, subtly adjusting the sling on his arm as his eyes bounce around the room, clearly unsure of how to proceed.

"I wanted to check in on you, if you have a minute," he says, standing a little more confidently.

I nod and sit up, giving him my full attention.

Considering what we've been through and the fact that we've known each other for years, it seems weird that we're still strangers. *That we never spoke at school.* I always wondered why. It's not that I wanted to talk to him, because he always made me feel uncomfortable with the strange way he'd watch me, but he still had my mind reeling, always trying to work out if I'd done something wrong.

Now I know.

And I can't blame him for it. Whether he stared at me in disgust for what I did, or was freaking out that I'd one day remember, I still get it. I can't pretend that day wasn't hard on all of us. Jesse and Tate may have walked away and left me, but they never escaped the nightmare. None of us ever will.

"I'm so sorry, Willow. I should have tried harder to find out more, and I should have told you that I thought Alex was dangerous. I just didn't want to scare you too much if I was wrong."

I want to understand, only there are still a few missing pieces. "Why didn't you warn me sooner, when you were first worried?"

"God, I don't know." He pulls at his hair and shakes his head. "I honestly didn't think it was that urgent. I thought it was jealousy. I had no idea he knew Jade until he texted me to meet you both on the mountain. Before that, it was just a weird vibe I was getting, and I'm really fucking sorry."

"It's not your fault. You had no idea what Alex had done. What he was capable of. None of us did."

"Yeah, I'm sorry about that too. I thought I knew him. I still can't believe Jade was buying his drugs. No wonder she had so much money."

I almost ask how much, but since Alex was talking about reselling the drugs, it's safe to assume it was a lot.

"I guess Jesse was right not to trust him." I smile but it's a little forced.

Tate huffs out a laugh. "And here I was thinking Jesse was just jealous too, and maybe that was a part of it, but I also think he saw through Alex."

"Like he saw through me?"

"Yep." He chuckles softly. "That guy was completely gone for you from the moment he first laid eyes on you. His buttercup." He walks toward me and finally sits down before letting out a long, drawn-out breath. "You know he was prepared to take the fall for Jade to protect you," he whispers, making me sigh. I did know that. He never corrected me when I said Jade's death was his fault.

"And I don't mean that he was just going to make you believe that he did it," Tate continues, looking over his shoulder to make sure we're still alone. "I'm referring to when it first happened. The day Jade died."

What? My brow furrows as I try to think about what that means.

"He was going to find you in the hospital and beg you to let him confess. We never considered the possibility that you'd lose your memory, and he didn't want you to be punished for what happened. But then you couldn't remember and that was infinitely better. For all of us."

"Okay." It's all I can say as my heart jolts in my chest.

"After the other incident that night." He pauses, giving me a pointed look, telling me he knows Jesse told me about his foster dad, making my heart break for both of them. "After that happened, we talked about what we'd do if you one day remembered something. What we'd do if you remembered us, but not the incident itself. And despite everything we went through, he still wanted to play the martyr. He said he'd rather go down than have you live with that guilt."

He pauses again when I gasp, and tears prick my eyes.

"I wouldn't let him," he continues. "He'd found a new home. A *good* home. He was about to get a better life. So, I told him I'd keep an eye on you, and then prayed you'd never get your memories back."

Wow. I sit gobsmacked as a range of emotions overwhelm me.

Jesse has always loved me. It's one thing to hear it from him, but *wow*.

"He's a good man," I finally say. "Which is why I wanted to protect him. It's why I never told him about your texts...Alex's texts."

"I know, and I wish I'd realized that because it's the exact reason I didn't involve him or return his calls.

I'm sorry I never saw how much you cared about him, and that I assumed the worst. After all these years, I didn't want the truth to suddenly come out...if Jesse got too close to you. I couldn't handle the fallout, and I was certain you'd tell someone if you ever figured it out."

The police—he assumed I'd tell the police.

"I wouldn't. I won't."

"I know that now, and I'm sorry."

A throat clears behind us, and Jesse enters the room holding a coffee and a box of chocolates. "Okay if I interrupt?"

"Yes." Tate jumps up. "I was just leaving. It's good to see you're okay, Willow. And I'm sorry again."

"Thank you." I smile. "I hope you feel better too."

Jesse nods to Tate as he walks away, an almost silent transaction taking place. "Everything okay?" he asks when Tate's gone.

"Everything's good. But I think Tate needs a friend. Not just any friend. I think he needs you."

After giving my statement to the police, telling them about Alex's threats—or versions of them—and what happened on the mountain, we were all cleared to leave. Our corroborating stories left no doubt that the fall occurred in a moment of self-defense.

Even Jade's parents made a statement, strengthening our case.

In the weeks following the accident, Jesse worked tirelessly to make sure I didn't fall back into a dark place. And when he was on the ice, he had Sara or Pippa scheduled to look after me. Even Tate called every now and then, just to check in.

I'm happy to say, Tate and Jesse started talking again, and even caught up when Jesse played in Seattle. Tate may have taken a different path than Jesse, but in the end, they were both just doing what they could to survive, and no one can fault them for that. Especially me, not now that I know everything.

I still have days when I wish I had my memories back, but those days are becoming fewer and farther between. If anything, I'd just like to know what I felt about Jesse back then. If his version of events stack up against mine. He says we flirted and kissed—he even showed me what it was like—but was that a young boy's imagination or was he really my first?

My first and last as he continually tells me.

Lying here in his arms now, I've never felt so content. So safe. And I never want to let go. As he gently runs his fingers through my hair, I think about our life, and the complicated nature of it, and pray that I never have to.

When we officially went public after the Alex threat was gone, a lot of people told me it wouldn't work, Ashley and Mom being the loudest. How could I possibly have a relationship with someone from another state, someone who barely has time for sleep, while I'm here running a business?

To my surprise, Dad finally stood up for me, telling Mom that she'd already pushed one daughter away, and that if she kept going, she'd lose another. I didn't think she'd care with a grandchild on the way, but apparently it was enough, because she's since supported our relationship, despite the fact that she doesn't quite trust Jesse. No matter how many times we tell her Pippa and Jesse were never together, she doesn't get it.

And I'm done explaining it. I'm done thinking about everyone else's views and opinions. Today, my focus is on Jade.

"Are you sure I can't stay?" Jesse asks as I jump up and pace the floor, his eyes following my every move, his expression full of concern.

"I'm sure," I say without stopping. "I need to talk to them alone. I don't want to accidentally mention that you were there."

Jade's parents are coming to see me. They usually come back to town earlier than now, but were delayed this year. And this timing is much better. I want to know about Alex. Why he did what he did. Why he was blamed. And what the hell happened with Jade?

I want to read her diary.

Jesse sighs before standing up and wrapping his arms around me, forcing me to break out of my freak-out pattern. "They know I was up on that mountain. Everyone does."

"They know you were there when Alex died. Not when Jade died."

"Willow, I can't leave you alone knowing what you're about to go through."

I blow out a slow breath and pout. "Ugh. Fine. You can sit in my bedroom. But stay out of sight."

Jesse laughs. "Still not good enough, but I guess it's better than being shoved out the door. I'll accept it. But only because I prefer strong, independent Willow over the people-pleasing one."

"Thank you. I appreciate that." I laugh.

"Should I hide away now?" he says, with his eyebrows raised in mock annoyance.

"I think that's best. And it will help if I don't have to look at your sour expression."

He rolls his eyes. "Sorry for caring."

"Can you just flip over to asshole Jesse for a second? You know, the guy that doesn't care."

Jesse grabs my face in his hands and leans forward until our noses touch, his eyes locked on mine. "I will *never* not care when it comes to you. It's just not in my nature. I've cared for too long."

My gaze softens and I smile. I know this is hard on him. He wants to help. He always wants to help, but in this case he can't. I have to do this alone. "I love you with all my heart."

"I know. I guess I love you too." He pouts again, making me burst out laughing just as someone knocks on the door.

"Okay. Time to go."

As Jesse mopes toward the bedroom, I walk slowly to the front door, my heart lodged in my throat. I have so many questions, but I'm not sure I really want the answers.

"Oh, Willow," Heather says, curling me into her arms the second she sees me, as tears prick her eyes. "I'm so sorry you went through that. We should have told you. I'm sorry."

She's sorry?

"No, I—"

"Heather's right. I wish we'd explained what we knew back then. We just never expected Alex to do anything," Jade's dad, Tom, adds, his face ashen with regret. "Especially not to you."

"Please stop," I say, motioning for them to come inside. "I don't blame you for any of this. I promise. And after a lot of heartbreak, I've come to realize that telling me back then would have completely broken me. I needed to heal before learning the full truth."

"The full truth?" Heather asks, her eyes wide as she sits down. "You remember?"

"No, I've tried, but still nothing. I..." *God, how do I tell them what really happened? How do I admit that it was my fault?* "I found out a few things, and I... I'm so sorry, it was me," I blurt. "I'm the reason Jade fell and..." I burst into tears, struggling to get the words out as I watch their faces pale, heavy emotion shadowing their features.

"Willow, no," Heather gasps, standing to pull me into another hug. "We don't blame you. Jade wasn't herself. She was doing a great job at hiding it, but she was in a bad place." *Oh God, how did I not see it?*

My tears thicken as I add to my guilt. If I'd only noticed something...

"We knew what happened," Tom adds and I freeze.

"What?" I sniff.

"Tate got in touch with us all after he started school at Hepburn. After he found out who we were. He told us he was up there with you, and what had happened."

"He said he was up there?"

"Yes, he admitted that Jade was there to meet him and why. No one even knew what that poor kid was going through, having to sell drugs for his foster father. Anyway, we all agreed with his choice to stay quiet. You didn't need to know what happened. It wasn't your fault, Willow. We don't blame you. No one blames you. This goes back to Alex, and—"

A thought occurs to me and I interrupt them. "When you say 'all,' you don't just mean the two of you, do you?"

Heather's shoulders drop as she shakes her head. "No. Your parents knew too. And Ashley."

Jesus. That cuts so deeply but explains so much. Why they always wanted me to move on. Why they never tried harder to discover the truth. Why Ashley felt she couldn't talk to me. *God*. I don't even know how to process that.

"Will you tell me about Alex?" I ask, needing to change the subject.

"Willow, I'm sorry, I—"

"No, please... I want to know about Alex."

Heather sits down again as Tom nods, both looking apprehensive. I'm sure that, like me, they spent years trying to recover from everything they went through, and having to rehash it can't be easy.

"After Tate told us about the drugs, we searched Jade's room, and that's when we found out what was really going on."

I sniff and frantically rub under my eyes. Through this entire conversation they haven't mentioned Jesse. Did Tate tell them what happened but leave Jesse out of it? It seems that while Jesse was acting as my protector, he had a protector of his own.

"Jade and Alex had met a few years earlier, but only seemed to get close a couple of months before she died. At a family function. He wasn't technically related to us, but he was there because his dad is my brother-in-law's brother. Jade's uncle's brother."

What? I'm sure that makes sense. I just have to process it.

Jade's uncle's brother's son. Not blood related. Oh yep, I'm there. Wait.

"Does your brother-in-law still live here?"

"With my sister, yes. That's who we come to visit and that's who Alex stayed with when he was here.

Of course, we had no idea. When we gave the police information about Alex, it caused some tension, and we all agreed he would not be a topic of conversation between us if we wanted to remain civil."

"Okay." I don't even know what to say.

"Anyway, he was a few years older than Jade, and she fell for his charms." *Like a lot of people.*

"They spent the entire night together at that party, but then she never mentioned him again. If we asked, she changed the subject, so we assumed he'd broken her heart and she was being a teenager. Please don't react to that; we will always regret that assumption."

"God, I'd never." *I didn't see it either.*

"When we searched her room," Tom continues, his voice a little rough as he takes over, "we found her diary. Most of it was about the two of you and your wild adventures." He smiles. "But there were a few pages near the end about Alex. Detailing how confused she was, how she was falling for him and how he was telling her he felt the same, but then he'd hurt her, or tell her she wasn't good enough." He pauses, running a hand down his face. "Her last entry was all about how she wanted to be good enough. That she wanted to prove to him that she wasn't the innocent little girl he said he couldn't fully love. That's why she tried to help him secure the drugs. We later found out that Alex would have continued to use her if given the chance. Her death ruined his plans."

Oh God. I can't hold back my gasp, but I do try to hide it as a tear slides down my cheek.

"Why didn't she tell me?" I whisper, wrapping my arms around myself. "We were a team."

"Oh, sweetie. She didn't tell anyone. She was embarrassed. She had no idea he was manipulating her. She truly believed she wasn't good enough, and part of her wanted to prove it to everyone. Not just Alex. I think she wanted to wait until they were together. Because she honestly believed they would be."

"But...why?" I never made her feel that way. She was *everything* to me. She was perfect just the way she was.

"We don't know. I'm sorry. And I'm sorry he came after you. We always assumed if he was going to come after anyone, it would be us."

A shiver runs through me, but I'm not concerned about myself or what he could have done to me. All I can think about is Jade and the way I let her down.

I try to hide my pain from Heather and Tom—they've been through enough—but I'm sure they see it.

"We all wish we'd seen the signs back then, Willow. But none of us did. I'm sorry we never told you."

We cry and hug until Heather and Tom have to leave, the conversation draining us all.

As soon as I turn around after closing the door, Jesse's there, pulling me into his arms, knowing I'm about to break. And break I do.

The past few months have been more than I can handle, but I want to believe that's it. That I have nothing left to go through.

"Promise me that's the end of it, Jesse," I say as I cry. "Promise me, there's not some other kind of fresh hell waiting around the corner."

Jesse holds me tightly, his lips pressed against my head. "It's over, Willow. We just have to process everything that happened and then it's over."

Short of me actually remembering one day.

Although, if I'm being honest, I'm no longer convinced that my memories are buried. I think they're gone. And after everything I've been through, I'm kind of okay with that.

"All happy from now on?" I ask, pulling back to peer up at Jesse. "Deal?" He smiles down at me with tears coating his eyes, but also with so much love that I have my answer. Even if it's not all smooth sailing. It doesn't matter, because I know that we will help each other through it. We'll make each other happy.

47
Willow

I wake early the next morning and consider going for a run to watch the sunrise. But with Jesse's fingers brushing across my naked skin, sending a tingle down my spine, I change my mind, snuggling back into his arms, a content moan leaving my lips. This is heaven. If only he didn't have to go home.

After speaking with Jade's parents yesterday, Jesse and I spent the afternoon talking through everything they'd told me, including the fact that *my* parents knew.

While I was reluctant to see them, Jesse thought it was best if I spoke to them right away, so off we went to dinner at my parents' house, armed with their biggest secret.

Mom did most of the talking—and crying—making out as though she's suffered more than anyone else, barely even apologizing. But it was Dad's words that hit me the deepest.

"No one wants to see their kid in a hospital bed. Ever," he'd said, gripping my hands between his. "No one wants to see their kid hurt. Period. So, when we found out the truth, and you couldn't remember it...

Willow, there was no way in hell we were going to knowingly cause you pain. It was done. There was nothing you could do about it. We thought we were doing the right thing."

"But—"

"I know. Your mother doesn't always handle things as well as she should, but I should have been better. We shouldn't have held you back. We were just both terrified of losing you again. But I'm so proud of the woman you've become. And can't wait to see you finally spread your wings."

Though Dad's eyes were filled with tears, I didn't cry—I'd cried enough for a lifetime of late—but by the time we walked away, I'd forgiven them both. It's going to take a while to forget, and we've got a lot to work through, but how could I not forgive them? After all, they were only doing the same thing Jesse was. If only I could tell them that, maybe Mom would accept Jesse more easily.

But for now, the plan is to keep Jesse's name away from that fateful day.

I know. Tate knows. And that's it. We'll take it to the grave, just like Jade did.

After falling into bed that night, Jesse and I were both emotionally exhausted, but in a much better place than we had been in a while. I felt an inner peace I hadn't felt in years, the exact feeling I'd assumed would only come if I got my memories back.

I was wrong. I know enough now to have a full picture, and that in itself is freeing. I'm no longer trapped in my head, searching for a missing piece I never thought I'd find.

I can be me. *I am me.*

Jesse pulls me tighter, and I can't resist wiggling my ass against his morning wood, relishing in my newfound happiness. I really could get used to waking up like this.

He groans into my hair as his cock twitches between us, making me giggle. "Careful," he says, almost painfully. "What time do you have to leave?"

"Never," I wish out loud. "I never want to leave."

I feel his chuckle before I hear it as his body shakes against me. "That wasn't the question."

"I know." I sigh. "I have to be there at eleven. Sara's got an appointment."

"Eleven's good. We still have a few hours. I'll head off when you do."

"Ugh. I hate this." I groan, turning to face him, taking in his mussed hair and sleepy eyes.

"You hate getting a few extra hours with me?" he teases with a wink.

"I mean, I hate that we live apart."

Jesse nods. "I've told you how to solve that problem."

"We don't have a private jet *or* a helipad."

"I'm sure I could get one. I know a guy who knows a guy."

I roll my eyes because we've joked and laughed about this many times before, but at some point, we'll have to discuss it seriously.

"How about I take your mind off things?" he asks as his hand moves between my legs.

"Oh yeah," I gasp when he runs a finger through my heat, drawing circles across my core. "And how would you do that?" I ask breathlessly, my head dropping back to the pillow.

"You'll just have to wait and see."

He maneuvers around until he's positioned on top of me, and then pushes his fingers inside, scissoring them around before he pulls back out, reaching for his length.

"Should we be doing this?" I blurt, putting a hand in between us. "You have a big game on Friday; how's your blood pressure?"

"I'm up for some nurse play, if you are," he says, ignoring my concern—like always—as he rises to his knees. "Oh nurse, my cock aches and—"

"Shut up, I'm being serious."

"As I keep telling you, it's good. I promise. Yes, my blood pressure spiked after you went and got yourself hurt again. But my life is a lot more stress free these days. And now that you've spoken with Jade's parents and everything is out in the open, it's only going to get better. Trust me, I'm good to go."

"You wouldn't admit it even if you weren't."

"Nope, I probably wouldn't, especially when I know how ready you are for me. I'm not wasting an opportunity." He licks the fingers he just had inside me and raises an eyebrow in challenge. Knowing he's got me... *Because how can I say no to that?*

I smile, rising to my knees to meet him before gripping his length, pumping it a few times, working him as he groans. "Okay, sir. Where exactly does it ache?"

Without responding, Jesse jumps off the bed and sheaths himself before lifting me in his arms, groaning when I wrap my legs around him, squeezing him between my thighs.

"These legs will be the death of me," he grates. "And this ass." His fingers bite into the flesh of my ass cheeks, and I tense but stay quiet. "God, this body." He groans again, rolling his hips, making my thighs clench again. "And this heart." He pauses when my back hits the wall, and I melt into him. This man is my everything.

"Jesse," I cry out, unable to form words.

"I know, Buttercup. I know."

Releasing one hand from my ass, he positions himself at my core and pushes inside me. We both groan when our bodies connect, pausing for a moment to savor it all, eyes locked.

Jesse's the first to break away when he presses his lips to mine, grabbing my hand to secure it above my head, stretching my body. He sinks deeper with this new angle, causing a spark to shoot through me.

"God, Jesse."

"Fuck. I'm so deep. I need to move."

"Yes," I rush out. "Move."

I don't wait for him to go first, circling my hips instead, seeking the friction. Jesse growls as I take control, before squeezing my ass and slamming into me, taking everything back.

We move breathlessly, messily grinding against each other, pushing and rocking, desperately chasing that high. And when I'm almost there, Jesse releases my hand and spins us around, before dropping me to the bed and crawling on top of me, his gaze running over my body, making me melt.

He grips my legs under my knees and pushes them against my chest, exposing me, opening me up before staring between my spread legs. He watches as he pushes inside me again, and the carnal look in his eyes has me crying out as my walls clench around him.

"That's it, Buttercup. Give me everything."

Pressing against me, he opens me wider before rocking his hips, hitting me so deep, I'm not sure I can take it, but God, do I try. Biting down on my lip, I let out a high-pitched mewl as he moves his hand up my body, settling it at my neck, as the other holds his weight above me, the new angle increasing the sensation, almost sending me over the edge.

I fight to keep going, to give him more, but I'm at his mercy. The best I can do is grip his hair and pull his face to mine, kissing him with fervor, biting down on his lip instead of my own.

"Fuck, Willow. Fuck. Yes."

Jesse's movements quicken and it's too much for me to handle. It's too good. My orgasm rips from within me as I scream out his name, thrashing around beneath him, my body shaking uncontrollably.

He pumps into me a few more times before grunting through his own release, dropping my legs as he falls to the bed beside me, flipping me to my side before tucking me into his hold.

"I love you," he whispers with his lips pressed against my hair. "So. Fucking. Much." He tightens his grip around my waist and sighs. "What time did you have to get up again?"

"We've got a few hours." I giggle a little breathlessly.

"Good. I don't plan on moving until then."

"Good." I want to stay like this forever. "And I love you too."

Sara and I are closing up the shop later that day when an unfamiliar black car pulls up in front of the window.

Sara squeals, drawing my attention, my brows raised in suspicion. "What did you do?"

"Me?" She mocks offense. "What makes you think it was me?"

"Fine," I say, folding my arms over my chest. "What did *Jesse* do?"

Sara cringes but she can't keep the smile from her face. "Okay, it was me. Jesse has no idea."

I turn back around to see a petite older woman stepping out of the passenger seat. She pauses, her eyes bouncing around the front of our store like she's judging it. After a moment, she takes a single step and Sara hisses before rushing to my side. "Please don't hate me for this. I think it's the best decision for both of us."

With a frown, I look back at the lady to see her stop again, talking animatedly to a man dressed in a business suit. "What decision? What's going on?"

"She wants to buy the shop?" Sara says, her voice soft and hesitant.

"What shop?" I say absentmindedly, trying to make out what the couple are saying.

"Ours."

What? Abandoning my task, I spin around to face her. "It's not for sale."

"It is now."

"How do I *not* know this?"

"Because you would have told me I was crazy," Sara says with her hands on her hips, making a stand. "You would have tried to get out of it because of some kind of misplaced guilt, and you don't owe this town anything. You don't even owe me."

"But..."

"But nothing. I want you to go and live in the big city, designing your jewelry or selling your scents online. Hell, be a trophy wife if that's what you want. But I'm not letting you stay here."

I rest back against the shelf behind me and huff. "What about you? What will you do?"

Sara's face scrunches, and she looks away. "I didn't want to tell you like this. I didn't think they were coming until next week." She pauses, taking a deep breath, scaring me a little. "I'm pregnant. We're having another baby, and I want to stay home."

"You're pregnant?" I gasp in excitement, my hands flying to my mouth. "Sara, that's amazing. I didn't think you could..." I trail off because she knows.

Happy tears well in my eyes but guilt pools in my belly. I made her work while she was pregnant. All those times I disappeared to see Jesse...

"Uh-uh, stop."

"What?" I smile because she knows me so well. One of only two people that do.

"Before you get any ideas in your head, I'm *okay*. If I was too tired to work, I had someone fill in. You needed this. I wasn't going to stop you."

"I should have been there for *you*. That's what's important."

"You will be. Now. When you sign over the shop. That's what I need."

My eyes flash to the people outside to see them staring at something down the street. "Are you sure?" I ask, because deep down, I want this. I want out.

"I'm positive. It's time we both started new adventures."

I smile before pulling Sara into a hug, careful not to hold her too tightly. "They're coming," I say, when I notice them out of the corner of my eye. "I guess it's show time."

"Oh, before she arrives," Sara rushes. "I told her she might not get the essential oils, and that would be your decision. I didn't know what you'd want to do."

"Thank you." I don't know either, but maybe it's time for a fresh start.

Maybe it's time for my new beginning. My sunrise.

"Did we just sell our store? Our livelihood?" I ask with an incredulous smile.

"We did." Sara laughs, her hand resting across her belly, drawing my gaze.

God, I've been so deeply rooted in my own world that I didn't even notice her wearing baggier clothes. Or that she was tired. And I didn't even question her the day she was sick. I need to be a better friend.

"I'm sorry, Sara. I wish I'd been here to help."

"Don't. I told you I was fine. I had help."

"I am curious, who do I have to thank for that?" I say with a grin, making Sara laugh as her cheeks pinken.

"Anyone I could get. Your mom, your dad, Grant."

My stomach churns at the mention of my parents as I think about our talk, but I block it out. "Why didn't you tell me? And what did you tell them?" I don't want to believe they knew before I did.

"I told others I had to look after Benji." *Her son.* "And I didn't tell you because I knew you'd race back here. I hope I did the right thing?"

"You did. It's just going to take some time to get used to. But I am happy for you. And excited!" I hug her again before pulling away to look at her bump. "When are you due?"

We talk babies and the future until well into the night, with Grant apparently informed that he'd be solo tonight. By the time I get home, I'm tired and emotional. Sara did the right thing by selling the store. I'm not happy here, and I would never have made the decision on my own. But the thought of packing up and actually moving away is a completely different story, and I'm not even sure where to start.

There's also the fact that I'd be leaving Sara, who I can't live without...and my family. But while my family and I still have a lot to work out, this is what's best for me. I've been living for others for too long.

My mind races as I try to make sense of everything, until I realize the first thing I need to do is tell Jesse. He'll be there to help.

I arrive at Jesse's apartment in the early evening, two days later, with my heart racing. I've been on edge since I boarded the flight, trying to decide how to tell him, hoping he'll be excited and not worried that I'm giving up my life for him. Just like I would have been worried if he'd done the same.

I take a deep breath and gather all my strength before unlocking the door. But the second I see Jesse, his eyes light up, and everything I've been feeling for the past forty-eight hours—all the fear and apprehension—instantly fades away. Because I'm home. Jesse's my home. And it's about time we started our life together.

Our forever.

Jesse stands up and walks over, pulling me into his arms. "Of all the joints in all the towns in all the world, she walks into mine. I'm a lucky man," he says, half quoting *Casablanca*, making me smile.

But I have to disagree. This isn't about luck anymore—it's all *us*, and we're going to have one hell of a story.

EPILOGUE ONE
Willow

One Month Later

"You're actually here," Jesse says, grabbing my face in his hands as he presses his lips to mine. He slowly walks me backward until my body meets the wall and then he groans, sinking one of his hands into my hair before releasing me from the kiss. "You being here makes everything right with the world. Makes all the pain worth it. Mostly."

My lips curl into a smile, because "mostly" is exactly right. Neither of us deserved the pain we went through, and there were moments when it felt like we'd never get through it, but we found our light at the end of the tunnel, and now things are looking up.

After the longest month, Sara and I finally handed over Audrey's and I sold my house, ready for my move to the big city. Well, a city anyway. Since visiting New York City, I can say that San Francisco is like baby steps. It's still big but it's not *huge*. It's the perfect place for me. Plus, I'm close to the water, something

I've discovered is my second favorite place to be, with the first being right here, with Jesse.

"Now that you've mauled me, can you help with my bags?" I say, stepping out of his hold to gesture to the bags sitting in his doorway. I brought two with me when I visited a couple of weeks ago, and the last two with me today.

Four suitcases.

My small-town life fits into four suitcases. Easily. It's probably more like three and a half. Mainly because I chose to leave a lot of it behind, including my anger and pain. Things with my family aren't perfect, but I don't think they ever will be. I'm hoping that in time we can move on, but for now...this is *my* new beginning. Right here. Right now. I'm starting fresh. We're starting fresh. Jesse and I. But keeping the nicknames. I've grown quite fond of jokingly calling Jesse Robin, and I think I'd feel lost if he stopped calling me Buttercup. His voice changes when he says it—whether he's whispering softly into my ear or grating it out as he slams into me, it's always packed full of emotion. Reminding me that he's loved me for years, not just the months since we reconnected.

Jesse groans, but grabs my bags and moves them to his bedroom—our bedroom—before returning with a cocky grin. "Done. Now where were we?"

He lifts his hands to my face again, but I duck out of the way, giggling as I run down the hallway. "Now I move in."

I fall onto the couch and sink back into the cushions, exhausted from unpacking. "Ugh, why did that have to take so long?" I whine, as though it wasn't my idea.

"No one said you had to do it all as soon as you arrived," Jesse laughs as my eyes fall shut. "We've got a lifetime."

I bite back a smile. "Such a romantic notion until I'm looking for my bed socks at four a.m. because my feet are cold."

"For one," Jesse says, holding up a finger, "we have heating here. And two, please tell me the bed socks thing is a joke."

I shrug, giving nothing away until he huffs out a laugh.

"You'll love them; they're so cozy. I'll get you a pair." I grew up in a mountain town. Thick, warm socks were necessary in the winter, and I'm not ready to part with them. "I can't spend all my time naked or in sexy lingerie. Now that we're living together, you will see me at my worst."

Jesse playfully rolls his eyes before a smile brightens his features. "I can't wait...and ditto." He chuckles, making me laugh.

The irony is that I think we've both seen each other at our lowest points. I think we can handle the little things like bed socks, or clothes on the bathroom floor, or blanket hogging. The little things will be easy. As long as we support each other.

"Now that that's done..." Jesse hedges again, dropping to his knees in front of me just as my phone rings. "You've got to be kidding me." He groans.

"Who is it?" I say with a smile, too tired to even lift my head. "Maybe we can ignore it."

Jesse grabs my cell and checks the screen, shaking his head. "Nah, you're not ignoring this one. I owe her big time."

"Pippa?" I thought they were calling it even these days.

"Hell no. Sara. Without her genius and sneaky plan, you wouldn't be here. Plus, she looked after you when I couldn't. So, like I said. I owe her. Here. Take your time."

He hands me the phone and stands up before walking into the kitchen, giving me some privacy. Not that I need it; we no longer have any secrets. It's the one promise we made to each other. Unless they're good secrets. Like if he wanted to surprise me with a trip to Paris, I wouldn't be complaining.

As soon as I answer the phone, Sara's at me in her motherly tone. "How was your flight? Was Jesse on time to pick you up? Are you settled in? I miss you."

"Order of importance?" I say, with a smile, my chest tightening.

"Always."

"I miss you too." I pause and hear Sara sniff. "The flight was only a little delayed, Jesse was on time, and I'm all unpacked and settled."

"All unpacked? That's impressive. I didn't call right away because I assumed you'd be having welcome home sex."

I bark out a laugh because so did Jesse. "Jesse's been trying."

"Ha, I'll bet. Grant tries for welcome home sex even if I've only been to the grocery store these days. He's picturing life with two kids and trying to get as much as he can now."

"Smart man. Although, we all know you're a superwoman. You'll work it out."

Something bangs in the kitchen, drawing my attention to see Jesse pulling a pot from the top cupboard before grabbing bits and pieces from the pantry. "I think Jesse's given up. He's now making us dinner."

"You've got all the time in the world. You don't need to rush anything."

"You're right; we don't. But I do need to figure out what I'm going to do with my life."

"Nope, that fits into the 'anything' category. You don't need to rush that either. Take a breath, enjoy the peace and the little moments. Just *be* for a while. You deserve that. You deserve the chance to figure out what you want on your own, in your own time."

I bite back my emotions and quietly thank her. Once again, she's my sounding board, calming me in a way no one else could, except Jesse.

"Are you sure you don't want to move here?" I ask, walking over to join Jesse in the kitchen. "I'm sure they have ranches nearby. Horses travel."

Jesse chuckles as Sara laughs. But then she pauses, and I can imagine her actually contemplating that idea before she laughs again. "Maybe one day." She giggles. "For now, I'll just be jealous. But..." She trails off, leaving me waiting with anticipation. "Before this baby makes me too uncomfortable to travel, we are coming to visit. Grant agreed that we deserved a mini escape before she arrives."

"Yes!" I cheer, before realizing what she said. "She?" I gush. "You're having a girl."

"We are. And we can't wait."

"I'm excited for you." I smile as Jesse wraps an arm around me, continuing with his meal preparation. "And I can't wait to see you."

"Soon. It will be very soon. I'll call you again in a couple of days."

"Yes, please do. I miss you."

"Miss you too, Willow. Bye."

She hangs up and I curl into Jesse, burying my face in his chest. "I'm happy, I really am, but this is going to take some getting used to. It's been years since I spent a week away from Sara. She's been my rock."

Jesse kisses my head, adding salt to his now boiling water. "I know. But trust me when I say, I will be working double time to make sure you feel comfortable here. And safe. I want you to be happy. I want this life to become ours, whatever we want to make of it."

"Thank you. That means the world to me. And right now, I want whatever amazing thing you're cooking. That smells delicious."

"It's just pasta and sauce. San Francisco style."

"Oh." I look at him curiously. "Is that different from other styles?"

"I have absolutely no idea; it's just the way I know how to make it."

"I'm up for that."

I follow him around the kitchen, tucked under his arm, most likely annoying the hell out of him, but he never says a word. He just continues on like this is normal, like we've always had this life. And right now, it feels that way. It feels nice.

"I think it's time I attended another game. Or two or three. Or all of them. I better get used to it now that you'll be playing for another few years."

Four days ago, Jesse finally signed a new contract, and the relief he felt was evident. Mind you, they haven't lost a game this season, so there's a good chance they'll win the cup this year.

"I might even accept an invite into the Wives' room if Lauren offers again," I joke but then cringe. "Or maybe not."

Jesse barks out a laugh and abandons his stirring spoon, curling me into a hug. "I would love for you to come to a game, and you can go wherever you want; sit wherever you want. But there must be a jersey with my name on it covering this sexy as hell body of yours."

"Is that so?" I say with a yawn. "What if I want to wear Ryan's? You know... to support my sister's man." I shrug before stepping back, knowing I've just started something.

"Well, now I'm regretting that I helped them sort their shit out," he grates as I step back again, getting ready to run around to the other side of the counter. "Come here!" He reaches for me but just misses my arms as I squeal out a laugh and make a run for it.

"But it's such a sisterly thing to do," I call out as he chases me around the apartment.

"*Buttercup*," he warns. "You're asking for trouble."

"Oh no. Really?" I come to a stop and spin around to face him before lifting myself up onto the counter. "Maybe I want it."

Jesse releases a deep guttural groan as he reaches me, spreading my legs before stepping between them. I expect him to start stripping me immediately since he's been wanting this since I first walked in the door, but he surprises me, his face softening.

"I'm so proud of you, Willow. No matter what you do from here on out, you'll always remain my hero. Your strength, your courage, your heart. You are everything I never knew I needed, but the one person I always missed. Thank you for moving your entire life for me. Thank you for becoming my home."

My heart pounds in my chest as an overwhelming feeling takes over me and tears prick my eyes. Because this is it. Jesse is my forever. He's my person. And I can't wait for our next life to truly begin. I love this man, and always will.

My mind may not remember him, but my heart *always* did.

EPILOGUE TWO
Jesse

Two And A Half Years Later

I glance around the room packed full of people closest to me, and yet I only recognize a dozen that are not part of my team. While I'll admit, the number of "friends" I have has grown since finding Willow, I'm still the same reclusive asshole they all know and love.

I'm talking to Seth and Amber when Pippa comes sashaying over, an exaggerated smile on her face. "ESPN—"

"No," I cut in. I don't need to hear anymore.

But of course, Pippa continues. "They want to interview you and—"

"Fuck, no. Tell them I'm not interested. I'm out."

Pippa gapes while Seth chuckles beside me. "You didn't even let me finish."

Crossing my arms over my chest, I stare at her deadpan until she huffs. "Pippa, we just won the cup. I'm all interviewed out. I've given you everything I can."

"And here I was thinking you'd changed," she grumbles, making Seth laugh even harder.

"You just caught him on a championship high," he says, elbowing me in the side. "Before that he was still his asshole self."

"Not true." Pippa wags her finger. "He did a few more things than he used to."

Now it's my turn to chuckle. "I did. On Willow's insistence. She said I had to go easy on you every once in a while. But if she'd asked me to agree to everything, I probably would have—lucky for me she didn't."

"Wow, you really are pussy-whipped," Seth says with another laugh until Amber shoots him a glare.

"Actually, I'm Willow whipped," I say and own it proudly. "Speaking of, where did she disappear to?"

Pippa points in the direction of the door and my gaze follows. "Tate just arrived with his new girlfriend," she informs me. "Willow rushed off to meet them."

Of course she did. She and Tate have grown closer since we became friends again, and it's nice to have him in our lives.

As if we've summoned them, they walk over to join us, with Tate holding his hand out for a shake. "Congratulations, my man. What a year to bow out."

"It was time. What can I say?"

Tate smiles before turning to the young woman beside him. "This is Emily," he says with a proud grin, curling her under his arm.

"Nice to meet you. I've heard so much about you." Not a lie. Tate won't shut up about the feisty young girl he met at a football game of all places. We don't talk about the fact that he never came to any of my games.

Willow curls herself into me as she tucks her elegantly styled hair behind her ear, smiling to a brunette beside her. "And this is her sister, Cory."

Cory steps forward, lifting her hand for me to shake. "Sister-in-law, but close enough. It's great to meet you; my husband's a huge fan."

I can't help but chuckle. "Tell your husband I said thanks."

"Oh, I'll be telling Nate *everything* about this encounter. I didn't know we were coming here. Emily told me it was a retirement party, so naturally I pictured old people." She grimaces and I laugh.

"There are some old people here. Let me introduce you to Seth." I point over my shoulder, right as Seth shoves me in the back.

"You're retired now, so I can finally kick your ass."

"True, but you still need me. I've got people lining up for endorsements."

Seth groans. "I hate when you're right. How long until I'm done with you?"

"Never and you love it."

As soon as the formalities are over, and I've done the appropriate amount of mingling, I seek out Willow, ready to take her home.

She's once again talking with Tate and his girl, keeping her friends close. Despite being a hockey girlfriend for almost three years, and having a successful and extremely popular jewelry business, she still prefers to stay out of the spotlight and stick with what she knows. Or in this case, who she knows.

I watch her as I walk her way, taking in her easy smile and the overall lightness she projects. The warmth. The happiness. Like petals in the wind, my Buttercup is free. And there's no better feeling than knowing that.

"I'm at the end of my rope; are you ready to blow this joint?" I whisper, wrapping my arms around her waist from behind.

She startles at the sudden intrusion but relaxes almost instantly, sinking back into my hold. "You can't leave; it's your party."

"Care to wager on that?" I say, spinning her around to face me. "I'll bet you a hot tub that I can walk right out of here with no regrets."

"A hot tub?" Willow deadpans while the others chuckle beside us.

"You heard me. I've been thinking we need one. I'm kind of partial to the warmth."

"First, where would we fit a hot tub and... Nope, you know what, I'm not even going to go there." She throws her hands in the air. "What do I get if I win?"

"What do you want?" I shrug.

"A house. There's no place like home," she jokes, quoting *The Wizard of Oz* like she's started doing lately, always making her bets outrageous, trying to see how far I'll go. And the house one has come up a few times.

"Deal. I've got this in the bag. Hot tub, here we come."

She rolls her eyes and turns to the others. "I guess we're leaving," she says exaggeratedly. "The man of the hour is out."

"Bye all. I'll see you for golf next week," I joke to Tate. "You know, now that I'm a retired old man."

While everyone laughs, I shoot Seth a pointed look, getting a subtle nod in return. Slipping my hand into Willow's, I say goodbye again and guide her toward the door, waving to guests as I pass by.

"You're really going to do this?" she asks, completely bewildered.

"Did you really think I'd behave otherwise?"

She huffs out a laugh. "No, I guess not. But Jesse, it's only been a few hours. They haven't even done speeches yet."

"Even better. Come on."

When we reach the door, Seth rushes over as planned, sliding to a halt in front of us. "Where are you going?"

"Home, Seth. Where else would I be going?"

"You can't leave. We have speeches planned and there's cake."

"Ooh, I like cake." Willow beams. "And houses. I like houses."

I try not to smile as she plays right into my plan. "Fine. I'll give you thirty minutes. But then I'm done."

"Deal," Seth says, holding back his smile until Willow turns her back on him.

Willow guides me back to the middle of the room, pointing toward the cake they're wheeling out. "You're lucky I'm nice, otherwise you'd owe me a house."

"You mean you're not going to hold me to it?" I mock surprise.

"Come on. As if I'd do that."

When the excruciating speeches are finally done, and Willow's full of cake, we make our escape, driving away with Willow behind the wheel. It took me a good two years to convince her to try driving here, but it still freaks her out. I offered to drive tonight but she insisted I was free to drink. To which I easily agreed. Not for the alcohol, but because it makes my plan so much more fun.

"Can you turn left up here?" I say when we're almost to the apartment.

Willow's eyes flash my way before she looks forward again, her face pinching in confusion. "Why?"

"I need to pick up a bottle of red; we're celebrating."

"We have plenty of red at home."

Home. I still love when she calls it that. "It's my retirement celebration. Humor me."

"Nope," she says, popping the *p*, trying to rile me up on purpose.

"Don't sass me. Left *now.*"

She bites her lip, and I know my gruff tone turns her on. It's the reason she did it, but I can't focus on that now. For as much as I'd love to demand she pull over so I can take her in the back of the car, in the middle of downtown San Francisco, I have other ideas.

She obediently follows my directions as we continue on. As long as I'm firm. If I say please or thank you, she turns a different way to piss me off. And fuck, does it turn *me* on. I'm just about ready to abandon my plans completely when the street I need comes into view.

"Left here and hurry up."

"Yes sir," she says with a nod of her head, and *fuck me.*

Not long now, Jesse. You can do it.

"And stop."

Willow pulls to the curb and slams on the brakes, turning to me in her seat. "They don't sell wine here, Jesse," she says with a raised eyebrow.

"No, they don't. I'm just fulfilling our bet."

Her brow furrows as she runs through some of the other bets we've made. I'm sure the thought of me buying her a house never crosses her mind. "We already did the public sex thing," she says after a beat.

"Oh, I know. And God was it hot. But that's not what we're doing here."

"Jesse."

"Look left."

Willow turns to look out her window, and her eyes lock on the house I want to buy her. Well, the garage anyway—she'd have to look up to see the rest. It's tall and skinny. "You didn't," she says with a soft tone.

"No, I didn't," I confirm and she relaxes. "But this house is for sale, and I've booked a tour for us tomorrow."

"What?" Her voice comes out screechy, but with the way her eyes are lighting up, I'm going to guess the "what?" is a good thing. "You want us to move into a house?"

"Don't you?"

"Well, yes. But it's a big step."

"We don't have to fill it with babies yet, but it does have plenty of space for an office *and* a workshop. Plus—"

Willow gawks at me, making me chuckle. "Back up. Back up. You're talking babies now? Who the hell are you?"

My laughter continues as she stares at me like I'm a stranger—a stranger that she happens to find very attractive judging by the heat in her eyes. But I have one more surprise.

"The house itself isn't even the best part. Can you drive forward a little? There's an empty block up ahead."

Willow does as I asked, and when she turns her head she gasps.

"That's the view from the back balcony. And I've been assured that because of the direction we're facing, you'll get to see the sunrise *and* sunset."

Willow's eyes glisten with emotion. "So, we didn't stop here for sex?" she asks after a beat, making me laugh again.

"It wasn't my intention, but..." I trail off and she unbuckles her seatbelt before reaching down to hitch up her dress. *Fuck, this is happening.*

I slide back my chair and unbuckle my own belt, pulling down my zipper just as she awkwardly springs across the center console, straddling my legs when she lands.

"Hi," she says when we're face-to-face, forced closer by the tight space.

"God, I love you," I say in response, not wasting any time in taking her lips, my hands snaking under her dress.

If we weren't parked in front of an empty block, I wouldn't be doing this. No one gets to see Willow like this except me, but since it's dark and a quiet street, I take my chances, lifting Willow's dress above her head, revealing a red silk corset and garter belt.

Double fuck. Happy retirement to me.

I gulp as she sucks her lip into her mouth, a nervous energy pouring out of her. "Willow, you are by far the best thing to ever happen to me. Whatever you want, it's yours. I'll never make up for everything you've given me."

Willow giggles as though I'm joking, and it's like a symphony I'll never tire of. "I should wear these more often if I get that response."

"It's not the corset, Buttercup. It's you. Always has been. Always will be. Forever."

I'll never stop questioning how I got so lucky with Willow. For all the darkness in my world, I never thought I'd find my light. But I did. And God, is she amazing.

Willow often points out how many times I've saved her, always catching her when she falls. But the truth is, she saved me long before she even knew I existed, and I will never do enough to make up for that.

But I've got forever to try.

Thank you for reading Jesse and Willow's story. These two hold a special place in my heart and I'm so grateful to you for taking the time to read the duet.

If you want to read any of my other books, you can find them all on Amazon and Kindle Unlimited. If you haven't started the Heartstrings series, a few of the characters are mentioned during this story... Dylan from When Nothing Else Matters, and Cory from Ain't No Sunshine (Novella). Keep reading for a sneak peek.

BOOKS BY KATHERINE JAY

SYMPHONY OF SOUND DUET
The Sound Of Silence (Jesse and Willow)
The Sound Of Forever (Jesse and Willow)

HEARTSTRINGS SERIES
When Nothing Else Matters (Summer and Dylan)
Still Here Without You (Joel and Delilah)
It Had To Be Us (Logan and Dani)
Truly Madly Deeply Mine (Wes and Lucy)
A Sky Full Of Stars (Thomas and Lainey) – coming
soon
Ain't No Sunshine (Nate and Cory) – novella

For more information, visit
http://www.katherinejayauthor.com

And if you want to stay in-the-know for all things
Katherine Jay, come and join my Facebook Reader
Group The Angsty Lovers Playlist for fun, exclusive
content and sneak peeks. Or sign up for my
newsletter here for monthly updates.

Are you following me on social media? If not, you can
find me below:
Instagram
Facebook
TikTok

HEARTSTRINGS SNEAK PEEK

D ylan – Twelve Years Old

She's here again. I know I shouldn't look. As the quarterback, the coach needs me to focus, to lead this team, but I can't help myself. I didn't think she'd show today, considering the weather, but there she is, long blonde hair stuck to her face and clothes soaking wet from rain. For the last three weeks she's been in the same position—hiding in the tree line, watching my football team practice. Alone. She doesn't look older than ten, so at first, I thought she was the younger sister of a teammate, but no one else has mentioned her. She always arrives mid session and leaves before it's over, like she doesn't want to be seen. But she has to be here for someone, right?

I try to keep my eyes on the play but keep stealing glances her way. She must be more confident today, because for the first time, she's stepped out from the trees and is standing by the fence. Now that she's closer, I manage to catch her eye. She's watching me, not the team. Me. And I gotta say it feels good to know that. Because at twelve years old, I finally understand the appeal of girls. I used to think they were annoying, but now, I get it. And every part of me is now focused on her, practice forgotten.

"Heads!" Someone yells from behind me, but I stupidly ignore it. *Big mistake.*

Thump. Direct hit. *Dang, that hurt.* Rubbing my head, I look back at the team before shaking off my thoughts and running to my starting position.

"Head in the game or the laps are on you!" the coach yells, and my team collectively boos as they set up for the next play. For the next twenty minutes, I ignore the girl and play my best, determined to give it my all, even showing off a little. *Okay, maybe not completely ignoring the girl then?*

I'm in my element, showing everyone how it's done. Every throw, every move, every second. I'm not going to be the reason for the extra laps today; someone else can deal with that. I'm focused now, or at least, I'm trying to be, until we set up for the fourth run of the same play, a play I know inside and out. Confident in myself, I check out the girl near the trees, and then all focus is lost.

I watch in horror, frozen, as the girl falls to her knees in the slosh as a man towers over her. From what I can see, he's tall and solid, so while she's trying to use her strength to pull away, she's helpless against him. The rain makes it hard to see properly, but it's impossible to miss when he rips her to her feet and drags her toward a car. She doesn't scream, doesn't make a sound. She just lets him drag her without even fighting back. *Why isn't she screaming?*

It seems I have a split-second decision to make. I look back at my teammates to see if anyone has noticed and see that they haven't. I'm just about to alert Coach when I glance back to see the girl cry out in surprise when the man slaps her across the face. That cry finally snaps me out of my shock and kicks my ass into gear.

"Hey!" I yell. "Let her go...Stop! You're hurting her..."

The man doesn't react, but his movements become faster and less violent. He can definitely hear me, and yet, no one else is moving.

Without a plan, I take off in a run, knowing I need to reach her. *But what am I going to do? I'm a kid.* I need backup. Without stopping, I yell over my shoulder.

"Someone help...by the fence...help her!" *Why hadn't anyone else noticed?*

I feel like someone has answered my prayers when I see Dad's car pulling into the parking lot. As soon as he spots me, I wave frantically and point in the girl's direction.

"Dad, help her. Please!" The panic in my voice is enough to rattle my dad into action.

"Get your hands off her!" he yells as soon as he spots what I'm seeing. "Hey! I'm talking to you!"

He's running now too. I'm fast, but I got my speed from him. He'll catch them. He has to. My eyes remain focused in the girl's direction. The man now has her in the car and is making his way to the driver's seat. No!

Yelling and loud footsteps start up behind me. Finally, others have noticed, but no one will reach them in time. I reach the fence just as the car speeds out of the parking lot, and seconds later, my father follows. I hadn't even noticed he'd gone back to his car. Relief hits me.

There's nothing more I can do. Dropping to the ground in a heap, I rest my head in my hands and take a deep breath. It's only then that my teammates catch up.

"Who was that?"

"What happened?"

"Does anyone know them?"

"Do you think she's okay?"

The questions are firing, but I have no answers. I have nothing left. When the coach reaches my side, I brace myself for the lecture, but it doesn't come.

"You did a good thing, kid," he says as he squats down in front of me, patting me on the back. "Alright boys, show's over. Off to the locker room. No laps tonight."

Cheers ring out at his words. The girl is clearly forgotten as everyone heads back across the field, met by their concerned parents.

I look back toward the parking lot and can't help but think about the questions my teammates had asked. *Who was she? Who was he? Is she okay? At least I could answer that one. She will be. Dad will find them. I know it. She'll be okay. She's got to be.*

With a sigh, I get up and follow the team back to the locker rooms, completely unaware that what I just witnessed would not be the worst thing to happen that day.

You can find out what happened to Dylan and the young girl in When Nothing Else Matters – book one in the Heartstrings series of interconnected stand-alone novels. The series is available now on Amazon and kindle unlimited.

ACKNOWLEDGEMENTS

F irst up, to my fabulous readers. Your love for Willow and Jesse has blown my mind. As I said in book one, I've wanted to write this story for a long time, but wasn't sure I could pull it off. Having my readers cheer for me and these characters has helped me immensely. And now you've reached the end. The end. Ahh I'm not at all ready to let them go, these two will stay with me for a long time.

To Sara. I've never been good at expressing my feelings, despite the fact I write emotional books, but if I had the right words, Sara, you would be getting them. I couldn't do life with out you. Thank you. For all that you do. And for your friendship, which I will cherish forever.

Lauren, you are a godsend. So glad to have connected with you and Jess. I'm so excited to be on this journey with you. Thank you for your guidance and support on this duet.

To my incredible beta/proof readers – Adi, Anna, Cindy, Inka, Jenn, Mim, Nikki and Sarah — This book wouldn't be the same without you. From the first draft to the very end, you've helped shape this story. I will forever be grateful for you all.

To my amazing author friends, I'm going to say the same thing I said in book one because it means a lot to me...thank you for the chats, support, laughs, check in's and most importantly for knowing we're all colleagues instead of competitors. I'm so blessed to have you in my life and can't wait to meet you all one day.

Thank you to my phenomenal Influencer and Street teams. You give me life. Every time I see a post, comment, share, or DM, my heart bursts. I will never be able to express how grateful I am for you all.

To Rudi, thank you for your wealth of ice hockey knowledge. I could not have finished this book without you. You are an absolute gem.

Books and Mood – I've said it before and I'll say it again... These covers are EVERYTHING! Pure perfection. Thank you.

To Ann and Ann, I don't think I tell you enough how in awe I am of you both. You constantly go above and beyond and I honestly could not do this without you. You're stuck with me.

To my wonderful kids and hubby, I could thank you everyday and it wouldn't be enough. You are my everything. Sorry this one kept me busy. It was a long journey.

To my family and friends... I miss you and I'm sorry.

And thank you all for supporting indie authors. If you enjoyed this book, please shout it from the rooftops and leave a review on Amazon or Goodreads.

Here's to Willow and Jesse!

ABOUT KATHERINE JAY

Katherine lives in Australia with her hubby, two kids and a mind full of characters. She spends her days partaking in role play, building fortes and dancing. While her nights are spent reading and writing.

Katherine writes emotional and angsty romance with love that's worth fighting for and characters full of heart.